LORDS OF LIGHT

Also by Steven Spruill

RULERS OF DARKNESS

DAUGHTER OF DARKNESS

LORDS OF LIGHT

Steven Spruill

Hodder & Stoughton

Copyright © 1999 by Steven Spruill

First published in Great Britain in 1999
by Hodder and Stoughton
A division of Hodder Headline PLC

The right of Steven Spruill to be identified as the Author
of the Work has been asserted by him in accordance with
the Copyright, Designs and Patents Act 1988.

10 9 8 7 6 5 4 3 2 1

British Library Cataloguing in Publication Data

Spruill, Steven G.
Lords of light
1. Physicians – United States – Fiction 2. Angels – Fiction
3. Vampires – Fiction 4. Horror Tales
I. Title
813.5'4 [F]

ISBN 0 340 708115

Typeset by Hewer Text Ltd, Edinburgh
Printed and bound in Great Britain by
Mackays of Chatham PLC, Chatham, Kent

Hodder and Stoughton
A division of Hodder Headline PLC
338 Euston Road
London NW1 3BH

To Nancy
A True Angel

I gratefully acknowledge the invaluable healing touches of three doctors to this novel: Al Zuckerman, DFA, Nancy Lyon, PhD, and F. Paul Wilson, MD.

ANGELS

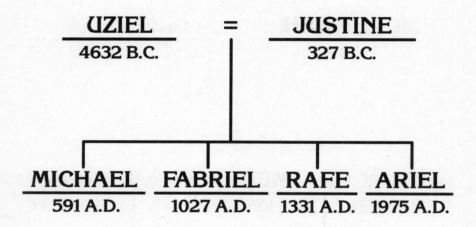

UZIEL = JUSTINE
4632 B.C.   327 B.C.

MICHAEL   FABRIEL   RAFE   ARIEL
591 A.D.   1027 A.D.   1331 A.D.   1975 A.D.

PHAGES

CHEMOSH = Elrida
1304 B.C.   1034 A.D.

Blythe = MERRICK = Katie
1440 A.D.   1058 A.D.   1954 A.D.

Gregory
1982 A.D.

ZANE = Anne
1462 A.D.   1949 A.D.

JENN = Hugh (died)
1972 A.D.   1966 A.D.

PROLOGUE

14 October 1986

I have done all I can to make sure no one but me will ever read this diary. I do realize that, in keeping the secret of these frightening and magnificent creatures, I may be failing my duty to my own kind. But if I were to reveal what I know, the dangers to humanity might be far greater than if I keep silent. So these words will exist only as electrons inside my computer. I'm using a good encryption program, further protected by a password that is not my birthday, the name of my dog when I was a kid, or any other thing that could be guessed.

For I must tell someone, even if that one is me.

Today marks two months since I learned what Merrick really is. Will I ever truly get my mind around it? It can't be easy for him to reveal what he has kept hidden for so long, but he has answered every question I can think to ask, and each new revelation only stuns me more. If I had not seen so much with my own eyes, I doubt I could believe anything he has told me about hemophages, even though I still love and trust him with all my heart.

I am now in awe of him as well.

It will take more than a few months to slip back into the comfortable delusion that he is solely as he appears, a handsome, vital man. Those smoldering eyes, the thick dark hair, the broad shoulders. Are all phages so attractive? What I'm seeing now in his granddaughter suggests that, once activated, the gene that transforms phages in so many other ways also enhances their appearance. The changes in Jenny Hrluska since her father gave her first blood have been striking, and they continue. Only a little over two months ago, she was a thin, pale child. Lying there on my ward, so deathly ill, she had a certain fragile beauty, but now she is stunning. Looking at the princely, unlined face of her grandfather, it is impossible to comprehend that he has lived more than a thousand years. He could pass for twenty-five. His son put me through terrors I could not have imagined. But now that I am safe from Zane, I can remember how striking he, too, was – is. Taller even than his father, with that sable hair, the startling jade eyes. Maybe it's another part of the genetic endowment of phages – a beguiling attractiveness that makes it easier to get close to their prey.

For that is what the gene compels them to be – predators. They must have fresh blood every few weeks or they will sicken and eventually die a horrible, lingering death. Bad enough, but the compulsion that goes with it is even worse, for the act of drawing blood triggers in them an overwhelming urge to kill. Merrick may be alone among phages in his ability to defy this instinct each and every time he takes blood. It chills me to imagine murder trying over and over to possess such a good heart, and if I am to go on loving Merrick without fear – as he deserves – I dare not dwell on it.

And the truth is, there is much to admire in them, just as we feel awe and wonder for the tiger so long as we're not in the same room with one. If I had not become a physician, I'd have studied anthropology, but I never dreamed that one day I, Katie O'Keefe, would discover a new race. Where did the gene for hemophagia come from? Did phages split off from humanity long ago in the mists of prehistory, or was the gene introduced by visitors from another planet? Merrick does not know. Scattered across the earth, phages have no society, no history. If they are entirely of

2

human origin, the genetic fork must have occurred near the beginning, because the differences are so great, right down to the cellular level. Zane's blood stayed fresh and viable in my lab long after a normal human's would decay. Their tissue can regenerate with incredible speed — I pumped three bullets into Zane's brain and he was down less than a minute. Merrick has survived, uninjured, falls of several hundred feet.

With such amazing levels of cell function it is no surprise that their muscular strength is tremendous. Zane tore open the roof of my house to get at me. Merrick recounts being trapped inside a flaming car once and escaping by tearing the door off with his bare hands. His burns were slight and healed in minutes. Phages are graceful and dexterous as well — I have that dim memory of Merrick racing up the side of a building after his son, the two of them propelling themselves across the mortar seams with their fingertips as easily as if they were sprinting along level ground.

And their minds are at least as fascinating as their bodies. From a distance, they can cause blood vessels of their prey to constrict or dilate. Influence, Merrick calls it. Normal humans have no control over parasympathetic nerve impulses. How do phages manage to stimulate them in their prey? It makes them nearly invincible as hunters. Not only can they use Influence to create blind spots on the retina, so you won't see them coming, they can drop you unconscious from thirty yards away by dilating your jugular veins and dumping blood from your brain.

With such remarkable powers, I wonder that phages have not set themselves up as gods among us. Maybe they have, at different times and places in history. But Merrick says most are solitary. Having no social group of their own, they haunt the periphery of human society. He estimates there are no more than a hundred thousand phages scattered around the world. Fortunately for humanity, the gene must be both rare and recessive. Though they are far stronger and more capable than any ten men, there are fifty thousand of us for every one of them. Better to keep moving, stay in the shadows. They seem content to be rulers of darkness.

God help us if they were ever to come into the light. Imagine a being that has lived a thousand years — when Columbus set sail for the new world, Merrick was already three times as old as any normal man can live. Think of all they have seen, all they know. A human face must be as easy for them to read as street signs. In a world that worships beauty and power, they could all be kings. Much as they fascinate me, I pray each night that whatever genetic constraint has kept hemophages rare will continue. Right now they *are*, in a sense, tigers, hunting alone, staying out of sight. If ever they were to become lions, to emerge from the shadows and band together, mankind would end up little more than a herd of zebras.

In the grand scheme of things, my other prayer is smaller, but no less heartfelt: I pray that Merrick will be able to teach his granddaughter what he was unable to get across to his son — how to satisfy, without killing, the terrible urge that now flares up in her every few weeks. For thirteen years, until puberty triggered the gene, Jenny was not only a normal child, but an extraordinarily sweet and good one, according to her mother. I witnessed her final months as that child. Watching her slip to the edge of death despite everything I could do, I prayed that she would live, and I will not now regret that she has been saved, however Faustian the bargain might be. If I had known what her leukemia really was, and that the nameless thing she hungered for was blood, I might have given it to her myself. How ironic that it was the lethal Zane who discovered who she was and gave her what she craved. If he had not pieced together that she was his daughter, she would now be dead.

For better or worse, she is alive, but what horrors she must face. Six months ago, a little girl with dolls and comic books and now she must drink blood to live. And the murderous urge that goes with it — how can she live with that? But she must, for there is no escape. Merrick is her best hope. Only he knows what she is going through and how to fight it. He could not love her more. If, after losing his son, he can save her, it will be his redemption, too. But will even his wisdom and love be enough to keep Jenny from becoming the killer she was born to be?

I must go on doing all I can to help. A powerful bond formed between Jenny and me while she was my patient, and she seems to admire me. I am the one normal human who knows her secret. By loving her still, maybe I can keep her from fleeing the life that has been hers. She is still so young, she may not realize nearly everyone is hiding something. That she is forced to do the same does not make her less human. I'll do my best to help her see that.

Still, I worry. Where will Jenny Hrluska be in a year, in ten years?

What will she be?

From the diary of Mary Katherine O'Keefe, MD

Chapter One

17 February 1999:

Jenn steeled herself as she headed for the last room on the coma ward. The air seemed dense, smothering, as if she were trying to push forward under water. Blue tiles slipped beneath her feet; a gurney drifted past, nuzzling the wooden guard rail. From the doorway ahead, she could hear the clicks and sighs of the respirator that, for a week, had kept Neil Hudson's body alive.

So we could heal him.

At the threshold, she paused to shape what she would say, the painful words, because unless a miracle had turned Neil around since this afternoon, she must now tell his wife that his brain was dead.

That's why they pay me the big bucks, Jenn thought, but could find no trace of a smile. With all the hundred-hour work weeks, resident pay averaged out to six bucks an hour, which meant she would earn seventy-five cents ripping Cheryl Hudson's heart out.

At least, I know how it feels. I can give her that.

Her readiness to use her own experience with death to help Cheryl encouraged Jenn. Even a year ago, she could not have mentioned Hugh to a patient, but the pain was small enough now to take out and put away again. Life was looking up. She had her work to challenge her, and her family to love — three generations of extraordinary men who vied with each other to coddle and look out for her. None of them would ever replace Hugh, but they would not die on her either.

Cheryl sat in her usual spot, tight against her husband's bedside, curly head down, seemingly intent on her needlework. After a week, the prospective cat still consisted of a single yarn ear, and Cheryl's pastel slacks and sweaters were starting to drape on her. In the constant summery heat of the ward, a sweater would seem out of place to most people. I always felt chilly, Jenn remembered, those nights in here with Hugh.

She tapped on the doorpost. Cheryl's head jerked up, the big, round glasses magnifying her look of surprise. 'Dr Hrluska, come on in! I wasn't expecting you — didn't you get off at four today?'

'Just finishing up a few things. How are you doing?'

'I think Neil's a little better.'

'Let's have a look.' Jenn saw that Neil's color was actually a bit worse, the dusky tinge of cyanosis tainting his pale cheeks. A faint, sweet scent rose from his skin, the lotion nurses used to fight bedsores. Jenn pinched his earlobe hard; no response, he was still oblivious to pain. Tension ringed the top of her throat. Taking out her penlight, she peeled Neil's left lid back and shone the beam onto his eye. The pupil did not constrict, and the last of her hope died away. Pupillary response was the key, and Neil's had been poor since admission. At this point, the chances of his ever waking up were slim to none.

'I saw him move again, Dr Hrluska, just a few minutes before you came in. That's a good sign, isn't it?'

'It can be, Mrs Hudson, but coma patients will also move as a result of a spinal reflex, which doesn't really involve the brain.' Releasing Neil's eyelid, Jenn inspected the sutures where the windshield had cut his forehead and cheekbone. His face was healing nicely — no higher order brain function required for that, either. He wasn't handsome, but she liked the laugh wrinkles at his eyes and the deep creases on either side of his mouth that gave him a slight smile even now. She imagined Neil striding the aisles of his American History class, looking his students in the eye, gesturing with enthusiasm as he lit them up with Lewis and Clark or the Gettysburg Address. He had been good, she knew, because every night kids from Fairfax High would drift in, eyeing Neil with dread fascination, their voices hushed as they kept their pained vigil. Good kids – most of them had been to the junkyard to see Neil's car, but they never talked about it when Cheryl was in the room. All of them were working on hope, and none more than Cheryl, but Neil had now reached the point where allowing further hope would not be a mercy.

Jenn's stomach tightened. She turned to Mrs Hudson, but before she could begin, Cheryl started talking, launching a nervous torrent of words, as if she knew what was coming and was determined to ward it off. She told how clever Neil was, how he could fix most anything, but always got filthy and managed to tear his clothes doing even the simplest tasks. Jenn listened, letting her talk, knowing it was important, Cheryl starting to gather to herself the parts of Neil nothing could take from her . . .

From across the hall, Michael Avalon, as he was now calling himself, watched Jenn through the door, observing with admiration her easy way with the frightened woman. Her shift was over. She could have put her grim task off until tomorrow. Just being on this ward, day after day – and many of the nights – meant reliving her own pain, but she did not shrink from it. Her big heart drew him as powerfully as her beauty – the long legs, her green eyes and leopard grace. He loved her hair, thick and short, that tawny golden color. Her tall body, now hidden beneath the shapeless white coat, possessed tremendous strength, he knew, almost as great as his own. Her mind was quick and strong. She had an irrepressible vitality just standing there, a thumb under her chin, one elegant finger curled over her full upper lip, listening with full attention as the woman talked about her dying husband. Even in her sadness, Jenn glowed with the flush of health common to her kind.

No one had bled to death to give her that flush.

Watching her now, Michael felt a surge of desire. I must know, he thought, if I could make her mine. No one has the right to deny me that. Just that much, and then I can face my fate.

Footsteps sounded up the hall and he turned. A short man with a ludicrous comb-over, a thousand dollar suit, and the aggressive, head-forward stride of a bantam rooster came on fast, shoving a gurney against the wall as he passed it. Rich Sikorsky, chief of neurology and Jenn's clinical supervisor. Michael held still, resenting the intrusion, making sure the man's gaze slid blindly across him. Rich marched into Neil's room and Michael retreated up the hall, frustrated. He wanted Jenn, so powerfully it made his chest ache. If he was going to make a move, it must be soon.

I will do it, he thought, the next time I find her alone.

Jenn heard Rich's footsteps several rooms away, that characteristic fast clip that carried him everywhere. She willed him to turn aside into another room, but no, here he came. Plucking the chart from the foot of Neil's bed, he rifled through it, frowning, then shook his head. Jenn felt Cheryl stiffen beside her. Didn't Rich realize she was standing right here?

Jenn said, 'Mrs Hudson, you remember Dr Sikorsky.'

'Sure. Hello, Doctor, how are you?'

'Fine, thank you,' Rich said absently. He replaced the chart and pushed Neil's eyelid up with a brusque, practiced motion, holding it there as he reached for his penlight. Shining the light into Neil's eye, he sighed. 'I'm afraid it's not looking good, Mrs . . . Houston, not good at all. You should be aware that your husband has virtually no chance of waking up. Zero, I'm afraid. His life can be sustained, of course, by the respirator and he can continue to be fed through I.V. lines like this one. There are long-term facilities that can see to those needs as well or better than we can. I'll let Dr Hrluska fill you in on all that.' Rich patted Cheryl's shoulder, glanced at his watch and sailed back into the hall.

Heat rushed to Jenn's face. *Bastard!* You can't even keep her name straight, but you couldn't wait to crush her.

'Is it true?' Cheryl's voice shook.

Hiding her anger at Rich, Jenn said, 'I'm sure you've known from the start that Neil is in a bad way. As we discussed on Monday, the odds against him grow each day he remains unconscious. His pupils still show no response to light, and at this point, we must begin to accept that his brain is too damaged to regain consciousness.'

'We? You don't have to accept it, I do.'

'Mrs Hudson, I know how you feel—'

'How could you? Neil is just another patient to you doctors. He's my whole life.' Tears spilled from Cheryl's eyes and ran down her cheeks, etching thin tracks through her makeup. 'And now you talk about farming him out someplace that'll keep his body alive with tubes and a breathing machine, as if that's all that mattered. Well, I won't let you do that, do you hear me? I'll fight it with everything I've got.'

Jenn reached for her hands, but Cheryl jerked them away and turned back to the bed, clutching Neil's arm, sobbing silently. Stung, Jenn longed to touch her shoulder, comfort her. Five minutes ago she could have done it, but that was before Rich had shattered her trust.

'I need to be alone with my husband now.'

'I understand. Maybe we can talk later.' *After I've done what I need to do.*

Jenn strode down the hall, looking into each room for Rich, feeling her blood sizzle. A voice in the back of her mind warned her to hold up, to think about what she was doing. Rich Sikorsky could ruin her career.

But Neil is *my* patient, she thought. I'm the one who knows him and Cheryl and who cares about them. I should have been the one to tell her. I could have helped her through this, I *do* understand. Rich, you bully, where the hell did you *go?*

'Hey, Jenn!'

Turning, she saw Wes Faltier bearing down on her. With an effort, she returned his smile. Wes was handsome, still sporting his California tan and bleach blond hair six months into his residency. He continually tried to be funny, and even made it much of the time, but now was *not* the time.

'Seen Rich?' she asked before he could say anything.

'What's he got that I haven't got, besides a BMW, a condo in Florida and two hundred thousand a year?'

She gave him another, tighter smile.

'Sorry, haven't seen him.'

Jenn stopped at the nurses' station. The charge nurse, Silvie, stood within the circular enclosure at the junction of neurology's two corridors, leaning on the counter top and gazing down the hall to where an LPN was trying to herd a patient with a bandaged head back into his room. The confused man submitted and Silvie turned, arching a dark eyebrow in question.

'I'm looking for Rich.'

'He's in the PET scan lab with his baby. Said he wasn't to be disturbed.' Silvie's eyes took an expressive upward roll.

Jenn hurried down the hall to the steel door Rich had installed when he'd begun working nights in the lab. The knob held firm as she tried to turn it, and for an instant she had the urge to tear it off. Easing her key in, she turned it and the knob together.

Rich squatted beside his prototype, fooling with one of its servomotors. He threw her a glance devoid of welcome and turned back to the equipment. Easing the door shut, Jenn leaned against it, knowing the only way to beat one of Rich's power silences was to wait it out. After the cosseting heat of the ward, the lab felt cool despite the blazing floodlight Rich had set up to illuminate the prototype. Rich's baby – Silvie was right – and as charmless as its daddy, a gray, steel armchair from Navy surplus to which two vertical rails had been welded. The rails, poking up from either side of the back, supported a metal crosspiece on which a helmet the size of a beautician's hair dryer had been mounted. Once Rich got the servomotors going, they would slide the helmet up and down the rails, adjusting it to the height of the patient in the chair. Ungainly, but that was probably true of most inventions in their infancy. At this point, smooth edges and ergonomic perfection weren't important.

Jenn found herself looking beyond the prototype to the round door set into the back of the lab. The porthole in it always made her think of a laundromat dryer rather than a miracle of modern science. But if Rich was the prototype's father, the cylindrical chamber behind that door was its mother. When the door was opened, a table-like cot slid out. The patient, having received an injection, lay down on the table, which then slid back into the chamber. There, sensors in the encircling wall scanned the patient's brain and other organs for positrons created by the injection. A computer displayed the organs, portraying their biochemical activity in vivid colors on a monitor screen. Called Positron Emission Tomography – or 'PET' scan, it was a powerful new tool, favored by neurologists because it allowed them to observe ongoing action in the brain, rather than the static 'snapshots' of its anatomy provided by CAT scans.

If Rich's idea worked it would be even more powerful.

Despite her anger, Jenn had to admit it was clever. No longer would patients have to lie prone inside the big chamber – Rich had managed to load the same scanning power into the helmet, which he had then wired, like the big chamber, into the lab's computer. The helmet limited the scan to the brain area, leaving patients free to sit and watch their own cerebral activity on the computer's monitor. Rich would use the prototype to try and teach people to home in on the activity they were seeing and learn to control it, using basic biofeedback techniques. If it worked, patients might be taught to regulate errant signals in their brain that caused high blood pressure, migraines; epilepsy. Rich would be hailed as a genius.

And he would still be a horse's ass. If only a PET scan could show him the mean streak in his own mind.

'You want something, Hrluska?' He continued to work on

the equipment. Deliberately, she stepped closer and bent as if to examine the chair. He fended her off with an alarmed expression. 'Don't touch. This equipment is one of a kind, very fragile at this point.'

'Like Mrs Hudson's feelings?'

'Mrs Hudson?'

'The woman you left in tears back on the ward.'

Rich eased back from the machine, rose and faced her. 'You are disturbing my work because the wife of one of your patients is sad that her husband is brain dead?'

'She isn't just "sad," Rich. She's broken-hearted, furious and scared.'

'Put it however you like. She needed the truth.'

'And she was about to get it, from her doctor. That's me, Rich, not you.'

'You object to my helping you? Most residents find it hard to tell patient families the bad news. It's my responsibility to show you how to do the hard things.'

Jenn stared at him. Was he faking sweet reason, or might he really be so clueless about what he'd done? She said, 'Mrs Hudson trusted me. By preempting me the way you did, you made it seem that I had held out on her, and then you further aggravated the situation by giving her the impression that you and I had discussed the "details" of moving her husband into a maintenance facility, which we have not. It trashed the bond we had formed, making me seem as callous as you, and it shattered what little sense of control she has right now.'

'So now you're instructing me on how to break bad news. Tell me, *Doctor* Hrluska, what would you have said to her? "Your husband probably might be dying?"' Rich gave her a cold smirk.

'I would have told her that I could offer her no further hope that her husband would wake up. I'd have explained that the man she knew and loved is gone beyond all suffering. Then I'd have put my arm around her and confided that coma took my husband too, and that I know it's going to hurt so bad she'll

14

want to scream, and it will seem like the pain will never end, but she can come through it and feel like living again. I would have stayed with her as long as she wanted, answered any questions, including about Hugh and me. I'd have held her if she needed it. I would *not* have talked about moving her husband out of his room, much less the hospital, or keeping his body alive with machines — not until she felt ready to ask about that.'

Rich shook his head with an air of weary superiority. 'Right, I've been waiting for this. Just because your husband died in a coma, you think you, a resident, know more about how to handle patient families than a board certified neurologist, chief of this service. Well, I'm sorry to tell you, but you don't know squat. Your experience with your husband is useless — worse than useless, because you're letting it screw up your objectivity. This is an eight hundred bed hospital, Hrluska, the biggest and busiest in the city. No matter what they told you on your psych rotation, the more time you spend holding hands with relatives or friends of patients, the less time you can spend treating the patient. Whatever you irrationally wanted doctors to do for you back when your husband died, it wasn't their job then and it's not your job now. I'm sorry your husband died in a coma, but Christ, Hrluska, it's been three years. Get over it.'

Rage flashed through Jenn. All at once she could see the carotid artery pulsing in Rich's scrawny neck, sense the blood rushing through it. The rich smell of it filled her head and she felt the muscles in her legs tensing to leap at him—

Alarm coursed through her and she took half a step back, her face tingling as if she'd been slapped. 'Keep your mouth shut about my husband,' she said in a low voice. 'You know nothing about him and a lot less than you think about me.'

Rich's eyes widened.

Watch it! Jenn's pulse thundered in her ears; she could not seem to stop the words boiling up in her throat. 'And with all due respect, in the future, if you feel you need to intervene in my treatment of my patients or my care of their relatives, would you have the courtesy to take it up with me, not them?'

'Hah?' He stared at her, popeyed, his face turning red.

No resident had ever talked to him like this before, Jenn realized. *And I shouldn't be, either.*

'Get something straight, Hrluska. I'm your supervisor, and I'll intervene whenever and however I judge necessary. I want that patient out of here tomorrow.'

'You should have thought of that before you did your charming little act with his wife. She told me she'd fight us moving Neil with everything she's got.'

'I won't have him taking up a bed from someone with a better shot at recovery.'

'We have three beds open right now.'

'One bad moment on the beltway could change that.'

'What is it, Rich? You're worried about the paperwork if Neil dies on your ward, the inconvenience of having to present his case to the morbidity/mortality board?'

Rich took a step toward her, and she saw his fist tightening. She fought off a powerful urge to laugh. On his best day, Rich Sikorsky couldn't lay a hand on her.

But he can kill your career.

Rich took a deep breath and relaxed his fist. 'You're way out of line, Hrluska. I could terminate your residency for this kind of insolence. I demand that you apologize for that last remark.'

'I apologize.'

He looked taken aback, then glared at her sullenly, as if her apology had cheated him. 'When I tell you to get that man out of here, I'm doing what I know is best for him, not me, understand?'

'And if Mrs Hudson calls in the patient representative?'

'Christ, she knows about that?' Rich grimaced. 'Bleeding heart social worker. Worst mistake the hospital ever made, as if we doctors aren't already representing the patient's best interests.'

Jenn kept silent.

'Well, talk to her. Get her to see reason with all this rapport you think you have with her.'

'Had, Rich.'

'All right then, run an EEG on the guy. Prove to her he's brain dead. Also it will give us ammo with the patient rep.'

Jenn knew she had no choice. And if the EEG people were overbooked it might win Neil another day or two on the ward, give Cheryl time to adjust.

'And in case you're thinking of dragging this out,' Rich said, 'don't. I'll be watching for that, I mean it. Don't take any crap from them about "standard environment" and having to schedule him in their lab. A coma patient has got his own built-in freedom from distraction. Tell them to bring their portable rig down tomorrow. Get the wife in to watch the test, show her the flat lines and explain in no uncertain terms what they mean. Then dry her tears and get her husband out of here and into maintenance. Now if you'll stop wasting my time, I have important work to do.' Rich turned away to his machine.

Just dump the blood from his brain, watch him collapse into his precious prototype—

Alarmed by the intensity of the impulse, Jenn hurried from the lab and shut the door behind her.

Heading back to Neil's room, she unclenched her teeth and shook her shoulders, trying to purge the tension. It almost seemed as if Rich had deliberately come gunning for her tonight, and Cheryl had simply been a convenient tool. The timing alone was suspicious, him rushing in practically at the very moment it first became necessary to give Cheryl the hard news. It was the first time she'd suspected him of baiting her, but lately he was always on her case about something. Why? *I've worked hard*, she thought, *done my best for all my patients, and my best has been pretty damned good.*

As she walked, her anger bled away, and she began to think more coolly about what she'd done. *I could terminate your residency.* Her scalp prickled. How could she have taken such a risk? *I have life where I want it*, she thought — *right where I've got to keep it, and then I rock the boat, hell, I stand up and start stomping a hole in the bottom. What's wrong with me?*

Reaching Neil's door, she found it closed. She tapped once,

then pushed the door open a foot. Cheryl wasn't in the room. Her needlepoint materials sat beside the chair, but sometimes she left them there overnight. The soft sheen of the window drew Jenn's eye, night pressing like black water against the glass. She went to it and looked down at the parking lot, searching for the old VW Cheryl's brother had loaned her. There it was, the dents in the yellow paint visible even from seven stories up. She probably just went to repair her makeup, Jenn thought. I'll wait — I've got all night.

Then she remembered that tonight was family dinner at Merrick and Katie's. When she'd decided to hang around to talk to Cheryl, she'd called Chemosh and invited him to meet her here and ride along with her. Dinner was usually around eight and it was six-thirty now, so he'd probably left his apartment, but at his leisurely, strolling pace, it usually took him an hour to walk uptown to the hospital from the Watergate. Surely Cheryl would be back before that.

But will she even let me talk to her?

Jenn put the negative thought from her mind. Somehow she must get through to Cheryl, win back her trust.

And then put things right with Rich. Neurology residencies were hard to come by, and if Rich terminated hers it might well torpedo her chances of getting another shot elsewhere. Then, the best she could hope for would be a general practice.

She'd be all done fighting coma.

A terrifying emptiness yawned open inside her, and then she felt the only thing she feared more than emptiness — the red thing that waited, always, to fill it.

Chapter Two

Waiting for Cheryl to return, Jenn watched Neil's chest rise and fall to the ceaseless rhythm of the respirator. With his wife gone from his side, he seemed smaller, lifeless despite the forced tides of air.

Jenn opened her mind to his pulse, swallowing against the rasp of thirst aroused by the faint, steady beat. Neil's body still lived. Oxygenated blood bathed his injured brain with each involuntary breath. Did he feel anything in the primitive centers of emotion that might be left to him? He reminded her so much of Hugh three years ago, Hugh's face serene night after night, his arms arranged along his sides atop the blankets. She remembered worrying that he might be feeling pain, trapped under all that calmness, unable even to moan.

Stop it!

Jenn busied herself checking the line on Neil's I.V. drip. The rate seemed a little slow; she increased it, fighting a sense of futility. A faster infusion of dextrose and amino acids wasn't going to help Neil if the most important part of him was already dead.

What would she say to Cheryl? First an apology—

Jenn's neck prickled. Suddenly she could feel the window behind her, the black glass — *someone watching her!*

Impossible — this was the seventh floor.

The feeling intensified, rippling down her spine. Turning, she froze. The face beyond the glass peered at her for a second and then vanished.

Stunned, she continued to stare. A phage, using influence on her? But that only worked on normals, didn't it? Maybe not. If this one was very powerful . . .

Jenn's mouth went dry. For a second she stood, petrified with fear, and then she thought of Neil, lying helpless behind her. Had the creature out there come to feed on him?

A desperate resolve seized her. Powerful or not, he wasn't getting her patient. She rushed to the window. In the parking lot below, an old man bent with difficulty to get into his car. No one else was in sight. Pressing her face against the glass, Jenn strained to see down the side of the building, but the brick sill outside cut off the angle. He could be clinging to the mortar seams just below, staring up, his keen predator hearing bringing him the hammering of her heart through the glass.

She listened for the trickle of mortar dust.

Nothing.

The roof, Jenn thought. I could see the whole wall from there.

Hurrying from Neil's room, she turned right into the stairs and raced up two flights. From the top floor landing, a narrower, side stairwell led to the roof. Unlit, it was nearly dark, but her predator eyes adjusted at once to the murk, making the passage flare into a semblance of daylight.

The door at the top was locked.

Frustrated, Jenn turned away, thinking of the helipad atop the hospital where the Medevac choppers brought people in to ER. But that was at the other end of the long wing, and by the time she could get to it and follow the roof back here, whoever had been at the window could be well away.

Jenn grasped the knob and tore it, shaft and all, from the door. Pushing her finger into the hole, she found the sheared end of the deadbolt and drove it sideways into the jamb, burying it in the wood. The door swung open and she ran across the gravel rooftop to the edge two stories above Neil's room. The wall plunged away to the grassy strip that bordered the parking lot. No one clung to the brick.

Or no one she could see.

The cold, February wind swept up the wall, scouring her face. She sniffed it for any trace of him but smelled only bus exhaust from the street beyond the parking lot. How long had it taken to get up here? Thirty seconds, a minute at the most. She listened again for the fall of mortar dust. The wind was too loud, moaning through the air-conditioning compressors behind her, an eerie sound that raised her hackles. Turning, she looked down the wing toward the heliport—

There!

Her breath caught. Tall, his height emphasized by the long, black coat that fanned like a cap around his ankles. Her eyes tingled as she drank every glimmer of light from his dark form. A gust of wind whipped his hair to the side. Was it red? Hard to tell through the greenish tint of night vision. He stared back at her with an intent stillness that made her spine crawl.

Then vanished again.

Jenn sucked a breath. Her knees felt weak, as though she might faint. Was he striking at her with Influence? The thought sent fresh fear pumping through her.

She forced her mind back to Neil. Not just Neil, hundreds of other patients in the huge, sprawling complex of wings, all of them vulnerable, and then she was sprinting along the roof, barely feeling the gravel beneath her feet, sailing through the darkness. Her heart pounded. A shivery buzz, like a fly trapped inside her skull, told her he was still there, tampering with her vision. Would he attack her? How could she fight someone she could not see? She slowed as she reached the edge of the roof, searching for any hint of him, a scatter in the gravel, a trace of shadow.

'Are you there?' she asked softly. 'What do you want?'

A flapping sound startled her – *wings?* – and then she realized it was the flag at the front of the hospital, snapping to the wind.

Catching movement at the corner of her eye, she whirled and saw a security guard in the parking lot, starting to look up at her. She struck out, constricting the capillaries of his retinas to create a second blind spot where her image would fall. The guard gazed up a few seconds longer, then shrugged and continued his rounds, walking away from her. She felt a mixture of relief and dismay. Another second and he'd have seen her vanish, maybe gotten enough of a look to identify her, and that would have caused real problems.

She headed back across the long roof to the stairwell and down. The lights of the ward blazed with painful intensity in the instant before her eyes readjusted. The hallway, so familiar to her, looked strange, a mock-up, not quite real, somehow.

Cheryl Hudson's things were now gone from her husband's room.

Jenn felt a small relief. She was too rattled to talk to Cheryl right now anyway, even if she'd allow it.

I have to think.

Heading up the hall toward the residents' break room, Jenn tried to make sense out of what had just happened. *What was he doing at that window?*

The break room was empty this early in the next shift. All eight chairs sat well back from the communal table, skewed this way and that. The familiar sight soothed her with its potion of normalcy. Circling, she restored order, Jenn the den mother. Did guys lack a gene for pushing chairs back under a table? Wes Faltier had argued that the male residents were just being polite, sparing her the trouble of pulling a chair out. What would be his alibi for this litter of styrofoam cups — hey, Jenn, it makes the place look lived in? Smiling now, she policed up the coffee dregs and emptied them into the sink, then settled at the table, feeling calmer.

A new phage in the area — she must let the family know. Chemosh would be showing up soon to ride to dinner with her, but maybe she should hold off and talk to Zane first. He was trying so hard to be a good father, and he might be hurt if she took this problem to her great grandfather. Besides, Zane had developed some unusual abilities of his own back when he'd been running for his life. If anyone knew whether a phage could blind one of his own with Influence, it would be Zane.

But why should a hunter that powerful need to turn to prey lying helpless in their hospital beds?

Or was he just looking?

Jenn focused her memory on the face at the window, those few startled seconds when she'd seen it up close: Square jaw, long red hair swept back from a broad forehead, falling almost to the shoulders. Handsome, in a hyper masculine way. And curious, yes. Like he'd never seen a hospital before and just wanted a look. Then, when he realized I was seeing him, he somehow upped the wattage and I lost him. But why climb the wall when it would be so much easier just to walk in? And why, after he knew what I was, did he let me see him again on the roof? Maybe his control isn't perfect.

The door squeaked open and Jenn looked up. Goosebumps rippled along her arms and then she realized the man in the doorway could not be the creature from the roof – not unless he'd been to a barber in the last five minutes. His hair *was* red, though – a deep auburn actually, thick on top but tapered to a fine buzz cut around the ears and at the nape of the neck. About the same height as the creature on the roof, too, the same broad forehead and powerful build, so muscular at the shoulders and thighs that loose khakis and a baggy black sweater couldn't hide it. His face was different from the one at the window, though, the line of his jaw strong but not square. The straight nose and generous forehead seemed oddly smooth, flawless as a child's, but there was something knowing in the composed line of his mouth. His eyes were almost too vivid, the warm, rare blue of sapphire. He was not so much handsome as . . . *arresting*.

I *have* seen him, she thought. Not on the roof tonight but somewhere.

You're staring. 'Hi. Can I help you?' Her voice seemed to startle him. He blinked, and she realized he'd been staring at her, too. A pleasant warmth crept into her face.

He said, 'Just giving myself a tour of the hospital. I'm Michael Avalon, the new guy in psychiatry.' A low, mild voice.

'Jenn Hrluska, second-year resident here on neurology.'

He nodded. 'Actually, I'm semi-new. I've been here almost a month, but I haven't had much time to explore. I don't want to disturb you.'

'I was disturbed before you came in.' Jenn felt startled at herself. Why had she told him that?

He smiled and spread his hands. 'Then maybe I can undisturb you — we shrinks live for that.'

She watched her hand, seemingly on its own, pull a chair out for him. He sat and tipped back, lacing his hands behind his head, as relaxed as if they were old friends, though he did not look at all old. In fact, he looked young to be an attending in psychiatry. Then it hit her, who he was. 'Avalon — I've heard about you.'

'Oh?'

'Hospital grapevine.'

'I'm afraid to ask.'

'Single, independently wealthy, nice to everyone — which, by the way, is considered a rare trait among senior staff.' OK, and handsome — admit it. For weeks, female staff from neurology had been trumping up errands to Psychiatry. Michael must have slipped, unseen, past the nurses' station or he'd never have made it this far. If I had ever met him before, Jenn thought, I'd remember. So why does he seem so familiar? He looks sort of like that actor, Matthew McConaughey, but that's not it. This is a feeling like I've *been* with him before.

For the first time in years, Jenn remembered what it had been like to dream. That's what this felt like, that she might have dreamed of him, shadowy images of him sitting companionably with her in her living room, or watching while she worked in the garden — strange, nonsensical, but there. If she *had* dreamed this face with the brilliant, knowing eyes, this marvelous body, it was long ago, because she had not slept since the change; thirteen years.

'Nice to everyone.' He looked embarrassed. 'I sound insipid. What would this hospital grapevine say about you?'

'That I come here, treat patients and go home.'

'That's it?'

'Pretty much.' And that's just the way I want it, Jenn thought. 'And which of those three things has you disturbed tonight?'

That there used to be more than three. 'None of them, actually.'

He gave an expectant nod.

I have to give him something, she thought. But it certainly can't be that I saw a face at a seventh-story window. 'Just a little problem with my clinical supervisor,' she said.

'A little problem?'

'He's been coming down pretty hard on me lately.'

'Has he been like that with his other residents as well?'

'Not that I've observed. I can't figure it out. He seemed fine with me at first — in fact, I thought he liked me. Then it just slowly went bad.'

'He desires you.'

Jenn looked at him, startled. *Does he think that because he finds me attractive himself?* She felt her pulse picking up. A lovely thought, yes, but it could go nowhere. 'Excuse me?'

'A professional surmise. I've met Sikorsky. The fact that he's married is an obstacle to his desire, but an even bigger one is that hospitals have strict rules against romance between supervisors and residents.'

'Romance with Rich?' Jenn felt disgusted.

'Romance might be too fine a name for it.'

'I hope you're wrong, but if you're not, do you have any professional advice?'

'Nothing you can do. The problem is entirely his, and he must take care of it. I'm afraid that's what he's doing by giving you a rough time — trying to convince himself that you are *not* wonderful, and beautiful, and desirable.'

He didn't seem to be coming on to her, just stating a fact that everyone would find obvious. Flustered, she could think of nothing to say.

Michael said, 'Something happened between you two tonight?'

'I was easing the wife of one of my coma patients into preparing for the worst. Rich bustled in and told her that her husband's coma was irreversible and we needed to transfer him to a maintenance facility. Just tossed it off and breezed out. She burst into tears and became angry at me, too. I was so mad at Rich I went after him.'

'Are you always so protective of your patients' families?'

'Shouldn't I be?'

'You'll get no argument from me.' Michael eyed her. 'I have a confession. I've heard of you, too — the neurology resident who used to be in pediatrics but changed specialties when her husband died . . . after a prolonged coma.'

Jenn hesitated, thrown off stride. From the beginning, she hadn't talked at the hospital about Hugh's death. He'd died here, and neurology staff who'd been around back then all knew about it, of course, but it surprised her that anyone would still be talking about it.

And further that she didn't mind Michael bringing it up. 'Are you saying I can't be objective about coma?'

'Why would you need to be?'

'Exactly.' Take *that*, Rich.

'But it must be rough sometimes, especially if one of your coma patients happens to remind you of your husband.' He leaned forward, giving the back of her hand the briefest touch. 'I'm sorry. Maybe you'd rather not talk about it.'

'That's all right. I'm curious, though. What did you hear?'

'That your husband was injured trying to rescue someone from a fire.'

'He did rescue them. Two little girls. I was here at the hospital when it happened. Hugh was a novelist, so he worked at home. He was taking a break, jogging around our neighborhood in Alexandria when he saw smoke coming from a house. The downstairs was on fire and the girls were trapped upstairs. He ran in and carried them outside, then asked them if anyone else was in the house. They must have misunderstood because the older girl said yes, even though the house was empty. He ran back in and the ceiling collapsed on him.'

The remarkable blue eyes turned dusky. 'How horrible. I'm sorry.'

Jenn felt pressure building in her throat but continued, knowing she could keep control. 'He was in a coma for three weeks. I'd hold his hand and try to get through to him — you know, concentrating, willing my thoughts into his mind. I got pretty weird. Sometimes I . . . even imagined I heard him calling my name. But he died without ever waking up.'

'What the little girl told Hugh . . . is that why you left pediatrics?'

Cutting close to the bone now, but she found it didn't matter, she wanted to answer. 'For awhile I couldn't get it out of my mind. If only she'd answered "no," I'd still have Hugh. But it wasn't her fault. She must have been scared out of her wits. What I couldn't stop thinking about was how Hugh and I had decided to put off kids until I could finish my residency. We both wanted children. We never imagined . . . After he died, I . . . just . . . found myself unable to go on seeing kids every day.'

'And you had a new passion, fighting coma.'

'That's right.'

Michael's eyes watered and he blinked. 'Must be mildew in here. I'm allergic.'

'We grow our own penicillin in the fridge.' *Is he about to cry for me?* The thought touched and, at the same time, dismayed her. She didn't want pity. She just wanted her life to be normal, stable, under control.

'How about you?' she said. 'Why psychiatry?'

'There's no blood. I faint at the sight of blood.' He made a drooping motion with his hand toward the table.

She smiled, doubting it. *If he knew what the sight of blood does to me . . .*

'To tell you the truth,' he said, 'I thought psychiatry would be like Ann Landers, giving everyone advice. What fun. Boy was I wrong. The first thing they teach you is never to give advice—'

Michael's watch began beeping; he shut it off and looked at her with regret. 'I've got a patient in ten minutes. Good luck with your coma case. Maybe we can talk again.'

She nodded.

Again, he touched her hand, this time lingering. Her heart quickened. For an instant, the sapphire eyes openly admired her, then he was gone.

Jenn felt her blood simmering in places she'd half forgotten. And she had better forget them again now.

At the sink, she studied herself in the mirror, trying to see what Michael had evidently seen. The uncanny illusion that she knew him persisted – not just knew him, but had spent time with him. Impossible. She didn't know him and wasn't going to know him, except casually, because sooner or later, she'd owe him the truth about herself. *By the way, Michael, I'm a hemophage – like the vampires in the stories, except I'm the real thing. I can go out in the sunlight and I don't turn into a bat, but I do have to drink human blood or I'll die. Is that a problem?*

And even if it wasn't, even if Michael could get past that, as Hugh had, she could not risk the pain again. Hugh had looked strong and indestructible, too.

But they die.

Jenn released a pent-up breath. *Easy, Hrluska. You are not going to let yourself fall for Michael, so you don't have to be afraid of him. He matches some kind of ideal that has taken root in your unconscious, and that's why you feel you know him, but it's just illusion. He made you feel good just now; take that for what it is, and don't wish for more.*

The door opened again, and she looked up with anticipation, but it was not Michael. Chemosh eyed her with an odd distraction, as if he'd forgotten why he'd come. For a second, his befuddled look reminded her of the ancient being hidden inside his youthful, phage body, but the ghostly impression

28

quickly faded. How could this smooth-skinned man with the deep tan, straight back and warm brown eyes be anyone's great grandfather, much less ten or more centuries old? His gleaming hair was black as onyx, so dense he has to pin it back to keep it off his forehead. The way he carried himself, his grace and dignity, made her think of a young sheik — a role he might well have played sometime in his long life. She could imagine him striding through a bazaar in Cairo or Damascus, a dozen servants in his wake. Centuries of canny investments had made him rich as a sheik, and the surging bull market of the past few years had redoubled that wealth several times over. He could afford a fleet of stretch limos with full-time chauffeurs, but that did not stop him from hoofing it or taking public transportation whenever he could. She could smell the subway on him now as she gave him a welcoming hug. He stiffened, then hugged her back, and she savored the contact, mindful of how rare it was. Chemosh might be a little shy of physical affection, but it was a small enough flaw among many virtues.

He stood back, studying her with concern. 'You all right?'

'Fine.' Had he sensed in her some lingering anxiety about the creature on the roof? Michael had distracted her so thoroughly she'd all but forgotten the phage, but Chemosh's long life had made him uncannily sharp at reading people.

'Ready to go?' he asked.

'You stopped off for an espresso.'

He raised an eyebrow, and she felt a little foolish. Why try to match his clairvoyance when it would be obvious to him she'd merely smelled his breath?

'A cappuccino, actually,' he said. 'They have a Starbucks at the DuPont Circle Metro — two of them, in fact. Can't pass them up.'

'DuPont Circle? That's nowhere near your place, not even on your way.'

'Don't worry. I'll do justice to Katie's fine cooking.' He barely smiled and she realized the stiffness was still on him, a troubled look in his eyes.

'Are *you* all right?' she asked.

'Of course.'

'And you would tell me if you weren't?'

He gave her a small smile. 'I might.'

'You do realize I'm going to get seriously upset with you if you keep stonewalling on yourself.'

'What stonewalling?'

She pushed a finger against his ribs, hard enough to make him blink. 'I'm serious. You're always ready to listen to my problems, but you never seem to have any of your own, and I don't believe that.'

He took her hands. 'Jenn, I've never been so happy as this past year. Finding my family, becoming a part of your lives — it's all I could ever want.'

'You're upset about something right now.'

'So are you.'

'No you don't. We're talking about you now. I saw it in your face the minute you walked in.'

'It will probably come to nothing. There's no sense in talking about a problem that might not even be a problem. If I'm wrong, I'll come to you with it, I promise.'

She realized she'd won ground. She had seen enough of him to know he would not use the word 'promise' lightly.

He said, 'And now we get to ride in your splendid little car?'

'I'll even let you drive, if you like.'

'No, thanks.'

'You *can* drive?'

'Of course.' He gave a small sigh, and she realized she was starting to try his patience. It frustrated her. Couldn't she at least know why he loved riding the subway, or in her MG, but had no interest in driving and refused, despite all his millions, to buy a car? What could he have done or suffered in his life that would make him so reserved about himself, leery even of being touched, when he so obviously cared for her?

Outside in the hall, she started to turn toward the elevators, then caught herself and led Chemosh the other way, toward the stairwell. He'd never objected to using elevators, but he didn't have to. No phage would like the security camera in the upper corner – a bloodless eye, immune to Influence. And if an elevator broke down, it turned into a trap. Thinking about it now, she realized how far she'd let herself drift from her own instinctive wariness. As a resident, you rushed everywhere, so if you needed to go to labs or psychiatry or the cafeteria, and the elevator was there, you took it . . .

And why was she questioning herself? Usually, she accommodated Chemosh without giving it a thought. The strange phage at the window had raised her awareness of what she and Chemosh were, and she did not like the feeling. She just wanted Chemosh to be her great grandfather and herself to be Jenn Hrluska, neurology resident.

So the thing to do was put the phage from her mind as quickly as possible. She'd get Father aside after dinner tonight and tell him what had happened, let him check it out if he thought it necessary. It would please Zane to be asked for help, and she could then put it from her mind and get back to being herself, just herself.

Following Chemosh from the stairwell into the parking lot, Jenn bent into a gust of wind. She heard the flapping flag again, and this time it did not sound like wings.

Chemosh said, 'That handsome fellow I saw coming out of the break room – who is he?'

'Michael Avalon. He's a new psychiatrist here.'

'Is he?'

His odd inflection made her wish she could see his face. *Does Chemosh think he knows Michael too?* The flag stopped flapping, and in the sudden stillness her spine tingled with foreboding, and in that instant she knew, somehow, that the safe and orderly life she'd been building was starting to tip over.

Chapter Three

Guard mankind. For this hath thy Creator made thee strong, delivering thee from sickness and from sleep; yea even from the weight of years that draggeth men down to their graves. Divide thou the earth among the families of thy kind, first the cities, then the towns and villages, even to the wilderness at the ends of the earth wherever any man shall set one brick upon another. Keep ye each family to its chosen ground. There shall ye protect and shield man, but enlighten him not, for his Creator alone shall save his soul. Only shelter thou his body from harm, bearing him up lest he dash his foot against a stone, for he is weak and darkness hath fallen upon the earth.

Codex Angelorum I, 1

Following his patient into the theater, Michael tried to focus on the task at hand. Only an hour ago, he'd been with Jenn — and she, for the first time, with him. His mind glowed with her, and at the same time his stomach churned over what he'd done. That she might respond to him had been his greatest hope, but what next? Could he really cast aside his duty?

Your duty right now is to your patient. Think about Jenn later.

Screen C was one of the larger theaters of the multiplex. Entering, Michael overrode the impulse of his eyes to neutralize the darkness, relishing the cozy feeling of anonymity it conferred. The buttery aroma of popcorn made his mouth water; knots of people chattered and laughed as admonitions flashed on the screen — no talking, no smoking, please leave from the rear exits when the show is over. Michael followed Julius down the long aisle, the screen expanding until it filled his vision. At the fifth row from the front, Julius turned and filed into the land of the young, the popeyed and the rubber-necked.

'This all right, Doc?'

With an effort Michael resolved giant swirls of red into jumbo colas dancing across the counter of a concession stand. 'Perfect.'

With a skeptical laugh, Julius tugged him down into his seat and offered his tub of popcorn. Scooping out a handful, Michael chewed, dimly aware of salt and grease, seeing Jenn through the shifting play of light on the screen — Jenn's beautiful eyes, green as jade, gazing back at him for the first time.

How long had his eye been on her? Ten years now; looking in on her every few months at first, then monthly, and then, as he got into the rhythm of her feeding cycles, every two weeks. Finding her ever more fascinating, until finally her courage after her husband's death had utterly won his heart. Fifteen hundred years he had lived, and in every one of them he had witnessed death and every shade of mourning from relief to collapse, including incredible bravery. But he had never seen anyone handle it quite the way Jenn had. She did not act brave. What she did was make herself laugh and smile at the hospital despite her grief, faking it so her misery would not spread to her co-workers. She wept only at home during the long, lonely nights. Though it gutted her to talk about her loss, she did so with Kate, the human who had become like a mother to her, and with her hemophage father and grandfather, knowing if she did not, their worry about her would deepen into torment. And finally, the Jenn she had willed for the comfort of these others had begun to be her true self again. What joy to see her once again finding pleasure in working that tiny back garden of hers, down on her

34

knees lifting the leaves of her violets to water under them, cooing as if they were favorite nieces. Her hunger to learn had returned and she'd buried herself in medical journals, fending off the lonely hours after midnight when her tireless phage body denied her the oblivion nature allowed normal people. Sometimes, in the absolute quiet of 2 or 3 a.m., she would look up from her desk and he would see a flicker of recognition, almost as though in some deep, unconscious part of her brain she were actually seeing him.

But that had only been fantasy.

Tonight, reality. Finally she *had* gazed back at him, and in that instant, he'd felt like he'd grabbed a power line.

Amazing that he could have lived so long and never felt such a jolt before. Women of his own kind observed him every year at the conclaves. He'd looked into their eyes too, all of them beautiful, with their symmetrical faces, each half a mirror of the other, perfect, always perfect. But Jenn — such voltage behind that direct gaze, all that she was and all she fought not to be, sitting there looking at him while they'd talked about coma and commitment.

What will Father do when I tell him?

Michael felt the lightness flee from him. Clearing his mind, he focused on Julius again. Had it been a mistake to bring him here? Watching a kid watch a movie was hardly accepted diagnostic procedure. He could imagine the prissy voice of the chief of psychiatry: *Doctor, is that what they taught you at Stanford?* Possibly followed by more dangerous questions to deans or registrars: *Take a look at this photo of Dr Avalon. According to his records, he was in your med school class of 1993 . . .*

A risk, yes, but not a mistake. Three 'real' doctors had done nothing for Julius. If I let him get worse so I can play it safe, Michael thought, then 'Dr Avalon' is only a means to an end, a subterfuge to get close to Jenn, and I will have sinned.

The movie started off with a car chase and a fight. From the corner of his eye, Michael monitored the boy's face in the flickering backwash from the screen. Wesley Snipes, kicking ass in an alley, and Julius's rapt expression was right on specs for a fourteen-year-old male.

What was not on specs was that Julius Nash kept sticking hats pins through his hands.

Michael winced inwardly, feeling a phantom spike through his own palm as he tried to fathom the desperation that must drive this kid's self-destruction. The only son among three daughters of a middle-class black couple, Julius was intelligent and likeable. Not an obsessive compulsive or a masochist, nor was he on drugs. Julius had no idea why he felt compelled to hurt himself. His parents and sisters clearly loved him and all joined in family therapy sessions, but they had no insights either. Rorschach inkblots elicited only ordinary responses. TAT cards, with their suggestive tableaus, suggested little to him. Brain scans appeared normal. Julius wouldn't – or couldn't – come to the doctor, so it was time the doctor went to him. Or the day would come when the boy would trade pins for razor blades and his palms for his wrists.

Wesley Snipes, having run off the bad guys in the alley, was now accepting the thanks of the woman he'd saved. Their faces drifted together, Wesley preparing to lay a gentle first kiss on her. Michael saw that Julius was now gazing with half-lidded eyes at the bottom of the screen, turning out this mushy part. His expression was neutral, neither engrossed nor grossed out, though most boys his age would have been one or the other.

Interesting. When was a non-response a response?

'You're so fine,' Snipes murmured.

His tenderness to the woman made Michael think of Jenn, the apple-peel fragrance of her skin. He felt suddenly hollow, the air prickling in his lungs. What had he done? He'd told himself he had to know. Maybe Jenn would be indifferent, or merely polite, and he could turn away at last and accept his duty, the fate that awaited him. But Jenn had not been indifferent. She had responded to him, he had felt the power of it, as if something in her had been waiting for him to walk into that room. He could love her truly, and she could love him, he felt almost sure of it. So instead of release, he'd taken the first real step, and gotten her to take it with him. The dream had become reality.

But what next?

Michael suppressed a groan. The plans were set, Philippa would be arriving in three days and they would then be officially engaged. The marriage would come soon after. Could he really back out at this point? *What will Father do when I tell him I love a phage?*

Gunfire exploded on the screen, the action resuming in torrents of breaking glass. Snipes and the woman ran from the alley, chased by friends of the earlier bad guys. Michael made himself concentrate on Julius again. The movie raced along to its finish, a final violent confrontation, another kiss, and then the credits started to roll. Julius heaved a sigh and turned in his chair as the lights came up. 'All right!' he said.

'Glad you liked it.'

'It was all right.' This time his inflection was blasé, as befitted a homie on the edge of manhood, except that he gave himself away by grinning. Michael followed him back up the aisle, marveling at how his loose stride worked to help keep his baggy, ultra-low-slung pants from falling down. The bill of his Orioles baseball cap hid his thin neck; the black NWA sweatshirt, at least three sizes too large, made him seem all the skinnier, but somehow he made it all work, proving that teenagers had more grace than often it seemed.

The theater exited to a sprawling parking lot of Springfield Mall. Drey had pulled the car up and was waiting for them. Michael gave the nephilim's sloping shoulder a squeeze as he slipped into the back seat with Julius. Drey's head cocked – had he sensed more than a greeting in the touch? *That's right, old friend, I'm troubled, And I've no one but myself to blame.*

In the soft radiance of the car's dome light, Michael saw with a pang how much gray now peppered Drey's cropped fringe of hair. It was easy to forget the nephilim's age. His bald head, larger toward the top, was curiously like an infant's. The ears stuck out, and his dainty chin heightened the impression of a grave, outsized baby. Drey was only a hundred and a score, but that was old enough for the senescence genes from the human half of his parentage to start dragging him down. Still a few years left for him, but not enough, never enough.

An image of Drey lying still and cold in the round funeral chamber deep inside the mansion brought a dull pain to Michael's chest, as though his heart had twisted inside him. The urgency of the emotion startled him, and then he realized what he was really afraid of – that if he went ahead with Jenn, he could lose them all – Drey, Mother and Father, his sister and brothers.

Surely not.

'My man,' Julius said to Drey, 'where you been while we in the movie? Doin' wheelies in the lot?'

The nephilim swivelled and gave the boy a tolerant smile. 'I trust you enjoyed the movie, Master Julius?'

Michael felt a sharp longing at the easy rapport between Drey and Julius, each comfortable in displaying his very different and uncompromised self to the other. If only everyone could look beneath the surface as keenly as these two had with each other. Drey's habitual dignity, ingrained by decades of service to the Loyola clan, could make him seem aloof, even cold, but Julius had recognized the kindness in the mild, brown eyes and responded to it, just as Drey had seen through Julius's street talk and hardcase poses to the sweet, troubled kid beneath.

But could Drey, could any of the family, see the divine in an eater of blood?

'Home, Drey.'

'Yes, Master Julius.'

The boy popped a wobbly, green gummy snake into his mouth and slouched down, as if riding in an antique Chrysler limousine was an everyday occurrence for him. With only the mall theaters open after ten, escaping the huge parking lot was easy, and Drey soon had them cruising up 395 toward Washington.

With an effort, Michael turned his mind once more to

Julius's therapy. Tonight's session wasn't over yet. 'What part of the movie did you like best?'

'When he went over the falls,' Julius said. 'Those rocks – I thought he'd had it. Extreme.'

'What about when he put the moves on the woman?'

'Huh?' Julius gave him a blank look.

Michael saw with surprise that the boy had no idea what he was talking about. Probing, he was unable to find any mental images of the romantic parts of the movie in Julius's mind. The youngster hadn't merely ignored or disdained those parts, he hadn't registered them to begin with. *I've depended on being able to tell what he's thinking, when it's what he's not thinking that may tell the story.*

Michael looked out the window at the massive floodlit fortress of the Pentagon sliding past on his right. The building blurred and he saw instead his own pained eyes reflected in the glass. Did Julius have brain damage after all, something too subtle to show up on scans?

'You OK, Dr Avalon?'

'Fine.'

'Good, 'cause you *look* like some dude just stuck you up for your Jordans.'

Michael found a smile.

They pulled up in front of Julius's home on a narrow, gently sloping street in Adams Morgan. An inviting house, cream-painted wood and green shutters, a big front porch, looking like it belonged in the country, not on this small lot in Washington, DC.

'We still on for day after tomorrow?' Julius asked.

'You bet.' Michael resisted an impulse to hug him, knowing it would embarrass him. Instead, he gave the boy's minutely scarred hand a pat and watched him slide out and bound up the steps to his house. The door opened before he reached it, spilling a yellow square of light across the porch. Julius's father raised a hand and Michael gave a cheerful return wave as Drey pulled away. But he did not feel cheerful. He wanted to protect Julius, save him, but first he must know from what.

He caught Drey observing him in the rearview mirror.

'You seem troubled, my lord.'

'Yes.'

Drey glanced into the mirror a few more times, then tightened his grip on the wheel and fixed his gaze resolutely on the road. Now I've embarrassed him, Michael thought. He's afraid he's been too forward. But that's nonsense. We've talked of so many things over the years.

Dare I tell him about Jenn?

His mind swept back over the century they'd been together. Drey was only eighteen when he'd first taken up his duties, and from the first he'd kept a certain distance. Nothing seemed able to penetrate his reserve — jokes, comradely hands on the shoulder, calling him, 'my friend,' nothing. Then, seeing that it was not aloofness but awe which stood between him and the nephilim, Michael had begun to ask Drey's advice on various matters. The power of this small gift had been truly astonishing, as Drey had begun to open up, to look him in the eye — in short, to become the friend Michael wished. Asking his advice, at first something of a kindly pose, had developed into more as, over and over, the nephilim had helped him, often merely by listening. And now that Drey was beginning to see in his mirror the age that would never show on Michael, he had grown almost comfortable in offering his fatherly advice. If anyone would make an effort to understand how he could have fallen in love with a phage, it was Drey.

And if he can't, Michael thought, I need to know that too, before I go to Father.

'Promise you'll tell no one?'

'My lord.' Drey's voice was soft with rebuke.

'You don't yet know the scale of it.'

'You're having second thoughts about your marriage to Philippa.'

Michael stared at him, astonished.

'Asa has seen you pacing the trails in the woods near the stables. Morian, in the kitchen, tells me you haven't finished your supper in weeks. And I, myself, am hardly blind, Michael. You're more quiet than usual. I see the distant look in your eyes. This marriage is a huge step for you and the Loyola clan. Who wouldn't get the jitters?'

Michael had a sudden sense of the intimate interconnection of the estate's twenty nephilim, who carried out all the mundane duties of running the household, from gardening to cleaning to buying the food and cooking, maintaining the grounds, even keeping the family's finances straight. Clearly, they were all more attuned to the moods and nuances within the family than he had ever imagined.

'If it were me,' Drey said, 'I'd be plenty nervous.'

'What do you mean?'

'Philippa is beautiful, Michael. So tall, with those long legs and lavender eyes. I may be over a hundred, but as I say, I'm not blind. And she has a powerful mind. No sharper than yours, of course, but formidable. Your last wife was many years ago, when I was still young, and now, at last, you will be marrying an equal, one of your own kind. I would be amazed if you did not have many questions. Perhaps even some anxieties about how it might go in bed?' Drey kept his eyes on the road.

A sense of unreality swept Michael. Sex with Philippa? Whenever he'd thought of it, his mind had shied away. Beautiful, certainly, but he kept remembering her at the last conclave. Everywhere he'd turned, she'd seemed to be there. He'd talked with her several times, and she'd given him a long, rather patronizing discourse on how best to decide which person to save when several were in immediate danger at the same time. He had thought her chilly and superior, and had come away feeling vaguely guilty at his aversion to her. Then to find that she was smitten with him, so smitten that Amator, patriarch of the Evangelines, had approached Father to suggest marriage.

And even now, with that marriage so close at hand, it did not quite seem real. He barely knew Philippa. It was Jenn he knew, Jenn he wanted.

Michael turned to the window. Outside, an unpopulated

stretch of the parkway slid by, a band of woodland bordered on its far side by the Potomac. The oaks had not yet budded, and their blue-black branches stood out against a silvery bank of moonlit clouds above the Potomac. He could feel the life in them, waiting to burst out, and it filled him with yearning, for he could feel it in himself, too.

'I'm in love with another.'

One tire ran onto the shoulder before Drey corrected, his eyes wide in the mirror. 'Michael!'

'Believe it.'

Drey slowed, turning in at the Washington Yacht Club. He pulled the limo to a stop in the overflow lot of the restaurant. Well back from the water, surrounded by trees, the lot was empty this late at night. Sliding away from the wheel, Drey set his back against the passenger door and gazed at Michael with a mixture of wonder and alarm. 'Another angel?'

'No.'

'A human woman, then. But Michael, surely you see—'

'Not human either.'

Drey blinked.

'She's a doctor at the hospital. The most loving and caring woman I've ever seen.'

'I don't understand. If she's not human and not an angel . . .' Drey trailed off. 'A *phage*?'

'Not like any you ever heard of.'

'Dear God.' Drey put his hands to his face.

'She doesn't kill. She's a doctor – a healer.'

The nephilim's hands dropped, revealing eyes moist with shock and dread. 'Doesn't kill? How could that be? How does she get blood? No. I . . . I can't believe I'm hearing this.'

Alarm bubbled up in Michael's chest. *You always thought I could do no wrong. If you're this horrified, how can I hope to persuade Father?*

'Michael, you've only been at the hospital a couple of months. How could you have fallen in love so quickly?'

'It wasn't quick. I've . . . observed her for ten years.'

'But why? Why would you do that – a phage?'

42

'Listen to me. The time I first saw her, she was sixteen. It was late at night, pure chance. I was checking a neighborhood in Falls Church and I heard the grate of a foot against brick, the trickle of mortar dust. I moved in and saw this teenager climbing straight up the chimney of a house, just her fingers and toes in the mortar seams. That's a scary sight, Drey. It raised my hackles. I knew what she was, of course, so I followed her through an open upstairs window into the master bedroom. There was a young couple in the bed and the woman rose up on an elbow, but Jenn dropped her right down again, then dilated the man's jugulars, too, so he couldn't wake up. Very quick, very practiced. I got ready to grab her, but then she whips out a couple of transfusion packs. That stopped me dead. All I'd ever heard from Father was how vicious they are, how deadly. But she was gentle. She tapped into a vein in the woman's ankle and drew off a pint.'

Drey's shoulders twitched in an involuntary shudder.

Michael felt dismay; he was not getting through. 'She was as repulsed as you are, my friend. I read her, and I could feel it — horrible torment. Just a girl, but forced to drink blood or die. Not a quick death, either; a normal human could starve to death in a tenth of the time and with far less pain. It horrified her that she had to drink blood, I felt that very clearly. Think of it, Drey. For the first thirteen years of her life, she is a normal little girl, who plays with her friends and rides her bike and goes to school with no inkling that puberty will activate a gene that will strike her down with a terrible illness. She lies in her hospital bed, growing sicker by the day with what the doctors all think is leukemia. Fever burns in her; the pressure of the mattress against her aching joints drives out sleep, making her groan with each breath. She is dying, and her mother and the man who thinks he's her father can do nothing. Then a mysterious man comes in the night. Her true father has discovered her, and recognizes her illness for what it truly is because he has it too. He gives her blood, and the sickness fades away. From then on she must drink every few weeks or it will return. But even that is not the worst, because hemophagia drives its victims not just to feed but to kill. Every second she was in that bedroom, she was fighting a powerful compulsion to jump on that man and woman, rip their throats open with her teeth, shake them around the way a cat kills a mouse. Instead, she bit down on a wet rag as she drew the blood. I could see her trembling. Tears ran down her cheeks. She took a pint from the woman, then the man, and then she got out of there as fast as she could.'

'I've heard they take great pleasure in killing,' Drey said doubtfully.

'Maybe they do, most of them. But I wonder if pleasure is the right word. Pleasure is something we elect to do — listen to a beautiful symphony, or savor a fine wine. Is it pleasant to breathe? Only if you've been unable to. It is *necessary* to breathe. Breathe or die.' Michael grabbed the front seat and pulled himself forward, willing the nephilim to understand. 'Look, at first I felt just like you. I was sure she must be a killer if she was a phage, and the only reason I followed her home that night was so I could keep track of her and protect her future victims. But there never were any. I saw her slip into other bedrooms after midnight, and it was always the same — she longed to kill, lusted for it, but somehow always resisted. More and more her self-denial fascinated me. As far as she knew, there was no one to stop her, but she just wouldn't do it. She was *determined*. She became a woman, not a girl anymore, a doctor — a healer — and she was just so beautiful in every way, inside and out. That's who I fell in love with Drey, not an evil phage, but a remarkable and rare woman. Even then I resisted, telling myself her kind were forbidden to me and I could never have her. Ironic. Like her, I had come to want something desperately which I would not allow myself. For the first time, I truly understood how she must feel every time she sips at what she was born to devour.'

Drey covered Michael's hand on the seat. 'You must continue to deny yourself. This cannot be.'

'Have you heard nothing I've said?'

'Everything; it changes nothing.'

'I don't love Philippa. I love Jenn. And you say it counts for nothing.'

'Of course your feelings matter. If you come to me for sympathy, you have it. What a burden you must bear. But you are strong enough.'

'I'm not sure I am.'

'You must be, for the sake of your family. This is far more than a marriage, Michael, it is an alliance, as surely as any medieval English prince marrying a Spanish Princess. The Evangelines have become the most influential of all the clans while the glory of the Loyolas has steadily faded . . .'

'You would have me marry for influence, power?'

'Surely you don't consider these means beneath you if their end is the greater glory of God? But I forget how pure your heart is. And you do not hear what is said.'

'What are you talking about?'

Drey looked pained. 'Maybe I shouldn't—'

'Come on.'

'All right. For years there have been whispers at the conclaves. Rumors about the Loyolas. Such things are not said in your hearing because you angels are so serious about maintaining unity and comity, especially at the conclaves. The burden of righteousness is not so heavy, I'm afraid, on the shoulders of us nephilim. We hear what our masters say in the privacy of their homes, and we are human enough to discuss it among ourselves, while you are up there in the clouds, having your meetings.'

Michael felt a dread fascination. *Why have I not glimpsed this other world of those who keep our households? That is not pureness of heart, it is arrogance, for which I should be ashamed.* 'And what have you heard while our heads are in the clouds?'

A meager smile touched Drey's lips. 'I meant no disrespect, my lord.'

'Perhaps you should have.'

'Never.' Drey gazed out at the lot. Michael waited, watching gnats swarm outside the window, glinting in the brassy glow from the light poles. At last the nephilim turned back. 'It is said that, long ago, Uziel stood at the left hand of God.'

45

Michael felt a thrill, deep in his stomach. 'Father? He's never spoken of it.'

'He may have reason. The stories also hold that he fell from favor. That he rebuked God and ran from Him, and that this is what began the long silence all the clans have endured.'

Michael stared at Drey in shock. 'Outrageous. It cannot be true. In all my life, fourteen centuries, Father has never shown anything but full devotion to God.'

Drey held up his hands. 'Please, Michael. I'm not criticizing Uziel, only repeating what I have heard. The stories may well be false. They are from long ago, beyond the limit of memory.'

Michael felt a superstitious chill. The limit of memory, yes. But it *was* true that, for thousands of years now, neither Uziel nor any other angel had heard the actual voice of God, and even the old stories of it had nearly faded from the shared memory of the clans. The true ancients, like Uziel of the Loyolas and Amator of the Evangelines, were thought to go all the way back to heaven itself. But no mind except for God's could possibly hold onto a past so impossibly remote. New experience continually crowded out the old, and even those things written down came, in time, to lose the charge of reality they might once have carried. No one questioned the divine inspiration of the *Codex Angelorum*, but its purpose was to set forth the duties of angels, and it had almost nothing in it of history.

How many thousand years, Michael wondered, before I forget this night, that I sat here, terrified of bringing disgrace on my family before the other great houses? I will forget that I was so desperately in love with Jenn, that Drey ever existed, even that I knew Jenn, because too much will have happened between.

A vast weariness passed through him, leaving an ache in his chest.

'My point,' Drey said, 'is that your marriage to Philippa will create close ties to the leading clan of angels. Amator will be giving the house of Uziel the most powerful sign of approval any father can give another. Uziel has felt his isolation, I know it, but this could redeem him, give him new life for the glory of God. If you and Philippa are blessed with children, it will be a further sign of divine approval, of immense importance to all the angels. But if you refuse the marriage, the shock of it will be felt throughout the clans. The *Codex* makes mention of fallen angels, Lucifer and his followers. None are known to exist any more, but the idea persists and has great potency. If you refuse Philippa for a blood eater, you must face the possibility that you will be seen as fallen.'

Michael felt a cold tremor. Defiant, he shook it off. 'Not if they look on Jenn's heart.'

'But Michael, you have said yourself that there is evil in her heart — that she longs to kill.'

'A longing that was coded in her genes before she was born. She did not ask for it and does not want it. Her only choice is to give in or defy. She defies. Who is more noble, Drey, someone like Philippa, who is virtuous because she's not tempted to be anything else, or someone who fights to be good every day of her life?'

Drey's eye turned thoughtful, and Michael felt a small hope. 'Would it please God for me to marry without love, to do so for politics, to aggrandize the name of my clan?'

'You really feel nothing for Philippa?'

'Nothing at all.'

Drey looked sad. 'Michael, I cannot say what God wants for you, but I know that, as your friend, I would not want to see you trapped in an eternal, loveless marriage. If you must refuse Philippa, it cannot be for a phage. If you could propose an alternative to your father, a marriage into some other clan, it would help soften the blow. Haven't you met someone at the conclaves you find attractive?'

'Maybe others could fall in love in a week, Drey, but I can't. If it were in me, it would have happened long before now.'

'Surely a hemophage can't be your one and only hope of love. If your father could find your mother—'

'That was different. Father fell in love with Mother nearly two thousand years ago. At that time, there were only two hundred and fifty million people on the planet. As many as ten clans guarded each protectorate, and the protectorates were far smaller. Father was in daily contact with Mother in Jerusalem for years as part of his duties before he came to love her. There are now more than twenty times as many people on the planet. They breed like rabbits while we can produce a child only rarely. Two thousand years ago, a family covering one neighborhood of a city could stay close enough together to converse in each other's minds. Now we are spread so thin that if cell phones had not been invented, we would not be able to stay in touch as we patrol. Look at our family, Drey. Five of us to guard all of Washington. We're overwhelmed. We try our best to protect people from harm as the *Codex* tells us to, but we fail to save so many, and the burden of that failure weighs on us every day. We do what we can, but it is never enough. Knowing Jenn, loving her, has eased my burden, given me new strength and resolve. Would you deny me that?'

Drey sagged back against the door. The fear was back in his eyes. 'I would deny you nothing, my lord, even if I had the power. Your father does have the power if he commands you to go through with the marriage, then what?'

A chill went through Michael. 'I'll reason with him.'

'And if he refuses your reasoning? Michael, as his son you feel his love. You have never clashed, and so you have no sense of how powerful he is, how determined to do God's will as he sees it. We nephilim all feel it. It's almost scary sometimes. No one could hope to oppose him, and you must not try, Michael. Promise me.'

'I love and honor my father, you know that. If I come before him with Jenn, I promise I'll do what I believe to be right before God. Even Father has no right to demand otherwise.'

Drey's mouth opened, then closed again. He slid back behind the wheel and started the car. The headlights stabbed out, illuminating a tangle of brush at the far border of the parking lot. 'I owe you everything,' Drey murmured. 'My life has been joyous because of you, and if the Loyolas are now headed for dark times, I will stand by you to the gates of hell. You have honored me over the years by asking my advice. I have never cared if you took it — to be asked was enough. If truly you love this phage, I can't condemn it. But I beg you now to bear in mind that passion can cloud judgement, even yours. Please don't do anything hasty. Have you told this phage how you feel?'

'Her name is Jenn. Dr Jenn Hrluska.'

'Yes, my lord.'

'I haven't told her, no.'

'Then you've made no commitment to her.'

'I have in my heart. And tonight I took the first step. I approached her and she responded to me, I could feel it.'

'Of course she did. What woman could fail to?'

'Are you trying to flatter or annoy me?'

'I'm sorry, Michael, I'm just saying you are handsome and an inner light shines in you. Dr Hrluska started out as a human, and no human who saw an angel could fail to respond. It says nothing about whether you would truly be compatible. If you tell your family about her, and then it doesn't work out between you and her, you'll have caused terrible anguish for nothing.'

'Drey, Philippa will arrive in three days. I must talk to them before that.'

'Fine. Tell them you're nervous, you have the jitters, that you are not yet quite prepared emotionally — whatever — but do not, I beg you, tell them you can't marry Philippa because you're in love with a phage. Just ask for a postponement. Give yourself time to see whether this can even go further between you and Dr Hrluska.'

Michael hesitated. He would feel a certain relief if he could put off the confrontation, but then it would just hang over him. 'It isn't honest.'

'What isn't? That you aren't quite ready? That you need more time? Michael, listen to me. You have never asked anything of your father that he might deny. As an angel, you have such great power, each of you more mighty than a thousand men. You hold the world in your hands. And that is why you have never needed

49

to develop the tactics of persuasion we lesser mortals must master. Listen to me, please. The course you are considering could set your father against you and two great houses of angels against each other. It could shake the pillars of heaven itself. Uziel has the power to deny you, make no mistake, and you cannot begin by asking the impossible of him. Ask the possible. Ask for a delay. That will be hard enough.'

Through his frustration, Michael felt a grudging wonder. This old man had been on earth only a hundred and twenty years. All the mortal frailties thinned the blood of angels in him. *And his very limitations show him things I cannot see.*

'You're right, Drey. I'll do as you suggest.'

The nephilim turned to him, relief lighting his face. 'I know that was hard for you, my lord. I have spoken of your father's power, and it is awesome. But you, Michael — your ability to listen, even to the likes of me, to look for truth in unlikely places, gives you a strength not found in the rawest power.'

'It is also what got me into this mess in the first place,' Michael said.

'I wasn't going to mention that.'

Reaching forward, Michael ruffled the fringe of hair at Drey's neck. 'Let's go home, my friend, while it's still home.'

Chapter Four

Beware the blood eater. Shouldst thou come upon him, preserve thy charges, but assail him not, lest he smite thee sorely. Except God willeth unto thee his death, suffer him to flee, for all that liveth draweth breath from the Creator, who shall judge each soul in His time. And is not the blood eater even now cursed among all creatures, few in number, scattered across the earth, driven forth alone in the night to slay lest he perish? Though he take himself from the eye, doth not his prey reproach him with his own image? At his peril cleaveth the blood eater unto his kinfolk, nor hath he a city of his own, nor record of his race to succor him. Yea must he fear to tarry a week with his fellows lest the trace thereof undo them all, to be snared like lions for the pit.

Codex Angelorum III, 14

Chemosh hid his inner turmoil as he followed his son and daughter-in-law into the living room, where they always had their coffee. He must get Merrick alone and explain how dangerous this so-called Dr Michael Avalon was to Jenn — to all of them. But there were risks even in explaining, and he still wasn't sure how to handle it. Time was passing, winding tight inside him. All through dinner, he'd kept up a calm front while rehearsing what he might say. Now, still unsure, he found himself settling into the old wingbacked chair that had become his on Tuesday nights, just as if everything were fine. How good it had been, these evenings with his family in this cozy room, with its Persian carpets and creaking floorboards, its overstuffed couch and pretty knockoffs of tiffany lamps. But the horror was back. They were all in danger, and only he had a hope of saving them.

Watching Merrick and Katie arrange themselves on the couch, he could hear Jenn below as she and Zane started up their weekly game of pool in the basement. The lilting sound of her laugh tore at his heart. She's so precious to all of us, he thought; so *young*. I've lived longer than I've any right. If I end, no great tragedy, but I can't bear losing a child, not again.

With an effort, he calmed himself. That Jenn was still alive meant Uziel, as yet, knew nothing about her. Michael, on the other hand, must be assumed to know everything. With the ability of his kind to read minds, he was certainly aware Jenn was a phage — and didn't care. Her dedication to healing must have hooked him, together with her refusal to kill. He'd found a way to overlook her *lust* to kill — an amazing open-mindedness for one of his kind — but Uziel would not overlook it. He'll be appalled and outraged, Chemosh thought. He'd burn in hell before letting his son join with a hemophage. He will not merely be enraged, he will *destroy* her. Doesn't Michael understand that?

Somehow, I must stop it.

'More coffee?' Kate leaned across Merrick to lift the carafe from the end table.

Chemosh realized he'd already drained his cup. He brought his cup to her then returned to the chair. The wooden 'tock' of a pool cue sounded down in the rec room, followed by the thump of a ball falling into the pocket. Jenn's voice drifted upstairs and more laughter, this time from Zane. See how Merrick cocked his head, no longer able to hear such distant sounds clearly. I'm noticing everything tonight, Chemosh thought, every expression, each little gesture, all so vivid, because I know I might lose them. A lump rose to this throat. How close Katie and his son sat now, like young lovers. They were beautiful together. He had to admit, the physical signs of age Merrick was bringing on himself with the injections actually suited him, letting some seasoning of his long life show in his face without yet eroding the rugged proportions of his body. Aside from the silver hair, he looked only late forties or early fifties, deep chested, with dockyard shoulders and the warm eyes of a parish priest.

Katie didn't look her age either, though there wasn't a drop of phage blood in her body. At forty-five she was still lean and limber as a girl, looking good in jeans as she walked around barefoot in her house, or sat now with her feet tucked up under her. Her dark hair, with its red undertones, looked windblown and a bit wild, as if she'd just come striding in from the moors instead of taking the garbage out to the back stoop.

I can see why Merrick thinks she's worth dying for, Chemosh thought, when death seems far off. But it's closer than they think. Can I persuade Merrick? And if I do, will he follow my lead? He's accepted me now, and we've begun to grow close, but he's used to leading the family, and that must end if we're to survive.

'I'd better go upstairs,' Katie said, 'and make sure Gregory is studying as opposed to fighting Zorlons from the planet C-minus.' She gave them each a quick kiss, then bounded upstairs.

When she was gone, Chemosh said. 'How *is* Gregory doing in school?'

'The nuns complain that he's not applying himself. He keeps bugging us to let him go to public school. Fine with me, but you know Katie.'

'She wants to shelter him. You can understand it.'

'Sure.'

Chemosh drew his chair closer and leaned forward. 'That doctor Jenn was talking about at dinner. What do you think?'

Merrick smiled. 'She seems quite taken with him. If she'd known him longer than twenty minutes, I'd say she was in love.'

Though it matched his own perception, the emphatic way Merrick said it made his heart sink. 'So you don't believe her when she insists she isn't ready to start dating him or anyone else.'

'Not for a second. You weren't around when she was falling in love with Hugh. Tonight I saw an eagerness in her eyes that I feared might never be there again. Did you notice the way she kept sighing at dinner? She must have done it half a dozen times, as if she has three years' worth of stale air trapped in her and she's finally pushing it out.'

Chemosh managed a nod. He had not known Jenn when she'd fallen in love with Hugh, no, but he had seen love on the faces of more people than he could remember and in the eyes of hundreds of women who had found him irresistible. Jenn might not yet know it, but she *was* falling in love. People could do it in a single day, from nothing more than a whiff of pheromone. How powerful must the animal magnetism of one like Michael be? He'd gotten close to her, touched her, no doubt. His compassionate air, his seeing gentleness would be as enticing in their own way as his physical allure. How could Jenn resist an angel?

Chemosh felt a galling bitterness. That's what they called themselves. Angels, lords of light.

'You seem upset,' Merrick said. 'Isn't this what we've all been hoping for, Jenn to come out of her emotional coma? Do you know something about this guy?'

'He's Uziel's son.'

Merrick looked puzzled, then the dark eyes narrowed. 'Uziel — the one who——?'

'Yes.'

Merrick leaned back into the couch, pressing a hand against his forehead. Chemosh gave him time to remember what they'd talked about that night a few months ago, when they were still deep into each other's histories, trying to make up for a thousand lost years. The grandfather clock in the foyer measured off the seconds with dull clacks as his own mind, against his will, raced back in time to the royal palace at Per Ramesse, the year 1236 — very near the end of his reign. He stood again in the immense bedchamber of his son. He could smell the sweet fragrance of lamp oil. Soft light flickered. He tiptoed to the canopied and cushioned pallet far too vast for the little boy who lay sleeping on it. Chemosh touched his son's round, mahogany cheek, wondering at the fine down on it, then stroked the thick black hair, so like his own. The child went on sleeping, wrapped in a loose silken nightshirt, his beloved cat nestled close to his face. Chemosh felt a fierce love for his son, so wonderful and perfect.

Someone else entered the room. Turning, Chemosh saw a tall, glowing shape at the far end of the chamber. The noble face, the square jaw and the shaggy mane of red hair sent a tide of fear and wonder through him.

I am Uziel. I sit at the left hand of God. I bring His judgement now upon you.

The voice sounded in his mind, loud and brassy, eerily split, like two trumpets sounding in different pitches. Suddenly, he was unable to move. Uziel raised his left hand. The three fingers between the thumb and little finger flamed with light, sending a brilliant white beam across the chamber to strike the forehead of Chemosh's son. The little boy began to twitch and jerk. Seized by an overwhelming panic, Chemosh tried to break his paralysis and help his son, grab him away from the beam of light, but still he could not move. He felt as if a great hook had pierced his spine, pulling him up to dangle, his feet thrashing inches above the floor, unable to move him closer to his son. He could only watch, helpless, as the boy's twitches deepened into spasms and then convulsions. *He's dying! My son is dying!*

'Stop!' he screamed. 'Take me. I'll do whatever you want!'

With a fierce effort, Chemosh threw off the memory. His teeth had clamped together. He forced them apart, but the fear remained, clenching now in his gut. Uziel, the destroyer. *And now he will want Jenn, then the rest of us.*

'Are you all right?' Merrick asked.

Chemosh gave a stiff nod.

'When you told me about Uziel killing your son, you didn't mention that he had a son, himself.'

'I don't know that he did, then. I found it out much later. I didn't tell you this, but five hundred years ago in Barcelona, I spotted Uziel again. His was not a face I'd ever forget. Four others were with him, two males and two females. The one I saw at the hospital tonight – Jenn's "Michael" – was one of them. I've been assuming they were still in Spain, but if Michael's here, so are the rest of them.'

'Maybe Uziel has died by now.'

'I doubt that very much. They live a lot longer than we do.'

Merrick studied him. 'Seems you know more about them than you've told me.'

'I didn't think it would ever be important.' Chemosh hesitated, swallowing against a sudden dryness in his throat. This was where it got tricky. The parish priest in Merrick's eyes was more than an illusion. He had the mind of a Jesuit, a strict, even harsh morality that had driven him out to hunt not just his own kind, but his own son, back in the days when Zane had been a wanton killer. If he decides my own failings have given me a distorted view of Uziel and his kind, Chemosh thought, I'll never persuade him of the danger. But he'll want to know how – and why – I know so much, and he'll smell the slightest dishonesty.

The truth, but carefully.

'Most of what I know about Uziel I learned in Barcelona. After I saw him, I followed them at a great distance and was able to track them home. When they went out the next day, I reconnoitered the place, a big villa. They had fifteen servants, all what they call nephilim – the result of matings between one of Uziel's kind and a human. Interesting creatures. They live longer than most people and are quite strong, but at the same time docile, happy to spend their lives as servants to the "lords of light," as they call them. I waited my chance and waylaid one of Uziel's nephilim as he went to market. Using Influence to dilate his jugulars, I dumped just enough blood from his brain to put him in a semi-conscious, compliant state so I could question him.'

'What were you after? Revenge?'

'I . . . Yes. I wanted to find out if his kind could be killed.'

Merrick's expression darkened. Chemosh hurried on. 'More than a century before I spotted Uziel in Barcelona, I had encountered one of his kind in Persia, I'd carried off a sick old man and was preparing to feed when this strange buzzing sensation began in my mind, and then this tall, blond-haired creature materialized right in front of me. Called me a blood eater and the next thing I knew, my brain was on fire. He apparently had no fear of my powers, because he came so close I was able to strike him with Influence. I managed to pinch off the blood to his brain; he went down and I ran like a terrified field mouse. I had no idea if he was dead or just stunned. It turns out I was lucky he came close. From Uziel's nephilim I learned that they can strike with lethal force from quite a distance, certainly much farther than we could deliver a killing blow with Influence. Maybe the one I struck down in Persia was young and inexperienced and didn't realize I could fight back at close range.'

'So did you attack Uziel?'

So easy to lie now, simply by omitting the truth. 'It was Michael I wanted to kill. A son for a son.' Merrick looked away, shaking his head. His disapproval stung. 'Damn it, I wanted to see the same grief and pain on that bastard's face as he had burned into my heart.'

'Though his son had done nothing to you?'

'My son was innocent, too, only a child.'

Merrick raised a palm. 'Clearly, you didn't kill Michael. Why?'

Chemosh gave a bitter laugh. 'I decided instead to prove to myself that I was better than Uziel.'

Approval softened Merrick's expression; he nodded and sat back in the couch, and Chemosh knew with relief that he had found the right words. The truth, in fact, but that could not stop him from feeling like a hypocrite. Better than Uziel? What a joke.

Another memory engulfed him, of standing on the wall of his new palace, watching a hundred slaves, chained together in two long lines, drag a huge block of stone toward a nearby site where construction was still in progress. They moaned in pain and exhaustion but the overseers kept them going with the long whips. It tore their skin, Chemosh thought, and the warm, dry breezes carried the smell of their blood to me. Each night my vizier brought me the weakest slave so we could drink deep.

They were former enemies, after all, taken in battle. Life was new and grand — was grand, the most mighty of all kings. I had no choice in any case but to drink blood, and it freed me from having to harm my own subjects. Has any other phage ever done as much as I did for the masses? In ruling them, I also protected them. Under my command, their armies conquered and their people prospered. I built up their cities and their civilization. Surely I gave more than I took.

But now the temples are empty, reeking of age, scoured down by the sand of ten thousand windstorms. Dirty, fuming buses disgorge crowds of tourists, who shuffle through the ruins with wide eyes, trying to see them in the light of other days. They *were* magnificent, but they are dead and I am not. I, who forced slaves to build my cities while I drank their blood at night. Uziel was right to hate me, but I have changed. Must more of my innocent heirs die because I was once a monster?

'I wish I *had* killed Michael. Our Jenn would not now be in such terrible danger.'

Merrick frowned. 'Aren't you overreacting? Just because they ran into each other at the hospital doesn't mean he has any interest in her.'

'Michael didn't just happen across Jenn. They read *minds*, Merrick. He knows she's a phage. He'd never have come near Jenn unless he was attracted — so powerfully that he doesn't care what she is. If Uziel knew about it, she'd be dead already.'

Merrick's face paled. 'Maybe Michael won't tell him.'

'I'm certain that he will. That family is tight as a wolfpack. No way will Michael give them up for her, which means he'll bring her to them.'

'Even knowing how his father feels?'

'He may have worries, but clearly he thinks he can overcome any objections his father might make. He can't have a clue of what Uziel will really do, or he'd never have started this.'

Merrick looked down at his hands. He was silent for a long time. 'You know how fond I've become of you,' he said in a low voice. 'I would hate to lose you, but if Jenn is truly in danger, maybe you need to think about leaving us, going somewhere else. I would miss you – we'd all miss you terribly. But we must face the fact that you're the one Uziel truly hates. If, when he finds out about Jenn, you are gone from her life, maybe he'll let her be.'

Chemosh felt a piercing sadness, than saw the sheen of tears in Merrick's eyes and realized what the words had cost him. *He raised her from first blood, twelve years with her before he even knew I existed. He'd do anything to protect her – and so will I.* 'You were right to say that. And if I could save her by leaving, I'd catch a plane tonight, but it would do no good. The only way Uziel can be sure his son won't join with a blood eater is by destroying Jenn, and he *will* do it.'

Merrick looked frightened. He blew out a breath. 'You sound so *sure*, but how can you be? I know you believe everything you've told me. I'm not questioning your honesty, but how do I know you are *right*?'

'Trust me.' Desperate, Chemosh leaned forward and touched Merrick's hand. 'It's hard, I realize – we haven't been together that long. But I know Uziel and you don't. I'm the only one with a hope of getting us out of this, and you must follow my lead now.'

Merrick got up and went to the living-room door. Alarm filled Chemosh. Was he going to tell Jenn? They mustn't – not yet. Rising, he took a step toward his son, then Merrick turned back. 'What do you propose to do?'

'Go right now and find Michael. Persuade him he must leave Jenn alone or his father will kill her.'

'*I'll* do it.'

'No, Merrick, it has to be me – just listen, will you? I'm going to invite Michael into my mind, where he can see what his father did to my child at Per Ramesse. Uziel can't have told him that, or he'd have known better than to think he could bring Jenn into the family. When he sees the truth, he'll give her up – he has to.'

Merrick looked like he still wanted to argue; finally he nodded. 'All right. Where does he live?'

'I don't know. There are no Michael Avalons in the phone book, and his answering service was no help. But the hospital must have his address in their personnel records – they'd never employ a doctor who wouldn't give them that.'

'I'll go with you.'

'And if the night watchman sees you? I can hide myself, but the injections have taken that away from you.'

'How will you get in? Can you pick a lock?'

'I'll manage it.'

'Do you think you can just slip a credit card in and wiggle it like they do on TV?'

Sounds of protest rose from downstairs, Zane accusing his daughter of being a hustler. In that second, inspiration struck. 'Your son!' Chemosh said. 'He's the world's expert at getting in and out of places. And he can hide himself if we need to.'

'I'll wait in the lot and keep the engine running.'

Chemosh hesitated, reluctant to turn the knife, but he must. 'Merrick, I'm sorry, but there's too much chance you'll be a liability. Michael may well be living with his family – if he'd taken his own place while masquerading as a doctor, why keep it out of the phone book? We won't know until we get there if it's just Michael or the whole clan. If Uziel senses us, Zane and I will have all we can do to get clear.'

'Damn it . . .' Merrick's shoulders slumped and he sat down heavily on the couch.

Chemosh put a hand on his shoulder. 'I'm sorry, son. I know it must be hard. You were stronger than any of us. When you decided to give that up, you couldn't have anticipated this danger. Zane and I must move quickly, but tonight will only be the first move. If you're willing to try reversing the injections . . .'

Merrick gave him a sharp look. 'What makes you imagine that's possible?'

'I asked Katie about it.'

'You had no right. After what she and I went through getting the issue settled, she didn't need you raising it again.'

'I'm sorry, but what did you expect me to do? I'm your father. I don't want you to die, and neither does she, you know that—'

Seeing the anger on Merrick's face, Chemosh stopped,

frustrated. So stubborn. Surely he must know what it cost his wife to draw toxic blood from her young patients, knowing she would soon be injecting it into him. Progeria was a vile and appalling disease that turned children into withered ancients before the age of twenty. Its extreme rarity was no comfort to the kids dying on fast forward. Katie had dedicated years of her life to fighting the disease. How it must gall her that her attempts to isolate it and find a cure had instead given her the one substance in all of nature that could speed the death of the man she loved.

'Even if I stopped the injections,' Merrick said, 'it might take months or years for my cells to regenerate.'

'Not if Jenn and I and Zane gave you transfusions of our blood.'

'That's pure speculation.'

'Katie thinks it would work.'

Merrick stared at some distant vista, his eyes haunted. Chemosh remained silent, hoping.

'Did Katie also tell you that the first thing my rejuvenated cells would do is produce immunity to the injections?'

'She believes it's a possibility, yes.'

Merrick shut his eyes, pressed his thumbs into the lids. 'I would have lost my one chance to grow old with her. If I stay young while she ages, I will have to leave her, you know that. I can't be the cause of her moving every few years, uprooting herself over and over, dropping all her friends, her medical practice. And that's the least of it. I'll look twenty-five again. How long before she begins to feel that a man with a body that young couldn't love a woman of sixty, seventy? How long before she begins to fear, then hate her own aging face in the mirror? I love her as I have never loved before. I want to stay with her to the end.'

'I know.' Chemosh felt his agony, the same anguish he'd experienced so many times himself. *But if Uziel comes after us all? Stay as you are and you'll have to stand helpless while he kills your beloved Katie and the young son you both love so much.*

He did not say it. It was too soon to be sure what would happen. If he could head the crisis off, Merrick could still have

61

his wish. 'Let's wait and see how Michael takes what I tell him.'

'Yes.' Merrick released a breath. 'If he is staying with his family and you have to back off tonight, what then?'

'I'll be waiting at his office when he comes in tomorrow morning.'

'And you'll guard Jenn's place until then.'

'Of course.'

Merrick hesitated, holding his gaze. 'If Uziel does come after her tonight, would you and Zane be able to stop him?'

'There's really no point thinking about that, is there?'

'No.' Merrick stood and embraced him.

'Don't worry. We'll be all right.' Chemosh wished he could believe it.

Waiting on the front stoop while, inside, his grandson finished his goodnights, Chemosh gazed around the neighborhood. He loved this sleepy street, high enough up the hill to escape the noise, lights and hustle of the Georgetown business district. The houses were old by the standards of their occupants, many smothered in ivy. The azaleas on either side of Katie's front steps were starting to bud out, he saw, though it was only mid February.

Will we see the spring, any of us?

Zane came out, and Chemosh followed him to his old Peugeot. The seat was cold, making him shiver, but he resisted the urge to reach for the heater control as Zane pulled from the narrow driveway. The real cold was inside him now, and it would stay there until he knew his family was safe from Uziel.

Zane's silence began to register. Was he upset at being asked to leave the daughter he adored to drive his grandfather home? Maybe, or it may just be one of his normal silences. Chemosh studied him covertly. Lately, Zane had taken to cutting his black hair short; it hugged his head like the glossy pelt of a panther. He had the nose of a Caesar, perfectly straight when viewed from the front, but in profile showing the slightest hawkish curve. My face, Chemosh thought, except for those wonderful green eyes, vivid as Jenn's. If there was any doubt Merrick was my son, all we'd have to do is look at Zane. Pride swelled in Chemosh. With Jenn's help, Zane had overcome his compulsion to kill. He was a good son and father now, adoring of his daughter, big enough in heart to love Merrick despite the horrors they'd put each other through back when he was killing and Merrick was trying to stop him. He *has* changed, Chemosh told himself firmly, and I know how hard that is. Have I told him how much I admire him for it?

The words rose to his lips, and then he realized this wasn't the moment. Tonight, he might want Zane to be dangerous again.

'So what's up?' Zane asked, as he turned down 34th Street toward M.

'Am I that obvious?'

'No, but I've been on edge enough to know it when I see it.'

'I need your help. This doctor Jenn met tonight. I saw him as he was leaving the break room, and there's something about him I want to check out.'

'You think he might be a phage?'

Chemosh looked at him, surprised. 'What makes you ask that?'

'Jenn saw a strange phage at the hospital tonight. She was going to tell you, but she was afraid it would hurt my feelings if she went to you first.'

'She said that?'

'No. But I know her better than she thinks.'

Chemosh felt startled at Zane's insight, and a bit unsettled. He did not want Zane to view him as a rival for Jenn's affections.

Zane threw him a small smile. 'Relax. I wouldn't have been offended.'

'A strange phage,' Chemosh said. 'How did she know it was one of us?'

'He had climbed the wall of the hospital and was looking into the room of one of her patients. When she saw him, he vanished.'

Chemosh's heart sank. 'What?'

'Yes, that surprised me, too. She ran up to the roof and glimpsed him again, and then he again disappeared. I've got a few tricks of my own, but I could never manage to Influence another phage's retinas, and believe me I tried. If I could have made it work back when Merrick was after me, I'd have had a lot less running to do. Have you ever heard of a phage doing that?'

'No.'

But Uziel and his kind can do it, by bypassing our retinas and striking directly at the visual cortex with neural Influence — it isn't easy for them, but they can do it.

Chemosh felt a building pressure in his chest. 'What did this phage look like?'

'Tall, long red hair, a square jaw. Quite handsome — no surprise there.'

Red hair, Chemosh thought. And the jaw. Uziel?

No. Or Jenn would never have made it off the roof. But the resemblance was chilling. 'It climbed the wall, you say?'

Zane gave him a questioning look. 'How else could it get up there, seven stories high?'

'Of course, you're right,' Chemosh said quickly.

'I told Jenn the phage was probably checking out the hospital, looking for the blood bank, maybe, because he didn't want to go to the trouble of setting up and concealing a kill.'

No, Chemosh thought. He didn't climb the wall, he flew up it.

'You seemed startled when I described him,' Zane said. 'Have you seen a phage like this one before?'

'No.' True enough. Chemosh found himself wishing he'd told Zane about Uziel and his kind, even though the knowledge was a poisonous burden, like being told you had a rare but lethal cancer you could do nothing about. If one of them ever ran across you and attacked, knowing about them in advance would not save you. Why dump that fear onto Zane when it was so unlikely to be realized? Clearly, the two species almost never crossed paths, or Uziel's kind would be no secret to phages by now. I'm one of the few ever to see one, Chemosh thought.

Or to live to tell about it.

Zane said, 'You look like you want to say something.'

'No.' *There isn't time now. You'll know soon enough, and one image will be worth a thousand words.*

64

'Jenn was worried, but I told her the phage would probably move on to another city now that he knows she's around. Too many hunters spook the deer.'

'Yes.'

'What is it you need me to do?' Zane asked.

'To check Michael Avalon out, we need his address, and it's not in the phone book. Think you can pick the lock on the personnel office at Jenn's hospital?'

'If I can't,' Zane said, 'no one can.'

'What a grand place.'

Though Zane had spoken in the barest whisper, Chemosh had the urge to hush him. But surely not even Uziel could hear a whisper from dense woods a hundred yards away. It *was* a magnificent house, a colonial mansion with two wings. Tall pillars in the Doric style supported an extension of the center roof out over the drive, forming an elegant *porte cochère*. The front of the white house blazed under floodlights; a long black lawn ended in a downward roll that probably turned steep as it fell away to the Potomac below.

Chemosh felt a small shock as a drop of water fell from the treetops onto his forehead. The earlier wind must have blown a shower through while they were at the hospital; now it was eerily still, the carpet of dead leaves absorbing the sound of falling drops.

Would Michael have this perimeter patrolled?

Probably not. Why bother to set a watch when you were as powerful as one of them?

'What are we waiting for?' Zane asked. 'Shouldn't we move in now? If Michael is a phage, two of us can surely handle him.'

'Let's just watch a few more minutes.' Chemosh said it so softly he could barely hear his own voice. A whippoorwill sang out deep in the wooded stretch at their backs, making the nerves in his neck jump. He felt an almost unbearable tension. This house was too big, too grand. Were they all in there together? In

Barcelona, and before, they'd always lived together. Surely this was far more room than Michael would want or need alone. The thought that Uziel and his clan might be in that house right now made Chemosh's scalp crawl. If so, there was nothing to do but get out of here, as quietly as possible.

He checked his watch. Near midnight. The murders, assaults, traffic accidents and other mayhem that threatened humans would be tailing off now to the north, where the nation's capital cast a red glow against the night sky. In Barcelona, the family had always returned home around midnight, taking a break from their self-appointed role as guardian angels, to eat dinner together. If this was not only Michael's home but the stronghold of the ret of the family, they'd be returning soon.

'What was that?' Zane asked.

At the same instant, Chemosh saw a flicker of light in the sky north of the house. His heart began to hammer. There it was again! Zane drew a sharp breath. Chemosh gripped his grandson's arm, willing him to silence. An instant later, the breath stopped in his lungs as the flickers of light coalesced into a man-like figure sweeping in across the black sky. The aurora of distorted gravity, so very like wings, trailed out behind the figure as it drew closer and descended toward the *porte cochère*. The illusion vanished as the creature landed gracefully beside one of the tall columns. The floodlights blazed off its face for an instant before it turned toward the door.

Uziel!

Chemosh's stomach clenched in fear and loathing.

Uziel started to reach for the door, then paused in an attitude of listening. Chemosh felt his fingers digging into Zane's forearm. Could the old bastard sense them, even at this distance?

Someone, probably a servant, opened the front door, pouring a golden glow across Uziel. Without a backward glance, he disappeared into the house.

'What in *hell* was that?' Zane hissed. 'And don't tell me it was a goddamned phage.'

'No,' Chemosh said.

Chapter Five

Reveal not thyselves to mankind, for if the scales be lifted from their eyes that they should see the mighty ones who bear them up, they would lay down their mantle and become as sheep. Rejoice in the rumors of My glory, but confirm it not, for the will of man to choose his own way is the gift by which his Creator doth ennoble man, and cursed be thy name if thou pluckest that crown from him.

Codex Angelorum I, 16

Drifting above the rooftops near Catholic University, Uziel was imagining the grand wedding of his son to the splendid Philippa Evangeline and her noble house when he realized someone was in trouble below.

There – that grubby rowhouse near the middle of the block!

Terror rose through the aging shingles, paining him even as it drew him down. As he got closer he could hear their voices, the woman's, soft and frightened, the man's, hectoring. On the narrow front lawn, mostly bare dirt, a child's tricycle lay on its side. Hand prints smudged the peeling door jamb. The door itself was unlocked, as if no threat from outside could rival those within.

His heart heavy, Uziel followed the sounds of the argument,

passing down a dim hall redolent of grease and fish. In the kitchen, the man sat at the table, waving a phone bill at the woman, who shrank against the kitchen counter. A wiry guy, plaid shirt, sandy hair thinning on top. Perfectly ordinary, except for the fury that reddened his round face and powered him like a drug.

'What have I tole you about calling your sister?'

'But it was her birthday—'

'Long distance! Calfornya, four doller and thirty-nine cent. You called her to whine about me, didn't you? Don't lie to me, I can get a tape, the phone company keeps 'em. Telling her how you suffer. Did you say how you waste money? How you sit around the house all day?'

Uziel felt his own anger rising.

'I didn't—'

'Don' inerrup me. Where is the four doller comin' from? You gonna' get a job and pay me back?'

'Mark, please. Jeremy's out back. If he hears us—'

'Mark, puhleease,' he mimicked.

Uziel saw the evidence on her pale, pinched face, a fading blue-green crescent under one eye, a scar across her forehead. Janey, her name, was thinking Mark would kill her this time. Having gleaned enough, Uziel tried to stop, but he could not keep her terror out, seeing in her memory the chaotic images of past beatings, her husband's fist swinging, the room careening around her, such a miserable, appalling life. A vast sadness filled him.

The brute called Mark stood at the table and flung the bill down. 'We in debt up to our necks, can't make the car payment, how'm I gonna' get through to you? Huh? You tell me.' His voice soft now with menace.

Uziel read him, *gonna hafta beat the stupid bitch*, felt the pressure peaking in him, which could only be released in blows, after which he would cry and beg forgiveness – sorry, but not sorry enough to keep his temper next time.

With an effort, Uziel kept control of himself. *I'm a guardian, not an avenger. Stop this man's hand, make him slip, but don't hurt him. God is his judge. God will punish.*

Mark took a step toward his wife.

Uziel reached mentally into his brain stem, found the nerves leading to his legs and gave them a pinch. Mark sprawled over a chair, tipped sideways and crashed to the floor with a curse. Lunging up, he staggered, then stared down at his legs. 'Wha'd'you do?' he said plaintively.

Janey stared at him, popeyed. 'Nothing, I swear it. I didn't touch you, honest.'

Mark took a clumsy step toward her, trying to raise his fist. Uziel blocked the nerve at his shoulder then, unable to restrain himself, he cut off all feeling to Mark's left leg. The man flopped down again, thrashing on the floor like a beached fish, then lying still. The red fury drained from the face, leaving it the pale, shiny color of toothpaste. 'Call the docter,' he gasped. 'I'm havin' one a them strokes. Hurry up, woman!'

Janey shrieked and knelt beside her husband. Uziel shook his head. How many times had he seen this, yet always it amazed and confounded him? Look at her, weeping as if her heart would break. How could women be so foolish, loving someone who beat them? What good could this man ever do for her that could make up for the horror of his fists?

Still sobbing, Janey rushed to her phone and dialed 911, restraining her hysteria enough to get her address out, then returning to her husband's side.

Uziel slipped out and rose into the sky, his hands clasped together above him, letting the cool air scrub him clean of what he had witnessed. *Where will I be when he does it next time?*

Justine was waiting patiently for him at their usual noon rendezvous above the Shrine of the Immaculate Conception. He touched her hands, drinking in her love, marvelling at the beauty which never failed to move him, even when they'd been separated only for an hour or two. Her hair was beautiful and long, the color of darkened mahogany, soft and fine to the touch. When he'd delivered her of Fabriel, that was the first thing he'd looked for on the red, squirming newborn — to see if she had her mother's dark hair. At first it seemed so, but when Fabriel's hair later turned blond, Uziel had not minded because it preserved Justine's uniqueness. None of the children had that golden cast in Justine's eyes either. How tiny she was for an angel, only five-six, but strong inside, rare and beautiful and mysterious, and he loved her more than he would ever be able to say. Fortunately, he did not need to say. He opened his heart to her now. She gave him a happy smile that lifted playfully over him, her small, strong hands finding the tight cords of his neck and massaging.

'My poor baby,' she said in his mind. 'How that upsets you.'

'I had unworthy thoughts,' Uziel admitted. 'I wanted to strike the bully down for good.'

'But you didn't. That's what matters.'

'No, the wish itself is a sin. I'll pray for forgiveness.'

He let her fingers work blessed relief into his shoulders and the base of his skull. Sunlight gleamed off the Byzantine dome below him, electrifying the dazzling blue background and setting ablaze the inlaid embellishments of red and gold. Catholic University students and professors strolled the sidewalks around the shrine or sped along on bikes, a lovely and familiar sight that further soothed him. He savored the light even as he scattered it from himself, as Justine was doing, saving himself the effort of editing his image from each mind below. If it weren't for his impure thought earlier, he'd be at peace. As soon as he got home, he would go to the prayer room on top of the house, yes, and beg God to forgive him for wanting to kill the man.

And in return, I will hear nothing, feel nothing.

Uziel blocked the thought at once, a greater sin by far than the passing impulse to take the bully's life.

Clearing his mind, he returned his attention to the wedding. Philippa would be arriving in only two days. She'd take up the guest room over the garden maze for the weeks before the wedding. A new face at the dinner table, from now on. Her father, Amator, would be visiting from time to time, and that alone would bring the Loyolas back closer to the inner circle of the clans. Uziel felt a small rush, its sweetness filling his head like a sudden scent of honeysuckle. Amator had initiated the alliance, not he. Might this possibly be a sign of God's returning favor?

Might more powerful signs follow — possibly even a grand-child? Happiness welled up in him, startling in its unaccustomed power.

Justine gave his shoulders a quick squeeze. 'Tell me again about Philippa.'

Uziel considered. 'Amator tells me her senses are extremely keen. She can speak in his mind at a distance of ten miles — he rarely needs a cell phone with her, and that's in Chicago. Their metro area is much larger than ours. Apparently, she's also very quick. We can use her in the hot spots of the city. Best of all, Michael will have to drop this foolishness at the hospital in order to help her become oriented, so we'll have him back too.'

'I miss him too, but he is doing good where he is, I'm sure.'

Uziel felt the slightest disharmony, not quite irritation. Doing good was not the same as protecting, and protecting was the mission — but he did not want to argue that point.

Justine rolled around to drift beneath him. The sun made her blink, so she maneuvered into his shadow and regarded him seriously. 'I just wish I could be sure this is what Michael truly wants.'

'What do you mean? Of course he wants it.'

'He might have preferred to make his own choice.'

'Nonsense. He knows what this means to our family. He's a good lad.'

'Uziel, he's fifteen hundred years old, hardly a lad.'

'You know what I mean. Philippa is just what he needs. He's gotten a bit lonely, even with us around him. Why else would he go native? Being seen gives him the chance to look for another human wife, I'm sure you must have considered that. This will be far better,' Uziel said, 'for him and for everyone. Now that Ariel's reached adulthood, I know you've been longing, as I have, for an infant of our own flesh and blood in the house again.'

Justine closed her eyes, and Uziel immersed himself in her

reverie. She could almost feel the baby in her hands, the downy touch of its cheek on her own as she basked in the glow of an innocent new life.

She sighed. 'You're right, of course.'

'But?'

A reflective frown marred the smoothness between Justine's gently arching eyebrows. 'I was only going to say that Michael seems a bit distant to me lately. It's been some time since he invited me into his mind. Don't you think he's just a bit . . . guarded?'

'Maybe, but it's only natural right now. Remember, he spends hours every day inside the heads of disturbed people. I'm sure he simply doesn't want to spread that kind of gloom to the rest of us. He'll be glad enough to trade the strain of the hospital for the joys and responsibilities of marriage, you'll see.'

'No doubt, dear.'

She drifted up and kissed him, but he could see in her eyes that she was still worried about Michael, and when he plumbed his own recent impressions of their son, he found misgivings of his own.

Maybe I should glean him, see what's going on.

And if I do, what would stop him from probing my mind, unasked, and seeing the parts I don't want him to see?

Uziel felt frustration edged with a familiar anxiety. It was for good reason he had stressed to the family that they must never enter each other's minds without asking. But a lot was riding on this alliance with the Evangelines, too. With it, the Loyolas could regain the stronger voice they'd once had among the clans. Whether or not Amator's offer of alliance had been divinely inspired, it could only help for God to see the head of the Loyolas moving back into the company of His favored ones. My isolation has gone on long enough, Uziel thought.

The most important thing, of course, is that my son be happy to receive Philippa. I must pay closer attention to him. I'll watch him tonight at dinner, and then decide whether I must look more deeply.

The butterflies began fluttering in Michael's stomach as he walked into the hospital. The next step with Jenn was to ask her for a date. He had a play picked out, and then dinner after, and all he had to do was ask her. He had patients all day, but maybe one of them would cancel and he could do it then. Just thinking about it made him nervous. He'd seen people ask for a date thousands of times.

And bungled more thousands.

She hasn't gone out with a man since her husband's death, Michael thought, and she's turned a lot of guys down the past year. That will be her automatic response, and somehow I have to get past that. I must make sure she's in a good mood and relaxed, and I mustn't seem keyed up myself—

He stopped, startled, just outside the hall that led to his office. He could sense someone waiting around the corner at the end of the hall, beyond his door, the aura vaguely familiar—

Chemosh!

After a second of blank surprise, his mind raced. What could Jenn's great grandfather want with him?

Rounding the corner, he saw the phage standing motionless at the end of the hall, where no one would accidentally bump into him. A tingle at the backs of his eyes told him Chemosh was projecting Influence, trying to remove his image.

Good, Michael thought. I can ignore him.

He slipped his key into the lock of his door, acutely conscious of the phage only two yards away, perfectly still, watching him. Fear swarmed from Chemosh — and something else, like heat from a summer pavement . . . anger?

'You needn't pretend you don't see me,' Chemosh said.

A cold shock ran down the nerves of Michael's arms. He whirled toward the phage, avoiding eye contact. 'Who said that?'

Chemosh gave him a faint smile. 'I've come to talk to you about your father, Uziel.'

Michael's heart thumped suddenly at his ribs. *My God, how could he know Father's name?* Abandoning pretence, he gazed at the phage, so strikingly handsome, lean and dark like Jenn's father, Zane. 'Shall we step into my office?'

'Thank you.' Chemosh indicated he would follow, and Michael had a fleeting sense of danger, as if the phage were considering attacking him from behind. He readied himself, but nothing happened. He indicated the chair his patients usually took.

'Thank you, I prefer to stand.'

'How do you know my father's name?'

'I know a great deal about your father. The most important right now is that, if he finds out you have fallen for my great granddaughter, he will kill her.'

Even in his surprise, Michael noted the slight emphasis on the 'fallen.' But what a charge – crazy! 'You are mistaken.'

Chemosh studied him. 'In a way, I'm glad to hear you say that. I couldn't understand how you could love Jenn and yet put her in such horrible danger.'

'My father does not like phages, it is true, but—'

'He loathes us. And I am why.'

Michael needed to sit down, but was unwilling to let the phage tower over him. A mystifying wave of pain – and, yes, rage – radiated from Chemosh. How could this phage, who hadn't even been around until a year ago, know Father, when Father had never mentioned him? Was this some kind of desperate bluff? Somehow, Chemosh knew about angels, and he clearly was paranoid about Father. But that gives him no right to try to take Jenn away from me, Michael thought.

And then he realized something else: Chemosh wouldn't be here if he didn't know Jenn is interested in me. Did she tell him, or did he see it in her eyes, as I did?

Michael felt his heart lifting, then cautioned himself. He could not be sure until he heard it from Jen. But suddenly he felt like smiling.

74

He said, 'Whatever you may believe, my father will not harm Jenn. He may be angry and disappointed with me, and he may refuse to accept her, but once I've had a chance to make him understand about her, he'll let her be.'

'You couldn't be more wrong. Look inside me. See how your father killed my innocent son, only a child.'

Michael's anger returned in a rush. 'That's preposterous.'

Chemosh gave a bitter smile. 'So Uziel has never told you. Is he afraid of what you'll think of him?'

'I want you to leave now.'

Chemosh raised both hands in a placating gesture, looking frightened. 'Please, hear me out. You resent me attacking your father, I understand that. Words aren't important, anyway. If you care anything at all for Jenn, you must look into me now. You can do that. Just look, and you'll see the truth.'

Michael felt a deep disgust. 'If *you* care anything for Jenn, stay out of this. She has been unhappy, desperately unhappy, and I can end that—'

'You will end her. Your father will—'

'Get out.'

'No, I beg you—'

Before he could stop the impulse, Michael grabbed Chemosh by the shoulders to spin him around so he could push him out the door, but the phage brought his hands up inside and knocked his wrists away. Shocked, Michael resisted the urge to rub at his tingling wrists. *So strong.* 'Neither of us can afford a scene in this place, Chemosh. I'm asking you again to leave.'

'You are going to listen to me—'

'I have listened, and I reject what you say. You will never persuade me to doubt my father.'

'If you would just look into me, that's all I ask.'

'Looking *is* doubting.'

'Then I will tell you again. My son was only six years old, and Uziel killed him. Your father came into his bedchamber when I was there and an evil light poured from his hand into my son's brain, and he convulsed and died.' Chemosh's voice remained low, but it shook with conviction.

He believes it, Michael thought.

His anger at Chemosh cooled and a familiar sadness settled over him, the melancholy he felt each time a patient entered this room and poured out his inner demons.

Chemosh took his arm. 'Please, Michael. Would I dare make such a charge and then invite you to see it all in my memory if it weren't true?'

'If you were delusional, you would. I'm sorry, but you must go.' Michael started for the door.

Chemosh released his arm and stayed where he was.

'Don't make me force you out,' Michael said.

Chemosh threw up his hands. 'All right, I'm crazy. You help other people. Take me as a patient. Then you won't be doubting your father, you'll be helping me to get over my delusion.'

'I could not do good therapy when I and my family are at the heart of your delusion.'

'Who else can I go to? Shall I tell some ordinary shrink that a being who thinks he's an angel killed my son thousands of years ago, and that soon he'll kill my great granddaughter?'

Michael felt a dread fascination at the distorting power of Chemosh's hatred, so intense he could not bear to acknowledge that Uziel was an angel. 'You don't want therapy. You don't believe you're deluded.'

'Damn you, if you don't listen to me, Jenn will die.'

'I'm sure you believe that.'

'I'm staying here until you read my mind.'

I've had enough of this, Michael thought. At the same instant, he released a jolt of energy into the phage's spinal cord then pulled back, startled at himself. Chemosh gasped, and his knees buckled. Michael felt energy flowing into his arms and legs, buzzing in his brain, making it difficult to think. Whatever he had done to Chemosh, he wanted to do it again, harder. With a fierce effort, he held himself in check. 'Go,' he hissed.

Chemosh stared at him with wide, frightened eyes, then

turned and stumbled for the door. Michael strode after him, pushing him out. Shutting the door, he leaned against it, trembling with excess energy. *What is wrong with me? I hurt him. I struck him with my mind. I've never done anything like that before . . .*

Michael pressed his hands to his face, sick with remorse. The idea that Father would murder a child — or the woman his son loved — *was* insane, but that did not excuse what he had done. Chemosh *was* Jenn's great grandfather, her flesh and blood.

Flinging the door open again, Michael hurried into the hall, hoping to find Chemosh, to ask his pardon, but the phage was gone.

Alone in his room near the back of the great house, Michael prepared to go out on night rounds. An unpleasant charge lingered in the nerves of his spine as he changed into the dark clothes that would reduce the need for hiding himself. *The way Father watched me at dinner,* he thought — *my half-hearted smiles, the way I held back when everyone was rhapsodizing about the wedding. But how could I help it, when the very idea repulses me?*

For a minute, I was afraid he would glean me.

A chill went through Michael. *Nothing could be worse. If Father finds out that way, digs Jenn out of my mind while I'm still trying to hide her, it will shatter his trust in me. Then what chance would I have of persuading him how different she is?*

I should have told everyone tonight that I want a delay. It would have explained my tepid mood to Father and dimmed the chances of him gleaning me. But they were all so happy, talking, anticipating. The National Cathedral at midnight, before the ancients of all the clans, a thousand angels, brilliant as the sun, a great choir from the Cherubinis filling our minds with anthems. The coronation of a king would not be more grand . . .

Michael went to the window and leaned on the sill, feeling pressed down, as if the house around him were settling on his shoulders. He must tell the family tomorrow night, without fail. Philippa was due to arrive the evening after. He wouldn't hit Father with all of it at once — Drey was right. Just get a postponement. There had been no chance to ask Jenn out today. They hadn't yet taken a second step together, and they must have time to do so if he was to know whether her response to him was more than just physical — Drey was right about that, too.

Surely Father won't push if I ask for a little more time.

And if he later gleans me, to see exactly why I'm hesitating?

Michael groaned, feeling trapped. Whichever way he turned, the potential for disaster loomed.

Movement in the garden maze below caught his eye — the top of Fabriel's blond head bobbing between the bristly walls. She was having her usual after-dinner stroll before going back to the city . . .

Michael gazed at her, his mind quickening. Fabriel — what if he told her, only her? Swear her to silence and give her the whole truth. She's independent and open-minded, he thought. She'll surely hear me out. At worst, I'll be on record with one of the family — far better than merely having intended to tell, which Father might view as a self-delusion. At best, with time to think about it, Fabriel might even be ready to side with me when I tell the others about Jenn. An ally would be a great help.

Slipping into the hall, Michael hurried past the other bedrooms to one of the back balconies, leaping from there down to the lawn. In the moonlight, each blade of grass glistened with its own silvery radiance. Approaching the maze from the river side, with the moon at his back, he saw with the clarity of noon. The tall hedges were beginning to bud; in another few weeks they'd be as lush as the holly that had stood its prickly watch all winter. Here and there, Brother Rafe's giant stone creatures peeked above the maze as if they too were trapped and trying to find a way out.

Rising above the maze, Michael spotted Fabriel again, on the far side now. She waved him down and he settled beside her, managing to return her smile. How lovely she was, still in her dinner clothes, that simple, dark blue dress to the knee graced by a pearl pendant at her throat. At some point, she'd gathered her dazzling hair into a tight twist behind. The curious, faint smell of cigarette smoke he'd noticed at dinner still wafted from her. 'Has the tobacco lobby gotten to you, too?'

Fabriel winced. 'That! How embarrassing. I changed all my clothes and washed, but it must be in my hair too. I was passing the Pole Vault Bar on Fourteenth Street, when I picked up someone, thinking, "I'm going to stick this guy." So I ran in and, while blanking myself to everyone, managed to deflect the blade without anyone bumping into me — but, Michael, you can't believe the smoke in that place. Forget the knife, it's a wonder they don't all fall down choking.'

'They do sometimes seem in a hurry to end their short lives.'

She studied him with her clear, light blue eyes. 'You're upset. I could see it at dinner. Want to tell Sister Fabriel?'

'That's exactly what I want. But just you. I'm not ready for the rest of the family to know.'

She looked troubled. 'Michael . . .'

'Could we talk down by the river?'

'Of course.' Lifting from the maze, she sped away across the darkened back yard, disappearing down over the high bluff. Michael followed, plummeting over the edge, descending a hundred feet to where she had settled on the ribbon of shore. On either side, bushes and kudzu vines covered the steep slope and obliterated the beach with splayed networks of root, but here there was just ground enough to stand together. Fabriel said nothing, staring out at the broad Potomac. Clouds slid away from the moon, pouring down shafts of light to stripe the sluggish water in milky bands that crawled nearer, then sped away before vanishing again. Farther down, at the bend in the river, water trilled over stone.

In profile, Fabriel's beautiful face was harder to read, the straight lines of nose and mouth yielding no hint to her thoughts. Michael found himself wondering if his glamorous sister had ever been in love. Every day on her rounds she must encounter romance, people holding and caressing each other, murmuring loving words, but she never gave any sign of loneliness. Staying hidden deprives her of seeing herself desired, Michael thought. Concealing ourselves is second nature, but until Jenn looked at me, what I felt for her was a pale fantasy.

Fabriel sighed. 'It's so beautiful down here.'

'Yes.' Michael looked upriver to the north, where the horizon blushed with the lights of Washington; he could feel the distant human clamor fading to a whisper in the center of his brain; midnight, the city settling into sleep.

'Would you like me just to look inside you, Michael?'

'After I've told you. Better if I first present it to you.' Michael took a deep breath, heard his heart thumping in his eardrums. 'I'm in love.'

She gave him a questioning grin. 'You say that as if it's a bad thing.'

'Not with Philippa. Someone else.'

Fabriel gave her head a little shake. 'Michael! Who, what clan—?'

'She's not one of us. She's a doctor at the hospital. She's also a hemophage.'

Fabriel's mouth fell open and she stared at him. For a second, she seemed merely astonished, and then all color drained from her face. 'Michael, no . . .'

His heart sank. 'Fabriel, she's not like any phage you ever heard of.'

She turned away, grasping her own hair above her ears, staring at the river in shock. Her anguish stabbed him.

'Michael. Dear God. What will Father *do*?'

'What can *I* do? I love her. Her name is Jenn. She is as virtuous as any of us, noble and loving, a healer. I know it's hard to believe—'

'Oh, I believe you.'

Michael's heart leapt. But no, this was too easy. How could she accept such a thing, just like that?

'Listen to me, Michael. Do you imagine you're the only one ever to be surprised by a phage? You're not.'

He felt a dread fascination. 'Tell me.'

'It will change nothing.'

'Fabriel, please.'

Her jaw set. After a second, she made a throwaway gesture with one hand. 'It was while we were still in Spain, near the end of that time.'

Michael let his mind roll back, back to the family's service in Barcelona. At the point Fabriel was talking about, Spanish Catholicism was in one of its cruel stages — the Inquisition — and Father had been agonizing over Torquemada's torture of Spanish heretics. Before long, Uziel would decide to take his family to the new world for which Columbus had just set sail. Michael remembered his regret at leaving Barcelona. In memory he felt the warm sun on his back, saw the great hill called Montjuich that looked protectively down on the city from the south. He remembered drifting along above the beautiful trees that lined the *Rambla* on its way to the Plaza de Catalunya.

'I'm warning you, Michael, I'll tell you my story, but nothing in it will help you win me over.' She drew a deep breath. 'It happened that time Father sent me to Madrid to help the NeSeraph clan for a week. I was returning across the Spanish countryside when I saw a small castle miles from any town. I thought it was abandoned, but when I got closer, I could feel several auras within — very powerful. At first I assumed they were angels, but a strangeness in them made me hold back. If they were Lords of Light, why would they stay in the castle all day instead of watching over the countryside? Curious, I watched from a distance. That night around midnight, the castle gate clanged open and four of them rode out on these magnificent Arabian horses — just came thundering out of the gate and dashed away into the night. They did not call out to each other. They were eerily quiet, only the drumbeat of hooves, but I could feel their jubilation.

'I followed them from above. After awhile, I realized they weren't just riding, they were hunting for something, and then I realized it was men they were hunting — the sort of men who hid in the woods at night to waylay straggling travellers. They found one, and I saw that they meant to kill him. He was screaming and begging, kneeling within the circle of their horses, calling them "Lordship," and I was trying to think of a way to rescue him without hurting anybody or revealing myself. Then I caught something from his mind. Not far from him, in the woods, was the body of a young girl he'd kidnapped and stabbed to death after raping her. I was sickened, and then I realized the horsemen knew it too, could smell her blood on him, and then I gleaned one of them and realized that these must be phages, the evil ones Father had warned us about.'

Fabriel shuddered and stared out over the river. Michael imagined himself in her place, a guardian of mankind, but revolted by what this murderous human had done. But the rule was clear: angels were sworn to guard all men, not to judge and punish them − even a man so thoroughly depraved and horrible.

'I let them kill him,' Fabriel said softly.

Michael nodded.

'After they all had drunk his blood, two of them went off to find the girl. Her blood was fresh too, but they drank none of it. Instead, they dressed and cleaned her up and took her body back to the nearest village so it could be found by her relatives or someone who knew her. Watching the two phages prepare the child's body, I felt the most incredible confusion. These were the lowest of the low, bestial blood drinkers, as Father always told us. Before that, on three occasions I had been lucky enough to catch a phage going in for the kill, always on an innocent victim. But these were different. Not only did they refuse to drink the girl's blood, in fact they mourned her − I could feel it in them − even though they hadn't known her. I was glad they had punished the filthy brute who could do such a thing to a child.' Fabriel turned to him in appeal. 'Haven't you wanted to do that, Michael? When you saw someone so evil, so unworthy of life.'

'Yes.'

'But you never have − I don't even have to ask. And neither have I. The taboo is so ingrained in us. But I let them do it. I . . .

admired them. More than that. One of them was so striking, tall and broad shouldered, with kind, dark eyes. I . . . desired him, Michael.' Her head gave a convulsive shake.

She could have been describing the power of his first attraction to Jenn. Michael wanted to take her hand, show her that he understood, but her grim expression forbade contact. She seemed to have shrunk into herself, staring down at the black water lapping at her feet.

She feels guilty, even after all this time.

'I would have *fallen*, Michael. The phages did not drink the girl's blood, but it did excite them. I felt that, too, but in my confusion, my attraction to that one phage, I set the knowledge aside as if it had no importance. Had I actually acted on my . . . lust, it would have been a betrayal of Father, my family and God. I came so close.' She swallowed; he caught her inward prayer for forgiveness. He wanted to tell her he did not think she had sinned, that goodness and evil lay in what people did, not what they wanted to do.

She turned to him. 'Michael, you can't do this to God and to us, and you must not do it to yourself. Phages are evil and powerful. No one knows how many people they kill every year, covering it all up with auto accidents and fires and missing persons statistics. They may even have killed some of us over the centuries. Father says four angels have disappeared in the last thousand years, never to be seen again. He says that, in close, phages have powers almost as great as ours, and our *Codex* bears that out—'

'I keep telling you, Jenn isn't like other phages.'

Fabriel shook her head. 'You think she's good because she seems good and does good. But look at her effect on you. You lay aside your duty of protecting humans to enter the world posing as one of them. Instead of saving their bodies, you tamper with their minds, which we were never meant to do. At best, you are neglecting the many to trifle with the few. Why? So you could be with this phage. Oh, I know, Michael, she doesn't *seem* evil. But think. Would evil seduce us with a snarl, a hideous face, a wicked laugh? No. We'd run in fear for our souls from that. Evil wins us over with a gentle hand, the semblance of good. Liking those phages, weeping for the poor little girl murdered by the devil no one could mistake, justifying their own murder of that sick, twisted man on the highest of principles, as if they were God, sitting in judgement.'

'Jenn has never killed anyone.'

Fabriel stopped, her mouth still open to speak. She frowned, thrown off stride. 'How can you be sure?'

He did not answer.

'Of course. You've looked into her. But Father says they all kill.'

'Father is mistaken.'

'But they have to drink blood to live, don't they?'

'Jenn sustains herself by drinking what she can safely transfuse. The people she visits are not harmed and never even know she was there.'

Fabriel stared at him. 'How about in her heart? Does she desire to kill them?'

Michael felt exasperated, then defiant. 'Yes! She longs to kill each and every one of the people she visits in the night, she can imagine no greater thrill, which is precisely what makes her refusal to do it so noble.'

Fabriel shook her head. 'Listen to yourself, Michael. You have just praised her for having evil in her heart.'

'No, for making sure it never gets out.'

'I can't help you with Father, Michael.'

Her voice was flat and final, pressing him down like a weight on his shoulders. 'Will you at least keep silence? Jenn might refuse me. If so, it will be better if Father never knew.'

'If she refuses you, will you marry Philippa?'

Michael hesitated, feeling a leaden weight in his chest. 'Yes.'

'Then I pray that she will refuse you. But I doubt that will happen. You are an angel of God. You'll dazzle her, and she'll fall for you — especially if, as you say, she does have some good in her.' Fabriel gripped his arm. 'Give her up, Michael. Escape her now, while you still have your soul.'

Chapter Six

Falling in with the pack of med students and residents who trailed Rich Sikorsky, Jenn noticed that he'd left his medical coat open. Showing off another new suit, this one a dark blue pinstripe that had probably set him back a grand. No surprise, the color. Rich's tastes ran from blue pinstripes to blue chalkstripes — and everything in between, as Hugh would have quipped. With luck, he'd be feeling confident in the new suit and wouldn't start firing off obscure and aggressive questions to show how much smarter he was than everyone else.

Keeping an ear on him just in case, Jenn thought about Cheryl Hudson.

Should she try to set Cheryl up with Michael — Dr Avalon? He's good, she thought. He got me talking about Hugh, saying things I've never said to anyone. Cheryl could really use the help, especially after what Rich did to her.

But will she take any suggestions from me right now?

Jenn realized Rich Sikorsky was leading them into the room of Mr Leavitt, one of her patients. Her heart skipped a beat. Rich had said nothing to her about presenting Leavitt.

'Dr Hrluska, I believe Mr Leavitt is your patient. Would you care to fill us in?'

She summarized the facts: Forty-two-year-old male found in an alley, victim of an apparent mugging. Contusion on his right temple, no evidence of serious bleeding on the CT scan. Pupils responding to light, pulse and BP now normal and his reflexes were equal on both sides.

'And yet,' Rich said in a mildly reproving voice, 'your patient has remained unconscious since admission.' With a flourish, he pulled a roll of surgical tape from his pocket, tore off two pieces and taped Leavitt's eyes open. Grasping his head above the ears, Rich tilted it sharply forward so that Leavitt's plump, receding chin almost touched his chest. 'Note how the eyes roll up briskly. This is called the doll's head eye response.' He nodded the unresisting head up and down several more times making sure the crowd around the bed could see Leavitt's eyes rolling. Jenn hid her distaste. Did he do that to Hugh, she wondered, when I wasn't there? Use him as a show-and-tell prop?

'What does this response tell us?' Rich asked.

'Uh, it rules out brain stem lesions?' offered one of the med students.

'Did not Dr Hrluska say the CT scan was normal?'

'Yes.'

'Then I think we've already ruled out brain stem lesions, don't you? So what does it mean, Dr Hrluska?'

'Cortical depression and a lighter versus deeper coma.'

Rich made no acknowledgement. Rolling the patient's head to the side, he picked up a pitcher of ice water by the bed and dribbled some into his left ear. Leavitt's eyes rolled slowly and steadily toward his left ear. Stepping forward, Jenn wiped spilled ice water from her patient's cheek. Rich cleared his throat sharply. 'If Dr Hrluska will get out of the way, you can see how the patient's eyes turn toward the caloric stimulus.'

She stepped back, suppressing an urge to dilate the blood vessels in Rich's calf and send him to the floor writhing with a muscle cramp.

He tried a few more times to catch her out, then stalked on to the next room, his medical coat flaring like the mantle of a small, agitated stingray.

After rounds came outpatient clinic, and it was nearly noon before she could grab time to call Michael about Cheryl.

She decided to walk over to Psychiatry instead.

As she entered the hallway of the attending offices, her mouth went dry and the palms of her hands ached with a fierce nervous tension. Annoying – she had business with Michael, nothing more.

Or was she fooling herself?

Because if she was, she'd better turn around right now.

But then who would help Cheryl Hudson?

She heard Michael's voice, the droning stop-and-go doctors fall into with a dictaphone. Two inches of oak could not keep his words from her, an intake summary on a forty-five-year-old man who'd been 'downsized' out of a job and was now suicidal. Realizing she was eavesdropping, she backed away with a guilty start – and the voice on the other side stopped. The squeak of a chair inside sent a mindless alarm through her and she spun away and headed back up the hall.

The door opened before she got three steps.

'Jenn!'

She turned, embarrassed. 'Hi.'

He gave her such a pleased smile that her heart melted. *My God, he does attract me.*

'I was just about to come looking for you,' he said.

'I wanted to talk to you about a patient,' she put in before he could go on. She felt her heart thumping.

He looked a bit deflated. 'Come in, please.'

Entering his office, she heard a flutter of wings. A bright green parakeet swooped from a window sill to Michael's shoulder and pecked daintily at his earlobe, making her laugh. He stroked the bird's head with a gentle fingertip. 'This is Budgie. Budgie, meet Jenn.' The bird pecked insistently at a delicate trough in his earlobe. Did he sometimes put birdseed there for it? The thought deepened the warmth she felt for him – damn, this was hard enough already.

'Have a seat.' He motioned to the leather recliner which

apparently served as his psychiatric couch and settled in a straight-backed chair across from her. Beside him was a low table with the dictaphone, the only thing here that might pass for a desk. She was impressed by how he had converted the room from the sterile utility of a hospital into a place where patients could feel comfortable. Movie posters covered the walls, peeking between the fronds, leaves, and shoots of a lush menagerie of plant life. She could smell green all around her, feel it soothing her spirits. The office was alive and friendly, and she liked it very much.

'Pretty bird,' she said, and Budgie flew off to a ficus and chirped with either excitement or annoyance.

Michael gazed at her, and she realized he was waiting to hear about the patient. Clearing her throat, she said, 'Remember the coma case I mentioned when we . . . met the other night?'

He nodded.

'The patient's wife is still pretty burned up at me, thanks to Rich — my supervisor—'

'I recall.'

'I . . . I've tried talking with her, but she's freezing me out, and that worries me. She really could use some help. Her husband's condition is hopeless — I'll be overseeing an EEG on him in about half an hour, and it's probably going to show flatline.'

Michael gave a sympathetic grimace. 'Rough.'

'Yes. If she's willing to talk with you, are you available?'

He picked up a notebook from the table and paged through it. 'I believe I can manage it, if she doesn't mind coming in fairly late. I could fit her day after tomorrow at ten o'clock at night.'

'I don't think that would be a problem. She's here every evening until late. Thank you, Michael, I appreciate it.'

Get up, she thought, you've done what you came for.

Instead, she said, 'So why did you want to see me?'

'These.' He held up two tickets. 'The Arlington Theater is putting on *Waiting for Godot*. It's not Broadway, but I've been impressed with them in the past.'

Jenn felt that everything had speeded up around her. He was asking her out, and she must say no, but she hadn't prepared herself for that.

'They're for next Tuesday,' Michael said in a more hesitant voice, 'so I don't have to know right away.'

'I appreciate it,' she said, 'but I don't think I'd better.' God, that was graceless. She saw both surprise and dismay in the wonderful blue eyes. It made her oddly ashamed, as though she'd broken some unspoken promise between them.

'I know we've only just met,' he said, then gave a pained laugh. 'The truth is, I wanted to ask you yesterday, but I thought that might be pushing.'

'I'm flattered to be asked, really. I like you, I guess you can tell, and I'm sorry if that led you on. I know this sounds silly, but I'm just not ready to . . . start dating again.'

'It doesn't sound silly.'

'I realize it's been three years since Hugh, but . . .'

'It takes however long it takes,' Michael said, 'and that's nobody's business, including mine.'

His understanding made her feel even more attracted to him; she wanted to take his hands, to thank him for standing back, but she knew his touch would instead undo her resolve and bring them closer. How wonderful it would be simply to let herself fall for him, as she had for Hugh, but how could she put aside what she had learned? Hugh's death had scalded her. The scar tissue was on the inside, as smooth and dead to the touch as burned skin, but now Michael had found a part of her that hadn't been deadened, a new place to burn and she knew she couldn't bear that again. If only I wouldn't have to lose you, she thought. But I would, even if you live to be an old man.

Michael seemed to be waiting for her to say more, but what was the point? She got up, startling Budgie from the ficus tree, and Michael stood too.

'I'll let you know about my patient's wife.'

'That will be fine.'

Everything seemed a trifle blurred as she headed back to

neurology. Her stomach ached; she felt low, so miserable it was almost like being sick, a sensation she'd forgotten in the perfect health that came with being a phage. She had used Hugh to hold Michael away, credible enough and true in its way, but it made her feel shabby, somehow.

A memory popped into her mind, of the time Hugh had snapped a bunch of Polaroids of her digging in the little garden out back on one of her rare days off. He'd shown them to her that evening as they continued the luxurious ease of that day with a glass of wine before dinner. Early spring, but mild enough to sit in the lawn chairs and smell the fragrant earth she'd turned up with her hand spade. Such love in his eyes as he'd gazed at the photos. What was it he'd said? *Jenn, in eighty years, when I'm on the wrong side of the lawn, you'll still look like you do in this picture. I realize no one could ever be as magnificent as me, but after I'm gone if you don't go out and fall in love again, the part of me still alive inside you is going to start kicking you.*

Jenn's eyes flooded, and she turned aside into a rest room and rinsed her face with cold water.

I can't, Hugh. I just can't.

She realized she had to hurry to get to Neil Hudson's room before the EEG machine. Blotting her face, she resolved not to think about Michael again today, not to let her blood fizz at the thought of him, or to visualize that wave of auburn hair above his smooth forehead—

Stop it!

She had plenty to do, and she would do it, and it would help her, as it always had.

Back in the hall, she nearly ran into Wes Faltier. His eyes lit. 'Hey, Jenn—'

'Hey, Wes,' she said, and kept on going. The hospital was full of women, hundreds of nurses and dozens of other residents. Wes was handsome, bright and funny enough to have his pick. *I like you, Wes,* she thought, *but not enough. Don't feel bad. It seems like I can't like anyone enough.*

On the elevator, she forced her attention to Cheryl Hudson.

Better be ready for more abuse, unless Cheryl had calmed down by now. Anger is easier than grief, Jenn thought, and if she has to yell at me to bear her pain, then go ahead, Cheryl.

But what's Rich's excuse?

Annoyance welled up in her. Yelling at her this morning even though the portable EEG had been out of service all day yesterday for maintenance. *That's routine, Hrluska, you could have gotten them to put that off a day. You're stalling to keep your patient here, and I warned you about that. I want him out of here, right away, do you understand?*

Actually, no, I don't, Rich.

But she'd nodded meekly and fantasized a quick slash to his throat, and that bothered her more than anything else. As long as she didn't do it . . . but how far could she let herself go with the wish before it became the act? Such urges came each time she fed, but with Rich it was the first time she'd found herself deliberately imagining such a thing, letting herself *enjoy* the thought.

Dangerous.

Cheryl stood as she entered, said hello and smiled, and relief flooded Jenn. If there was one person in all the world she didn't want to fight, it was Cheryl. 'Hi, Mrs Hudson. Ready for the EEG?'

Cheryl took a deep breath. 'First, I want to say something. I didn't realize about your husband. I feel like such a fool.'

Jenn felt a mild surprise. 'How could you have known when I didn't tell you?' *And how do you know?*

'The patient representative told me,' Cheryl explained. 'I was in there mouthing off about how you doctors didn't care, and she explained about your husband. I get what happened now, night before last. You were on the verge of telling me about . . . Neil not having much chance when that other doctor came in and beat you to it. I'd never have been so mean and said all that about you not being able to understand, if I'd known about your husband.'

'I didn't want to tell you while we still had reason to hope for Neil,' Jenn said.

Understanding showed in Cheryl's eyes. 'You were right not

to – hope was what I needed then, not hearing about someone losing her husband, which I was already so scared about. I'm so sorry for the way I've been acting.'

Jenn took her hands. 'Cheryl, I never held it against you for one minute. I was really angry when Hugh died.'

'But I'll bet you didn't dump on his doctors.'

'I wanted to.'

Cheryl gave her a wan smile. 'I . . . I might want to talk to you some more, but not now, you know?'

'I know,' Jenn said. *Because you're still hoping Neil might make it.*

She heard the EEG cart trundling down the hall toward them, a sound too faint for Cheryl to pick up yet, but as loud in its way to her as an onrushing locomotive. 'Ready for the EEG?'

Cheryl tensed. 'Can you go over that test again – I'm afraid I wasn't listening very well yesterday.'

'Sure. EEG is short for electroencephalogram. The technician will bring the machine in here and hook up some electrodes to Neil's scalp, and we'll be able to see a readout of the activity in various areas of his brain.'

'His brain waves?'

'Yes. It will tell us whether there is any higher order activity remaining in Neil's brain.'

Cheryl took her hands again and squeezed tightly. 'That really scares me.'

'I know. But you need this, believe me, for your own peace of mind, one way or the other.'

Cheryl closed her eyes. 'It's just that I want him here. What if he started bleeding inside his brain again, and he was in some nursing home and they couldn't get him into an operating room fast enough?'

'It wouldn't be a nursing home, Cheryl. They're trained for complete care of coma victims . . .' Breaking off as she saw tears welling up, Jenn said, 'Let's not worry it until we've seen the results.'

Cheryl nodded, her lips pressed tight.

The technician rolled the machine in. Jenn led Cheryl back a few steps and stood with her while the tech smeared paste on the small electrode disks and winnowed through Neil's hair, clearing pale bits of scalp to which he pressed the electrodes. He was careful to keep the wires that led back to the amplifier from tangling.

'Is it going to shock him?' Cheryl whispered fearfully.

'No,' Jenn said. 'The electrodes are receiving, not sending. See how that amplifier is connected to the recording machine, which has a roll of graph paper in it? When he flips on the amplifier, it'll start recording electrical signals from Neil's brain and converting them into wavy lines, which that bank of pens will draw onto the graph paper.'

The technician flipped on the amplifier and the paper began to roll. Jenn held her breath, hoping for a miracle. The pens stayed steady instead of flipping back and forth, inking out lines straighter than anything alive. Even though she'd expected it, Jenn's heart sank. If higher level activity existed in Neil's brain, the pens should be clicking back and forth now.

The technician started checking the connections, his face impassive, the look of someone who hoped not to be noticed.

'When do the pens start?' Cheryl asked.

Jenn moved to the bedside to check the connections for herself, just on the off-chance—

The pens began to move.

She caught her breath. The technician blinked at the un-rolling swath of paper, and then smiled. The pens were jiggling, plenty of life in there. Jenn stared at the unrolling paper, stunned, and then her spirits soared. She'd hoped for a miracle, and this was it. Let Rich try to move Neil out now! She went back to Cheryl to give her the good news—

And the pens stopped moving again.

Hearing the clicks die away, Jenn turned to the tech again. 'Must be a short in there.'

'I don't think so. I just used this machine on another patient and it worked fine. Besides, we ran the maintenance check yesterday and it passed A-OK.'

Going back to him, Jenn bent to look at the amplifier.
The needles started clicking again.

She felt the little hairs standing up along her arms.

'Weird,' the tech muttered.

It's me, she thought. When I'm closer to the machine, it works.

Or maybe it's when I'm closer to Neil.

No, that was crazy.

Easy enough to test — just walk around to the other side of the bed from the tech and the machine. Then she'd be close to Neil but as far from the equipment as when she'd stood with Cheryl.

As Jenn rounded the foot of the bed, the pens slowed, then speeded again when she stopped near his head. The tech, bending over his equipment, didn't notice the correlation. Her mind spun. Was there any way the machine could be picking up waves from her own brain? No. The wires were insulated against any outside electrical activity. When I stand close to Neil, she thought — no, close to his head — it causes activity in *his* brain, which the machine picks up. When I move away, that activity dies down. I can't explain it, but it's happening.

Astonished, she managed to give Cheryl a smile and a thumbs up. Signalling the tech to pause the recording, she took out her penlight and peeled Neil's eyelid back. When the light hit the pupil, it constricted slightly. The tiny response enthralled her. It wasn't just the EEG, something real was going on in Neil's brain — but only when she stood close to him. The pens continued to click busily, a sweet symphony of reprieve for Neil that sent goosebumps along her arms.

What am I doing? How am I doing it?

She stayed close to Neil's head until the tech had collected a standard-length readout, making sure she did not move until he shut the machine off and pulled the electrodes free from Neil's scalp. Only when he handed her the complete electroencephalogram did she step away from Neil's head.

She took it to Cheryl and partially unfolded it, showing her the darting activity from all sixteen electrodes. Cheryl's eyes shone, her smile this time transforming her face with hope. 'He's in there,' she whispered.

'It's a good EEG – better than I'd dared hope.'

'Thank you, God.' Cheryl gazed at her husband's face, smoothing his forehead. 'Oh, Neil, what are you thinking of? I wish I knew what all these lines really mean!'

So do I, Jenn thought. 'I need to show this readout to Dr Sikorsky.'

'Yes!' Cheryl beamed. 'I'd like to be there to see his face, but I'm staying right here with Neil.' She bent over her husband again. 'Honey, I'm here. You're going to get well, I know it.'

'We still have a long way to go,' Jenn cautioned.

'That's all right. We'll go it, Neil and I.'

On her way to Rich's office, Jenn walked slowly, trying to figure out what to say about these readings. She didn't dare tell him that she, herself, had somehow caused the activity recorded on these pages. He'd think she'd gone nuts. But how could she explain it? I don't have to, she decided. Let *him* explain it.

But he couldn't, of course.

She watched his face as he stared at the electroencephalogram spread across his desk. His eyes widened, then narrowed, and she heard uncertain little sounds deep in his throat. He looked up sharply at her. 'This can't be right.'

Not knowing what else to do, she shrugged.

'You were there and watched? The tech did everything by the book?'

'Yes.'

He looked at the jiggling lines again, shaking his head. 'I don't understand this.'

Jenn felt a fleeting disgust that he seemed to have no happiness for Neil. And then, in the midst of her own joy for her patient, what she appeared to have caused began to sink in and a chill passed through her. Modern medicine had its miracles: severed hands could be reattached to grasp again, and people could play basketball on prosthetic feet. Patients whose lungs had turned to slag could be given new lungs, stopped hearts could be restarted or even replaced.

But brain death — pupils fixed and dilated, flatline EEG — had always augured the true death, final and irreversible.

Until now.

Was it possible she somehow had just brought a dead brain back to life?

How?

And if she had — and could do it again, whenever the need arose — what would become of her?

Chapter Seven

Sorrow not that the children of thy kind be few, for as the lowly grass of the field by its seed doth spring up anew each season while the lofty oak reneweth itself in the fullness of years, so must it be for thee in thy splendor. Yea, this is the way of all creation and no life may arise outside it. Therefore hold not back from joining in Godly love to increase thine own kind.

And if a man or woman be pure in heart thou mayest join with them also, providing ye take any nephilim beget therefrom into thy service with love that they may bind thy hearts to mankind.

Only join ye not with the impure nor any who might yearn to reveal thee, recalling always that thou shalt not suffer the presence of angels to be proven, lest man cease to mind his own ways.

Codex Angelorum IV, 27–29

Dressing for dinner, Michael fumbled, stiff-fingered, at the buttons of his shirt. In minutes he must go down and drop his bombshell: *Call Amator Evangeline, tell him not to send his daughter tomorrow, I'm not ready.* Then the argument, what did he mean not ready? Did he realize how insulting such a message would be to the head of such a great clan? Father, shaken and dismayed, would point out why each of his excuses was no good.

And if he guesses I love someone else? *If he gleans me?*

Michael's scalp prickled. It was Father who decreed that the family must never probe each other without permission. It would be awkward for him to break his own rule.

Awkward, but not impossible.

In his closet, Michael ran a hand along the coats, deciding on the white dinner jacket Fabriel had given him. Seeing him in it would remind her of their closeness and maybe help her hold back from telling the family about Jenn.

He closed his eyes, feeling his heart pound. The family would be upset enough over the delay and all it *might* mean. If they learned his love for a phage was behind it, it would pour gasoline on the fire — Mother crying, Father furious that he'd kept it hidden, a desperate resentment of Jenn blazing up in all of them before they knew anything about her. Any chance Jenn might have had of being accepted by the family would be ended.

Michael steadied himself with a deep breath. Fabriel wanted Jenn out of his life, but enough to betray a confidence, when he'd made it plain he didn't even know yet if Jenn would have him?

And my chances today are worse than yesterday.

He felt a sickening sense of uncertainty. She turned me down on the play, he thought. Because of Chemosh? I didn't get that impression, but how long before he *does* talk to her? The truth about me will shock her enough without Chemosh having poisoned her with his delusions. By now he may have told her that rubbish about Father killing his child. I might be about to throw my family into turmoil for nothing. And they'll have every right to be upset: Philippa is smart, highly capable, and we need her help. And the alliance will be good for Father, healing the breach that is starting to open between us and the other clans.

Michael had a sudden, dizzying sense of great wheels turning beyond his understanding. There might be far more at stake here than he could imagine. The *Codex* warned against disharmony.

According to its sacred texts, the ancient war in heaven had started with the envy of one angel. Could anyone at that time have imagined it would end in a celestial Armageddon, with a third of the angels being cast down?

But if I marry Philippa, will it truly unite our clans? She cannot help but see I do not love her, and that could lead to a greater breach than if I call it off.

Why can't I love Philippa?

Because I'm already in love.

Visions of Jenn filled his mind: Jenn through her kitchen window, standing alone at the counter to build one of her huge salads, making herself hum along with the oldies station to fill the silence left by Hugh.

The hope in her eyes as she asks Dr Avalon to talk with her coma patient's wife, trying everything she knows to soften the grief that had not been softened for her.

Jenn sitting in front of her TV with a huge bowl of popcorn at 3 a.m., riveted on a terrified Clarice Starling as the young FBI trainee creeps through the pitch blackness of the maniac's basement, a trembling green wraith in his night vision goggles. Cheering as Starling shoots back at his muzzle flash and kills the beast at last.

A beast like the one in her.

Jenn biting down on a washrag to keep from savaging a man's throat as his blood runs into the transfusion pack. Does God watch her at these, her finest moments, when she does what she must to survive, while denying the beast? Does He weep for her?

I want to hold her in my arms, Michael thought, and feel her strength. I want to live with her, to love her as long as she lives, to tell her how beautiful she is and see her smile. I want to kiss her mouth, make love to her, have children by her – girls, all girls.

But if she can't love me in return . . .

The thought stabbed him through.

He became aware of the aroma of corn pudding drifting into his room. His favorite dish, but he could scarcely imagine putting anything into his stomach. Running a comb through his hair, he was startled by the face that stared back from the mirror, pale above the black of his shirt, his eyes too wide, the mouth rigid at the corners. He must not go down looking like this. Rubbing gently at his face, he got the flinching muscles to relax. Jenn *is* drawn to me — she as much as told me that. She fears she's not ready to date again. I must convince her she is.

And for that I need time.

Rolling his shoulders to break their stiffness, he went downstairs.

Raphael and Ariel already stood at the table, engaged in one of their good-natured debates. Rafe gave him a cheery wave and Michael managed a smile, warmed despite his tension by the pleasure he always felt at seeing his brothers. Tonight, Rafe wore a dark silk T-shirt under a charcoal jacket by Armani. Despite its unstructured tailoring, the coat hung awkwardly on his rounded frame. Rafe loved style, and lately he'd been dropping by Alexandria's Torpedo Factory and other riverside art venues to see how the painters and sculptors dressed at their showings. He was more skilled than any of them, but he could dress all in black and stab an earring through his eyebrow and he'd still look like a merry, plump-faced cherub — that turned-up nose and tulip mouth, the sandy mop of tousled hair. His eyes, so like Mother's with their flecks of gold in the brown, were mild and gentle. Despite having seen a thousand years of human pain and suffering, Rafe had the gift of dwelling, instead, on whatever he found beautiful.

'Am I right, Michael?' Ariel said.

'Sorry, I wasn't listening.'

But Ariel had already turned back to Rafe, his blazing red ponytail swinging across his back. He tugged at the mandarin collar of his white dress shirt as he talked, as if afraid it would choke him. The unconscious gesture brought back to Michael the restless little boy Ariel had been not so long ago, always chafing over something, only to break out in joyous laughter the next minute. At twenty-four, Ariel no longer looked anything like a boy. Physical maturity had cemented his resemblance to

Father — the broad shoulders, Uziel's square jaw, the torrent of fiery curls that, unbound, would spill in Mosaic splendor. If Rafe was a cherub, Ariel, with his burning eyes and coked-up twitchiness, would be lead guitar in a group with a name like 'Bad Boys.' In truth, there wasn't a bad bone in his body. If he was the last one in at night, it was because he was protecting, not partying. His drug was action, the split-second timing, the gratification of saving a life. So young, Michael thought. Picking us all up, because no doubt has yet touched his heart. *May it never, dear Brother.*

'Can you really not see how absurd it is to sculpt a giant amoeba?' Ariel said to Rafe.

'It's a paramecium, as you would know if you applied yourself to your microbiology.'

'Fine, a paramecium, rendered large. An eight-foot stone microbe. How inspiring. Why don't you do a person some time?'

'Because people are already there for everyone to see,' Raphael explained in a patient voice. 'Paramecia are so small only a few ever see them, and that is sad, because they are really quite beautiful.'

'What next, Monsieur Rodin, an eight-foot flea?'

As Rafe started to answer, Fabriel came in. Abandoning his brother in mid-sentence, Ariel hurried over to grab her in a bear hug. He danced her around, toe to toe, then released her and whirled in a tight circle, tapping one foot and clapping his hands above his head like a flamenco dancer.

Smiling, Fabriel shook her head, and smoothed down the smart, red sheath dress she had picked out tonight. She'd let her hair fall in a straight sweep from one collarbone around back to the other, like Cleopatra in the relief on the temple wall at Dendera. A dazzling, blonde Cleopatra, tonight with the forbidding air of a queen. *Because she knows what's coming.* Michael tried to catch her eye, but she avoided his gaze. His stomach knotted. *She must let me do this my way. Surely she knows that.*

'Hey, everyone,' Ariel said, 'I was in this guy's house today, because I picked up a lot of anxiety. Turns out he was only late to work, looking frantically for some socks to go with his suit. He pulled the drawer out too far, dumping it all out on the floor. "There is no God," he groaned, and I whispered, "Yes, there is." He jumped like a frog and stared around the room for five minutes.'

Rafe laughed, and Fabriel managed another smile.

'You must never do that again,' Rafe said. 'I mean it. You know what the *Codex* says.'

'Sure, but you should have seen him.'

Mother hurried in from the kitchen, her face flushed, unable as always to refrain from last-minute hovering behind cook. She circled the table, planting kisses on each of their cheeks; Michael smelled cardamom on her hand as it touched his chin, and then she was past. Despite his anxiety, the presence of the others ran through him in a soothing current. If he were blind, he could still feel them around him, nearly as much a part of him as his own flesh. During the day, even miles away, he could usually locate them by winnowing through the constant neuroelectric spill all creatures radiate. Here, with them all close, he could feel the strengths of each of them — Mother's wisdom, Rafe's gentleness, Fabriel's sharpness and poise, Ariel's energy, all soaking into him and becoming a part of his own outlook when they were near. He loved them for making him better, more complete.

What if it came down to him choosing between them and Jenn?

His head swooped with vertigo, as if a chasm had cracked open at his feet. I can't lose them, he thought desperately. But I can't give Jenn up, either, not until I'm sure she won't have me.

Uziel entered from the conservatory and walked around the table, hugging each of them. Michael hugged back, then let go, but Father clung an extra second, keeping hold of his shoulders, gazing at him. He and Ariel looked alike, but they'd never be mistaken for each other. The uninformed eye would see Father as no older than thirty, but to one who knew what to watch for, the economy of his movements, the vast wisdom in his eyes, gave away the ancient being inside the young body. Father had a gravity, a majesty the fidgety Ariel could never imitate, though at times he tried. If Father said the sky was green, it would be hard not to see it so. I've never gone against him, Michael thought, not in a millennium and a half. Can I really do it tonight?

For Jenn.

Uziel strode to the head of the table. 'Sit, sit,' he boomed loudly enough for the kitchen staff to hear. On cue, Ruth carried in a salad of greens, raw broccoli and cauliflower and behind her came Simone with citrus and avocado. 'Wonderful,' Uziel exclaimed, and the faces of the two nephilim shone with pleasure. Michael remembered them as wide-eyed, burbling babies, brought to the Loyola household ten years apart by the NeSeraph family of the Dallas protectorate.

'You're not touching your salad,' Father observed.

'Just trying to figure out which fork to use.'

'You seem preoccupied,' Uziel persisted. 'Anything we can help you with?'

'This one, right?' He picked up the salad fork and, forcing a smile, began to eat.

Father looked at him a moment longer, then turned to Ariel. 'Jesus, Moses and another old man are playing golf. Moses hits first. His ball sails into a pond, so he orders the waters to part, and chips his next shot into the hole for a birdie. Then it's Jesus' turn. His first shot splashes too, so he walks out on the water, commands the ball to surface, then chips it onto the green and, plunk, into the hole for a birdie. The old man, hitting last, also hooks the ball into the pond, but a fish swallows it, then a hawk scoops up the fish, loses his grip and drops it on the green, dislodging the ball, which rolls into the hole. Moses shakes his head and says to Jesus, "I like playing golf with you, but I hate it when you bring your old man along." '

Michael found himself laughing with everyone else, but not as hard as Ariel, who threw his head back, then punched Father on the shoulder. Watching the two, he felt a touch of envy at their easy rapport.

Ruth served the vichyssoise, and everyone exclaimed over it.

Several times, talk turned briefly to Philippa, speculation about when she'd arrive tomorrow, jokes about Michael the nervous bridegroom, but the conversation quickly veered away again when he failed to join in.

Tell them now, Michael thought, before you explode.

No. Let them at least enjoy the main course.

Simone brought in a spicy ratatouille with pumpernickel rolls. Michael drank glass after glass of the rich '94 Sonoma merlot from Sebastiani, wishing it could affect him as it did mortals and dull the growing panic in his stomach. Dessert was an agony, everyone taking their time, enjoying the coffee and cheeses. At last Simone cleared away the dishes. Ariel started to get up.

'Wait, brother.'

Ariel settled back into his seat. Michael took a final gulp of wine, feeling a minute tremor in his hand as he set the glass down. 'Someone called me a nervous bridegroom earlier. I'm sure you've all noticed it by now. I want to apologize to you all, for what I am about to ask. My nervousness is deeper than it might appear. The truth is, from the beginning I've been unsure about marrying Philippa. I thought my uncertainty would go away, and it may yet, but at this point it hasn't. I'm asking that we postpone her joining us.' For a few seconds, the room was utterly quiet, like the compression of sound after a loud explosion. Then Rafe gave a nervous cough.

'Michael,' Mother said in a low voice. 'Do you realize what you're asking?'

'It's awkward, I realize. I kept hoping I could resolve my feelings before we got to this point, and that's why I didn't speak out sooner.'

Uziel stared at him. 'Awkward doesn't begin to describe it, son. You would have me call the noble Amator and tell him my son isn't ready to receive his daughter?'

'He is no more noble than you.'

An indescribable pain flitted across Uziel's face and was gone. He leaned forward. 'What is this, Michael?'

'I'm not ready.'

'What does that mean? The plans are made. Philippa is lovely, beautiful, smart. How can you have any hesitation?'

When he said nothing, Father tipped back in his chair, touched both hands to his forehead then flung them up. 'I don't understand you. Do you feel no desire whatsoever for a mate?'

I *burn* with desire, Michael thought, but I don't know if Jenn will have me. And if she will, how long before I could bring her to you as my love, without you seeing instead not only a blood eater but a trespasser who has dashed your hopes for me?

'Well?' Father prompted.

'Do I feel desire for a mate? No. I want to be in love.' *And able to share it with all of you.*

Father studied him. 'Is that why you've insisted on this charade as a human doctor? Your wish to "get closer to people" is actually a hope that you might fall in love with some human woman again?'

A chill went through Michael. Father was burrowing close to the truth.

'*Have* you fallen in love with a human?' Mother asked.

'No!' Conscious of Fabriel, he knew he must press on, but fear blanked his mind. In thousands of years of watching faces, Father had seen every conceivable nuance of deceit. What was he seeing now?

Fabriel leaned toward him. 'Michael—'

He held up a hand. 'All I'm asking is a little more time to consider this, to try and settle my mind about it.'

'You speak of time as if it were not precious to us,' Uziel said. 'We need you back with us, Michael, and we need Philippa to help us do God's work. Things are heating up in the city. The Haitian crew and Damon Malcolm's gang are getting ready to fight over drug territory. Drive-by shootings, Michael, innocent bystanders at risk. When I visited the Evangelines to discuss the marriage with Amator, I happened to see Philippa approach their compound. She is very fast in the air, and from what her father said, she's able to maintain mental contact over larger distances than any of us. She'd add great strengths to our family. I truly believe you could fall in love with her, if you worked on it – and after all love does take work. Compared to what your mother and I feel for each other now, what we had in the beginning could scarcely even be called love.'

Glancing at Mother, Michael saw her look down at the table. An instant later, she raised her head and smiled at him, but he could see a sheen in her eyes. That hurt her, he realized. Did she love Father at first sight? His face warmed with indignation. Must Father be so clinical, so remorselessly analytic? If his heartbeat had not picked up the moment he first saw Mother, if he hadn't felt a rush in his veins and thought, 'I must contrive to meet this lovely creature,' if it had started as a marriage of convenience or duty, couldn't he keep that to himself?

And then Michael felt shame. This is happening because of *me*, he thought. I must end it, before we all start cutting more deeply. But how can I even imagine accepting Philippa while there's still a chance Jenn might have me?

'Hey, brother,' Ariel said, 'if you don't want Philippa, I'll take her.'

'All right.'

Ariel's eyes widened, and nervous laughter burst from Rafe, then quickly died as Father raised a hand. 'Amator has not offered Philippa to Ariel,' he said in a soft voice.

'How about Rafe, then?' Michael said.

Taking a sip of wine, Rafe nearly sprayed it out again. 'Me?'

'Are you saying you wouldn't want her?'

Rafe hesitated, and Michael could almost see his mind spinning as it tried to find the path of least conflict. If Rafe said he'd want Philippa, he'd risk annoying Father, and if he said he wouldn't want her, he'd be validating his brother's reluctance, which would also displease Father.

'You're not being fair, Michael,' Fabriel said in a low voice. 'It's not a matter of what Rafe or Ariel would like, but of what is being offered.'

'You're right, I'm sorry.' He must keep Fabriel out of this, at all costs.

Father relaxed a fraction. 'Surely I don't have to tell you how important this is, not just to you, but to all of us.'

'I do understand.'

'It is only natural that you don't yet know how you feel about Philippa. You barely know her. But the answer is not to keep her away but to start spending time with her as soon as possible. We could lengthen your engagement if you like, give you more time to come to appreciate her. This alliance between our two families is vital. It must go forward.'

'Is that all you care about?'

For a second Father's eyes seemed to flick to black and Michael felt a freezing jolt of terror, and then Father looked himself again. Had it even happened?

Mother leaned forward quickly. 'That is certainly not all your father cares about, Michael. He wants you to be happy, as we all do. Have you thought about children? In the years since our family was blessed with Ariel, in all the world only a few hundred more of us have been born. You and Philippa might have a son or daughter.'

Father said, 'You've been lonely, I know you have, though you've tried to hide it. Love takes time. Just go around with her, be with her for awhile. Sit with her at this table and give her a chance, and maybe you'll find you could love her as a husband.'

It sounded so reasonable, how could he refuse? And yet he must.

Father sighed. 'It saddens me to see you thinking so little of your duty.'

'It saddens me that you think *only* of duty.' The words were out before Michael could stop them.

'Michael!' Fabriel said sharply.

Uziel's eyes widened and he put his hands flat on the table, as if to steady himself. 'Well, now . . .'

'I'm sorry,' Michael said, reaching toward Father's hand. 'I watch you carry the burden of protecting the people of this city every minute, every hour, year after year, and I'm amazed at how you bear up. But sometimes I feel so sad for you. You're tired, Father. Whenever the papers report another murder or rape, a mugging in some alley, you take it on your shoulders. *Why wasn't I there?* I know. When people sit in my office and pour out their hearts to me, I feel I must save them — *must* — even if they then resist every bit of help I try to give. Yesterday Fabriel made a joke out of how she saved a man from a stabbing in a bar, and at once I felt lighter inside. That's what we need, more joking and less of this eternal, crushing "duty." '

'You're talking rubbish!' Ariel's voice had an angry edge. 'What's wrong with you? Can't you see how we've missed you working with us? I don't like you being away at this hospital. The *Codex* tells us not to mess with people's minds—'

'I'm not messing with anyone's mind. I look, but I don't touch. I use what I see to help them, but only in the same ways as a human therapist would.'

'What a waste. You're not a doctor, you're an angel of God, and you're supposed to guard people from harm. That *is* your duty. Sometimes I want to come over to the hospital and push aside the people that are taking you away from us so I can grab you and drag you out!'

'That's enough, now,' Father said softly.

Ariel looked stung, his face turning red.

Pained for him, Michael said, 'I know you miss me during the day, Ariel, and I miss you, too. But, I love working with people's minds, helping them that way.'

Ariel said nothing, his jaw set tight. How hard it must be for him, Michael thought, to be twenty-four among all of us. Even Fabriel has five hundred years on him.

He wasn't joking about coming to the hospital. Might he make trouble?

Michael felt a twinge of foreboding as he imagined Ariel discovering Jenn, deciding to push *her* aside. *I must keep an eye out for him.*

Turning back to Father, Michael said, 'Surely it can't be

wrong for us to make our work as much a joy as possible, or for me to want to be in love if I'm to marry, instead of feeling it's my duty.'

Father said, 'Our lives are not about fun, Michael. We have a commitment to the Amator clan. We cannot break it.'

Defiance welled up in him. 'You made that commitment. Did it ever occur to you to consult me first?'

Father's hand jerked, his glass thumped over, a red stain of wine spreading on the white damask. Ruth stepped forward from the shadows, but Father waved her back, his face rigid. Michael gasped as a spot just below the frontal bone of his skull tingled, and he realized with shock that Father was on the verge of gleaning him. Terror raced through him and he gathered his legs under him. If Uziel saw Jenn—

Don't think about her!

But he knew in the same instant that trying not to think of Jenn was the same as thinking of her, and that Father would surely see it—

And then the tingle subsided, and he nearly sobbed in relief. Father's head gave a quick, convulsive shake, and he raised a hand in what might be apology, but his face remained grim. 'Michael, I am head of this clan, and for all our love and familiarity, I stand in the place of God for you. You seem to have forgotten that. Don't.'

'Two weeks, Father. Just delay Philippa's coming two weeks, that's all I'm asking.'

Uziel sat back, gazing at him. For nearly a minute, he said nothing. 'One week.'

Michael hesitated. This might be his only chance. But a week — how could he hope to win Jenn's heart in so little time? And every minute of the week would be filled with risk, that Fabriel would break down and tell Father, or that next time Father would overcome his aversion to pushing into his mind.

What had Drey said? *Ask for the possible. That will be hard enough.*

'A week,' Michael agreed. 'Thank you, Father.' Getting up, he walked out, torn between hope and dread.

Chapter Eight

At 2 a.m., Jenn sat in the study upstairs, the little room off her bedroom. It flitted through her mind that, if Hugh had lived, a baby might be crying in this room right now, and she'd be right here, picking it up and putting it to her breast before it woke its father. A baby, warm and soft, and Hugh coming in anyway with a yawn, rubbing at his hair, which stood up comically from his pillow—

Quickly, she refocused on the article. 'Examiner-induced Artifacts in Clinical Electroencephalography,' in *The New England Journal of Medicine*. All of the irregularities discussed by the authors came from accidental sounds or other forms of stimulation by the technician in the lab.

All involved conscious patients.

I was praying for activity on Neil's EEG, Jenn thought, and then it came, and his pupil also responded for the first time since admission. Could I have been Influencing his blood flow somehow, and that caused the readings?

Unlikely. The neural noise in even a damaged brain interfered with blood Influence into cerebral veins and arteries, so it wasn't something you did without knowing it.

Then how?

It had been so intense, but now it was losing focus and color, like a photo left out in the sun. If she'd turned lead to gold, at least she'd have the gold. When Rich had checked Neil's pupil for himself, the response had been there, slight, but enough to convince Rich he was improving.

But I was standing at his elbow, Jenn thought. If I'd moved away . . .

She planted her head between her hands, squeezing, trying to steady her whirling thoughts. She wanted Neil to be better. But she was afraid, too. What if she really could restore life to a dead brain? How long before she had mobs running after her, desperate people whose dear ones were in coma or had been diagnosed with brain tumors, pursuing her wherever she went, waiting outside her house, pulling at her if she ventured out, begging her to come heal the one they loved, touch them, stand close to them, do whatever you do—

She took a deep breath and eased it out, trying to slow her racing heart. She was getting ahead of herself. She didn't know what had happened, or if she could ever do it again. She was just rattled because nothing was under control these past few days. But was that really so bad? Being off balance and excited and afraid could also make you feel more alive — as long as things didn't get too far out of hand. She hadn't seen the strange phage again, and she would proceed carefully with Neil, and if she found that she somehow was healing him, she'd go on doing it and just make sure no one found out.

'Everything is sweetened by risk,' she thought. I used to like that saying.

She looked up at the clock above her desk. Hugh had given it to her on their first anniversary, when they'd thought time meant forever, red numerals on a lined notepad face framed by four outsized colored pencils. Two-thirty. The normal world was asleep now. How many times in the past three years had she found herself envying their oblivion? I used to sneak into the bedroom, she thought, and watch Hugh sleep. Then I'd go back and hit the journals, knowing I wasn't alone.

She thought of Michael, his clear sapphire gaze, so vivid it speeded up her breathing. That straight back, his contained grace, his hands, strong and well formed, his smile as warming as an embrace. What would he look like as an old man? Handsome still, but the back not so straight, the color of his eyes watered down by glasses, and she would feel a growing desperation, knowing he would soon be gone, and it would be worse than Hugh because she'd had Michael longer, grown to love him even more deeply, but it would not have seemed long at all, a twentieth of her life, perhaps, no more than five years to any normal . . .

Jenn slammed the journal shut and stalked downstairs. The house, envy of her fellow residents, seemed suddenly too big for her, too full of memories and unrealized dreams. Maybe she should have let it go after Hugh died, but he'd paid it off with the advance on his last novel, and a one-bedroom apartment fit to live in would be triple the taxes on this place.

Hurrying through the sunken living room, she escaped out the back way to the rear courtyard. The cool air, heavy with damp earth smells, felt good in her lungs. The grass was still a wintry gray, but crocuses had sprung up along the base of the privacy fence that hid the alley beyond.

Michael asked me out, she thought, and I turned him down. And that's the end of it.

She went back inside and checked the clock again: 2:40. Only four more hours, and she could head for the hospital—

The doorbell chimed, startling her, and then a warm anticipation filled her. Only one of the family would call this late. Morning would come a lot faster with company. Hurrying through, she pulled the front door open.

Chemosh gave her an apologetic smile. 'Sorry to call so late.'

'Don't be silly, come in.'

She led him through the dining area and down the three steps to the living room. He settled on the couch across from the fireplace and leaned back, then crouched forward to the edge of the seat, clamping his hands between his knees. His deeply tanned face looked almost sallow, his dense black hair pinned back so closely that the skin seemed stretched tight over the fine cheekbones and nose.

'What is it?' she asked.

'At the hospital a few days ago, you chided me for not opening up to you. I'd like to do so now.'

In the middle of the night? Why do I think I'm not going to like this?

Settling on the raised hearth beside the fire, Jenn waited attentively. Chemosh rubbed his forehead. 'To avoid confusing you, I have to give you some background, so bear with me.'

'I'm not due at work until seven,' Jenn said.

He did not smile. 'Zane told me about the face you saw at the hospital window.'

'The phage, yes.'

'It wasn't a phage.'

Mystified, she said, 'What do you mean? What else could it have been?'

'Phages are not the only off-shoot of humanity unsuspected by normals. We have a natural enemy. They believe they are angels of God, but—'

'Wait,' Jenn said. 'Slow down. You're telling me an angel looked in the hospital window?'

'Not an angel, one of the creatures behind the myth, just as we are the reality behind the vampire myth.'

Jenn shook her head, astonished. Had the whole world gone crazy? *First Neil's EEG improves without my doing anything but wishing, and now angels. What's next, Santa Claus?* 'Come on, Chemosh—'

'Listen to me.' His tone was not loud, but the command cracked like a whip. Unnerved, she stared, wondering at this side to him she had not seen before.

'They have very long lives,' Chemosh said in a gentler voice, 'longer than ours, and they may be true immortals. And they do have many of the powers you find in the angel myths. They can fly, for example, and when they're doing it, it even looks as if they have wings, but actually it's an aurora generated when they deflect gravity to flow around themselves. They control other forms of energy too, just as the phage affinity for blood allows us to Influence circulation. They remain unseen to normals by scattering the light energy that reflects from them. This doesn't work on our superior eyes, but they can blind us to them by interfering directly in the visual cortex, which runs on neural energy. That's why the one you saw was able to vanish twice.'

'Chemosh . . .' Jenn was having trouble getting her mind around what he was saying. 'How could I never have heard of them?'

'They rarely let themselves be seen. I'm still surprised you managed to spot the one two nights ago. He wouldn't have expected that a doctor might also be a phage. He was probably merely scattering light from himself, then when he realized you saw him anyway, he switched to direct neural Influence. It doesn't matter, the point is, it's part of their code for themselves that they stay hidden, and they are masters at it. I'm the only phage I know of who has tangled with them and lived to tell about it.'

Despite Chemosh's grim tone, a sense of wonder swept Jenn. 'I thought he was clinging to the building, but you're saying he was . . . flying.'

'That's right.'

She remembered the figure on the roof, tall, strikingly handsome with his chiseled jaw and luxuriant auburn hair. 'Why didn't you tell me about them before?'

'Just knowing these creatures exist is hard, Jenn. I so wish I had never heard of them.'

'But why?'

'Think. Do you really want to wonder if one is watching you, maybe getting ready to hurt you, and you can't see him or do anything about it?'

'Why would an angel hurt me . . .?' She trailed off. 'Because I'm a phage?'

'They believe their own myth. They protect humans.'

'But I've never killed.'

'They read minds. They can see what is in your heart and respond to it.'

A cold spasm went through her as she remembered just this morning wanting Rich Sikorsky's throat.

'Fortunately, they are rare, like us, and we don't cross paths often, but when we do, angels try to stop phages from feeding. They are certainly strong enough to fight us on even terms physically, which means they could bury us to die horrible, lingering deaths. They can also use their control of energy fields to attack the nervous system itself. One came after me once, and I thought my brain was being ripped from my skull. Fortunately, I could strike back with blood Influence and somehow escape.'

The fear in Chemosh's voice burrowed into the hollow of her stomach; at the same time, she felt disappointed, almost betrayed. She'd always liked the idea of angels. And now Chemosh was trying to make her afraid of them — or rather, of the 'reality behind the myth.' But if there was a reality behind the angel 'myth,' wasn't that the same thing as saying that it *wasn't* a myth?

'Why are you telling me this now?'

Chemosh took her hands. 'Because Michael Avalon is one of them.'

She stared, too astonished to speak.

'The one at the window could only have been his brother,' Chemosh said, 'a new member of the family since last I saw them. There are at least five others, including Michael, but it's the father who counts.'

'Michael's *father*? Angels have mothers and fathers?'

'I told you, they're not really angels. Michael's father is called Uziel, and I know him better than any of the others. He has hated our kind for thousands of years. If Uziel learns Michael is interested in you, he'll kill you. And there's no way you can escape him. He has allies of his own kind all over the earth. If you run, he can have thousands keeping watch for you. Nerves generate neurochemical electricity which spills from every creature. This aura is distinct for each of us. It's as if you glowed in the dark to them. You *will* be found and Uziel *will* kill you.'

Jenn found her voice again. 'Chemosh, this is insane—'

'You must tell Michael you can have nothing further to do with him. If he has your best interests at heart, he'll accept that.'

Jenn barely heard Chemosh. *They have very long lives — longer than ours. They may even be immortal.* I wouldn't have to lose Michael, she thought with a rising excitement, then realized Chemosh was looking at her with dismay.

'Jenn, why are you smiling? Have you heard a word I've said?'

'What if they *are* truly angels of God?'

'Are we vampires?'

'Aren't we? That people have some details about us wrong would hardly console someone being attacked by one of us. The truth is we drink blood. You may be wrong about angels, and you have to be wrong about Michael's father. Michael would stay away from me if he thought it would put me in danger.'

'Jenn, you have known him for exactly two days.'

'Do you have to drink a whole bottle of wine to know it's good?'

'It is likely he has been stalking you for some time.'

Jenn felt herself bristling. 'That's absurd.' She got up and paced to the courtyard door so Chemosh wouldn't see the indignation in her face. And then her anger dissipated as she recalled the powerful feeling of recognition she'd had at her first sight of Michael. What if that hadn't been her first sight. Could she, on some unconscious level, have been seeing him, sensing him, maybe for a long time? Sometimes, in her bleakest moments of grief and despair, she would feel a warming touch on her shoulder, and know she was imagining it. What if she had not imagined it?

Turning back to Chemosh, she said, 'When I was a little girl, before I was ever a phage, I used to imagine I had a guardian angel. Sometimes, at night when I was feeling a little afraid of the dark, I'd set a chair at the foot of my bed for him. Imagining he was in the room with me, sitting in that chair, made me feel better, not so afraid anymore. If Michael has been watching over me, I would hardly call that stalking.'

Chemosh looked exasperated. 'All right, if it doesn't bother you that Michael has been watching you for years, following you around, reading your mind, at least you must listen to what I'm telling you about his father. Uziel will kill you.'

'How could someone who sees himself as an angel go around committing murder? I've felt Michael's compassion and caring when we talked about Hugh. I can't believe he could have a killer for a father.'

'I could say the same about you.'

'Zane has stopped killing.'

Chemosh hesitated, and a tremor went through her. Did he know something he wasn't saying? 'Are you telling me my father has been killing and lying to me about it?'

He held up his hands. 'Absolutely not. I'm just reminding you that he *was* a vicious killer for five hundred years, and yet you are the soul of gentleness. Believe me, assuming Uziel is like his son is the worst mistake you could make.'

'He could be as different from his son as night from day and still not be a murderer . . .' Suspicion struck her as she realized Chemosh's expression had gone completely opaque. 'What aren't you telling me?'

His chest lifted in a quick breath; it was a long moment before he let it out. 'Uziel killed my son when I was pharaoh of Egypt.'

Jenn leaned against the door, dumbfounded. 'When you were *what*? How old *are* you?'

'Three thousand three hundred and two, to be precise.'

She stared at him with disbelief. 'I thought phages only live around fifteen hundred years, give or take.'

'Most, yes. I can't explain why I have lived longer but it is true. By the current system of reckoning time, I was born in 1304 in Egypt.'

He means 1304 B.C.!

'My father was the Pharaoh Seti I and my royal name was Ramses II.'

Jenn shook her head. 'I . . . I need to sit down.' She made her way back to the hearth and sank down on it. 'You were Ramses II?'

He said nothing, gazing at her, waiting. A chill ran up her spine. It was almost too much to comprehend. Ramses II had been a giant of history, millions had pressed their faces to the earth before him. Could this young-looking, vital being truly be both her own great grandfather and one of the grandest kings of ancient Egypt? 'So that mummy in the museum—'

'One of my accountants whom I caught stealing from the royal treasury. I awarded him the dubious honor of being buried in my tomb.' There seemed a bitter edge to his voice, as if the treachery wounded him even now.

'How did Uziel come to kill your son?'

Chemosh hesitated.

He's making me drag this out of him. Why?

'If you've read your history, you know I was quite a builder. You also know, I'm sure, that the actual work was done by slaves, and among the people I used in this way were the Hebrews. They built my capital of Per Ramesse in the eastern delta of the Nile. Uziel took offense at the merciless way I was driving them. He put their man Moses up to demanding that I free his people. If I had been then who I am now, I'd never have abused them in the first place. It shames me that I once kept a whole nation in slavery, but you must understand, back then the rules were different. When I governed Egypt, I was still within the life span of a normal man, too young to have risen above such barbarity . . .'

Chemosh seemed to sag in the couch. He waved a weary hand as if dismissing his own words. 'The truth is, I have no defense. I didn't just drive the Hebrews and my other slaves to the limits of human endurance so I could have my grand temples and palaces. Each night, my head overseer would bring to me a slave who had displeased him. The lower reaches of my palace were accessible through only one door. I would release the slave into that part of the palace, set guards at the door, and hunt him during the night, feasting on his terror, toying with him until the lust for blood won out and I killed him. Some nights the overseer would bring as many as ten. I would even arm them, but of course they stood no chance against me. I did this every night, Jenn. Phage metabolism was no different then than now. A few pints of blood every two weeks would have sustained me, but I loved to hunt and kill. I was drunk on my power as a pharaoh and a phage, utterly heedless of the pain and grief I caused, not just to the endless string of doomed slaves but to every loved one, every wife and child each of them left to grieve, thousands of people as the years went by. No commandant in any Nazi prison camp could have been worse than I . . .' He stopped and swallowed. Jenn saw that his eyes had filled with tears. She felt a harsh burning at the base of her throat. At the same time, she realized she felt no horror at what he'd said, but a deep sadness.

'You wanted to know why I haven't told you of angels before,' Chemosh said. 'Part of it *was* to protect you from fearing what you could not change. And the other part was this. If humanity were to receive justice for my crimes, I would not draw another breath, and though I have changed, I can never forget the monster that I was, those hunts through the hallways, the excitement I felt, down there inside me still, like the innermost rings of an oak. I did not want you to know. I was afraid of what you would think of me, that you might not understand how the centuries can reshape character, as surely as wind molds stone. Now you know – not just the adoring great grandfather I am now, but the monster I once was.'

The anguish in Chemosh's voice touched her. To carry the memory of yourself committing such hideous acts – how it must torment him. It would have been far easier for Chemosh if he had remained evil. She remembered him appearing almost a year ago, searching Merrick out because of his fascination with the notorious phage who had hunted down and buried others of his own kind who went on wanton killing sprees. Inquiring about Merrick's parents because he wanted to know what kind of people could produce a son with such moral courage. Finding to his astonishment that Merrick's mother was the woman who had served him at the inn of a small English village he'd passed through nearly a thousand years ago, and who had shared his bed the next two nights. It had seemed incredible to her that fate could have brought Chemosh and Merrick together, even given a thousand years to do so, but she saw now that it had not been fate at all. Something deep within Chemosh had recognized his own moral dilemma playing out in the life of this other phage. He had been drawn to Merrick by the part of himself that was stronger in his son.

Jenn said, 'I doubt that true monsters regard themselves as monsters. And do you think you have described to me anything I have not felt myself?'

'But you've *kept* it a feeling, never acting on it. What strength you have! You can't know how I admire you – how I wish I had been so morally strong at your age.'

'When you were young, the world *was* far less enlightened – that is not an excuse for you, Chemosh, it's reality. I *have* read history and I took a college course on ancient civilizations, and one of the things I remember is that the Israelites went on from their days in Egypt to become fierce as lions themselves, slaughtering whole armies that came against them, sometimes including the camp followers and the livestock. Whatever you did back then, you *have* changed.'

His eyes turned luminous; he seemed unable to speak.

'So when you enslaved the Israelites, Uziel was watching?'

He cleared his throat. 'Yes. The Nile delta was apparently his territory back then. I had no inkling about angels, self-styled or otherwise, and it seemed absurd to me to let a multitude of able-bodied workers walk off simply because one of their number asked me to. If Uziel had come to me himself, shown me his powers . . . but no, he let me think it was all Moses, and Moses insisted he was speaking for Yahweh, the Israelite God.' Chemosh gave her a bitter smile. 'As the son of Ra, I was a god myself, you understand, so I wasn't impressed. When I refused to free the Israelites, disturbing things began to happen – a terrible plague of locusts, prodigious hailstorms, crop failures, a dense cloud that hovered over the entire country for three days, making it nearly as dark as night – other strange and unsettling phenomena. Moses kept coming, taking credit for these natural calamities in the name of his God. He had me wavering a few times, but I wanted to go on building, and how could I if I let the work force go? Natural calamities had happened before and would again. I knew Ra was a fiction, used to keep the masses in line, and I wasn't superstitious enough to believe some other unseen deity, some competitor of Ra, was really at work.

'Then Uziel struck, not an imaginary god but a real creature, with terrifying power. He paralyzed me, made me watch help-lessly as he killed my son. He also murdered thousands of other children, not just in Per Ramesse, but all across Egypt.'

Cold horror welled up in Jenn.

Her great grandfather stared past her, into the ashes of the hearth, the last fire she and Hugh had enjoyed together. She had the distracted, familiar thought that she ought to sweep them out, but knew she would not.

'I can still hear the wails that shattered the night,' Chemosh murmured. 'The cries of my people. My own screams.'

'That's a dreadful story,' she whispered.

'It's not a story. My son was real. He was only six years old when he died, a beautiful innocent. In all of Per Ramesse, only the firstborn died, except for my son. How long I wondered about that, and then I realized the truth. He must have had the phage gene in him. He was my firstborn phage, and somehow Uziel had detected that. But my son was innocent, all the same. The disease doctors now mistake for leukemia would not have come for another six or seven years. His life was blameless. He played with the children of my courtiers, he loved to sail his reed boats in the pool. He had a cat named Narmer that he loved. After he died, Narmer stayed in his bedroom three days, refusing to eat or be touched.' Chemosh looked away, and she saw tears in his eyes. More than three millennia had passed; according to history, Ramses II had fathered many sons, but clearly that had not made the horrible death of the one any easier.

'He must have been a wonderful little boy,' she said softly. 'What was his name?'

'Chemosh. When I slipped away into the desert, leaving another man in my tomb, my son's name was the only thing I took with me.'

She went to him, putting a hand on his shoulder. He covered

it with his own. My great grandfather, she thought with wonder, one of the greatest pharaohs of ancient Egypt.

'I understand why you must hate Uziel,' she said softly, 'but it was a long time ago. If Uziel warned you before he struck, surely he'd warn me, too, and he hasn't. I've done nothing wrong. I appreciate what you've come here to tell me. I know it wasn't easy, and I know you're concerned for me—'

'Jenn,' he said urgently, 'this is *real*. Everything I've said is true. Michael means death for you. I'd give anything if it weren't so. You know I want you to love again, but you've only known Michael for two days, and surely you can back away. There will be other men—'

'Who live as long as we do?'

'A phage, then – one who doesn't kill, one like us. They do exist, I've met them here and there over the centuries.'

She took his hands. 'Chemosh, it's too late. I may have known Michael for two days, but I believe I've felt his love much longer than that. It's possible he sustained me through my grief, and that his presence at my most dangerous moments is what has helped me not to kill—'

'Jenn—'

'And whether or not that's true, the point is he has known me for years – you said so yourself. He knows what I am, and he wants me anyway. Can't you see what that means to me? Hugh thought he understood what I am, but he didn't, he couldn't. He softened and blurred me in that great novelist's imagination of his, never saw me at my worst, when all I want in the world is to kill. Michael has seen all that, and wants me anyway. You can't ask me to give him up just because his father may not like me.'

'To save your life—'

'What you'd be saving wouldn't be much of a life. I now have a chance really to live, and I won't give it up.'

Tears welled up in Chemosh's eyes. 'Then we are lost.'

Chapter Nine

At the door to Michael's office, Jenn heard Budgie chirping and Michael talking to him in a gentle voice. Soothing sounds, but her stomach kept churning. What if Chemosh was right about the danger from Uziel?

It was all so long ago, Jenn thought. Surely it's over.

And, anyway, everything is sweetened by risk.

Now it's my move. But what do I say? Hey, I understand you're an angel.

Is there another way?

An idea struck her: Last time she'd come here she'd gotten cold feet and turned away, but then Michael had pulled the door open, as if he'd sensed her through two inches of oak. Had he heard her? It seemed logical that the senses of angels would be as keen or keener than a phage's.

She whispered, 'Michael?'

Seconds later, the door swung wide, and he stood there, drinking her in with a look that made her heart race.

'It's true,' she said, dizzied. 'You're actually an angel.'

Taking her hands, he pulled her inside. 'How did you know?'

'My great grandfather told me.'

He paled. 'Chemosh?'

Jenn nodded mutely. Her knees felt weak — Michael *did* know all about her. People at the hospital had seen her with Chemosh, but who could imagine that a man who looked so young could be her great grandfather?

'Chemosh says you can fly.' The words rode out on her breath, as if another person had said them.

Michael smiled. Keeping hold of her hands, he seemed suddenly to grow taller, and then she looked down and saw that his feet had left the ground. In the bright light of morning flooding through his office window, the illusion of wings was faint, a golden nimbus arcing up from either shoulder. It took her breath away. She was afraid to look at his face.

Releasing one of her hands, he placed a finger along her jaw and gently steered her gaze back to him. 'Don't be afraid.'

She stood, paralyzed, suddenly remembering the nativity play at Gregory's school last Christmas. The child who'd played the angel had said almost those same words, 'Be not afraid,' in such a piping, quavery voice that some in the crowd had chuckled. 'Be not afraid,' and why should anyone fear an angel, but she *was* afraid, terrified.

'I . . . I'm on duty. I'd better get back. I . . . we can talk later—'

'Jenn, don't run from me, I beg you.'

He had foreseen her fear. His face looked suddenly too bright, as if it might blind her. The nerves in her legs pulsed with the need to back away from him, to turn and run.

'This is why you pretended to be a doctor,' she whispered.

'Pretended?' He sounded offended.

'You went to medical school?' she asked, surprised.

'Sort of, yes. I've read all the texts and taken the exams at Georgetown, though no one ever saw me, of course. I have a certain . . . expertise in the human mind. And I organized some records to show I graduated from Stanford.'

'Angels can lie?'

'Can we call it protective coloration?'

She found herself relaxing a little. 'You're starting to seem human again.'

He held her gaze. 'I'm as human as you are.'

126

She realized he had said precisely what he meant to. 'An angel. I sort of believed in you when I was little, but then I decided you were more of a wish, something written into the Bible with all the other things men hoped or believed but didn't know.'

'Not just the Bible,' he said, 'Jews and Christians, yes, but Moslems, Hindus, Zoroastrians, and many others have also sensed and written of us. Never with total accuracy, but that's true for hemophages, too, isn't it?'

She thought of the vampire myths and nodded. His hand was still on her face, warm and alive. Wanting to look away from his eyes, she found she could not.

'Jenn, come with me for a moment.'

She was not aware of answering, only of being led by the hand down the short hall. The receptionist did not look up, and Jenn realized Michael had edited their images from the woman's eyes. She felt caught up in a dream, as he led her up to the roof, where two nights ago she had seen another of his kind, one of his family perhaps — a brother, Chemosh thought.

Oh, Michael, have I been feeling your presence all along? Have we already been together in ways I could not recognize but always felt? I have so much to ask you.

But she could not find her tongue.

A cool wind, moist with the early promise of spring, blew across the rooftop, ruffling Michael's hair. The sky over his shoulder was a bright, crystalline blue, dotted with puffy, snow-white clouds. Taking her other hand, he stood with her for a moment, then drew her to him, embracing her gently, as if they were about to dance. She stiffened but did not pull away. His breath, warm along her neck, brought a thrill low in her stomach. Once more unleashing the glowing arcs of energy from his shoulders, Michael held her close and gently rose into the morning light. He drifted with her above the hospital, cheek to cheek. With a gasp, she tightened her grip on him as she looked down into the dark throat of a chimney — the hospital's power plant. The two massive wings of Adams Memorial, queen of the city's hospitals, lay spread below them, then they crossed bustling 16th Street, over some office buildings and then into the residential neighborhood to the north. From above, the bare oaks and maples along the yards looked curiously like giant tumbleweeds, blown up against the houses. Twigs and branches, fallen during winter storms, littered the rooftops. Michael carried them across a playground, the happy shouts and cries of children rising up.

'I love you,' he whispered. 'I have loved you for so long.'

Her heart melted. For an instant, she felt more intensely happy than she had ever been, and then the fear washed through her again. 'Michael, I . . .'

'Do you want me to take us back inside?'

'Yes.'

In his office again, surrounded by the lush potted plants and movie memorabilia, she stood away from him, against a large, framed poster from the film *Michael* – John Travolta, the man, posing as an angel, eyeing the camera with that surly sensitivity, scruffy wings protruding from the black topcoat. She gazed at the again-wingless Michael Avalon, posing as a man in his pleated pants and white medical coat. Looking like a man, but he filled her now with awe.

'Jenn!'

The parakeet's wiry voice startled her. It sat atop a small cart with a TV and VCR. 'Jenn,' it chirped. 'Jenn, Jenn.'

Michael flushed slightly.

He's taught it my name! A powerful sense of unreality gripped her. Could this really be? 'You say you love me, but how could an angel love a hemophage? My kind kill people and drink their blood.'

'Your kind, not you. You've never killed anyone.'

'But I want to.' She swallowed, feeling tears well up, battling them. She must have this out if there was ever to be anything between them. 'Chemosh says you've watched me. Have you seen me feed?'

'Many times.'

'Do you know that each time, what I want most is to tear that throat open with my teeth, to . . . watch the person kick and struggle and die, the way a cat would watch a mouse. Do you know how that would *thrill* me?'

'Yes,' he said calmly.

'No matter how much good I do, Michael, the greatest accomplishment I can hope for in life is that I can die in twelve or fifteen centuries without ever having killed anyone.'

He reached for her, and after a moment she leaned into him, feeling her stiffness melt away as she let herself be held. He was so warm. His clean, smooth skin had a faint smell of nutmeg.

'Dear Jenn,' he murmured. 'So afraid you could not be both known and loved. It's because I've felt the power of your murderous desire that I find your defiance of it so magnificent. *You* are magnificent.' His hands soothed her back. She felt hot tears flowing, soaking into the collar of his shirt.

'I know this is sudden for you,' he said, 'but not for me. I've watched you through all seasons. I've seen your sadness, your pain and heroism. I'm in love with a healer, not a killer.'

'Only because if I couldn't do something for people in return for the blood I take, I'd loathe myself.'

'You give yourself too little credit. You heal because you love people and enjoy helping them.'

It was the sort of thing people said to each other, ordinary humans, who could not see into the heart to know if what they so charitably theorized was true. Michael had seen, Michael knew: there was good in her. A pulse of joy spread through her, quickening her heart.

And yet the fear persisted. She pulled away from him and went to the window, keeping her back to him. 'Chemosh told me you read minds. This is how you know so much about me?'

'Before we met two nights ago, I looked into your mind many times.'

'And since?'

'No. My kind spend our lives protecting people. There aren't enough of us and we must use every tool we have, which includes looking into minds. It's another world, and when you didn't know that world – or I – existed, I watched over you and fell in love with what I saw, inside and out. Now I have stepped into your world to try and win your love. I come as a man, and I will never look inside you again unless you ask it.'

Her fear began to fall away; warmth for him spread through her. She found she could face him again. Turning, she said, 'You say this is sudden for me, but the moment you walked into the break room, I felt I knew you. I thought it was from some long-ago dream. But I've been sensing you, Michael, feeling your love and your comfort.'

He looked surprised. 'Really? Perhaps . . .'

She pressed her hands to her cheeks, feeling their rising heat. 'God. I'm surprised I can look you in the eye.'

'Because I've seen inside you? Jenn, if we're to be judged for everything that enters our minds, we're all doomed. I believe it's what we do – and don't – that counts. If God is truly good, if there's a heaven, a real one, not the one with harps and halos, you'll be there.'

'If?'

He smiled. 'A figure of speech. We can talk theology another time. Right now, what I want more than anything is to know whether you could love me.'

She wanted to say yes, could feel the word circling in her mind, pacing like a caged tiger yearning for release, but how could she love someone after only two days?

'This will seem strange, Michael, but I need to know this. Can you die?'

He hesitated. 'We can, in very rare circumstances, be killed. There are stories in the Bible and other sources about a war in heaven, long ago, in which a third of the angels who rebelled against God were cast down. No one is sure exactly what cast down means, but it might well mean they were killed. I have no direct experience of an angel being killed, but Father remembers an incident more than four thousand years ago, when it happened. He was fifteen miles away, but he felt the huge discharge of energy when the victim's neurochemical essence was ripped out of him.'

It made Jenn think of a fish being gutted. She shuddered. 'Who did it, another angel?'

'The killer was never identified.' Michael looked grim, and she realized this was upsetting him.

'I'm sorry, I didn't mean to—'

'That's all right.' He took her hands. 'What you are really asking is whether I could die of old age or of being shot or stabbed, or of cancer. Or from rescuing two little girls from a fire. The answer is no.'

He continued to hold her hands, his face expectant, and she knew he was still waiting for her to answer his question – could she love him? She wanted to love him, she could feel that she would love him. Would that be enough to say to him?

She said, 'Chemosh tells me he and your father are old enemies.' The light drained from Michael's face. *What am I doing?* Boldness seized her. 'But I say why let their fight, whatever it was, come between us?'

'Amen!' Michael said fervently.

She pulled him into her arms. She could feel him trembling, and then she realized with a shock that she knew what he was feeling, somehow receiving it directly into her mind, and it was both joy and fear.

Uziel tried to empty himself of all anger as he knelt in the small chapel he'd built at the top of the house. In a moment, when he felt calmer, he would pray . . . in a moment. He gazed around the room trying to absorb its soothing emptiness, the purity of the whitewashed walls, the perfect squareness – ceiling, floor and each wall precisely the same dimensions, each plane of each corner capturing a perfect quarter circle. In the beginning, he had considered enshrining sacred objects on each wall, a cross, a mezuzah, a prayer rug, the icons of the great religions, but the effort to size and position them all so that none was more prominent than any other had proven impossible, and he had come to savor the room's utter lack of furnishings.

Calm . . . calm.

He looked up at the central skylight, bathing his face in the chill light of a winter noon. In a few moments he must go back out to the streets — coming here in the middle of the day was almost a dereliction, but he had no choice. He was disturbed, angry, out of balance. He needed help.

Bending forward, Uziel pressed his head to the floor. 'God, hear my prayer,' he murmured. 'I'm worried about Michael. Your great servant Amator Evangeline has offered his daughter Philippa to my son for your greater glory. But Michael seems unwilling. This troubles me, God . . .' Uziel paused, realizing he was not being honest. 'It angers me,' he added. 'My son is on the verge of ruining this chance for the Loyolas to draw closer to you again, as we all long to do. I can't fathom it. I ask you to work on him, God, to speak to his heart and show him the way, so that he can accept Philippa and bring your servants closer together, and maybe even bring a powerful new angel into the world. Births are so rare among us, God, and we Loyolas are especially few. We do thank you for young Ariel. Bless us with another from Michael, so we can better protect your sheep.'

Uziel hesitated again, feeling the cold hardness of the floor against his head. 'Preserve me from doubt, God. I believe in you, even though you haven't spoken to me since Per Ramesse. Haven't I suffered enough for failing you? The other angels blame me for your silence. No one ever says so, but I can feel it. Once again, I beg your forgiveness. I need your help, God. If you could just tell me what to do about Michael. He guards his mind. Shall I read him, or will it break his trust of me? I need help, please, God.'

Uziel listened for the still, small voice inside his head that he could now barely remember. So long, the silence. Had the voice ever been there, or had he only imagined it? 'Give me a sign that you're still there, God,' he pleaded.

Nothing.

It's a test of my faith, Uziel thought. God is waiting to see if my belief in Him will fail. It will not. Never, God, even if you *never* speak to me again . . .

He waited, head to the floor, listening to the silence in his own brain, his blood hissing through the inner chambers of his ears.

Justine's tread was ascending the stairs. He heard her outside the door, each soft breath as she waited. At last he pushed up, feeling desolate, and still angry. Opening the door, he met her gaze and shook his head.

She put a comforting hand on his arm. 'Maybe tomorrow,' she murmured. 'He'll speak to us again through you, my love, I know He will. Just have faith.'

He nodded, but bitterness gripped him. If he could only dismiss all doubt when he prayed, but it was always there, slinking in the shadows but as bright as day to God. One day he would come to this room, and the doubt would never enter his mind, and God would speak to him.

Other feet raced up the stairwell. Justine raised an eyebrow as young Ariel burst in. His eyes were wide.

'There's—'

Uziel hushed him with an upraised palm, motioning him back, closing the door to the prayer room behind him. 'Now, son, what is it?'

'There's a stranger at the door. His face is tanned and he is quite tall. He's afraid and angry, both, and I smell blood on him—'

A fist closed around Uziel's heart. 'Wait. Slow down. Are you telling me you think it's a phage?'

Ariel nodded, the face so like his own filled with a sharp curiosity. 'He wants to speak to you, Father. He knows your name.'

Stunned, Uziel stared at Ariel. He heard Justine gasp beside him. The only phage in all of history he had let see him and know his name was Ramses. But surely the devil phage would have died by now. How could he be at the door?

Hurrying downstairs behind Ariel, Uziel motioned him back as he reached the door. Pulling it open, he looked into the eyes of the pharaoh, a face unmarked by more than three thousand years of time. The air seemed to freeze in Uziel's lungs. He could feel the hatred of Ramses, and an answering fury exploded in him. 'You dare come here, to my house?' A murderous power flowed into his arms, crackling at his fingertips.

Fear flared Ramses' face. 'Wait. Your son's life depends on it.'

Uziel felt the power coursing through him, building toward release, then faltering, dying back, leaving him shaken, as if he'd been struck. 'What? What did you say?' Michael and Rafe were both away at their work. Had Ramses somehow caught one of them, injured them? Who knew what one of these creatures, still alive far beyond its time, might be capable of?

Ramses said, 'Is there someplace private we can talk?'

Uziel realized the pharaoh had backed up several steps. Yes, away from the house; he must get this foul creature, this blood eater, away from his home, his family. 'The garden,' he said, pointing to the maze. Turning back, he saw Justine and Ariel behind him in the foyer, questioning him with their minds. He held up a hand. *Stay here. I will deal with him.*

Ariel's expression darkened with disappointment. Justine reached out to Uziel; he touched her fingertips, then wheeled and followed Ramses, who was already halfway to the maze. Launching himself into the air, he swept above the pharaoh and descended between the tall hedges, motioning him into the inner layers of the maze, striding ahead of him, leading him deeper, until they stood in the center.

Ramses looked around then cocked his head in an attitude of listening.

'No one has followed. Say what you came to say.'

Ramses gazed at him. 'Your son has become infatuated with my great granddaughter, a doctor at his hospital.'

The words shocked Uziel like a searing iron. He felt sick to his stomach. A lie, it had to be. He must simply kill this freak among evil freaks.

'Read my mind,' Ramses said.

A second shock rippled through Uziel. 'How do you know I can do this?'

'Does it matter? You are losing your son. Look inside me and you'll see.'

Sick with dread, Uziel reached into Ramses' mind. A memory closed around him, fresh, of Michael drifting above the hospital. In his arms was a blonde-haired woman, her face against Michael's face, their arms tight around each other. Ramses' great granddaughter, yes, and a blood eater like him—

I will kill you for this! Uziel reeled back out of the mind of Ramses, choking with pain and fury, feeling the strength, the lethal white fire flow into him again.

'I can stop it,' Ramses said.

Once more, Uziel fought back the killing thrust, absorbing it into his own cells; for a second, his knees buckled and he reached out instinctively for Ramses' hand, then in horror thrust his arm to the side, grappling in the thorny branches of the holly to hold himself up. 'You monster!' he gasped. 'Is this your revenge?'

Ramses' eyes glittered, but he said, 'I am as sickened by it as you.'

Uziel fought back a groan as everything fell into place – Michael's strange mania to take on the role of a human doctor, his resistance to Philippa. A sense of betrayal tore at him, nearly blinding him. *Amator would raise me up among all the clans. They would stop blaming me.* And what if Michael joined with this evil creature and produced a child? *My grandchild, born with the stain of evil in its mind, growing up to kill!* Uziel nearly retched, holding himself upright with an effort. How could Michael do this? *God forgive him.* 'Why did you tell me this?' he demanded. 'Are you so eager to hurt me that you'd give up your own granddaughter? I must destroy her, surely you know that.'

'As you did my son?' Ramses' voice was low, but sharp as any knife.

'God killed your son. I was merely His instrument.'

'Did he tell you that, or is it what you tell yourself?'

A shrewd stroke. Uziel glared at Ramses, determined not to respond, to let this blood eater, this most depraved of all blood eaters, see his weakness.

'I came to you,' Ramses said, 'because it was only a matter of hours or days before your son tells you, or you would have found out some other way, and you would destroy Jenn, not knowing there is another option, better for you.'

'She must die.'

Ramses' face paled. 'Kill her and I'll—'

'You'll what?'

Ramses held up his hands in a placating gesture. 'Think: if you harm Jenn, what will Michael feel toward you?'

'He'll understand. Oh, he'll be angry at first, of course, but when he comes to his senses and realizes that I've saved his soul . . .'

Ramses rolled his eyes contemptuously, and a hot fury again swept Uziel. 'You don't know my son, so don't pretend you do. I tell you, he will forgive me.'

'Never. He will loathe you, and if you can be honest with yourself for one moment, you will see it.'

Uziel felt his hands clenching into fists, the nails driving into his palms. He wanted to scream, to take this foul monster by the throat and shake him.

Because he was right.

'Why risk losing the love of your son,' Ramses said, 'when I want them apart as much as you do? Let me take care of it. If you restrain yourself and say nothing to Michael – and if he tells you, make no rash threats – then, when I have made her see reason and she's out of his life, he'll have no reason to suspect you had any role in their breaking up. In return, you will leave Jenn and the rest of my family alone. We will stay away from you and you from us.'

Uziel found himself considering it. 'How can you break them up?'

Ramses said, 'Leave that to me.'

Looking into him again, Uziel saw that Ramses would do

anything, even risk the hatred of his own flesh and blood, to keep her from Michael. Such resolve struck him with awe. Am I weak, that I don't want to risk Michael's hatred?

No. I love my son more than Ramses could love anyone. So let him try it his way.

'I'll give you two days, then I must act. Don't fail, Ramses.'

'I won't. And my name is no longer Ramses. It's Chemosh.'

The pharaoh's voice held a hatred so fierce it sent a chill through Uziel. Why did he emphasize the new name, as though it ought to mean something. It did not.

Leaving the maze, Chemosh felt relief and a grim determination powering his legs, lengthening his stride. He'd get out of this place, this nest of Uziel, as fast as he could and go to work on Jenn. He shouldn't need two days. The vicious bastard had made a direct threat to kill her, and surely that would be enough. All he had to do was relay that to her—

Who was that, slipping into the grand house?

Chemosh recognized the angel who had met him at the door and stopped short, stricken with unease. Uziel's newest son — too physically like him to be anything else — and a perfect match to Jenn's description of the one at the hospital window. Had he been eavesdropping? He already knew who Jenn was — the doctor who'd been able to see him. What if his father's murderous threats had inflamed him and he decided to take matters into his own hands and kill Jenn?

Surely not. Uziel had said two days, and surely no son of his would take it upon himself to break that word.

Chemosh loped across the lawn toward the road where Zane was waiting with his car. Only one thing mattered now. They must get to Jenn and make her give up Michael.

Chapter Ten

Michael stood at the window of his office, his hands clasped in prayerful ecstasy. How strange life could be. Only hours ago, he'd been deep in despair, trying to imagine how he could get the answer he needed from Jenn in only a week. And then *she* comes to *me*, he thought, *knowing* what I am — and despite all the vicious nonsense Chemosh must have fed her.

He savored Jenn's words to him again: *The moment you walked into the break room. I felt I knew you. I thought it was from some long-ago dream. But I've been sensing you, Michael, feeling your love and your comfort.*

Could that really be? He'd used every artifice to remain unseen, neurologic skills unique to his own kind — though it was true that phages did have their own, weaker version of Influence. Now and then he *had* imagined she was responding to him on some level, and if she had now made that fantasy hers, it could only be because she wanted it to be so. Chemosh meant to keep us apart, Michael thought, and instead drove us together. She took me in her arms! He could still feel Jenn along the length of him, her firm flesh, the sweet, trembling pressure of her hands on his back.

So now I can tell Father the truth — all of it.

Michael sobered. That was going to be hellishly difficult. But the reason for waiting was gone, so the longer he kept the secret, the greater risk of Father gleaning him — or failing that, the deeper would be Father's sense of betrayal when he finally confessed—

No, not confessed, proclaimed! Jenn was noble, beautiful – nothing like Father would first imagine – and now his one mission was to make the family see that.

Michael dialed the number of Father's cell phone. It rang once.

'Yes?' The deep voice was strained.

'It's Michael. Busy?'

A mirthless laugh came over the line. 'I just stepped between a rolling firing squad and a kid on her way home from school. The drug thing. Your sister managed to shield the guy they were shooting at, but they'll try again later.'

Michael had a plunging sensation in his stomach. *I should have been with you.* His fingers ground into the phone for a second, and then the guilt eased. 'Well done.'

'What did you want, Michael?'

'Can we meet tonight? I have something important to say.'

A pause. 'Really. We can talk at dinner—'

'No, not at the table. Before dinner – everyone in your study around ten, all right?'

'Fine. I'll tell the others. Good, Michael. Good.'

Michael realized the energy in his voice had raised Father's hopes. He held the phone away, his mind scrambling for the right words to leaven the false impression, but when he put the phone back to his ear, it was dead. He blew out a breath, his heart drumming. I should have kept it out of my voice, he thought. My joy will not be their joy, not at first, though I'll do all I can to make it so.

What will Father do?

Chemosh's words came back to Michael: *He killed my innocent son, only a child.*

No. Erase that from your mind! Chemosh is lying, deluded or outright insane. Father will not harm Jenn. The real danger is if he tries to make you choose – her or the family.

Fear squeezed Michael's heart. He remembered a thousand

summer nights with his brothers and Fabriel, rising together until the air was cool and they could see the earth curve, or drifting together in a circle above the Potomac on warm, September midnights, hands linked, thrilling to their moon shadow rippling across the water. To give them up was inconceivable, much less Mother and Father, but to turn away from Jenn — how could he? He loved his family and he loved Jenn. He could not choose, would not.

They love me too much to throw me out. They'll have to accept her, or at least give her a chance.

A soft footfall in the hall caught his ear. Julius!

The session had slipped his mind. For a second, he considered canceling it, telling the boy with the tiny scars in his palms to go home, and then an image came to him of Julius sneaking away, this time with a razor blade.

Two soft knocks.

'Come.'

'S'appenen, Doc?' Julius sauntered in, showing him a cool, deadpan face. He was dressed in a Nike jacket, T-shirt, baggy pants and the emblematic retrograde baseball cap. 'Hey, what's that?' he asked, seeing the push cart loaded with audiovisual equipment.

'A television.'

'I can *see* that.'

Michael inserted a tape into the set's VCR. 'Show time.'

'Awri-i-ight. You got style, Doc. All those other shrinks, all they wanted to do was talk, but you know what's important in life, man. Movies!' Julius's ardor chilled a degree. 'That is a movie, isn't it, not some kinda' training film like in health class?'

'It's an old TV show called "The Honeymooners." '

'Who's in it?'

'Jackie Gleason, Audrey Meadows, Art Carney, and Joyce Randolph . . .'

Julius gave a baffled frown.

'Of course, we could just talk if you'd rather.'

'No way, man. Bring on the flick, let's go, let's do it.' He flopped down into one of the slingback chairs, legs akimbo, eyes on the screen.

Instead of starting the tape, Michael said, 'You're good, Julius, but I still need to see your hands. That's the deal, remember?'

Julius's face fell. He held his palms out and Michael saw the fresh wound in his left hand, the small red hole in the flesh between thumb and palm. The skin around the wound had the faint sheen of Neosporin and did not look infected. With an effort, Michael hid his distress, which would only upset Julius for having shown his hands, not for wounding them.

'OK, ready?' Michael flicked on the TV and started the tape.

'Oh mah-yin, black and white?'

'Which of those shades don't you like?'

'I ain't touchin' that one, Whitey.'

The show started out as most of them did, Ralph and Alice Kramden talking peaceably in their threadbare, stage-set apartment. Pretending to watch along with Julius, Michael instead tapped into the leading edge of the boy's consciousness where all his attention was centered. Though Julius didn't smile, Michael felt his inner laughter as Kramden's goofy friend Norton, played by Art Carney, made his herky-jerky entrance.

'Good hat.' Julius paid close attention as Norton took Ralph aside and eagerly started laying out a questionable scheme for making money. Norton left. Ralph, inspired, started trying the notion out on Alice. As he talked up the scheme, Audrey Meadows fixed him with her classic stare of disdain and Gleason began the postural puffing up that always accompanied his famous 'slow burns.'

Michael felt alarm in Julius, which built quickly as Ralph began to pace up and down, raise his voice, and swing his arms to make points. Ralph was shouting now.

'Won-ah deese days, Alice, won-ah deese days . . .'

Alice shouted something back, but the words didn't register in Julius's mind. He wasn't alarmed anymore. He wasn't anything. Michael saw that his gaze was still on the TV set, but glassy and distant. His mind was blank, hearing nothing, seeing nothing, but then Michael went deeper, into his most primitive, unconscious mind, and there he found the fear. Julius was frozen, his calm like that of the mouse who has been thrown around by the cat and seems to be resting tranquilly, face to face with its tormentor, empty of all thought, because in its own mind it is already dead.

Appalled, Michael switched off the set. He knew all he needed to know. It *is* his parents! He doesn't know it because they never yell at him, and they don't know it either, because they think it's just between them, the screaming and yelling. They don't realize how it terrorizes him, how he worries that they'll hurt each other, leave, and he'll lose them both.

Now the real work starts.

Michael saw Julius out to reception, feeling charged up, pleased at the breakthrough, but by the time he had returned to his office, he felt the weight of his own situation settling back over him. *Jenn or my family, my family or Jenn.* As the afternoon wore on, his anxiety grew, making him fidgety and at the same time dull, as if he weren't getting enough air. He found escape working with his patients, but when his last one of the day called to cancel, instead of going straight home, he lingered in his office, caressing the leaves of his plants protectively, and gazing around. The movie posters jumped out with their color and drama. Here in this room, he had joined in with a score of people in the struggle against their inner demons. It was torturous work, harder than anything he'd ever done — and he loved it. But he must now be ready to give Father anything and everything he wanted in return for accepting Jenn. Which meant he'd be clearing out this office within the week, and some other doctor would be struggling with Julius.

And that's if I persuade Father to accept Jenn. Drey says he's more powerful than I realize. What if, somehow, he can force me to marry Philippa? Not only will I lose Julius and the others who came to me for help, I'll be showing a woman I do not love the haunts of people who spurn change, the back alleys of

Washington, the bad corners, the pimps and the crack houses, where people seek everything and anything but help.

And in the dark of morning, when even the wicked and the foolish have gone to bed, will come not Jenn's touch but Philippa's.

God help me, tonight, to find the right words.

Jenn hoped the man on the examination table wasn't sensing her distraction. Just this last 'walk-in' and then she was done with outpatient clinic for the day. Mr Reiss, a middle-aged guy, *and had she really felt Michael's emotions — that powerful mix of joy and fear flaring in her mind?*

You're being ridiculous, she told herself firmly. They were your feelings, not Michael's — had to be.

She said, 'Mr Reiss, do you recall if your father's hands trembled sometimes?'

As he thought about it, his eyes focused over her shoulder. His face had the round, bland geniality of the 'Charlie Brown' cartoon character. Flashier glasses or a mustache would do him good, but maybe bland and trustworthy was the best way to look when you worked at H&R Block.

Par, parky . . .

Jenn brushed the fragment of sound from her mind, making herself focus on how Reiss's left hand trembled as he searched his memory.

'Now that you mention it, doctor, I think I do recall Dad's hands shaking from time to time. Can this be hereditary?'

'It's possible. Ever feel any trembling in your legs?'

'No, never.'

'Are the hands worse when you're under pressure?'

He laughed. 'Definitely.'

She felt a flash of alarm that vanished so quickly she could not be sure of it. Unnerved, she tried to recapture her train of thought. 'Any effect when you have a beer or a glass of wine?'

His eyes lit. 'I'm glad you mentioned that — I wanted to be

sure and tell you. A beer stops it dead, but then it'll start up again before long.'

Another jolt of fear went through her. Jenn stared at her patient. *It's him — his fear I'm feeling!*

Shocked, she backed up a step.

But wait, Reiss looked perfectly calm.

No, he's terrified.

She felt her heart pounding now with her own alarm. Reiss was looking at her strangely. She must pull herself together—

—Parkis-parson . . . *Parkinson's*—

Jenn pushed the thought away again, confused that it would even enter her mind. This definitely wasn't Parkinson's disease.

I got it from him. I heard the word in his mind!

Her knees went weak. Could she really have read his mind? 'Mr Reiss, this is definitely not Parkinson's disease. You can put that right out of your mind.' *And mine!*

He released a breath, and she could feel his relief, a flood of warmth behind her eyes.

'Not Parkinson's. Thank God.' He laughed. 'What is it, then?'

She moved around him, groped for the edge of the exam table, steadying herself. 'Uh, I think you have what we call a benign essential tremor.'

'I like that word "benign," but I'm not so sure about "essential."'

All the fear was gone from him now. He could even joke. She swallowed, trying to collect her wits. 'This will probably be with you off and on,' she said, 'especially when you're under pressure. But it normally doesn't lead to any significant disability — unless you're a concert pianist or a draftsman, that sort of thing. And the good news is it can be treated.' *Just hold it together, get him out of here.* She gave Reiss's arm a reassuring squeeze. 'I'm going to prescribe a medication called propranolol. We'll start you out on a low dose, a sixty milligram tablet each day. I'd like you to call me in two weeks and let me know if it helps. If not, there's another we can try.'

'Good,' he said.

Grabbing her prescription pad, she scribbled out an order for propranolol, but her own hand was shaking now, so badly, she had to start over on a fresh sheet. He thanked her profusely and left.

What is happening to me?

She put her hands to her head, then laughed, though it wasn't funny, not at all. There were only two possibilities: she had directly read someone's feelings — and a fragment of his thoughts — or she was going crazy.

I'm not crazy. He looked so relieved when I told him it wasn't Parkinson's, I thought he was going to dance me around.

But I don't want to read minds!

She took a deep breath. She must not panic over this. It had to be another part of what was already emerging — the thing she'd done with Neil, whatever it was, and then sensing Michael's feelings. Where would this end? If the thoughts of people around her came pouring in, pounding at her constantly, eclipsing her own thoughts, she *would* go insane.

She had to find out what she was doing so she could take control, maybe. Biofeedback, she thought. That's how you learn to hit a baseball or sew up a wound or take your first bite off a spoon. You watch what you're doing while you're doing it, you feel it, and watch it, trial and error, until you've got it.

Rich's equipment!

He'll kill me if he finds out.

The air pressure changed subtly, and the light level went up in the room. Looking up, she caught the door closing, but no one had come in. Mystified, she went to the door and pulled it open.

No one there.

The nape of her neck prickled with the feeling of being watched. Whirling, she peered around the break room but, except for her, it was empty. A cool pocket of air brushed her face and she felt the hairs along her arms stiffen.

'Michael,' she whispered. 'Michael, is that you?'

No answer.

Her heart hammered. She ran into the hall, and there he was, coming toward her. Relief filled her and she hurried to meet him.

He looked at her with concern. 'Are you all right? You look as if you've seen a ghost.'

'Can we go back to your office? I need to talk to you, and the break room isn't private enough.'

'Sure.'

She walked beside him, resisting the urge to take his arm and run, mindful of the staff in the hall. When at last his door closed behind her, the relief and feeling of safety was wonderful. She looked around for the parakeet.

'Where's Budgie?'

'Home. The chief of psychiatry took exception to having a bird within the pristine sanctuary of the hospital. I tried to tell him Budgie put my patients at ease, but he informed me that was my job.'

Jenn tried to smile, but the feeling she'd had in the break room, of someone unseen passing so close to her, swept her again, making her shudder.

'Here,' Michael said in a concerned voice. 'Sit down.'

She let him guide her to a chair. He sat across from her, gazing at her with a worried expression. 'Jenn, what's wrong?'

'I don't know how to say this.'

'Straight out.'

'Something strange and frightening is happening to my mind. Yesterday I somehow improved the EEG of a man who was flatlining and then, this morning when we were together, I felt your fear. Just a few minutes ago, I read a patient's mind.'

He looked stunned, the color draining from his face, and she felt a cold stiffness, creeping up her spine.

He gave her shoulder a comforting squeeze. 'I . . . I don't know what to say. Angels can read minds, but I've never heard of it in a phage. Tell me what happened.'

She told him about her patient who was afraid of Parkinson's. 'Do you think this could be happening because of what I went through with Hugh, those weeks I sat at his bedside every night? I kept wishing I could enter his mind and heal it, or at least find a glimmer of thought or feeling to tell me he was still in there. Sometimes I felt I was sensing him. In my heart I knew it had to be just wishful thinking, but maybe it wasn't, Michael. Maybe my constant longing to reach him caused a change in my brain, or woke up a part of my mind that had been lying dormant.'

He chewed at his lip. 'Maybe. Or it might be me. I first entered your mind when you were sixteen and I spotted you going into an upstairs window. I kept checking back on you ever since, and I've been in your mind a fair amount in the three years since Hugh died. Maybe it somehow triggered a hidden potential in you.'

An eerie feeling came over her. She still wasn't used to the idea that Michael had been in her mind. 'Has that ever happened to anyone else?'

'It's taboo to interfere in minds; we are very careful to look, not touch. And I'd never have dreamed of trying to change anything in a mind as wonderful as yours.'

The love in his voice warmed her, settling her nerves a little. 'If I can just get control of this. I take it you have mastery over whether you read a mind or not.'

'I never even thought of it, but yes.'

'How do you turn it on and off?'

Michael looked puzzled. 'I just decide to do it, and when I'm done, I stop.'

'But see, that's what I have to learn. Right now it's happening even though I don't want it. Think back — was that how it was with you at first, or were you born with it fully developed?'

'No, we have to learn it, but I don't remember how. It was so long ago, and so natural, like learning to walk. You've walked from the time you were a toddler, but could you tell someone else how to do it?' He rubbed at his forehead, plainly perplexed.

'I have an idea how I might be able to use Positron Emission Tomography to help me, so I can watch what is going on in my brain when I read someone's thoughts. We've got that PET scan lab right on neurology and Rich has now built a smaller scanner into a helmet so you don't have to lie inside the big chamber if all you want to scan is the brain. He attached the helmet to adjustable tracks fitted onto the back of a regular chair, so the patient will be able to sit up, have the helmet lowered onto his head, and then be in position to watch the monitor along with the doctor.'

Michael looked impressed. 'For biofeedback?'

'Exactly. He got the idea from that classic experiment in tension reduction where they put electrodes on the forehead muscles of test subjects to show them their own tension levels on a monitor. When the subjects had watched the muscle spiking for a minute or two, they were told to try and make the spikes smaller. Most people got the hang of it fairly quickly. In just one session they learned to reduce tension in themselves. Rich wants to try a similar process with the PET scan. Instead of muscle spikes, patients could observe activity in their own brains — neurologic changes associated with epilepsy or migraine, for example — and maybe learn to control them.

'What I want to do is hook myself up, then try to read your mind. While I'm doing that, I'll watch the monitor screen. If I succeed in getting into your mind, the part of my brain that's doing it will show increased activity, and I can then try to dampen that activity down, just like in those old muscle experiments. How about it?'

He looked like he wanted to say yes, but he hesitated.

'Come on, Michael. I need something that works fast, and I need it now, before other people's thoughts start pouring in and I don't even know which ones are mine anymore. I can't ask anyone else to let me try and read their mind. If I'm going to try this, it has to be with you.'

'Let's go,' he said.

When they got to the lab, the technician was preparing to close up. Jenn promised she'd lock up for him after she'd shown Dr Avalon the new equipment.

The lights were low to enhance monitor viewing. The room,

as usual, was cool, but she knew the chill she felt had nothing to do with the temperature. 'How are you at giving shots? Phages have tough hides, but we've got to get a dose of marker solution into one of my arteries.'

'Arteries — those are the red ones, right?'

She laughed and felt a little calmer. 'There should be a batch of solution in that cabinet.'

Jenn flipped on the monitor that faced the chair and helmet. Rich had finished installing the switch that slid the helmet up and down on its tracks. The motor hummed as she elevated the helmet, then sat in the chair and lowered it again until it rested snugly on her head. She could just see the monitor below the front edge of the helmet. Actually sitting in the chair brought a cold feeling in the pit of her stomach.

Rich will never know, she told herself.

'Ready?' Michael asked.

'Ready.'

She kept her eyes on the monitor as she felt the needle sting her arm. The marker solution of glucose and fluorine rose in a cool column through her shoulder and up her neck. Controlling her breathing, she thought about what would happen next. As the solution reached her brain, positrons from the decaying fluorine would collide with electrons to form photons. The helmet would read these and send them to the computer which would interpret them and convert them to oranges and yellows on the monitor. The most active area in her brain would draw the most blood flow, causing the brightest yellow on the screen—

'You're on,' Michael said, and she focused on the screen. Yellow flared in a molten core at the center of her brain, the amygdala, the seat of emotion — not surprising, as frightened as she was. Yellow flames also licked along the speech cortex.

'Michael, I'm going to try to reach you now.'

But how?

Clearly, some form of mental contact was necessary between her and Michael, and the only thing remotely like that she'd ever done was with blood Influence. Sometimes she could detect blood vessels in a patient's brain, especially if there was a clot or hemorrhagic stroke. It was far more difficult than sensing blood flow outside the brain, where 'noise' from the nerves wasn't nearly as great. But maybe if she tried to reach Michael's brain with blood Influence, it would trigger the deeper awareness she was after. She envisioned the major artery supplying the lining of Michael's brain — the same one that had ruptured to cause Neil Hudson's coma.

'Anything?' Michael asked hopefully.

'No.'

Maybe she should start with something simpler. The femoral artery. Her brain stem flared yellow on the monitor.

'My leg just went a little numb,' Michael said.

'OK, good.'

She tried various veins and arteries, and her own brain stem continued to glow on the monitor, but nothing came to her from Michael's mind. She homed again on the meningeal artery in the lining of Michael's brain. The flare of yellow moved up from her brain stem a little, but she was still getting nothing from Michael.

Deeper, she thought, through the lining to the brain.

She felt a faint itch inside her skull above both ears, like the vibration of window glass from the passing of a distant train. On the monitor, a thin line of yellow crawled upward from her brain stem along the corpus callosum that connected the two hemispheres of her brain.

Nothing.

Her frustration rose, flaring yellow in the amygdala again. When she'd heard her patient's thoughts, it had been like a sound in her mind, his voice talking. She remembered Michael's voice, the warm, low strength of it, the soothing quality. The auditory cortex near her left temple flared yellow on the screen.

'I felt something,' Michael called out. 'And I heard my own voice.'

Jenn concentrated harder, willing the yellow area in her own auditory cortex to grow. It slid around, pulsing brighter—

She is so amazing, no one like her in all the universe!

'Dear God, you're reading me!' Michael's voice came to her distantly, nearly lost in the flood of his feelings for her. *He adores me!* – She felt it as a bright warmth that spread out from behind her eyes, down into her body, igniting a glow of wellbeing. Tears of joy flooded her eyes. A wonderful euphoria built in her, almost too much.

All right, now pull out.

She made herself focus on the monitor, trying to reduce the bonfire in her auditory cortex.

Michael's love kept pouring in; she felt almost drunk—

No, concentrate. It's in the auditory area. Try imagining a sound.

She imagined the lulling beat of rain on a rooftop. The yellow area on the monitor shrank and slid lower in the auditory cortex and, just like that, Michael was gone from her mind.

Closing her eyes to make sure she got no help from the monitor this time, she found the memory of Michael's voice and focused on it. She felt herself sliding back into the fabulous brightness of Michael's mind.

She loves me too – I can feel it!

Michael – his joy filling her, mingling with her own.

Out, she thought firmly, though she did not want it to end. Rain falling, and she was out. Ducking from under the helmet, she ran and threw her arms around him. 'Oh, Michael, I was inside your mind. It was all I could do to concentrate on the monitor. I've never imagined I could feel so deeply. It's fading now. God, I was afraid my heart might burst.'

'I know.'

'It was . . . rapture is the only way I can describe it. Oh, man, a little of that goes a long way.' She stepped back from him, smoothed her hair, tried to get her bearings.

'Did the biofeedback work?' he asked.

'Yes. I get in by focusing on your voice, and out by imagining rainfall. Other sounds would probably work too. For some reason, the auditory cortex seems to be the portal. All right. We don't want Rich finding me here. Let's go.'

Outside, the hall was empty. She walked with Michael part way back to the junction with the main corridor. Stopping, she faced him. 'Thank's for helping me.'

'I'd do anything for you,' he said, but he looked troubled.

'What is it?'

'Tonight, I'm telling my family about you.'

'Your father?'

'Him and all of them.'

A chill passed through her as she remembered what Chemosh had told her about Uziel. 'I'm supposed to meet with my family later tonight, too,' she said. 'Chemosh called me today, sounding very grim. I think he wants to warn me again about your father.'

'Don't worry, the worst that can happen is he'll forbid me to see you.'

'And if he does?'

'I'll find some way around it.'

The pain in his face worried her. 'Is there anything I can do? Do you want me to come? I don't have to listen to Chemosh again – I've heard it all, already.'

'Thanks, but it's better if you wait until I call. We're meeting at ten but who knows when it'll be over. I'm going to invite them into my mind, let them see you as I do.'

Jenn's anxiety sharpened. 'I don't know, Michael. When they see me feed—'

'What they will see is you refusing to kill. Believe me, it's our best chance of winning them over. If they will come in and stay in until they understand, it will put them on the path of accepting you. If they'll just give you a chance, they'll end up loving you, I know it.'

Raising on tiptoes, Jenn kissed him. His arms went around her and she felt the warming glow of his love again, and beneath it, the deep, bone coldness of his dread.

Chapter Eleven

It will be all right, Jenn told herself as she headed to the nurses' station. Every close family takes a hard look at the outsider who wants to take their daughter or son. Maybe I'll look hard at them, too. It doesn't matter. Michael and I will be together, and nothing — not Chemosh or his father — is going to stop us!

But a part of her mind told her this was the euphoria talking, Michael's love winning out over the dread she felt beneath.

'Oh, Dr Hrluska.'

Ev Bronstein was leaning over the counter of the nurses' station to flag her down. 'Your Mr Wainright says his shoulder is really hurting him. He wants more painkiller. He's on ibuprofen now. I was thinking maybe a short run of demerol?'

Jenn struggled to refocus. Wainright — the old gentleman in 604 she'd admitted yesterday with severe brachial plexopathy. He was in for a nerve biopsy and eval for possible surgical decompression. Demerol was a narcotic, but Wainright's history suggested no addictive tendencies, and his stay would be short. Ev, unofficial grandmother to the nursing staff, had been around forever, and her suggestions were usually sound.

Writing the new instructions in the chart, Jenn found herself starting to probe Ev's mind. She stopped, then reconsidered. She needed practice, to see if she really had control with someone besides Michael. I won't touch, she thought, just look, and when I'm sure I've got it, I won't ever do it again.

It took her only a second to find her way in using Ev's voice — far easier than it had been at first with Michael—

My God, look at Jenn. Her shift was over two hours ago and she looks like she could do another thirty-six. And where is that glow coming from? Has she finally met someone? Oh to be young and beautiful again, except I was never that young.

Jenn scuffed her foot on the tile, focusing on the sound, and as easily as that she exited Ev's mind. I *can* control it, she thought, buoyed. Going in, coming out — it feels almost natural. Michael compared it to walking, which means I probably won't even need to focus on sound cues after I've done it a few more times.

She marvelled at the flood of admiration she'd felt from Ev. Being told out loud how someone felt couldn't compare with actually receiving the emotion—

'Hrluska!'

Rich Sikorsky, barking at her from down the hall. Her heart sank, and then resignation settled over her. Whatever this was, no sense letting him chew her out in front of the nurses. She started toward him, but he stopped her with an upraised palm, bustling up to the counter.

'What's the idea, Hrluska?'

'Excuse me?'

'Are you going to deny you were just in the PET scan lab?'

Damn! The technician must have called him. 'Why would I deny that?' she asked mildly. 'Dr Avalon from psychiatry came by asking to see the lab, and I'm off duty so I took him over.'

'I'm sure you did. The new shrink might seem irresistible to you, but you had no right to use my prototype.'

With a sinking feeling, Jenn realized that, in her euphoria, she had not returned the chair and helmet to the position she'd found them. And of course Rich was paranoid enough to keep track of the settings. 'I merely demonstrated the helmet and chair for Dr Avalon.'

'You know I don't want anyone messing with that equipment. The servomotors were not fully tested and now you've damaged two circuit boards in the lift. Those boards took a lot of man hours, Hrluska. They're unique – I can't just go out and buy more at Radio Shack.'

Jenn felt confused. The chair had been in perfect working order when she'd left it. But why would he lie? 'I'm sure I didn't—'

'Don't contradict me.' His face was red now, his eyes bulging. She had never seen him so angry . . .

Except anger was not what she was picking up from inside him.

'Dr Sikorsky,' Ev said, 'if you could take this to your office so the patients don't overhear—'

'Shut up, Bronstein,' Rich said without looking at her. 'Who did you test, Hrluska, yourself?'

'No one.'

'Then what happened to the marker solution? It was down a dose and the tech didn't test anyone today. You shot yourself up, didn't you?'

'Certainly not.'

'Are you willing to prove that with a blood test?'

Cold alarm flashed through Jenn. No one must see her blood. 'Dr Sikorsky, please calm down.'

But he's *not* angry, she realized. It's an act—

—*get her to believe I can make big trouble for her, ruin her chances for a third year. Who would suspect I'd sabotage my own grant equipment? Chance I've been waiting for and now it's even better. I'll get that blood test. It'll come up fluorine, then I've got her lying. Wait until she begs me, then offer to let it pass if she'll show her gratitude. Such a gorgeous piece of ass. I'll never get a shot at her any other way – ha! what a lovely thought that is. Make her be nice to me—*

Jenn suddenly saw herself in his office, kneeling down naked in front of him – the ugly fantasy he was running in his head right now. It hit her like a blow, leaving her breathless with revulsion. She felt herself plunging into his brain, finding the feverish pulse of the images, gathering the streams of neural

157

energy as though they were a bundle of threads trailing through her fingers. She envisioned her fist closing over the threads, jerking them out of him—

Rich blanched and staggered back. As he fell, his head struck the counter a glancing blow and then he sprawled to the floor.

Jenn felt a rush of euphoria. Everything around her seemed vivid and beautiful, she was strong as a god!

Blood spurted from the nasty wound on Rich's head. She stared at the bright blood, frozen, then took a step toward Rich, and then Ev came between, kneeling to slap a wad of gauze onto the bleeding wound. Rich was out cold, his eyes rolled back, a spasm pulling his lips into a drooling grin.

Snap out of it — you've got to examine him!

But she could barely think, had no idea what to do first, all her years of training scrambled by the churning of her brain. Hands closed on her shoulders, and she let herself be pulled away.

'That's all right, Jenn,' Ev murmured, 'you're upset. Dr Faltier is on now, he's here, he'll take care of it. Don't worry about it. This only proves there is a God. The jerk just got so worked up he fainted, that's all. He'll be fine, more's the pity. You go on home, before he wakes up and starts chewing on you again.'

Jenn retreated down the hall, shaken and ashamed. Rich had not fainted and he was not going to be fine, she had hurt him badly — she did not know how she knew that, but she knew. For days she had fantasized about hurting him, and now she had come close to killing him, and it had taken no effort. She'd imagined using the new power inside her to heal but, instead, she'd made it a weapon.

Now that the meeting was almost upon him, Michael could scarcely bear the waiting. He sat with the rest of the family in Father's study. He'd picked this room because of the restful calm it usually inspired, with its high windows, curtained in graceful sweeps of blue damask, the leatherbound volumes of poetry and philosophy ascending on all sides beyond the glow of Father's desk lamp. But he felt no calm, only a growing turmoil in the pit of his stomach.

Where was Ariel? He surely would be as eager as the others for the next shoe to drop about Philippa, so why wasn't he here?

Michael looked around, anxious to size up the mood. Mother stood by the bookshelves, thumbing through Father's ancient copy of *The Pilgrim's Progress*. Rafe sat in the bow window, head down, meditating, and Fabriel drifted along the high ceiling, snatching wisps of cobweb missed by the household staff on their ladders. Only Father acknowledged him, returning his glance with a somber look, a slight cock of the head. They were all so quiet, a sign of their tension, wondering if he'd be their good son tonight, their loyal brother or would he deny the family not only Philippa's help, but the alliance that would raise them up in the society of angels? They were praying he'd say yes, and they had every right to.

Instead, he would be bringing to them a woman even harder to explain than he had thought a day ago. Jenn entered my mind, he thought with wonder. How could that be? I thought only we could do that. If I tell the family she's beginning to read minds, will it make them more, or less, likely to accept her? I love it, but it may frighten them.

See how it goes and play it by ear.

If Ariel ever gets here.

Michael was suddenly desperate to get it over with. 'Anybody have any idea what might be holding up our junior member?'

'Nope,' Fabriel chirped from the ceiling. Mother glanced up blankly; Father shook his head. Michael looked at Rafe, who should know if anyone would. Slowly, his brother opened his eyes and focused on him. 'He took off on his own this afternoon. Asked me if I could handle things alone; there was something else he needed to check out. He's getting more and more independent, you know.'

'All to the good,' Uziel said. 'I can feel him right now. He's not very close, I'm afraid.'

Closing his eyes, Michael picked up the trace too. Ariel, away to the north. He must be some miles distant because it was impossible to tell anything more — whether he was engrossed in something or thinking of home . . . the faintest touch of emotion, perhaps, a grim resolve?

'Maybe we can get started—'

'No, Michael,' Father said. 'This concerns the whole family. We'll wait. I'm sure he'll be here soon.'

Jenn hurried across the hospital parking lot to her car, still sickened by what she'd done. Running away — she should have stayed, seen if there was anything she could do for Rich.

Or if she could undo what she'd done.

And if she could?

He'd insist on the blood test, and that can't be allowed.

She started to slip her key into the door of the MG, then realized it was already unlocked. An alarm pinged in the back of her mind — she always locked the car . . . but maybe she'd forgotten this morning, she'd been so nervous about going to Michael.

Sliding behind the wheel, she pulled out of the parking lot.

All Rich had wanted was evidence of fluorine mixed in with her blood, but he would find so much more. Normal RBCs did not have cell walls. Hers did. And that was just for starters. Thirteen years ago her father, Zane, weakened from months of self-imposed starvation, had left a few drops of his own blood on a murder victim, and if Merrick had not been able to suppress that evidence, a police laboratory would have found that something far more durable than a normal human had killed the poor jogger.

From there, scientists could have figured out the rest.

Once normals knew that a deadly predator walked like men among them, they'd learn to use their video cameras to hunt and trap phages.

And for every phage buried, hundreds of normals would die.

What was Rich's life beside such carnage? To keep from being tested, she'd have been justified in killing him outright, if that's what it took.

Jenn shuddered. I'm a healer, yeah, right—

'Don't be alarmed.'

She clenched the wheel in shock. A man, right beside her! He must have already been in the car when she got in, but she'd never seen him.

Not a man, an angel — the one she'd seen before, hovering outside Neil Hudson's window!

Her heart pounded as she darted another look: Long red hair, the square jaw, so handsome. He looked young, but that meant nothing, in phages or angels.

Michael's father?

Her fear rose, spiking in her chest. *It's Uziel — he's going to kill me!* She started to pull to the curb.

'Please, keep driving. My name is Ariel. I just wanted to meet you, talk to you, if I may.'

She swallowed and her terror eased. 'Who are you?'

'Michael's brother.'

She glanced at him again. Yes, the same smooth forehead, and his curls nearly the same shade of deep auburn. Dressed all in black — black jeans, a black turtleneck, black cross-trainers.

'Is there someplace quiet we can chat?' he asked.

Her shock subsided and she grew curious. Michael had intended to tell his family about her tonight, but his brother already knew, and didn't seem distressed. Jenn's spirits rose. 'I know a coffee shop near here.'

'Someplace more private would be better. I want to know all about you, and you might have some questions for me, too.'

His voice sounded warm and friendly. If she could make him an ally, it might help Michael with his family.

'There's a little park around the Iwo Jima Memorial.'

'I know the place — right next to the Arlington Cemetery. Sounds fine.'

He chatted about the weather, asking her if she thought

spring would be early this year. Michael's brother! she thought with amazement as she kept up her end, driving south to Constitution Avenue, then crossing Roosevelt Bridge into Virginia. She got a glimpse of the Potomac, flat and dark under a sky dense with clouds. Exiting off Route 50, she crossed back above it and slowed. Low, brick garden apartments rose on the slope to her right to where the tall bulwark of the Prospect house dominated the crest of the hill, the lights of its rooftop restaurant blazing. Down slope to her left, on the other side of the road, the four giant marines of the Iwo Jima Memorial plowed their flag into bronze ground, the grand statue imitating the famous photo from World War II. Jenn pulled over to the curb above the memorial.

'A nice spot,' Ariel said. 'I've always liked it. You can see the city well from here.'

'Better up by those apartments, where you can get above the trees.'

'I can do that down here.' His teeth gleamed briefly in the darkness.

She realized he meant by flying. The boastful edge to his voice made her curious — surely he would take flying for granted. Or maybe he hadn't been doing it that long. I know nothing about him, she reminded herself. A nerve twanged in her stomach.

'Want to get out and walk?' Ariel asked.

'Sure.'

'Let's go in the cemetery — it's closed after dark so we'll be able to talk alone. And I love the wonderful oak trees.'

She hesitated, remembering Chemosh's warning about Uziel. Was Ariel deliberately drawing her farther away, isolating her beyond the mere needs of discretion?

But if she resisted, he'd surely take it as mistrust — a bad start if she were to make the best possible impression. And if she could not trust an angel, who could she trust?

She followed him beyond the apartment buildings to where the street dead-ended into another short road that ran along the border of Arlington Cemetery. Uphill to the right, one of the gates to Fort Myer blazed under floodlights. She started to reach out to the MP at the guard post.

'I've got him,' Ariel said companionably.

The guard gave no sign of seeing them.

A low brick wall marked the edge of the cemetery. Ariel rose into a slow arc over it, soaring higher than necessary, almost floating before coming down on the other side. It was eerily graceful, and Jenn felt a cool thrill in her stomach. She jumped the fence, putting some extra spring into it, but not matching Ariel's sailing leap.

He took off up a long slope, wending his way between the ancient, rounded tombstones. She lengthened her stride to keep up. 'So you're Michael's brother.'

'You sound surprised. Hasn't he told you about me?'

'I didn't even know *he* existed two days ago.'

'Really?' Ariel sounded skeptical.

'I saw you before I ever met him — the same night, in fact. You were outside the window of one of my patients, and then on the roof.'

Ariel gave a nervous laugh. 'Yes. It surprised me you could see me. I was drawn there by sharp distress from that room.'

'My patient's wife. She'd just learned her husband was dying. She must have run out just before you got there.'

'I didn't think a doctor could be a phage,' Ariel mused. 'Careless of me.'

The condescending way he said it annoyed her, but she let it pass. 'Does Michael have other brothers?'

'One, and a sister. How about you?'

'No.'

They climbed the hill until they reached a cluster of oaks that encircled a larger tomb. The inscription marked it as the burial place of Abraham Lincoln's son Todd. Ariel sat on one of the curving stone benches and gazed at her. His hands, clenching the marble curve on either side of him, showed that he was not so calm, after all. She realized she had only his word that he was

163

Michael's brother, not his father. And didn't her own father look young enough to be her brother?

Instead of sitting, she leaned against the sepulcher, maintaining distance, watching Ariel.

He said, 'So you've known Michael only two days.'

'That's right.'

'But you two are in love.' His voice was unreadable.

Something told her to be very careful now. 'Ariel, I don't know. It's all so sudden. But I have very strong feelings for your brother, yes.'

'And that's what he's going to tell the family tonight.'

'Yes. I know it will be difficult for your father, especially.'

Ariel stiffened. 'What has he told you?'

His tone, suddenly harsh, alarmed her. 'Take it easy—'

He stood, his eyes darkening. 'Why am I talking to you like this, giving you a chance to cast your spell over me, too? Listen to me, phage. I am not going to let you seduce and corrupt my brother.'

The sudden fury in his voice shocked her. 'Seduce him? I had no inkling of Michael until two days ago. He made contact with me – and I'm very glad he did.'

'Next you'll have him eating blood.'

'Ariel, or whoever you are, *I* would not eat blood if I had any choice.'

'There is always choice.'

'How old are you?'

'What difference could that possibly make?'

'It's just that you don't seem to know much about phages.'

'I know they kill people and devour their blood. And since we are protectors of humanity, your infatuation with Michael could hardly be made in heaven, could it?'

'I don't kill.'

'All phages kill. My father told me that, and he has been on earth a long time, and is no liar, as you seem to think I am.'

'I didn't say he's a liar, but he *is* mistaken. Did he send you to talk to me?'

'No one sent me. I'm perfectly capable of acting on my own. I see what needs to be done, and do it, like the rest of my family. And I know a liar when I see one.'

'Most phages *do* kill, Ariel, but I know of four who do not, and I am one of them.'

He shook his head. 'Amazing. You're doing it, trying to draw me in, seduce me too, make me believe you aren't evil. I don't want to talk about it. I'm going to give you one chance, which is more than you deserve. You are never to see Michael again. Promise me that — and, believe me, I'll know if you are lying. I will also know if you ever break the promise.'

She struggled to control her anger. 'It doesn't matter what you'll know, because I am not going to promise—'

She felt him rush into her mind, a dark, cold blow that almost blinded her. Instinctively, she pushed back with all her strength, scattering the darkness. Her eyes, soaking up the full spectrum of light in the grove, lit him up like a strobe as she pushed him out. With a surprised look, he struck at her again, a blinding pain inside her skull, as if her brain had swelled suddenly against the bone. She reeled against the stone of the tomb and fell. In a blurred glimpse of grass, she saw him jump toward her before her vision dimmed again, *killing me!*

She flailed out mentally, using her memory of his voice to cue herself into his brain, gasping as she felt his hatred sparking through her. *He means to kill me!* She tried to rise, but another blow in her mind hammered her down to her knees. She could barely see now. Focusing her mind within his, she imagined an explosion. Ariel cried out, and then pain tore inside her head, as though her brain were exploding. Wild with panic, she stabbed out at him with her own mind, felt herself clawing at his neurons, wrenching, and then she tore away from him, feeling the essence of his mind rip out with her in a flash of blinding light.

For a moment, nothing, and then she heard a hoarse sobbing. Ariel? She must have hurt him . . .

Feeling the raw jerks in her own throat, she realized it was she

165

who was sobbing. Fear rose in her again. Where was he? She couldn't see. Lying still, she listened. A distant hiss resolved into tires on pavement, the subliminal hum of the city across the river. She tried to ease her hand up to her stinging eyes. Her arm dragged along the ground, heavy as lead. She blinked, and a grainy, gray pattern swam into focus, the granite of the tomb, inches away. With a huge effort, she rolled over.

Ariel lay in front of the bench, utterly still.

Struck with foreboding, she pushed to her knees, then tried to stand but could not find the strength. Saying his name, she crawled to him. He remained still. She slipped two trembling fingers into the angle under his jaw. No pulse. He gazed up past her shoulder, his eyes dulling as the soft night breeze drank up their tears.

Jenn stared at the corpse, unable for a second to grasp what she had done. *I've killed him, killed an angel.*

Michael's brother.

For a second she was numb, as though she were shot and knew she would die, but could not yet feel the pain. Then, as she felt the grief massing inside her, she cried out and began to sob, her tears pouring down on Ariel's face, making his dead eyes glisten. No, no, she moaned, what have I done? I didn't mean to, I didn't *know.* Clutching her head, she bent low over Ariel. How could Michael forgive her? He couldn't, she had killed his brother.

Bowing over the fallen angel, Jenn wished that she could die, too.

Chapter Twelve

Worried about Ariel, Michael rose from the garden, hovering over the maze to peer at the sullen, red-black sky to the north. At eleven, the city's corona still boiled with the neural static of tens of thousands who hadn't yet fallen asleep. He could feel Ariel as a constant, faint presence in his mind, a sense of tense energy — anger, perhaps, and now something else . . . fear?

Michael's worry sharpened. What could possibly scare Ariel?

Rafe emerged from the house, where the others were still waiting to start the meeting. He drifted up above the line of trees to the north, staring toward the city.

'Can you tell where he is?'

The question came in Michael's mind. 'No,' he answered. 'I'm worried. He knew about the meeting. What could he think was more important?'

'I don't know, but it has him upset. Can you feel it?'

Without turning around, Rafe drifted back toward him, giving Michael an eerie sense of unreality, as if he were watching a movie in reverse. 'Yes, I can feel him now. He's angry and afraid, both, but I can't pick up any words. God, I think he's fighting with someone!'

Michael felt it too, a faint but furious surge that registered in the nerves of his own arms and legs, traces of intense physical effort, and then Ariel's rage evaporated. Michael froze, feeling shock from Ariel and then panic, maddeningly faint, but unmistakable. 'He's in trouble. We must—'

A phantom shriek tore through Michael's brain. All contact with Ariel vanished in the next instant. Michael sank to his knees, clutching at his heart, knowing in a horrified instant that Ariel had just died. Whoever he'd been fighting had killed him. 'God, NO!'

Dimly, Michael saw Rafe stagger away, hands pressed to his ears, and knew he had felt it too. An aftershock of agony ripped through Michael. *Ariel, dead?* He saw the dining-room window explode outward in a dazzling crystalline shower as Uziel hurtled through and rose above the house, his hands pressed to his face. Mother and Fabriel swooped out after him, faces frozen in shock. Michael felt Rafe pulling at his arm, tearing his shirt, his face twisted in grief.

'No!' Michael shouted. 'We can't lose him, God, he's just a baby!' He felt as if he was falling, plunging down into the dark heart of the earth. Covering his ears against the wails of his mother and sister, he tried again to reach Ariel.

Nothing.

'Father,' Rafe screamed in alarm.

Looking up, Michael saw Uziel twirling madly high above the house, then wheeling to plunge down toward the garden. Landing with a jarring thump, he stumbled forward, as though he'd lost all coordination. Righting himself, he stared at them, tears pouring from his eyes. 'Not Ariel,' he cried. 'Not Ariel, not my boy.'

'How could this happen?' Rafe cried in a pleading voice. 'How could he be dead?'

Did an angel do this? Michael wondered numbly. Or a phage? — the *Codex* says they can strike us!

Fabriel and Justine found their way into the maze, sobbing. Fabriel had torn her own clothes. Weeping, Michael held out his hands and they all came together in a ring, their arms grasping and pulling at each other.

'Father,' Mother urged. 'We must pray for Ariel!'

'I can't,' he cried.

Her eyes widened and then she bowed her head. 'Dear God, we have to find our son and brother now. Please help us. Guide us to him so we can take care of his . . . of him now. Thy will be done, Thy will.'

Fabriel and Rafe sobbed, their foreheads pressed together.

A breathless calm settled over Michael, his lungs stilled but his mind strangely clear. Chemosh, he thought. He *hates* Father, some ancient feud, thinking Father killed his son. Could he have found Ariel alone and somehow killed him? Dear God, I heard him spewing his hatred and I never warned Father or any of the others. If it was Chemosh, I could have stopped this!

A scalding pressure built in his throat. He realized Father was staring at him again.

'Did you pick up where he was?' Father's voice was harsh, desolate.

'What? No. I have a general idea, but we'll have to search.'

'There'll still be an aura once we get close. But it will grow fainter every minute. We must go now, all of us. We will grieve when we've found him.' Father made no move to do what he had ordered.

He has to be the strongest, now, Michael thought with dismay. What will we do if he can't function? We need him to lead us. 'Ariel was this side of the city, Father, I know that much. We should fan out and cover the ground north and within five degrees to the west. Stay in sight of each other.' He pulled Fabriel and Rafe apart. 'Come on.'

In the air, he resolved to preserve the deadness within him which now passed for calm. He must not let it shatter until they'd found Ariel. Rising up into the air, he pulled Rafe after him. At last Father gathered himself and rose. Movement seemed to help him, and he pushed into the lead, motioning them out from him, fanning them into a broader arc to search.

Staying off to Father's right, Michael flew across the dark terrain, widening his pupils until his irises disappeared, feeling the gaping blackness of his own eyes. Everything stood out in a parched brown light, his retinas leaching the darkness from the treetops, the marshes along the railroad tracks, and GW Parkway that ran north together toward the city. A sob beat at his lungs, but he kept it in, knowing that to release it would tear him open. His head swung back and forth as he looked for the corpse of his brother.

Chemosh. Warning me away from Jenn, trying to split me from Father with a vicious lie, and I did nothing, I let it go. If he did this, Jenn's great grandfather, what will I do?

Fury filled Michael. Whoever it was, he thought, Chemosh or a mad angel, or Lucifer himself, I will find him and kill him.

He faltered in the air, shocked and distraught that he could have such a thought. Father looked across at him and he regained his pace, his mind reeling. Vengeance belongs to God alone, he thought. I'm a protector. I've never killed anyone. I've stayed the hand of killers, I've questioned how such evil as murder could exist. But to become a killer myself?

No, I must not, even for Ariel . . .

But the killing rage went on burning, a hot coal in his chest.

Hiding his frustration, Chemosh waited for Merrick to answer. How could he look so relaxed, sitting there with one arm along the back of the couch? I just told him that Uziel is going to kill his granddaughter, Chemosh thought, unless we can get her to drop Michael. What is there to think about?

Zane, standing behind the couch out of his father's view, signaled patience with a downturned palm. Chemosh resisted the urge to spring up from his chair, his back rigid against the familiar curves that had given him comfort on so many long, lazy evenings after dinner. Merrick wasn't one to be pushed. We still have a day, he reminded himself. Uziel won't do anything before then, and neither will that son of his who eavesdropped in the maze. Jenn will be here soon and Merrick will persuade her right now, tonight. She trusts him more than any of us. She'll listen to him.

'You already warned her about Uziel,' Merrick said, 'and she refused to listen. What makes you think we can persuade her now?'

'Uziel explicitly said he would kill her if we couldn't keep her away from Michael. She can no longer pass it off as a guess on my part.'

'But you said she's determined to be with Michael.'

'Because he won't die on her like Hugh did.'

'Come on, it's more than that. She must have deep feelings for him, and he clearly must love her or he'd never have gone to such trouble to get close to her. Can't he handle his father?'

Chemosh struggled for patience. How many times did they have to go over this? 'He may think he can, but he can't.'

'Do you think Uziel will keep his word to leave her alone if we do manage to persuade her?'

'Yes.'

Pushing up, Merrick paced to the window and drew the curtain aside an inch, watching for Katie to bring Gregory back from his soccer practice. Chemosh's heart went out to Merrick. This had to be hardest for him. He'd raised Jenn, and he'd been longing for her to fall in love again.

But why did it have to be with Uziel's son?

Chemosh pressed a thumb and forefinger into his eyes, trying to black out the memory of Jenn and Michael, cheek to cheek, soaring in ecstasy above the hospital.

'I think we should listen to Chemosh,' Zane said.

Merrick turned. 'Do you have any idea what we'll be asking of her?'

'Of course I do. Losing Hugh was horrible for her, and now we're asking her to give up someone she could be with for a thousand years. It will break her heart.'

Chemosh felt torn by the sadness on Zane's face, hating the pain this was causing them all, but glad that Zane, after centuries of emotional isolation in which he'd lived only for the kill, had developed the empathy to feel pain for another. His adoration of his daughter had taught him to see life from outside himself.

'We must make her understand,' Chemosh said. 'If we don't succeed, Uziel will kill her. What he says, he does.'

Someone pounded on the front door, and the sudden clamor sent a current of fear through Chemosh.

Then he heard Jenn crying through the door.

Zane turned, his dark face going pale.

Chemosh raced to the door with the other two and pulled it open. Jenn staggered into his arms, clinging to him, sobbing as if her heart were breaking. Terrified that Uziel might be after her, Chemosh pulled her in and shut the door. 'What is it? You're trembling!'

'I've killed him.'

'Who?' Merrick moved in, his face filled with dread. 'Jenn, you didn't—'

'No, no,' she said. 'I didn't lose control feeding. It was an angel. He tried to kill me, but I killed him instead. It was awful, I didn't mean to.'

Uziel? Chemosh thought, stunned. No, it couldn't be, it isn't possible! He was torn between fear and a sudden, savage excitement. 'Who?'

'He said his name was Ariel. He was Uziel's son.'

Chemosh's excitement died stillborn, replaced by fear. 'He took one of ours, and now we have taken one of his. What has fate done to us?'

'How?' Zane asked.

'He . . . I . . .' Jenn's knees buckled and Chemosh grabbed her arm, bringing her upright.

'Here,' Merrick said, 'let's all go in the living room.' He led her by the arm, sitting her down on the couch. She looked white as chalk as though half dead herself. Ariel's attack must have taken a huge toll on her.

Chemosh suppressed a groan of pure fear. This was a disaster. They had to escape, at once, and Uziel would follow, oh yes, Uziel would hound them to the ends of the earth.

Zane knelt and took Jenn's hand. 'Can you tell us what happened?'

Chemosh listened, clutching his chest, as she told of Ariel surprising her in her car, feigning friendliness, then attacking her in the cemetery. Telling how she had fought back with her mind, she faltered and her voice broke.

Chemosh was staggered. He had struck down one of Uziel's kind with blood Influence and then run that time in Persia, but this was a confirmed kill. Had she projected Influence directly into Ariel's brain? She was lucky to be alive.

Chemosh felt his hands trembling. *We almost lost her!* That bastard Uziel and his upstart child who had turned a crisis into a catastrophe. Ariel's rashness, his blind hatred had not only ended his own life, but may have destroyed Jenn's as well.

Uziel would be insane with rage.

Chemosh put his hand on Jenn's shoulder. 'You must not feel guilty. It wasn't your choice — he's the one who made it him or you.'

She stared blankly. 'I killed Michael's brother. I feel awful.'

'I understand, but the important thing now is to save your life. Uziel won't rest until he has destroyed Ariel's killer, but — fortunately — in the next few hours nothing will be more important to him than claiming his son's body.' Chemosh turned away, planting his hands on the armrests of the wing-backed chair, trying to steady his reeling mind. Unless Uziel and his family were scattered far away, they'd have felt Ariel's death like a star going nova. 'They must find the body first,' he said, half out loud. 'If they don't, some jogger or tourist will stumble across it in the morning. It will be taken to a morgue, and they'll soon realize he's not human. It will be as bad for them as if the normals had found one of us.'

'Then *we* must go get it,' Jenn said.

Chemosh whirled. 'Jenn, no! We have to get out of here now, all of us, while we have a chance.'

'I'm going back,' Jenn said. 'The rest of you should go, get away, yes.'

Despite his alarm, Chemosh felt awe. What steel she had.

'I'm going with her,' Zane said.

'No,' Jenn said. 'You have to get out of here. Chemosh is right.'

'Not without you.'

'I never should have left,' she said in a low voice. 'I panicked. But to leave him like that, staring up at the sky . . . to make his family hunt for him . . . no.' Her eyes overflowed with tears.

Chemosh's mind leapt ahead. 'We can take care of it for you. If Uziel catches any of us, he'll see in our minds that we didn't kill his son and we may be allowed to live. With luck, we'll evade him. We'll get the body and leave it near their house while they're away, out hunting it. Jenn, you should get to National Airport and take the first plane to wherever you can. We'll fly to San Francisco, the Fairmont Hotel. You can wait two weeks, then—'

'No. You'll need me at the cemetery.'

'I recognized the spot from your description—'

'You need me to tell you if they're coming.'

'You can do that?' Chemosh was stunned.

She nodded.

What are you? What has happened to you?

If you can kill Ariel, might you in fact be able to kill his father?

The dark excitement returned, filling him with a feral longing, even as it chilled him.

Jenn sat next to her father in the back seat of the big Buick Roadmaster, determined not to sob, feeling the tears run down her cheeks in the darkness. An angel lay dead. How many lives had she ruined, besides her own?

Zane took her hand. 'Jenn, Chemosh is right, it wasn't your fault. If you hadn't fought back, he'd have killed you.'

'You're all in danger because of me.'

'Don't you worry about us.'

She nodded, but could feel herself trembling. Her family was all she had. Michael had shone into her life like a sun, and now he would hate her.

A fresh onslaught of tears took her; Zane fumbled out a handkerchief and Chemosh, from the front seat, reached back to pat her knee.

Merrick drew close to the cemetery; she pointed to the dark street above the Iwo Jima Memorial.

Again, the sentry at the Fort Myer gate did not react – Zane or Chemosh must have taken care of it.

She led them up the hillside between the tombstones. As they reached the grove of oaks around the sepulcher, she dropped to her knees. Her throat closed in a spasm as she watched Chemosh kneel beside the body and close the staring eyes of his ancient enemy's son.

And then she felt a pain so like her own that at first she thought it was hers . . .

Michael! Above and to the south, but drawing nearer – Michael, wracked with pain.

Michael, consumed with hatred.

She moaned, and then the fear hit her. 'They're coming!' she gasped.

Chemosh sprang up at once from the body. 'Run!' he hissed.

'You go. I'm staying.' *I'm who they want. I will beg their forgiveness. If they kill me, so be it.*

Jenn gasped as Zane picked her up, threw her over his shoulder, and raced down the dark hillside between the tombstones.

Chapter Thirteen

Standing in the shadows of the room of departure, Michael tried to wrap himself in numbness as he watched Drey prepare the body. How many times had he withstood sadness in this place of eternal quiet, deep within the mansion? Rafe had used his artistic skills to make the chamber as comforting as possible, dressing its circular wall in a fine tiled mosaic of a field of poppies under a cloudless blue sky. It was as beautiful as such a room could be, a fitting place for the family to say goodbye to its faithful nephilim.

Can it really now be one of us?

Everything seemed suspended, time stopping in its tracks, waiting alongside him to see if this could really have happened. He knew the body was Ariel, but at the same time could not fully accept it. This likeness on the slab was far too still; the real Ariel had never for a moment stopped moving

One of Rafe's sculptures, perhaps.

Might I be dreaming? Michael wondered. I've never slept, so how can I be sure?

I'm losing it.

He took slow, deep breaths, striving for calm. Ariel was dead; they could do nothing more for him but bury him. But I, Michael thought, how can I cool this aching for revenge?

If I could just be with Jenn.

He remembered the fleeting touch he'd felt as he'd neared the cemetery. Had that really been her, or merely a wish? It might have been real. Her route home did run through the area they'd been searching. He'd had to block her out to keep the fading thread of Ariel's aura, but her momentary nearness reminded him how much he yearned for her.

I promised I'd call tonight, he thought, and let her know how it went with my family. But now I must hide her awhile longer. Even if the murderer wasn't her great grandfather, my family is sure to suspect a phage. There could not be a worse time to try to persuade them about Jenn. Now I'll have to keep her at arm's length, at least until the family has finished mourning. Just when she needs me most, struggling with this mysterious new ability of hers, I must instead tell her we have to cool it for awhile.

The thought oppressed him, dragging him down when he'd thought he could sink no further.

Call her now, he thought. Get it over with.

His legs wouldn't move. He'd do it in a few minutes.

Now Drey was rubbing ointments on Ariel's face and chest and arms, the compounds of dissolution developed to speed the decay of nephilim. But Ariel was an angel, not half, and the special ointments would work more slowly on him. His body would doubtless remain as it now looked for decades before it began to deteriorate. That would be dangerous only if a human uncovered the body. Which will never happen, Michael thought. We will never leave this place now.

How could Ariel be dead?

I've seen thousands of humans die, and scores of our nephilim.

Now I truly know death.

He pressed a hand to his mouth to stop from crying out. Ariel, Ariel, no sorrow could be great enough.

Surely whoever killed him deserves to die!

Michael struck the wall behind him, the spark of pain calming him enough to regain his rigid control. Drey finished his work and stepped back. Michael could see sadness in his face, but his eyes were dry. 'I'm so sorry, my lord.'

Michael stepped forward to accept the embrace. The faint smell of mortality in the crepy skin of the nephilim's neck only added to his sorrow.

'Did you get a chance to tell them about Dr Hrluska before it happened?'

Michael glanced toward the door to make sure it was closed. 'No. We were waiting for Ariel.'

'This will make it harder.'

'Infinitely.'

'What will you do?'

'I dare not even mention Jenn now.'

'I agree.'

'Not until we've found out who killed Ariel and why. Once that . . . need is satisfied, maybe . . .'

In Drey's face Michael saw his own doubt reflected and his heart sank. A millennium would not heal Father's wound.

If I'm ever to have Jenn, Michael thought, I will have to go into exile.

His stomach contracted, pulling him partially down into a hunch. He felt Drey's hand on his shoulder. Could he bear separation from them?

He forced himself upright. It was tomorrow's pain. Now he must mourn Ariel, and help his family in their grief.

Drey said, 'Do you have any idea who could have done this?'

'Only a phage, and I know of only four in this area — Jenn, her father, her grandfather, and her great grandfather. Jenn didn't even know I had a brother, and if she did, she certainly wouldn't hurt him. Nor her grandfather. Metabolic poisons he's taking in order to die with his wife have made him into little more than a normal now. It might be the great grandfather, though. He warned me that I must give up Jenn or Father would kill her.'

Drey's eyes widened. 'He knows your father?'

'He claimed to.'

'Did he know Ariel?'

'Only if Ariel revealed himself to him, and if he did, he didn't tell me. My brother was both inexperienced and overly bold, a bad combination. I'm sure Father made it plain to him, as he did to all of us, that angels might, in some circumstances, be vulnerable to a phage, but Ariel was not a good listener.'

Michael turned away so Drey would not have to see his tears.

'I'm sorry, Michael. I long to comfort you and instead I aggravate your sorrow.'

'You do comfort me, Drey. As much as can be.'

'I'll be a go-between if you like, carry messages to Jenn while you're occupied.'

'I may take you up on that, my friend.' But he knew he must not. If Father was to learn one of his servants was trafficking with a phage . . .

Michael heard footsteps outside the chamber and signaled Drey with a tilt of his head. The door opened and Father stepped in. He glanced at the body of his son, then away quickly, turning toward the tiled wall, his eyes glazed with grief.

Drey bowed and headed for the door.

'Wait!' Father said in a low voice. 'Is he prepared?'

'Yes, Lord.'

'Our thanks.'

Drey bowed again and left. Michael moved to Father's side but something in his bearing forbade contact. Uziel took a deep, shuddering breath. Then he went to one of the curving divans set into the wall and sat, eyes fixed on the base of the table that served as Ariel's catafalque.

'How is Mother?' Michael asked.

'Inconsolable. Your sister is holding her grief away with that iron will of hers. But it's your brother I worry most about. Rafe is taking it very hard. He had a special closeness with Ariel, making it his mission to teach his young brother to appreciate art.' Father hunched over, fingers tightly interlaced, hands twisting. 'Rafe's heart is the gentlest of all of us. He can't comprehend this.'

Nor I, thought Michael. Father's bowed shoulders, his

broken voice, made him feel unbearably sad. Settling beside his father, he put an arm around him. After a moment, Uziel shifted away, making the contact awkward, and Michael withdrew, pained.

'We all waited so long for Ariel,' Father murmured. It might be centuries before we can have another child. Maybe never I'm old, so very old, Michael, and I've never felt it as I do this minute. I knew we could die — I still remember that one who was killed near me a few thousand years ago. And long before that . . . thousands of us . . . awful, terrible.'

Despite his grief, Michael felt a dread fascination. Could Father be having actual memories of heaven? How impossibly distant it had always seemed. Was it a planet or another plane of existence entirely? Were there rivers and trees, towering temples faced in gold? Was God really there, real and immediate, so that you could see Him, talk to Him? We are from there, Michael thought, exiles to this planet. A terrible, sharp longing tore at him, and he realized it was Father's longing, to be with God again as he once might have been . . .

And then the room faded and Michael found himself gazing up at a sapphire sky, bright as a thousand suns, and yet soothing to his eyes. He heard singing, a chorus of voices, each as clear and powerful as the tones of a great pipe organ. His blood stirred and then a deep uneasiness filled him as some instinct told him the music was martial, a contrapuntal song of war, rising from the throats of two converging armies. And then he saw them at either horizon, brilliant winged men and women sweeping toward each other like storm clouds before a great wind. Thousands and thousands of angels formed the ranks on each side, and as they came closer, an indescribable fear seized him. Somehow, he must stop this.

The great armies slowed advancing into each other now in stately ranks, poised and deliberate as sleepwalkers. Light began to flare, bursting in great flashes throughout the ranks, blinding gouts of light, white-hot, leaving scalded after-images on his retinas. He felt himself rising up among the quadrilles of contending angels, crying to them to stop, in God's name to stop. They seemed unable to hear him. Their faces shone like steel. Individuals began dropping from the clouds, hemorrhaging light as they fell, spinning down. Some were dead, he could feel it, but others were maimed inside, changed. He saw a plain below them, a vast field of golden grass, and in the middle a dark hole opened, and the stricken, falling angels vanished into that blackness, the utter void of space . . .

Michael gasped and, abruptly, the vision faded. He realized he was gripping Father's arm. He felt dizzy with the glory, the might, the horror of what he had seen.

'Father, was that heaven? The war—?'

'You gleaned me?' Uziel's voice was sharp.

'I didn't mean to. It came pouring out of you, so powerful I couldn't stop it. Was that an actual *memory*?'

Uziel passed a hand over his eyes. 'I don't know. Imagination, memory – after so long they mix together and you can no longer tell what is real.' He bent forward, clasping his hands between his knees. 'Ah, Ariel, Ariel. Who did this to you? We must find him.'

Shuddering convulsions took him, as though he were trying to heave up his soul. Terrified, Michael grabbed his shoulder, trying to steady him. 'Please, Father, you're scaring me. We'll find him. I'll help you.'

Uziel sagged and, after a moment, sat up again, gazing at him with reddened eyes. 'Son, I've asked the others, and now I ask you: do *you* have any idea who might done this?'

Michael gathered himself. There could be no holding back now. 'A phage named Chemosh.'

Father's eyes rolled up for a second, and his mouth drooped, as a man having a stroke might do. 'Chemosh,' he whispered.

He did not seem surprised. But how could that be? He came to my office with some lie about you having murdered his child.'

Father's eyes focused on him again. 'And you didn't tell me?'

Unable to bear the burning gaze, Michael looked away. 'I should have. I knew it was a lie, of course, and so I dismissed it. I . . . I didn't think . . . he would be capable of hurting one of us, even if he had the will.' Michael felt tears sliding down his cheeks.

Father made an incoherent sound, deep in his throat. 'Don't blame yourself. How could you have known? I should have told you.'

'Told me what?'

'About me and Chemosh.'

Michael felt a shock. Could it be true?

Father groaned, and his hands balled into fists. 'Chemosh, yes, it is what he would do, what he must have longed to do. How can that devil still be alive? I should have killed him in the beginning.'

Michael, stunned, tried to take it in. 'No, Father. You . . . you didn't really kill his son?'

Uziel did not answer. His face was pale. 'Do you know where Chemosh lives?'

'He has an apartment at the Watergate.'

Michael felt Father's hand under his chin, lifting his face. He wanted to look away, but the hand held him. Uziel's eyes glittered with a cold light, freezing Michael's blood. 'Good, son. Good. Now, you must not feel guilty. The guilt, if there be any, is all mine. We will bury Ariel, and then I will tell all of you why this has happened, and what we must do.'

The nephilim had dug Ariel's grave in the back lawn, about fifty yards from the precipice above the Potomac. The open hole bled a faint organic smell, like old leaves. It was deep — nearly ten feet; a tall horseshoe of dirt loomed around three sides of the pit, and the diggers had laid the sod out in neat rows nearby. Here at the foot of the grave there was just room for the five remaining Loyolas to stand together.

Michael was clamping his teeth together, but then a moan beside him caused his throat to convulse. Father or Rafe? — he could not pick out the grief of the others from his own. Mother's sable hair was carefully combed and she looked composed.

Father stood straight, rigid with barely suppressed rage, even as he comforted the sobbing Rafe with an arm around the shoulders. Fabriel had not changed her torn clothes. Her face was pale as alabaster. Her head turned toward him, a tormented question in her eyes. Michael felt a mild shock. Surely she did not imagine that the woman he loved could have killed his brother! He shook his head firmly; she gazed at him a moment longer, then tipped her head a fraction toward Father. Michael's heart sank. Her meaning was clear. She hadn't told Father about Jenn, but if he didn't, she would.

I must take her aside, tell her Father and I think we know who did it. Maybe then she'll wait.

And if Chemosh *didn't* do it?

Michael shook the thought off. Father had all but admitted the strongest possible motive, a son for a son. Who else could it be?

Six nephilim carried Ariel's body to the edge of the grave. Michael's heart lurched. His brother needed protection, a coffin to hold the dirt away, but that could not be allowed, he knew, because it would slow Ariel's decay. Slim as the chance of discovery might be, they could not risk that some human might someday find a rotted coffin surrounding a still well-preserved corpse that looked like a man but could not be.

Michael went to take the feet of his brother, but Father waved him away, his face hard and mottled. Gathering up his son's body, he floated down into the hole with it. Mother let out a soft cry; Fabriel took her hand. Father did not appear again, the minutes stretching, and Michael thought, I'll have to go in after him, but then Uziel emerged, his eyes nearly mad with anguish, and Michael felt a stab of pain around his heart. His knees buckled; he looked away from the terrible eyes, and his strength came back.

'Justine?' Father grated, and Michael realized with surprise that Mother would do the service. She began, a litany of thanks to God for all the blessings Ariel had brought, an expression of faith in His will. Mystified by Father's silence, Michael found it hard to listen. Uziel was their head, leader in all things, why not in this?

He's furious at God.

Michael knew he must be wrong, that Father was simply too choked with grief to manage words of comfort at this horrible moment. The mere idea of Father losing his faith unnerved him. Not Father, pillar of the faith, the most devout of us all.

Mother talked softly about Ariel, how loving he was, how beautiful and energetic, how he made them all feel younger and better for being around him. When she was finished, Father stepped forward. 'Vengeance is mine, saith the Lord. I will repay.' His voice had a hardness Michael had never heard before. 'And how does God repay? Through us, His servants. The power of God's vengeance slumbers in all of us, stronger in some than in others, but over the great epochs only a few are chosen. It is not an easy honor to bear.' Father passed a hand over his face, his eyes distracted now, as if by some distant scene. 'Sodom and Gomorrah,' he muttered. 'Pompeii, Atlantis — go forth and kill them all, the women and children, the sheep and cattle.'

Michael stared at him in shock. What was he saying — that *he* had been an angel of death? There were stories, in the Bible and other religious books, of God using angels to kill, but Michael had never believed it. Men wrote so imperfectly, always mixing their beliefs with fact, and how could angels, created by a loving God to love and protect, be ordered by that same God to kill?

'Sennacherib,' Father muttered. 'A hundred and eighty-five thousand Assyrians, killed by three of us in a single night. All those children in Egypt . . .'

Justine gripped her husband's arm. 'Dearest, Uziel — *Father*, please,' she whispered.

No, Michael thought, sickened. Not you, Father. Hundreds of thousands of people, the innocent with the guilty? *Children?* No, it was other angels, far away from us, long dead, their names never to be known. How *could* they live with it? Who could be their therapist?

'Tonight,' Father said, 'I have become death . . . again.' He stepped back.

The fury in his eyes made Michael aware again of his own simmering rage.

He stepped to the edge of the grave for a last look. Ariel, pale as ice, lay on his side, one hand under his cheek, the other palm on the ground, legs drawn up, the posture of an innocent, sleeping child. A sob tore up through Michael's throat. Stepping back, he felt the arms of Fabriel and Mother go around him. The others joined and they stood in a circle as the nephilim began returning the dirt to its domain.

Michael doubled over, bringing Mother and Fabriel down to the ground with him. He heard the damp earth showering into the hole behind him, a sound like rain driven by gusts of wind. When at last he let them bear him up again, he turned to see the lawn smooth and unbroken, the sod replaced, Ariel gone, as if he had never been, leaving only the pain.

'We will go in now,' Father said.

Michael tried to draw Fabriel aside, but Mother gave them a sharp look and motioned urgently. Panic welled in him. He must speak to Fabriel, tell her about Chemosh.

When they all stood together in the study, Michael implored her with his eyes. She drew a convulsive breath then said, 'I believe Michael has something to tell us.'

'That must wait,' Father said, and Michael felt a cool wave of relief. 'I pray God's forgiveness,' Father went on, 'and yours, for any unworthy bitterness I may have displayed at the grave. I never told you, because I was ashamed – not of what I did for God, but that in the end I failed Him. I have . . . suffered for that, but not enough, apparently. Now I have been repaid in full measure and you, who are innocent, are made to suffer too. Four millennia ago, before ever I met your mother, long before any of you were born, I was one of the chosen few who carried out God's judgements on the wicked. For five hundred years, I rained God's fire. Finally, in the city of Per Ramesse, in Egypt, I heard God tell me to kill the firstborn child of the pharaoh and his subjects. I did it, but then I . . . broke down. It was too much for me. I begged God to release me from the burden . . .

'He . . . did release me . . .'

Father looked upward, and Michael realized he was containing tears. 'I . . . have never again heard God's voice since that night. His silence has since descended on all of us, but I've never given up hope. Now I see that I may have been listening in the wrong way. I have learned that the phage pharaoh, Ramses II, is here in our midst. He calls himself Chemosh now. He is a blood eater, an abomination who has lived far past his time. He is the one who killed our Ariel. When I begged God to release me, Ramses, the doer of the evil, was still alive. I now see that God meant for me to kill him as well, that when I begged for release, I was leaving the most important part of God's will undone. This doomed us to this pain now, so long after. It is time to finish God's will, so I can hear His voice again. We will go out to search, and when we have found Chemosh, I'll do what I should have done three and a half millennia ago.'

'Vengeance?' Rafe cried. 'No, we must forgive—'

'It is *not* vengeance,' Father said in a sharp voice. 'Haven't you been listening? It is the final part of my work, ordained by God.'

Fabriel was shaking her head, a look of incredulity on her face. Father, are you telling us we are to kill? To *murder?*'

'If I can do it without your help,' Father said, 'I will. But Chemosh is a mystery. He has lived more than twice the normal life span of a phage. God may well have allowed it as a rebuke to me. It's possible that evil has grown powerful in him. As soon as we finish here, I'll call in help from the other clans nearest us. We'll blanket the sky over Washington. I pray you need do no more than help in that search, but once he is found, you, my family, must then stand ready to help me destroy him if I need you.'

'But how?' Michael asked. 'We don't know how to kill.'

'You *will* know. It's like gleaning, but you throw all your strength into it. You do not merely look, you touch. You strike into the mind, you gather it to you and then you pull.'

Fabriel looked appalled. Rafe moaned. 'Father, I can't—'

Father whirled on him. 'You can. And if necessary, you will. Even if you would disobey me, your father, you dare not disobey God.'

The power of Father's voice, its moral authority, filled Michael with a dark urgency. A sense of wrongness — something Father had said or not said — nagged at him, but who was he to question him for holding back, when he had held back Jenn? He would tell about her when this was over, but what mattered now was Ariel's killer. Michael felt his own desire for vengeance returning, flaming to a white heat.

Vengeance *is* ours, he thought. The murderer must die. If Uziel, the angel of death, says it is God's will, surely it is so.

Chapter Fourteen

'I am not angry.' Jenn pronounced each word.

'You *seem* angry.' Zane's hand rested near the lock, as if he feared she'd try leaping across him to escape the car. In the front seat, Chemosh sat sideways, his left arm draped along the back, no doubt ready to grab her if she tried the door on her side. Merrick had eyes only for the broad drive that circled the Lincoln Memorial, his hands still clutching the steering wheel, though they had been parked for twenty minutes. After midnight now, no traffic, everything still. The faint reflection of the memorial's floodlights cast a chalky glow into the car, heightening Jenn's sense of unreality. Did Chemosh and Zane really fear she'd run away now and deny Merrick her blood? Surely they trusted her more than that. She would wait for Katie to arrive with the transfusion equipment. She'd do her part.

And then she *would* go, and no one would stop her.

'I'm sorry for grabbing you like that,' Zane said, 'but I couldn't just let you stay and be killed, yourself. If you saw someone about to jump out a tenth-story window, wouldn't you grab him?'

'They wouldn't have killed me.'

'You don't know Uziel,' Chemosh cut in. 'I do.'

'You *knew* him. More than three thousand years ago.'

'And just one day ago he warned me if things did not go his

way, he would kill you.' Chemosh reached a hand out. 'Jenn, I know how this hurts. I wouldn't have had it this way for anything.'

Her love for him overcame her anger, and she took his hand, swallowing against the pressure in her throat, determined not to start crying again. Ariel was dead — it could not be undone. But she could tell Michael and his family how it happened and beg their forgiveness. If they decided to punish her instead, so be it.

But first, Merrick.

A car slid into view past the memorial, following the circle toward them — a red Cutlass. Merrick tensed. 'It's Katie!' Jumping out, he hurried to meet her. She scrambled from her car into his arms. The way they clung to each other broke Jenn's control and her tears overflowed; she blotted them away as she followed Zane out of the car. The night had grown cool, easing the feverish heat in her face.

Merrick stood back from Katie at last. 'Gregory?'

'On the plane to Baton Rouge,' she replied. 'Mom will take care of him until this is over.'

'You'll go too, as soon as we've finished.'

Katie looked away, but Jenn knew who would win this argument. Merrick was ready to give up all chance at a normal life with her in order to try to protect her and his family. In doing it, he would also be giving her what she had wanted — an end to his premature dying. Her part of the bargain would be to remove not just their son but herself as far as possible from Uziel's reach.

'We'd better get out of sight,' Zane said.

Katie turned back to her car and lifted out a flight bag. 'I'd feel a lot better if we could do this at home or the hospital. There's no one in my lab this late.'

'Too dangerous,' Chemosh said. 'We must assume Uziel now knows everything Michael does about our lives, which is probably a great deal, since Michael's been watching Jenn — and reading her mind — for who knows how long. We must avoid our normal haunts. You got in and out of the hospital because he's not after you, but believe me any phage will virtually glow in the dark to him.' He turned to Zane. 'Let's go.'

Jenn followed with the others, hurrying across the wide apron of pavement that encircled the memorial grounds, and onto the dark grass within—

Check out old Abe, then a donut — cream-filled . . .

Jenn stopped, startled by the voice in her mind. 'Stand still,' she hissed, turning as a cop car circled into view beyond the north edge of the memorial. Questing for the mind behind the wheel, she saw the head swing toward them and found his retinal capillaries just in time. 'I've got him. Just don't move.' From the corner of her eye, she could see the others frozen, small statues at the feet of the great one. She slid the cop's blind spot, compensating as the park police cruiser circled slowly toward them, rolled past and finally receded toward Memorial Bridge.

'OK.'

Zane loped ahead, Merrick and Katie close behind, but Chemosh remained still for a second, staring up at the brooding figure of Lincoln. Jenn caught an image from his mind — a long double line of men chained together, leaning forward halfway to the ground as they strained against the ropes girdling a giant slab of stone. She heard the crack of phantom whips, and smelled blood. Ramses the slaver, she thought, and Lincoln the emancipator. If people go to church to confess their sins, then this could be Chemosh's temple, as it had once been Zane's sanctuary.

'Here,' Zane whispered.

Taking Chemosh's arm, Jenn hurried him to the dense thicket of forsythia that hugged the massive flank of the memorial. Zane held the branches aside, and in the shadows against the wall, she saw a low steel door, flush with the ground. The lock on it had already been broken and it stood ajar. The branches raked her shoulders, and then she was through and into the dark tunnel. The air smelled musty, rich with earth. She could feel the hovering weight of stone above, as if it had packed the stagnant air down on their shoulders. Ahead, Merrick's flashlight picked out thick beams criss-crossed with cobwebs.

Katie made a disgusted sound, low in her throat. Zane, pushing into the lead, rounded a slight bend and vanished in the swaying shadows thrown by Merrick's light. Jenn followed with the others. Past the bend, the tunnel deepened, allowing everyone to stand upright. Old timbers, left by the builders of the memorial, criss-crossed the roof of the tunnel. Dirt trickled suddenly between two of them, as if the giant stone president had shifted in his marble chair above.

Chemosh looked around with a troubled expression. 'Reminds me of the worker tunnels under my temple at Abu Simbel.'

'This area has been forgotten for a long time,' Zane said.

Chemosh gave his shoulder a squeeze. 'You've done well. No way will Uziel detect us through all that granite and marble.'

Zane gave a grim smile, perhaps remembering how he'd hidden here twenty years ago, while Merrick, a detective sergeant of DC homicide, hunted him on the streets above.

Merrick laid his flashlight along a beam at shoulder level. Taking a second light from his pocket, he paced off eight steps and shone it back toward the first, creating a soft box of light that dwindled away to a black square in either direction.

'All right?' Chemosh asked Katie.

'Joseph Lister is spinning in his grave, but yes, it will do.'

'Who's Joseph Lister?' Zane asked.

'Pioneered antiseptic surgery,' Jenn said.

Katie spread a plastic tablecloth on the dirt floor of the tunnel, set her bag on it, and took out a one-liter Erlenmeyer flask, her movements as swift and practiced as if she transfused blood in tunnels every day. *She really wants this to work*, Jenn thought. *Even though if it does, and she and Merrick survive Uziel, there will be no old man to sit at the kitchen table with her when she's eighty. Instead, there will be a handsome, unwrinkled fellow who looks twenty-five. None of their life together will show on his face. She'll be tempted to wonder how many young women flirted with him on the street that day, and what he might have felt when they did. Merrick will stay with her, but in a very* real way she will lose him, and despite all that, she wants it, because he will not lose himself.

Jenn felt an ache around her heart. This was love, putting the life of someone else above your own. I felt that way with Hugh, she thought. And I could have felt it again with Michael.

Suddenly, Jenn felt that she was alone in the tunnel, that it was caving in on her. The feeling passed in a flash, and she made herself focus on the procedure ahead.

Katie straightened from her bag, holding the flask. 'We will need blood from each of you,' she said. 'Our best chance of reversing his condition quickly is to flood his cells, get as much healthy phage blood into him as possible. With your ability to recuperate quickly, the three of you can probably spare eight hundred milliliters each without ill effects. That'll give him about two and a half liters of phage blood, nearly half his total volume. Ready?' She looked at Zane.

With the barest hesitation, he nodded.

This has to be hard for him, Jenn realized. One reason I was able to get him back with his father was because Merrick no longer had the strength to hunt him, in case he relapsed into killing. Merrick assured him that part of their lives was over forever, but if this transfusion works, he'll have the strength. And if Zane ever did begin killing again, could Merrick really let it go, knowing he could stop it?

And yet Zane is rolling up his sleeve.

I believed him, but this is proof. He's stopped killing.

Jenn felt the dead weight of Ariel lift for a second.

Katie positioned Merrick in a seated position on the plastic tablecloth, making sure his arm was higher than the flask. Jenn bent to help her, fitting needles to both ends of one line and one end of a second, feeding the remaining end of the second line into the flask.

'First we're going to let blood from you,' Katie told Merrick, to make some room so the transfusion won't make you hypervolemic. A liter ought to be enough. Your spleen can take care of the rest — it should start throwing out your older, normal blood cells as soon as it gets the new. You might feel a little weak until we can get the phage blood into you. Relax and you'll be fine.'

Merrick nodded. His face was pale, probably not from fear but dejection. Katie found the median cubital vein in the crook of his left arm and set the needle. Blood spurted into the line, a dark red column that sped through and began dripping into the jug. Jenn looked away, feeling the thirst. How she hated it, and yet the blood smelled so good, making her think of a fine, aged Camembert.

To distract herself, she kept her eye on her watch, as Katie monitored her own. It took five minutes for the flask to fill; Jenn worked out the math — four minutes on the line for each donor ought to do it. Jenn removed the needle, pressed a wad of gauze onto the wound and bent Merrick's arm tight to keep pressure on, then had him lie flat on the tablecloth.

Katie said, 'Who's first?'

'Me,' Chemosh and Zane said at the same time.

Chemosh deferred to Zane, who offered his arm to Katie, gazing down at his father's face. 'If you had not given me blood,' he said softly, 'I would have died of the leukemia before my fourteenth birthday. Here's some of it back.'

Merrick's eyes grew moist, but he said nothing. How could he thank Zane for a gift, however grand, that he did not want?

Katie took Zane by the shoulders and positioned him so that his arm hung down directly above Merrick's. Jenn brought the other end of the line to the vein in Merrick's right arm and pushed the needle in. Gravity and Zane's heartbeat did the rest. Merrick lay still, receiving the blood of his son — perfect blood, with none of the Rh antigens that complicated human transfusions. Red blood cells with that strange wall that could turn porous to nourish and oxygenate the cells but close again at the first sign of trouble, becoming so impervious that it could repel even a massive dose of radiation.

We are so well made, Jenn thought, can it really only be to kill?

'It's coming out,' Zane said, and she realized the muscle

beneath his skin was starting to resist the needle as the tiny puncture healed.

'Run it back in,' Katie said urgently. 'You have to hold it in — I'm not strong enough.'

'I've got it.'

After a moment, Katie said, 'All right, that's enough from you.'

'I'll go next,' Jenn said, and Chemosh nodded.

Standing over her grandfather and struggling to keep the needle in, she had a quick image of Michael in his office, the parakeet sitting on his shoulder. Michael's gentle smile, the love she'd felt in his mind.

The air of the tunnel pressed like grit at her eyes.

Clearing her throat, she turned to practicalities: How would she contact Michael? Call him at the hospital? But surely he'd not be working during this awful time for him and his family.

He *will* be wondering where I am, she thought. He may even be keeping an eye on my place. I'll go there . . .

But what if Uziel has staked it out?

A chill ran through her. But why would he? Uziel knew about her, because of Chemosh, but none of Michael's family could know it was she who had killed Ariel. They must suspect Chemosh, who had the clear motive. If Uziel was watching anyone's place, surely it would be Chemosh's apartment at the Watergate.

And I'll be careful, she thought. I'll ease up to my house. If anyone's inside, I'll be able to sense them, like I did at the cemetery. If it's clear, I'll go inside and wait for Michael to come to me.

Chemosh stepped forward to take his turn. Looking at Merrick, Jenn felt a small shock as she saw that the small wrinkles around his eyes had disappeared and the muscles at his neck and shoulders looked thicker.

It was working — and fast!

Kneeling beside him, she took his pulse. His heartbeat was slow and deep, the muscle already regaining its power and efficiency. Thirteen years of aging, of pushing himself down cell by stubborn cell, reversing almost before her eyes. Merrick smiled past her shoulder and Jenn realized Katie had stepped into his view behind her. Oh, Katie, she thought. Now you'll never have to lose him.

But she could feel no joy. If Merrick's rejuvenated cells produced immunity to the injections he'd been taking, he would lose Katie, as he had lost all the other women he had ever loved.

'That's enough,' Katie said to Chemosh. As Jenn removed the needle from Merrick, she noticed the muscle mass of his forearm bulking up as it rebuilt itself. The puncture wound from the needle closed, then disappeared; his cells were healing themselves in the accelerated metabolic rush typical of a healthy phage.

Katie shone a penlight into his eye. 'Look at that,' she exclaimed. 'His pupil barely responds to light, which means the phage capacity of his retinas to handle it has already regenerated.'

'If you two are done prodding me, I'd like to get up.'

'Sure,' Katie said.

Merrick rose with a fluid grace and studied the back of his hand, flexing his fingers, rotating the wrist. 'There was pain in my hands,' he said wonderingly. 'I hadn't noticed until the transfusion drove it out.'

'A touch of arthritis, probably,' Katie said.

He pinched the skin on the back of his hand and let go. It snapped back, smooth, elastic as a teenager's.

'Tired?' Katie asked Merrick.

'I could run a marathon. I didn't want this but my body does. I feel wonderful . . . physically.'

Katie looked at him. 'If you'd rather be depressed, wait until you see my bill.'

'Isn't being turned back into a vampire covered by Medicare?'

Katie squeezed his arm, then hugged him to her. Zane watched them, his impassivity betrayed by shining eyes. Chemosh, smiling, put his arms around them both.

Jenn backed away, careful to make no sound. Her heart felt full to bursting. Merrick would live – if she now did her part.

She took a last mental picture of them, the three hugging, the fourth drinking it in from his safe distance, then backed quietly into the darkness.

Chapter Fifteen

As the sky to the east began to show pink, Uziel flew low over Old Town, searching for the she-phage's address. Hospital records had her on South Fayette, but it was hard to read the numbers from above. Swooping low down a narrow street lined with maples, he found it near the middle of the block. He breathed a quick prayer, *let her be here.* His confidence rose a fraction. She was not at the hospital. Unless she'd been in on Ariel's death with Ramses, she would either be here, or come here before long.

Settling on the roof, he winced as he heard a shingle crackle under his foot. Any phage could have heard that as far down as the basement. What was wrong with him?

Tired, so tired.

No. Angels did not tire.

He sank to his haunches on the slanted roof, resting his mind, numb and dazed. His tears for Ariel had stopped, leaving a parched feeling in his eyes, an emotional exhaustion of grief and rage. Not tired, but so similar to the weariness he had felt in humans that his body could not tell the difference. A lagging in his nerves and muscles, an ache in his throat, like thirst.

It did not matter. Physically, he was fine. He could go on for days, weeks, indefinitely. And that is what he would do.

But first kill the she-phage, Uziel thought, before Michael

realizes I know about her. With luck, he'll conclude she ran, taking Chemosh's side in Ariel's murder. I'll console him over her betrayal. And then he can marry Philippa and any clan who whispers against me will be whispering against Amator and the Evangelines as well.

I'll feel dirty for what I did to Michael, but my feelings don't count. Having lost his illusion of love, he would find it even crueler to have to hate his father for it. He'll need my consolation, and I'll give it. What's one more weight on my conscience, anyway?

Uziel shuddered, throwing off a sudden twitch in his shoulders. The guilt had started already, from having sent Michael to keep watch on Ramses' apartment as though it were an important duty. But I had to get him out of the way, somehow. Ariel is with God, but if I don't act at once I'll lose another son — not to God but to the she-phage. There will be time enough after I've killed her to hunt Ramses down and destroy him with God's fire, as I should have done in the beginning.

And then I will hear God's voice again.

Uziel listened to the house below, extending his mind down into it. He sensed no one, but if she were hiding in the basement, he might not be able to detect her from here—

Look out!

He flushed cold as he felt the human gaze lock onto him and freeze — a man who'd just stepped from the house across the street. Within a millisecond, Uziel had edited himself from the man's mind — Tom, his name was Tom, blinking now, and rubbing at his eyes.

I'm blind! I saw an angel and I'm blind! Up on that roof. Dear God, no one's going to believe me! They'll say I looked at the sun, but it's not even up yet!

Uziel bit back a groan. Truly, he was losing focus — remaining unseen was as natural as breathing. He looked through Tom's stunned eyes as the man squinted up at the roof again — ah, good, vision was coming back to the poor fellow, bleached and blurry, but no permanent damage.

It's gone, but it was there, I know it was. It looked like a statue made of fire. Magnificent!

Uziel could feel Tom's heart pounding in the ventricles of his own brain. Awed, but also afraid, even now that he realized he had not been blinded. Why? *Am I not an angel,* Uziel thought, *just like Justine or Fabriel or . . . Amator? There is nothing on the outside of me to show what I was once commanded to do. Poor humans, dreaming about angels, loving the idea of us, but if they manage to see one, they are afraid. If this man knew what lived across the street from him, then he would truly be terrified.*

Lifting from the roof, Uziel drifted over its peak and down the rear wall of Jenn's house, landing softly in the small, grassy enclosure of the rear courtyard. At the back door, he twisted the knob. Locked. He made a circuit of the house, checking all the windows and the front door, but all were locked, so he finished up at the back door again, where the high courtyard fence would seal away the noise from Tom or anyone else out at this early hour. Grasping the knob, Uziel twisted it until the metal sheared. He jerked the shaft out and threw it into the grass. Thrusting a finger into the hole, he wormed left, found the shank of the bolt, and pushed it on through, ramming it deep into the wood of the jamb. The door swung open.

Hurrying past the fireplace and up some steps, he went to the spiral staircase in the front foyer, which led both up and down. Descending to the basement, he listened for any sounds. The house remained silent above and below. The furnace fan kicked in and warmth bathed his face. Frustrated, he sped back upstairs, checking each room.

Not here.

Uziel felt his teeth clenching. *I hate her almost as much as Ramses,* he realized. *Ramses killed people's bodies, but she is after the soul of my son.*

Instead of heading back downstairs, he found himself in her bedroom. A faint aroma hung in the air, fresh, like a cut apple, and Uziel realized he was smelling her in the clothes that hung in her closet. Not the scent he had expected, that faint, carnal odor of flesh he could detect on most of her kind, a carnivore stench, which came not from the blood but from the skin and muscle phages accidentally consumed along with it, usually from the torn throat.

Uziel brushed the tendril of doubt aside. She must be eating blood, or she would either be sick with the false leukemia or dead.

Uziel felt something crack under his clenching thumbs. Without realizing it, he'd picked up the photo beside Jenn's bed. Beneath the cracked glass, a handsome face gazed out. 'My love always, Hugh' had been scrawled over the bottom of the photo. It was not the face of any phage he knew. A human boyfriend?

Why couldn't you have kept it to that, instead of going after my son?

Uziel set the picture back on the bed table. The room disgusted him suddenly, especially the bed, as if she slept — a prop to fool normals who might come in. A charade of life by an apostle of death.

And yet she sometimes lay here, thinking, perhaps, or reading. Otherwise, why put the photo by the bed, and on the other side a phone . . .?

Uziel gazed at the blinking red light on the phone's answering machine. The she-phage had some messages.

Circling the bed to the machine, Uziel found replay, and then stopped, his finger on the button. What if one or more of the messages were from Michael? Did he want to hear his son leaving messages of love to a daughter of darkness?

Sickened, Uziel started from the room, then hesitated. If he searched the place he might find a clue to where Jenn was. An address book, the names and locations of friends, people she might hide with.

Uziel pulled out the drawer of the bed table and spilled its contents on the bed — lifesavers, a hair pick, some bobby pins and a tangle of rubber bands. A door beckoned below the drawer. Locked. Ripping it from its hinges, he pulled the contents onto the floor. A photo album fanned open.

Uziel started to toss it on the bed, then the pictures captured him. Children, thirty or forty different photos. His stomach knotted as he flipped through them, unable to stop himself: the phage and a young girl, sitting together on the side of a hospital bed. Another child pretending to give the phage a shot while the creature made a frightened face. She and three kids standing beside an ambulance, a pale young boy sitting propped up in a hospital bed with a bandage on his head . . .

Uziel pressed the book shut, then pushed it under the bed. His eyes prickled in a tearless reflex. Ramses' son — that's who the boy had looked like. Three and a half millennia ago, but he would never forget that boy's dying face, all the tender, young faces that horrible night, the most ghastly night of his life.

Go out and kill all the firstborn of Egypt.

Had those been the exact words? He did not remember. He'd heard them only in his mind, as with all of God's commands. The voice of God, all right. Ramses was driving the Israelite slaves hard on his various building projects, and drinking their blood each night. His kingdom, Uziel thought, but *my* territory.

He remembered his horror: Children, Lord? Why not the pharaoh? He's the cause of all this. Surely his child is innocent, and what about the rest of them? The firstborn of the poorest farmer, the goatherd's child, the women who weave baskets, them too? Don't make me do this.

Go kill them, kill them all.

The voice of God, no question.

No question.

Thousands upon thousands of children, convulsing in their beds, their lives flowing around him in flashes prismed by his tears. Wails rising from the darkened streets of Per Ramesse as the people, from Ramses down to the lowliest gravedigger, discovered their dying children. I fled through the night, Uziel remembered, my hands crushing my ears, squalling as a child squalls, unable to draw a breath.

And now the pharaoh has his revenge.

Uziel's throat burned with bitterness. Damn you, Blood Eater. I had no choice in what I did to you. I was following God's command. You had many other children, a hundred of them just while you were pharaoh. In all my days I have had only four children.

Pain flared around Uziel's heart. His face felt stretched tight over the bone, and he realized his mouth had opened wide in an unvoiced scream. Gasping a breath, he forced his mouth shut. Somehow he had fallen to his knees.

Was it possible that Ariel was God's punishment for killing the children.

No, no, NO! He pounded the floor. Ariel died because I did not finish, because I ran.

Tell me it was you, God. Tell me it was not just an inner voice of my own, telling me to do that unspeakable thing. Talk to me this one more time, and I'll never ask again.

Uziel waited, his head pressed to the cool floor of the phage's bedroom.

Nothing.

And then he felt something.

Another mind, questing into the house, reaching for him.

The she-phage!

Michael hovered restlessly above the sinuous curve of the Watergate roof, trying to stay focused on New Hampshire Avenue below. He knew Chemosh's neurologic essence well enough to spot him with his eyes closed, but it seemed unlikely the phage would venture back to his apartment. Chemosh would know I'd tell Father about him, Michael thought. If he's the one who killed Ariel, he'd hide somewhere else in Washington or run. Is Father trying to keep me away from the real action so Chemosh won't kill me too?

Michael's legs seethed with the urge to run – or to kick something. By now, Father would have organized the angels he'd called in from the Baltimore, Philadelphia and Richmond clans. He's in the real hunt, Michael thought, watching one of the airports, or searching Washington with Mother, Rafe and Fabriel, while I'm stuck here.

Turning, he coasted back up the river side of the Watergate. The Potomac had turned rosy, the earlier mists burning off as Washington tilted toward the sun. The roof terraces of the Kennedy Center to the south and west glowed pink, seagulls picking through the peanuts and bits of cheese left during intermission by last night's concertgoers. How normal the world looked, as though no angel had died.

Michael's heart compressed, and he found himself longing for Jenn. If he could just call her, speak to her for two minutes, surely she would understand and wait for him to get through this. But she was not at the hospital and no one answered at her home, nor at Merrick's or Zane's.

Michael pulled his cell phone from his belt and dialed her number again. Four rings, then the click of the machine picking up: 'Hi, this is Jenn, if I'd known *you'd* call I'd have been here. I'll be devastated if you don't leave a message — wait for the beep, talk to you soon.'

Groaning, Michael cut the connection. No sense leaving his number yet again, or repeating his earlier pleas.

Where was she?

Damn you, Chemosh. Is it why you killed Ariel — to keep Jenn and me apart? Did you decide I was too much to handle, and then killed my brother?

Michael stopped above the west end of the Watergate, feeling himself on the edge of revelation — one he would not like. He had been fighting it off ever since the funeral. Why? What was he so afraid to see?

Something not quite right about Father. When I told him about Chemosh, the look in his eyes. Not surprise, just that deep pain . . .

He asked if I knew where Chemosh lived.

Michael went still, suspended in the air. Why would he think

I'd know that? I wouldn't, except that Chemosh is a part of Jenn's life, and I know all about her . . .

And so does Father!

Michael felt a sudden, choking pressure in his chest. Terrified, he rose and raced downriver toward Alexandria, praying he wasn't too late.

Chapter Sixteen

To avoid detection from the sky, Jenn entered the subway at Foggy Bottom, a few blocks from the Lincoln Memorial. The Metro closed at midnight – the tracks would be clear except for trains sitting at stations. Jumping down from the deserted platform, she passed under the looming arch of the westbound tunnel into blackness. At once, her eyes adjusted. Avoiding the power rail, she found a loping stride that matched the spacing of the railroad ties. All her senses sharpened; she could smell the faint vinegary tinge of mildew on the concrete, hear the tick of contracting metal and a whisper of subterranean wind. The tracks sloped down and the air went dead; in the silence, she imagined she could hear the faint rumble of the Potomac overhead. At Rosslyn she turned south into the Blue Line tunnel, surfacing at Arlington Cemetery, then plunging underground again. Eerie, running mile after mile through the earth. A rat bolted in front of her and she let out a little scream, then felt foolish. Clearly, the little girl who'd been terrified of rats was still somewhere inside her. Nothing in these caverns could threaten her now. If anything, it was the rat who should scream.

But she was glad when she emerged into the first light of dawn at the subway stop near Old Town in Alexandria.

Vulnerable now, she raced the swelling light into her neighborhood, feeling an itch of exposure between her shoulder blades. Chemosh had warned of Uziel's alliances. Was an angel overhead right now, searching for phage auras below?

Rounding the corner of her own block, she looked ahead to her house. At the same instant, she felt the contact in her mind, light as a moth's wing. Neck prickling, she halted. Michael? Jumping a hedge, she ran onto the yard of the corner house, up against its side, inching her head around until she could see her house again. The other mind lashed out at her and she felt his hatred—

Uziel!

She gasped as she saw him rising from her roof, his wings glowing red in the sunrise. He wheeled toward her with stunning speed. Fear sent strength surging to her legs and she dashed to the rear of the house. The contact broke – the brick must be blocking it. Desperate to throw him off, she turned back toward him, sprinting through darkened back yards, hoping the houses would continue to shield her. In the mad abandon of panic, she leapt a nine-foot chain-link fence, racing on until she reached the far end of the block. Stopping, she felt for him in her mind. Nothing. He must have passed her in the opposite direction – her feint had worked.

But when he couldn't find her, he'd retrace.

Across the street, the dark slash of a storm drain caught her eye. Sprinting across to it, she flattened herself on the pavement and swung her legs down into the blackness. As she tried to slither through, the underside of the curb caught at her head, holding her fast.

Planting her palms on the cement, she aligned her spine with the overhanging section of curb and pushed up against the massive weight of concrete. For a second, nothing, and then it gave way with a loud crack and she pushed herself backward, her hands finding purchase on the rough pavement. Dropping through and down, she twisted her ankle as she sprawled into black, stinking water.

She lay still. For a few seconds her ankle throbbed – it would surely have snapped if her bones were not phage. A cut in her scalp stung, and then the pain receded, evaporating in a torrent of adrenaline as the wound healed.

Can he pick up my fear?

Lying flat in the water, she tried to compose her mind. *I'm floating in a warm stream, no worries, the sun on my face.*

She saw that the storm drain stretched away in either direction. At this point it was about four feet wide and ten high. Above, where she'd come in, a narrow slice of sky showed, pink now, in the rising sun. The broken curb had fallen back into place, but the cracking sound had been quite loud—

A shadow flitted across, so swiftly she could not make it out. Her heart missed a beat. She should move away from the opening, farther into the sewer, but if she tried it now, Uziel might hear her.

A light stroke rippled through her mind.

She scurried away from the opening above, deeper into the sewer, feeling the stroke again, stronger now, a lash across her mind. She scrambled, sobbing. A steel grille swam from the murk ahead; she crashed against it, tearing at the crosspieces, then battering it with her shoulder, but it would not budge.

She could feel Uziel now, read his loathing. Gasping, she tried to think of Ariel, to focus her mind on it. If he could see—

But he wasn't interested in seeing. He wanted only one thing, to kill her.

Turning, she pressed her back against the grille, planted her feet and shoved with all her might, but her heels slipped along the scummy cement and she fell on her back, her head dipping beneath the filthy water for a second. She pushed up and saw him peering through the crease, a face much like Ariel's, same square jaw, the eyes burning with hatred and triumph. His arm appeared through the hole, glowing white, the hand rising to point at her, and she knew she was going to die.

And then his rage evaporated in surprise. His face and arm slipped back from the hole. She felt his trace dwindle then vanish.

Uziel was gone.

She wept with relief.

After a moment, she became aware of the stench. With a cry of disgust, she scrambled up, then laughed. A second ago she was sure she would die and now she was revolted because she'd gotten filthy water on her.

She slogged through the muck back toward the crease above. Looking up, she judged the distance, then leapt up to grab the opening with her hands. They slipped off, dumping her back down to her haunches and she sprang again, grabbing the edge of the gutter, clinging, chinning herself on it—

And felt the whisper of another mind, the faintest trace . . .

Michael!

In a burst of energy, she swung a leg up and out of the drain, hooking her arm over the ledge of the overhang, pulling and scrambling until she'd gotten herself half onto the apron of gutter, an arm and a leg thrusting out into the street. *Michael, I'm here. I'm here!*

She felt his joy as the trace of his mind swelled, filling her. Landing, he took her wrist and ankle and pulled her out onto the street. She rolled to her feet, filthy, reeking, and pulled him into her arms.

Ten minutes in her steaming shower scrubbed the smell from her pores. Michael stayed in the bedroom. As the hot water pounded her, she could feel her mind thawing, beginning to focus again. Michael said he had not detected his father, so Uziel must have sensed him coming, and that's why he'd broken off his attack. Michael had saved her. *My guardian angel.*

Toweling off, she pulled her terrycloth robe on, then went into her room and sat by Michael on the bed. His face was very pale. He pulled her to him. 'I'm so sorry. That my father would—'

'Hush. It *was* your father, not you.'

The dread of what she must do began to burrow in her, a hollow ache in her stomach. I killed his brother, she thought, but I'm letting him hold me. I must not.

But will he ever touch me again?

Pulling back, she went to her dressing table and sat before its big mirror, brushing her hair into a damp semblance of order. She must tell him the truth now, but she was afraid, so afraid.

Michael put his hands on her shoulders, hovering protectively over her, his blue eyes vivid and pained in the mirror. 'If Father would just look inside you . . .'

She longed to touch his hands. Instead, she said, 'Michael, I'm so sorry about your brother.' Her eyes filled with tears, blurring his face in the mirror.

'Chemosh told you.'

'No.'

'Then how . . .?'

Her stomach heaved. She blinked back tears, willing herself to be strong. 'You must look inside me now.'

Over her shoulder, his eyes turned baffled. Suddenly, his hands lifted from her as though seared, and he backed up a step. 'Ariel?' His voice was tight with fear.

'Yes.'

He turned away and she swung around on the little bench. 'Michael, you must look.'

'No.' He stared at her with wide eyes. His face was white.

Her heart aching, she closed her eyes, visualized Ariel sitting on the marble bench in the cemetery. She felt Michael enter her mind, see Ariel——

Dear God, she was there!

He started to pull back, but she could feel the sight of Ariel holding him, the brittle set of his brother's mouth, the angry eyes. And then Ariel blurred into motion, springing at her, and the ground rose up and struck her in the side and she felt cold stone pressing against her forehead. An overwhelming panic filled her, and she felt it in Michael as well, trapped, watching, powerless to look away.

He means to kill me!

And then she lashed out, plunging into Ariel's brain, finding the cords and lines of him, gathering them and twisting.

Michael screamed and Jenn sprawled forward onto her hands and knees, her head ringing, and then she realized the scream had been only in her mind. Raising her head, she saw him staring at her. His teeth had bared. Still linked to him, she felt his world collapse around him, crying out at the crushing weight of anguish. 'It was an accident,' she cried. 'Didn't you see? I didn't mean to kill him. You've got to believe me.'

Michael ran his hands into his hair and jerked at the roots. She reached out to him, but he stepped back as if her touch would pain him. His repugnance pierced her and she felt hot tears. 'Michael, you saw it. By everything that's holy, I had no wish to kill your brother, only to defend myself. He was going to kill me. Didn't you feel that?'

He stepped toward her, then halted, teetering, as if separate forces inside him were battling for control of his body. 'Dear God, you believed he would kill you, I saw that, yes, but that doesn't mean you were right.'

'Why did he attack, then?'

Michael shook his head, staring at her as if she had changed into something he had never seen before. 'To frighten you off.'

'No.'

She felt Michael enter her mind again, and this time he lurched inside her, all finesse gone, grasping at her mind, out of control. She stumbled back against the bench, knocking it over, falling against the dressing table, hearing the brush and makeup clatter to the floor. 'Michael,' she gasped, 'stop it . . . *please!*'

The room firmed up, and she saw him reel away, hugging his arms to his chest, as though his hands literally had been in her mind. She struggled to rise. He circled back to her, his eyes blazing. I love you so much, but I've lost you. You must run.'

Dismay filled her. 'No, take me to Uziel, explain—'

'You'd be dead in five seconds.'

'And if I had not fought back, I'd be dead already, and you'd be screaming at Ariel. Or maybe he'd just have buried me and let you wonder where I'd gone. He despised me, Michael, the same loathing I felt in your father.'

'Stop!'

'I beg your forgiveness, and your family's. Take me to them. Let me throw myself on their mercy.'

She saw that he was considering it, but then his hand slashed to the side. 'No. Father must have no more chances to kill you. I'll stay away from him, give you a head start. When I go back, he'll probably glean me, even if I resist. I'll try to block him, but I'm not sure I can.'

'Don't! *Let* him read what you saw in me. Let him see that it was not murder but a terrible mistake—'

'It won't matter, you're Chemosh's great granddaughter.' He pushed his hands against his face. 'I wanted you so much that I blinded myself. Jenn, all he'll want in my mind is where you're hiding, and I saw that – the Lincoln Memorial. Father will pry that out of me. Run, damn it. Don't go back with the others.'

'I have to warn them!'

'I'll do that. You must leave the city, at once. They'll be safe because he'll be after you. You'll be all he can think about. Find a cave – or no, a basement apartment in another city, with as many people around you as possible.'

She stared at him, appalled. He didn't know what he was saying. 'My *life* is here, everything I love and need, my career, my home and family . . . you . . .'

'There is only death for you here, Jenn.'

He held out his hands at last and she saw that they were shaking. She took them, feeling a suffocating pressure in her lungs. How could she stop this, she must stop it. He embraced her, holding her tightly. 'Ariel,' he murmured, 'Ariel, you *fool.*'

'Isn't there some way—?'

He squeezed her more tightly, stopping her breath, halting the words in her throat. 'I love you with all my heart,' he said, but if I'm with you it will make you far easier to find. I would fight Father, but he's so strong, the angel of death.'

She clung to him, feeling all the light and life drain from her. Even if Michael could defeat his father, it was unthinkable. The guilt would never leave him. It would be a wall between us forever, Jenn thought. Better to walk out now, and never see him again.

'Maybe we could meet somewhere,' she said, 'in a month, six months. Let's think of a place—'

'No. Father would read it in me. Get away, as far as you can.'

There was nothing more to say. Clinging to him, she felt her heart break, and his own.

Chapter Seventeen

Michael hovered to the east of Jenn's house, searching. His mind felt bruised and dull; with a fierce effort, he found Father's aura at last, nearly due north. Too far to make out any of Uziel's thoughts or feelings — or to fear having his own read — but it was him all right, the faintest trace, like incense lingering in the rafters of a cathedral. He took his cell phone from his belt. When Jenn picked up, he said, 'Eleven. Go. I love you . . .' His voice cracked under the strangling pressure in his throat, and he could say no more.

Eleven o'clock — Father's location to the north — so Jenn would know to head south. Michael watched as she left through her back door, got into her little MG and rolled from the alley behind her house onto Fayette Street. He stayed above her, a lowering bank of rain clouds at his back, keeping track of Father far out at the edge of his range, until she was safely on I-95 heading south. He resisted the urge to swoop down to her, to fly alongside her car and wave her over, climb in with her and go, fleeing Mother, Fabriel, Rafe, leaving them in their grief and running with Jenn. He could imagine himself with her tonight, on the rumpled, neon-lit bed of some roadside motel, her skin hot under his stroking hand, her name on his lips, feeling the rapture of being inside her body and mind at the same moment, of loving her fully.

And then the angel of death descending.

No. When he argued for Jenn's life, he must hope she was as far away as possible.

Father, how could you?

A gentle rain began, taking his tears with it down to the highway. He could barely breathe from grief and a helpless fury. He kept sight of the small red car for as long as he could, feeling her anguish grow fainter until it winked out in his mind.

He turned north, toward the Lincoln Memorial. He would warn her family, as he'd promised, and then he would face his own and pray to God that a spark of mercy might be found in Father.

In Uziel, the slayer of children.

Michael shuddered. How had Father known that horrible order came from God? Had it been a blinding light, a voice like thunder – God as a special effect? Or maybe you'd simply feel a compelling urge that God put inside you, but how could you tell such an urge from one of your own? Slaughtering children did not sound like God, but it did not sound like an angel, either. The air seemed to grow colder around Michael, raising goose-bumps. If Father could kill children and babies because he felt God willed it, how could he fail to destroy Jenn?

I must stay with him every minute, Michael thought. If he pursues her, I'll be with him, and if he tries again to kill her, he'll have to kill me first.

He saw that he was passing over the rail yards of Alexandria, ranging along behind the grubby auto supply stores, fast food joints and strip malls of Route 1. Veering east, he settled into a route upriver that would take him in minutes to the Lincoln Memorial. The rain soaked his clothes and sheeted down his body, plastering his hair back.

Father's trace swelled into a solid contact.

Michael?

Panic thrummed in his chest. He must warn Jenn's family before Father found them in his mind. But if he went to them now and Father followed, they'd be lost anyway.

Michael!

Here.

Come home with me, now. We must talk.

He felt shame in Father, but resolve, too – much stronger.

He'll assume I found Jenn, Michael thought, and that I know about him almost killing her. Both our secrets are out – that I love a phage, and that it *wasn't* a secret to him.

He tried to destroy the woman I love!

Tension flowed down Michael's arms, into his fists. He forced his hands open. *Yes, Father, we must talk – all of us.*

I'll summon the others.

Instead of turning south, Michael continued to face north-east toward the Memorial. Father's trace grew in strength, prodding, herding him. Damn! He must give up warning Jenn's family for now. He must go home.

And hope he was strong enough to keep Father out of his mind.

Michael swerved south. When he got to the house, Drey held the door open for him. The rounded head bowed as he entered, and then Drey raised his eyes, and Michael felt all his love and fear. His stomach clenched.

'My lord . . . don't let it destroy the family.'

Michael took his hands. 'Thank you for everything, old friend.'

'Michael—'

He shook his head and Drey fell silent, blinking back tears.

Father stood at the window of his den, Fabriel and Rafe to one side, Mother in a Queen Anne chair in the corner, where two bookcases joined. On her lap was the *Codex Angelorum*. She and Rafe looked frightened. The faces of Fabriel and Father were closed, watchful.

'Will you tell them?' Father asked.

Michael turned to Mother, feeling that someone else was doing this, a stranger who had taken over his body. He said, 'I'm in love with a doctor at my hospital. She is lovely and kind, and the most moral person I have ever known. She is also a phage.'

'Michael!' Mother's beautiful face drained of blood, her eyes burning against the chalky skin. Rafe bent forward, a hand to his mouth. Their shock tore at him but he felt no guilt.

'She has the heart of an angel.'

'Not the heart, Michael,' Fabriel said softly. 'She *acts* like an angel, but she has the heart of a killer. You admitted as much to me.'

Mother turned to her. 'You knew?'

'In confidence. Michael promised he would tell you if Jenn returned his interest.'

'Father knew too,' Michael said, 'didn't you?'

Uziel stood at the window of his study, his back to them now, watching the water pelt the glass and slide down. The sky beyond the garden was gray as shale. Wind lashed the house.

'Who told you about Jenn and me, Father? Chemosh? Did he come to warn you that I was in love with his great granddaughter?'

'Yes.' Uziel's voice was low, subdued. 'He was afraid you'd tell me, or I'd find out, and that I would then kill her. He warned me if I did, you'd hate me forever. He offered to break the two of you up so I wouldn't have to risk that. To my shame, I agreed.'

'To your *shame!*'

Father turned from the window. 'Yes. And to my greater shame, I fled when I felt you coming this morning. Michael, I want your love with all my heart, but not if we lose you to evil. I should have done my duty, but I was weak.'

'You listened to your heart—'

'The same sin I committed so long ago — *no, be quiet.*'

Michael's words died, stinging, in his throat.

'I put myself first,' Uziel continued, 'above God Himself. I begged Him to release me. *That's* why I haven't heard His voice — not because He turned His back on me, but because I abandoned Him. I didn't realize it. I kept praying, begging Him to come back. I felt abused, wronged.' Uziel's mouth twisted, as though he had tasted something bad. 'If I had finished God's work, destroyed the pharaoh, Ariel would be alive. Instead, Ramses lived to bear another phage, and the line continued, and now his great granddaughter has seduced my son.'

'She didn't seduce me. I went after her.'

'Michael, no!' Mother reached out as if to slap his words down.

'If you would just give her a chance. She's different from other phages—'

Uziel held up a hand. 'Decide who you're with, your family and God, or the eaters of blood.'

Michael felt a sudden, hot defiance. '*You* decide. I love you and Jenn both. Will you throw out a second son because you don't approve of the woman he loves?'

'I will do what is right before God. I failed that test once, but not again. You have one last chance now, Michael, my dear son, and I pray that you will take.it. You were with her an hour ago You must have seen where Chemosh is hiding. Give him up now, and we can work this out.'

Michael felt a freezing rush of fear. He must protect her family. He'd had no chance to warn them as he'd promised. But what could he do?

'I'm sorry,' Uziel said. Michael felt a prickle at the nape of his neck, Father starting to come in—

'Wait!' he shouted.

The tingle subsided, hope softening Uziel's face.

'Chemosh did not murder Ariel,' Michael said. 'No one did.'

Near Fort Belvoir, twenty miles south of Washington, the sorrow became too great. Jenn's foot, of its own accord, left the gas and hit the brake. Horns blared as other drivers swerved around her with angry gestures. Pulling to the shoulder, she sat, watching the wipers push the rain from the windshield. I can't do this, she thought.

I can't leave medicine, my patients.

I can't give up Michael.

He saw inside me and knows I never meant to kill Ariel. He still loves me. I can't run, I *won't*.

Her heart lifted. She would go back, find a way past this so she and Michael could be together.

Jenn accelerated along the shoulder and pulled back into traffic, looking for the next exit.

'When I was with Jenn this morning,' Michael said, 'she asked me to look into her mind. I saw Ariel die, and—'

'Dear God!' Rafe cried.

'—and I know without any doubt that it was an accident.'

Father stared at him with furious, bulging eyes. 'An *accident?*'

'Neural Influence has been emerging in Jenn—'

'*What?*' Father slammed a hand against the wall. Mother came to him and took his arm, her eyes frightened. 'How could a phage have acquired control over neural energy?' she whispered. 'The power to know the human mind comes only from God, and is invested only in us, His angels.'

Father looked shaken, but he said, 'It's not magic, it's physics. And striking the mind *would* kill our son, more quickly than anything a typical phage could do.'

Mother pressed her hands to her mouth and began to weep. Fabriel put an arm around her. Michael longed to go to her but something in Fabriel's face stopped him. How could he make them understand? 'Listen. I'm not making alibis for Jenn, I'm telling you the plain truth, what I saw in her mind. Ariel attacked her, no question. He ambushed her.'

'How did he know about her?' Rafe asked.

'He overheard Chemosh and me in the garden.' Father's voice was low, hoarse. 'I never dreamed he'd act on it.'

'However it happened,' Michael said, 'he knew. He lured her to the cemetery to "talk," then attacked without warning and struck into her mind. She collapsed. In panic and fear for her life, she tried to fend him off. But her ability is so new she hasn't learned to control it, and in her panic, she struck back too hard.

Ariel died from that one purely defensive blow. She is appalled, grief-stricken—'

'Stop!' Uziel snapped. 'I won't have you excusing my son's murderer in my own house.'

'I'm not excusing her. I'm telling you what I felt in her. She came to me to give herself up to us, to beg our forgiveness.'

Father blinked, clearly taken aback.

Michael pressed on. 'Jenn didn't even know I had a brother. Why would she murder him when she was falling in love with me? Ariel must have decided to break Jenn and me up before I caught on that you knew about her. He wanted to prevent a rift between you and me, Father. Maybe he planned simply to warn her, then lost it in the heat of the moment and decided to destroy her. Just kill her, bury her, let me wonder where she'd gone. No one but Father and he ever knows that I loved a phage, and the family is saved — by its youngest member, the one everyone patronizes and pats on the head. He couldn't have imagined that she might be able to hurt, much less kill him.'

'All right, son, if she came to beg our forgiveness, where is she?'

'I told her to run for her life.'

Father's face colored. 'What?'

'You already tried to kill her once.'

'We would have looked in her mind, to find the truth, as you say she wished.'

'And once there, what would you do when you see Ariel die? Could you control yourself? All it would take from you, Father, would be a push, a momentary "loss of control," a spasm of grief, and I would lose the woman I love as I have lost a brother.

'Did she tell you where she was going?' Father asked.

The flat calm in his voice chilled Michael. *I've lost.* 'She wanted to tell me, but I wouldn't let her.'

Father struck into his mind.

Michael felt himself reeling back, seeming to float, and he realized he was falling. He felt no impact; darkness closed in for a second and then he realized he was on the floor. They had gathered around him, stretching up and away, their heads lost in the blaze of a chandelier. Somehow, he must keep them out.

Father, do you remember that time you and I climbed Everest together? The air was thin, freezing, and we had to suck at it to get enough. Then we wasted it laughing, pointing at each other. That was the best day of my life, Father—

Michael realized Father had pulled back. A second later, a tear struck his face. Groping, he found Rafe's ankle and clutched it. 'Tell them to stop,' he gasped.

Rafe shook his head.

He felt Father plunging in again. 'The Lincoln Memorial!' Uziel's voice sounded not triumphant, but tormented. 'Chemosh, yes, and her father and grandfather.'

Above him, Michael saw Uziel press his hands together and bow his head. It seemed that a corona of blood shone all around him. Then Uziel's gaze settled on him again.

'Don't!' Michael cried.

Please, don't fight him, Michael, I beg you. Fabriel's voice in his mind, distant and terrified.

Father screaming in his mind, *give her up, give her up, GIVE HER UP!*

He steeled himself, thinking of Fabriel as a baby, cradling her in his arms, moving his finger back and forth and laughing as her eyes tracked—

Driving south, but will she really do it? Or will she come back to be with her family?

Michael gasped as the fear he had not let himself face tumbled into his view – and Father's.

'Let's go,' Uziel said in triumph.

Michael struggled to get up, but there was no strength in his legs, and he realized Father had scrambled the neurons.

'Wait, please – take me with you.'

'No,' Uziel said. 'If you had told us on your own, but you've chosen – the wrong side. Rafe, stay with your brother. If he tries to follow, stop him.'

Chapter Eighteen

Michael tried to move his leg. Nothing. His teeth ground together in an impotent fury of fear. Any moment now, Father and the others would be reaching the tunnels under the Lincoln Memorial. If Jenn had returned there to warn her family, she'd die.

He tried the leg again. This time it bent slightly.

Not enough – come on, come *on!*

He tried to focus his mind. If he could fly instead . . .

No.

He'd been doing it for centuries, but suddenly he couldn't remember how to reshape gravity, couldn't even reach Rafe mentally, though he was right there, only ten feet away.

What if Father had struck too hard and this was permanent?

Michael wanted to cry out in rage and fear, but his vocal cords produced only a groan. *He could have killed me!*

Michael tried to release the anger and fear. Only one thing mattered – getting to Jenn. From the corner of his eye, he could see Rafe hunched over in his chair, stunned and demoralized. Enough to disobey Father's orders?

Not without a push.

A savage determination flowed into Michael. He would do whatever it took, including turn Rafe against Father. Jenn was more important to him than family, duty, or honor – more important than God. If I were Adam, he thought, I'd eat from the tree rather than lose her—

He felt a distant horror at himself. Was he losing his soul? He did not feel evil, but the wicked often did not.

He flexed his knee again – ah, better. The feeling was coming back into his legs at last. His paralysis was only temporary; he might soon be able to stand and even walk. But he needed more than that. He must be able to control energy again. Making mental contact with Rafe would be a start. He focused his mind on Rafe. Nothing.

When Jenn had used the PET scan to help her make contact, where had the activity been? Auditory cortex.

He imagined the sunny timbre of Rafe's voice.

Help me!

The chair squeaked, and then his brother was kneeling beside him, his face creased with worry. 'What do you want? To sit up?'

Michael nodded. He could feel his heart pounding. Gravity – that was next. He must be able to fly. What did he do to bend gravity? It was lost to him, like certain words to a stroke victim.

Rafe sat him up, carried him to a wingbacked chair and settled him in it. *Hurry! They'll be there soon.*

Michael said, 'You must help me save Jenn.'

Rafe turned, biting at his lip. 'I can't. Father—'

'You think he's *right* in what he is doing?'

'It's not my place to question him.'

'Never? What if he told you to kill me?'

'That's absurd.'

'Don't be too sure.'

'Michael—'

'Two days ago, if I'd told you Father had slaughtered thousands of children and babies, would you have said "never" then, too? I would have. But we'd both have been wrong. Rafe, you are an angel, just like Father and me. You've been alive nearly a thousand years. You see with a sensitivity none of the rest of us have. I could never have fashioned those beautiful creatures in the garden.'

224

Rafe looked away. 'Ariel thought they were useless.'

'He was wrong. You see beauty where others don't even look, but can you find any beauty in what Father has done?'

Rafe held both hands in front of his face. 'Stop it, Michael. I can't listen to this.'

'Yes, you can. Listening and seeing is what you do best, Rafe, and you must do it now.'

'No! Father gave me a job — me, Rafe, the one he thinks is weak, and now you're trying to twist my thinking, because you believe I'm weak, too.'

The torment in Rafe's face made Michael's heart clench, but there was no time for shame. 'I'm appealing to the good in you, brother, not weakness. Do what you know is right.'

'Phages kill for blood. They—'

'Jenn is a healer, Rafe. I loved Ariel, but if you want evil, that was it — him trying to murder her. If you don't help me now, Father will compound that evil and split this family apart.'

Rafe took him by the arms and shook him. 'Damn it, Michael, do you know what you're asking?'

'Use the heart God gave you.'

'I . . . God!' Rafe stalked away, then turned back and grabbed his arms again, this time lifting him, slinging him onto his back. 'The Lincoln Memorial, right?'

Michael wanted to shout with relief. 'Hurry!'

Michael clung as Rafe ran onto the front lawn and sprang into the air. The rain had stopped, leaving the air heavy and cool. Clouds obscured the sun, and lunch-hour traffic choked the George Washington Parkway in both directions, as office workers scrambled for trendy spots along the river in Old Town. Michael closed his eyes, focusing inwardly on his own resurging strength. He began to feel the flow of gravity around him, a tingle in the muscles of his back. As they neared the memorial, he released Rafe's shoulders and pushed away. Rafe rolled onto his back, alarm on his face, then relief.

'Go back,' Michael said.

'Why?'

225

'I don't want Father angry at you. I'll tell him I overcame you, stunned you.'

Rafe's forehead furrowed. 'No. You'll need my help against Father.'

Michael's heart sank. *What have I done?* 'You mustn't ever fight him. He's too strong.'

'I mean in persuading him.'

'Come on, then.' Darting into the lead, Michael passed over the Washington Marina and followed the Potomac. He could see the Lincoln Memorial now, rising above in white splendor. Another presence impinged from the south, and he felt a cold spurt of alarm, then realized it wasn't any of the family but one of the searchers Father had called in from the Cherubini clan of Baltimore, hovering over Anacostia to the south. Head down, the distant searcher ignored him.

Five buses in front of the memorial disgorged a stream of students who ran toward the grand steps, laughing and calling out to each other. Michael dipped into the bushes to one side, the place he'd seen in Jenn's mind. Rafe followed him in against the flank of the monument, and Michael could feel his fear bristling along the nape of his own neck. Ignoring it, he ducked through the door.

An absolute darkness swallowed him; an instant later, his pupils dilated and the passage swam in a murky twilight. He could see no one, feel no one but the tunnel bent ahead — maybe the packed earth was screening someone. He plunged deeper, feeling Rafe at his back, then passing him. Light flowed from Rafe's arms, a rich, warm glow.

How?

I learned it in a bat cave. It's easy. You just—

Never mind. You send enough for both of us. Reaching the bend, Michael peered down a long central tunnel. No one. The smells of earth and old timbers filled his head, and something else, that made his stomach plunge. Blood? Running forward, he searched the packed dirt of the tunnel floor, finding a mass of fresh footprints. A dead flashlight perched on a beam.

'Phew,' Rafe said, wrinkling his nose. 'Iodine . . . and blood, I think.'

'Yes,' Michael said tightly.

Rafe looked perplexed. 'But that makes no sense. If Father fought them here, wouldn't it be with energy? I doubt it would open wounds.'

The weight on Michael's chest lifted. 'You're right. And in such close quarters, a fight with phages could be difficult. It wouldn't be over already. They must have been gone when he arrived.'

'Thank God. Let's go back home. If we could be there before they arrived, Father wouldn't have to know I defied him.'

Michael touched his hand. 'You go. I'm sorry, brother, but I have to find Jenn.'

Rafe took his arm. 'Michael, no. Isn't it enough that she escaped? She didn't come here, or if she did, she and the others are gone. With luck, Father won't find them, and he'll give up, and you'll know she's alive. What more can you hope for?'

'That I can be with her.'

Rafe's eyes glistened. 'Michael, we can't lose you.'

'Make Father see that.'

'Me?' Rafe gave a bitter laugh. 'Come back with me now.'

'I *love* her, Rafe.'

'And what about us, your family that loves you?'

Michael felt a raw pain in his throat. 'I pray we can all be together again, but that is up to Father, not me.'

Rafe shook his head. 'This will end badly, I can feel it. If you do find Jenn, Father will hunt you both. He'll never give up. He'll kill her, and I fear for you if you get in the way.'

Michael wanted to deny it, find the flaw, a part he could dispute. But no. Rafe was seeing the future.

'Come home with me now.'

'Tell Mother and Fabriel that I love them.'

Rafe swallowed, his eyes filling. 'And Father?'

Michael looked away. 'Him too.'

'Where might Jenn be? Do you know?'

'Maybe.'

'But you don't want to tell me.' Rafe's eyes showed a pained self-awareness. 'Right. I'm your man now, but in an hour, I'll be Father's again.'

'Rafe . . .' Michael hugged him, feeling the rounded shoulders convulse. His brother pulled back and walked away down the tunnel, melting away in a blur of tears.

Chapter Nineteen

Uziel felt a painful tightness in his chest as he looked into the face of the newest recruit, this one from the DelArroyo clan of Wilmington.

So like Ariel.

Not physically – his blond hair was clipped close around the perfectly shaped head. Throw a robe over him to hide the leather jacket, jeans, cell phone and Nikes and he'd look like a Buddhist acolyte. But he was intense, like Ariel, anxious to measure up. You could see it in his eager expression and the rigid way he kept his eyes front, not letting himself gawk at the austerity of the prayer room. The moon was perfectly centered in the open skylight now, glazing the walls with a pearly glow, but even that could not lure away his respectful gaze.

'Name?' Uziel asked.

'Melchiah.'

'How old are you?'

'Nineteen.'

Tears pressed at the backs of Uziel's eyes. He resisted an impulse to reach out and touch Melchiah's smooth cheek. Even younger than Ariel, rarest of the rare. He must be kept away from the she-phage. 'You understand that these blood eaters are extremely dangerous, capable of destroying you – that you are to search only? You must not approach any blood eater but must call me or one of my family at once?'

'Yes, sir.'

The youngster flushed, and Uziel could feel his frustration. So very like Ariel — desperate to be given the big job, taken seriously. If I had paid more attention to that, Uziel thought, treated Ariel with more respect, would he have gone chasing off after the she-phage?

And now Michael.

Uziel drew a labored breath, his lungs sheathed in lead. Michael, out looking for the phage, not to do God's will and kill her, but to *join* her. Why couldn't Rafe have been strong for once and stopped him, held him? I should have left Justine to guard him, Uziel thought.

Hindsight. If they'd found the phages in the tunnels under the memorial, Rafe would have been no good in the fight, while Justine — tiny, perfect Justine — would have been a tigress.

Never mind. With luck they would find the she-phage before Michael did. They *must* do that. By now, the word of Ariel's death had no doubt spread to the Evangelines. The offer to help in the search would doubtless come at any moment, and could not be easily refused. Uziel flushed with a horrid, cold premonition of Amator Evangeline being the one to find Jenn, descending on her, only to see Michael rush in to embrace and defend her. At that instant, all hope of regaining place among the angels would vanish in unthinkable scandal and humiliation. Our whole family might become outcasts, Uziel thought.

We must find the she-phage quickly, please, God.

Uziel realized Melchiah was looking into his eyes now, perhaps seeing more than was desirable. 'Very well. Thank you for taking time from the busy duties of your clan to help my family.'

Melchiah bowed. 'An angel has died. We grieve with you.'

Uziel's throat tightened. He put a hand on Melchiah's shoulder. 'Come closer and I'll give you the auras for which you must search.'

Uziel placed his forehead against Melchiah's and thought first of Chemosh, then of the she-phage.

Melchiah started, giving him a slight head-butt, then backing off with a crimson blush. 'Sir— I'm sorry, sir, but I sensed one of those on my way down – the she-phage.'

Uziel's heart missed a beat. 'Where?'

'Up the hill that backs away from Georgetown, near the top. It was such a strong aura I thought it might be a phage, so I veered off to get closer, but then I lost it, so I came here.'

'Where were you, exactly, when you lost it?'

'Near the great cathedral.'

How clever! Concealing his excitement, Uziel nodded at Melchiah. 'Very well. I'd like you to relieve the Cherubini who has been watching Union Station. Tell him he's to follow the rail lines up toward the New Carrollton Station.'

'Yes, sir.' Melchiah's shoulders drooped, but he turned away without complaint. When he was gone, Uziel rose up, exultant, through the skylight, dialing Justine's number on his cell phone as he turned north. The National Cathedral. Multiple layers of granite and stone, excellent shielding – the she-phage was right about that. But she had profaned sacred ground, and now she would die on it.

God is with me!

I *will* get back with Michael.

Though Jenn had no idea how to make the hope into a reality, she clung to it. Without it, she had only despair.

She gazed at the mural behind the chapel's altar, her night vision shifting its rich hues toward the reds, deepening its grimness: Mary, bent over in grief on the arm of one of the apostles, following the body of her son to the sepulcher. Here on canvas was Christendom's grimmest hour. To millions, the woman in mourning was the mother of divinity.

Might it be more than a good story?

Jenn realized she had never really thought about it. She didn't belong to a Church — what one would have her, if they knew what she was? Drinking the pretend blood of communion to remain alive spiritually was one thing, drinking real blood to survive physically quite another. Why me? she wondered. No Church, but I've seen angels, been carried up into the sky by one. Guardians. If they aren't angels, what?

And what am I, that I could kill one?

No, I will not cry again. If Michael can forgive me, I will forgive myself.

Behind her, a foot whispered across stone.

'Losing your edge?' she asked.

'Didn't want to startle you.'

She patted the seat beside her and Zane sank into it, glancing at the mural, then around at the chapel. 'This place gives me the creeps.'

'Surely it was your idea to come here.'

'Only because I knew you'd guess it. And we couldn't stay where we were.'

No chiding in his tone, but she felt uncomfortable anyway, reminded of the hole in her thinking. Instead of worrying about Michael warning them, she should have realized they'd clear out the minute they knew she was gone, in case Uziel caught her and looked in her mind.

Any further lapses in her logic might not be so harmless.

At least she'd figured out to come here. Three years since she and Zane had last been at the cathedral, but it was a night neither of them would forget. Above this very spot, they'd clung to the ramparts of the central tower, his blood spattering her face as she pursued him to the highest pinnacle and cornered him there. The memory made her shudder. But it had ended well, not in Zane's death but in his rebirth, from killer to loving father.

She saw that he was staring into the west arm of the Greek cross that formed the chapel. Two wrought-iron gates closed it off. Even in night vision, the area beyond the gates was dark.

'What?'

'I smell death in there. Decaying bodies.'

'It's probably where they bury the high and mighty of the cathedral.'

'They should bury them deeper.'

She touched his arm. 'Relax. We're in the right place. Look at those pillars – thirty feet in diameter if they're an inch. Thousands of tons of stone above us. If Uziel can detect us through all that, he's not an angel, he's God.'

'Plus I doubt he'd think to look for the likes of us in a church.'

'What's wrong with the likes of us?'

He gave her a mirthless smile.

'Where are Chemosh and Merrick?'

'Reconnoitering. There are other chapels down here in the crypt, other places to hide. But I told them we can't stay here long. It's midnight now; in another eight hours, docents will be arriving to prepare for the daily tours. We could keep to the shadows, hide ourselves, but a rambunctious kid could dart into one of us before we could stop it.'

'Where will you go next?'

'"You?" I don't like the sound of that.'

'I wanted to find you and make sure you're all right. I've done that. Now I need to find Michael.'

Zane started to shake his head; she took his hands, willing him to understand. 'He looked inside me and saw how it happened with Ariel. He knows the truth, and he still loves me. I think I've fallen in love with him, too.'

'That's fine, but—'

'You approve?' Surprise filled her.

'I'm not your great grandfather. I understand why Chemosh hates Uziel, but Michael isn't Uziel, any more than I'm Merrick. I'm just glad one of them is on your side. But if you mean to find Michael and disappear with him, you must take me with you. You've never hidden in your life, and I have done almost nothing else.'

'They can track the energy that radiates from us,' she reminded him. 'The more of us there are together, the easier we'd be to find.'

'But if Uziel does find you, you'll need help fighting him.'

'And get you killed too? Uziel isn't Ariel. He's the angel of death. Our best hope lies in evading him, and the fewer of us there are together, the easier that will be.'

She squeezed his hands, pained by the misery on his face.

'You said Michael was going to try and persuade Uziel to back off. Do you think he can?'

Jenn remembered her terror down in the gutter, Uziel peering through the slit at her, the hatred in his eyes as he'd pointed his hand at her. Nerves rattled in her stomach, like leaves kicked up in a sudden wind. 'I doubt it.'

'Then you must find him and get away together.'

Jenn was dumbfounded. She had expected Zane to go on arguing, maybe even try to restrain her, the way he'd carried her off at the cemetery. Did he hope that Uziel would be unable to kill her if she was with his son?

Or maybe he just wanted her to have the chance at love, no matter what.

Warmth spread through her and she leaned over and kissed his cheek. She had never loved him so much.

He cleared his throat. 'All right, then. How do you propose to link up with Michael?'

'I don't know. If he really believes he could stop his father from killing me, he's probably sticking close. If not, he may be looking for me on his own by now. Maybe if I went to his office at the hospital—'

'No. You mustn't go anyplace Uziel might expect you.'

'Then how do I find him?'

'You don't. Let him find you. You've only known him two days, but he's known you for years, watched you, seen where you like to go and spend time. Think where he might hope to find you, and go there.'

She felt like kissing him again. 'That's brilliant.'

He gave a faint smile. 'Not really. I spent a lot of years thinking where Merrick might hope to find me so I would *not* go there.'

Jenn thought of where Michael might look for her, and at once she knew. She resisted the urge to tell Zane; if Uziel found him, the less he knew the better. She said, 'If I can link up with Michael, we'll both need to get out of Washington. Tell me a good place to go.'

Zane sighed. 'It's not so simple. Running isn't just a place to hide, it's a state of mind. I ran from your grandfather for five hundred years. I got to where the nerves in the back of my neck would tell me when he was close. I learned how to leave no tracks, cast no shadow. These are not things I can simply tell you. You have to have lived it.'

'Then I'll live it now. Think of an escape you did that might be helpful for me. I'll enter your memory of it and absorb it, make it mine.'

He looked at her as if she'd gone mad.

'I'm not kidding. I've been in Michael's mind. Also in the minds of a patient and a nurse on my ward. It's a . . . vivid experience.'

'Have you been doing that to us?'

'No, and I wouldn't ever. Not without permission. But this could work. You think of a "great escape" you've brought off. When you have it firmly in mind, nod, and I'll come in. It should be easy — as father and daughter, we share a lot of DNA, which means our brain chemistry should be fairly similar, too.'

She saw that Zane had gone pale. Was he afraid she might hurt him? 'It's nothing like what I did in fighting Ariel,' she assured him. 'Don't be afraid.'

'All right.' But the tension remained in him; she could feel it. He closed his eyes. 'I got away from Merrick in Washington three different times,' he said softly. 'The one most like your situation was when Merrick was with the police and had men watching Union Station, Dulles, National and BWI . . .'

Jenn closed her eyes too, following his voice back into his mind. She heard the cry of an exotic bird, felt the warm, humid air of a jungle on her face. Suddenly his memory was pouring into her, the escape itself — in the hold of a plane. How clever she thought. She saw snow-covered fields, and then it was hot — a maze of trails through the bush in what had then been called Tanganyika. Then some mountains she knew in an instant were in a national park out west. Somehow, without knowing how, she had branched out from the first memory and was exploring in his mind. A dizzying flood of details poured into her, too fast to follow, and yet she could feel that her brain was absorbing them all, making the memories her own, as if they had happened to her.

She was in the hall of an apartment building now. The pit of her stomach throbbed, and she felt herself seizing the memory, slowing it down, wanting to see and experience every thrilling moment as she/her father—

thought of Sophie's slender wrist, how the blood would feel against his lips. It seemed so long since he had killed. Actually, only a few months, during which he'd managed to keep control, turning away from the exposed throat or wrist, running out with the transfusion packs, fighting off the gene's demand to kill that raged through him as powerfully as the hunger.

And now he was going to waste all that, just as he had after all the previous excruciating rounds of controlling himself.

Zane almost turned around and retreated down the hallway. But he knew if he managed to hold firm tonight, he would only start killing again with the next target, or the one after, no matter how he might wrestle against it. In the end he would do what he so craved, no matter the consequences. A groan turned like broken glass in his throat. He hated lying to Jenn. He'd do anything within his power for her . . .

But this was not within his power.

That's what Jenn refused to understand, would never accept. If he was honest with her, told her he had pushed himself to the limit of his endurance in an effort to win her approval and had failed, she'd stop seeing him, would have nothing more to do with him, and that he could not bear. So he must go on squirming on the gaff of her trust, letting her believe he had stopped killing.

Ironically, though he could not stop, he had changed. For five hundred years I never gave a thought to who I killed. If I saw someone and wanted to, I did. Now I learn all I can about them first. I make sure there will be as few as possible to grieve for them.

Galling. His love for Jenn had infected him, making him empathize, even with normals. Not enough to stop him from killing them, just enough to torture him with guilt.

Zane listened at Sophie's door. She was always in by ten o'clock, usually before, and it was now ten-thirty. Beyond the door, paper hissed across paper, yes, there she was in the corner, in her favorite chair, reading as usual.

You can still stop this.

An image of Jenn came to him — Jenn in that same chair, reading a medical journal. He sank to his haunches, trembling with sorrow and a vast frustration. He did not want to imagine Jenn now, of all times, but there she was in his mind, sighing in contentment as she turned the page, feeling safe and comfortable. What if another phage, older and more powerful, came after her? Phages could die, he had almost died himself, when Father had locked him away in that vault. If someone took Jenn from him, how could he go on living?

Damn it, Jenn was not going to die! She was predator, not prey, even if she never killed.

A door opened down the hall. Without moving, Zane blanked himself from the man's eyes until the elevator closed behind him.

He rose from his haunches, staring at Sophie's door, reviewing the weeks of research he'd compiled since first selecting her in a grocery store, picking the telltale single TV dinners from the frozen-food counter. She has no one. Her parents died years ago, no brothers or sisters. A quiet loner, who lives for her work and would rather read a book than go to lunch with the few who consider her a friend. No one will miss her much or for long.

Zane took the key to her apartment from his pocket — the copy he'd made from the one in her handbag. He eased the bolt over, opened the door and stepped inside.

'Who's there?' cried a frightened voice.

Reaching out with Influence, he dilated her jugulars and by the time he could take the three steps in from her foyer, she had sagged over in the chair, unconscious. The book plopped to the floor beneath her dangling hand. Excitement rode him like a hussar now. Goading him to her side, making him kneel so that his mouth was close to her exposed throat. He wanted her blood, all of it, now! With an effort, he turned his head aside, swallowing convulsively.

He must keep to the plan.

Carrying her into her bedroom, he put her on the bed and undressed her, taking care to pay no attention to the pale, slender body. She was not unattractive, but if he followed that thought, sexual desire would well up, blocking his lust to kill, and he had already gone too long without feeding.

Turning his back, he neatly folded her clothes and put them on the chair by the bed. In Sophie's bathroom, Zane stoppered the tub and turned the faucets on, adjusting the temperature, because he must not assume she would lie undiscovered until morning. Details; always and above all, details. While the tub filled, he went to the kitchen and took the Sabatier knife from its place in the drawer. The blade was very sharp. After reading, cooking was Sophie's second passion.

When he returned to the bathroom, the tub was full. He put Sophie in, taking care that her head did not slip below the water. Keeping his eyes on her throat, he felt his own pulse double the slow beat of hers. His throat crawled with hunger. He raised one wrist from the water and laid it along the edge of the tub. Curling the fingers of her other hand around the butt of the knife, he brought it over with a shiver of anticipation. After the few shallow, experimental cuts the medical examiner would expect, he guided her hand through a deep, clean slice. Blood gushed up and he fell on it, drinking, filling his throat with the food of the gods—

'No!'

Jenn's scream echoed back to her from the vaulted ceiling. Leaping up, she stared down at Zane. Her whole body ached, as if she'd fallen ten stories. Horror caught in her throat, choking her. She bent over and retched a dry heave. Feeling Zane's hand on her back, she twisted away and forced herself upright. His face was white, wincing, 'Jenn—'

'Don't.' Her throat crawled with the thirst for blood.

'I tried not to think of it,' he said brokenly. 'But that only made me think of it.'

'You lied to me! You swore you had stopped. You let me go on believing it!'

'Because I knew you'd reject me. Please, Jenn, you mustn't. I need you, I'll try again, I'll try harder—'

'No!'

Footsteps, running, Chemosh and Merrick. She turned as

they sprinted into the chapel. *Merrick! He's strong again. Will he feel he has to stop Zane? If he must hunt him again, it would destroy them both.*

'What is it?' Chemosh asked. 'What's wrong?'

'Nothing. Zane and I were arguing and it got out of hand. I have to leave now and find Michael.' She hurried down the row of chairs, tipping one over in her haste. She must get out of here, away from Zane, *now!*

'Wait,' Chemosh said. 'Don't go. With us, you stand a chance—'

'I have to. Zane agrees – he'll explain.'

'She's right. Let her go.' Zane's voice was hoarse.

She hugged Merrick, then Chemosh, feeling their confusion and unhappiness. 'I love you, Grandfather. And you, Chemosh. Stay here – you'll be safe.'

She ran from the chapel, through the dark crypt, feeling Zane cry out in her mind. She slowed, but only for a second.

Chapter Twenty

Michael ended his search back at Hugh's grave. Frustration burned in him, a desperate sense of time slipping away. He had felt so sure Jenn would come here.

Maybe she'd kept going south.

But I don't really believe that, he thought, and Father will act on what he saw in my mind. It's fine to hope she's somewhere else, but I must hunt her here in Washington, because that's where Father will hunt.

He scanned the slopes around him. From the knoll on which Hugh had been buried, he could see the back acres of Columbia Gardens. Ancient oaks that would, in summer, shield the graves from the hot sun cut off his view of Arlington Boulevard to the south, but he could hear scattered traffic, tires hissing through what was left of the earlier rainstorm. After midnight the temperature had dropped, and a light mist now hung over the tombstones, as the heat of the earth rose up and condensed into an eerie breath of the dead. He looked again at each of the mausoleums he could see from the grave. Good places for Jenn to hide from Uziel, but he had missed none of them.

Time to move on, but where?

If only he could commune with her dead husband. *You knew her before I did, Hugh. Where would she go?*

Michael remembered one summer afternoon among the

many, Jenn kneeling by this headstone, a mower droning in the distance. Two sparrows had tumbled over each other in the bliss of mating, nearly hitting her, but she hadn't even looked up. How his heart had ached for her, that she would heal, that she might one day love him half as much as she had Hugh.

Michael rose up above the trees. Arlington was all but dark, the huge enclave of early-rising federal workers snug in their beds. He headed east toward the lights of the city, veering back over Arlington Boulevard. A small car sped toward him – red, an MG! Hovering, he watched it slow at the gate to Columbia Gardens. His heart missed a beat, then pounded madly. Diving back below the sheltering branches, he swooped along the cemetery's roadway and dropped to the pavement fifty feet in front of the car. Jenn slammed on the brakes and leapt out, running to him. He threw his arms around her and she buried her head against his shoulder, sobbing as if her heart would break.

Dismay turned in him, sharp-edged. Had Father killed one of her family? 'Here,' he said, 'we must get out of sight.'

Lifting her, he sped to the nearest of the mausoleums, fashioned from thick blocks of granite faced in marble. Setting Jenn down, he opened the iron gate and led her down steps into the chill darkness. Stone benches lined the wall; she sat and he settled beside her. 'Now tell me what's wrong.'

She searched his face. 'Will you promise to do nothing?'

'Did my father—?'

'No, mine. His name is Zane—'

'Yes.'

'That's right, you . . .' She swallowed. 'Have you ever . . . read him?'

'No.'

'I wish I never had.' She struck the marble beside her with the heel of her fist. 'Damn him! Damn him to hell! Oh! I'm sorry.'

'It's all right. I'm an angel, not a nun.'

She bent over, staring at her fists. He could feel her anguish, cold as the floor. 'You must promise not to harm him.'

'I protect. I do not harm.'

She gazed at him, nodded. 'He's still killing. I saw it in his mind . . .' She took a deep breath, almost a gasp. 'He had sworn he would not, and at first he didn't – I know because I went out with him. But then he wanted to go on his own. Said I had to trust him, and I did, I did trust him, but he started killing again, months ago, and he let me go on believing he wasn't.' Her eyes glistened.

He put an arm around her. 'I'm sorry, so sorry.'

She focused on him. 'You're sad, too. Something has happened to you.'

'Never mind.'

'Michael!'

'It seems we both have father problems. Mine struck me down, paralyzed me, raped my mind to find where you might have gone.' He felt suddenly on the verge of tears.

She leaned into him.

'We must get away from them,' he said. 'Far away, and as fast as we can.'

'Yes.' She straightened. 'Can we do it, truly get away?'

'Of course. Nothing to it.'

She gave a shaky laugh. He kissed her hands and tried to think. She was depending on him now, and he had no plan, no idea what to do next. All he'd wanted was to find her, and now he had. But they would not be together long if he could not start *thinking!*

'I know how we can get away,' Jenn said.

'How? Father has over forty angels from other clans helping him. They're up there watching – not just the city but the suburbs. You were lucky to get this far—'

'We're going to catch a plane.'

'Impossible. He'll have all the airports watched.'

'What about the air *fields*? What about Andrews Air Force base? We can stow away.'

The crisp urgency in her voice lifted him. He would not have thought of using a military air base, and Father might not either. 'How do we get all the way down to Andrews without being detected?'

'How high is the surveillance?'

'Around a thousand yards. That cuts down on their acuity, but allows each to monitor a fairly wide area until more help arrives.'

'Has your father told them to look for you, too?'

A key question, Michael realized. By now Father would have returned home to check on him and Rafe, and would know he had gone looking for Jenn. But would he tell other angels to search for and restrain his own son? No. That would shame and humiliate him, Michael thought. *He'll be terrified that Amator will learn I'm in love with the phage who killed my brother. He dare not even mention me to the other clans and he has to be hoping no one even sees me.*

'Father won't have told them about me – not yet.'

'All right, good,' Jenn said. 'I drive. You stay close above me, screening me off from above. If you're seen, whoever spots you will assume you're helping your family search. All you have to do is stay between me and whoever's closest, and if one of them does spot me and close in, you can warn them back – they'll defer to you, won't they, as long as no one else from your family is there to overrule you?'

'Yes.'

'Then I think we can make it, don't you?'

Her conviction flowed into him, pushing him to his feet. 'Let's go.'

Crossing above the central 'Gloria in Excelsis' tower, Uziel first felt Ramses, then saw him, emerging from the crypt entrance on the south side of the cathedral. A savage excitement filled him, and then his heart stuttered as two others stepped out behind him, powerful auras – phages!

But no she-phage.

Maybe she was still inside.

If so, it would be three against four. Should he draw back and call Rafe in? No. God was with him, strike now!

Uziel felt a burst of anxiety from Fabriel as she saw the phages. *Be strong now! Just do as your mother and I do!*

Extending his left arm, Uziel felt the power flow into it, not as great as he would have liked. *God, I need more!*

And then the terrible white bolt flashed down and the ground flared in a sizzle of winter grass.

One of the phages fell, but then staggered up again.

I must get closer!

Uziel dived, calling Fabriel and Justine after him, as one of the phages, a powerful looking brute, picked up the stumbling one and leapt, sailing back through the dark entrance twenty feet away, almost as if he'd flown. Ramses dashed in behind him, all three phages now back inside.

Uziel felt his teeth grind. Could nothing be easy?

Hitting the ground running, he dashed down the steps into the crypt. The footsteps of the fleeing phages rang off the stone ahead. As his eyes peeled away the dark, he saw them dart aside into one of the chapels of the crypt. Uziel felt Justine close at his heels, and Fabriel right behind her. Brave Fabriel, *preserve her, God. I cannot lose another!*

Uziel raced into the cross-shaped chapel, then stopped, surprised, as Ramses stepped from behind a pillar. Motioning Justine and Fabriel to stay behind him, he readied himself to strike, but then the other two phages stepped out, flanking Chemosh. One resembled him strongly, the other was the broad-shouldered creature.

'This is my son, Merrick,' Ramses said, indicating the big one. 'And my grandson, Zane.'

Where did he think he was, a receiving line? Triumphant, Uziel raised his left arm.

'I'm sorry for the death of your son.'

Uziel stared at him.

'It was an accident. Surely you know that. But if you must have revenge, take me and leave my children.'

'No,' Zane said, pushing in front of Chemosh. 'Take me.'

Merrick stepped away from the other two, and Uziel felt a

warning shock in his knees, blood Influence – very strong, this big one. Uziel was aware suddenly of a faltering in Fabriel, a grudging admiration. He felt a chill jolt of alarm – he must not lose her support. Looking at Chemosh, he crafted his words for Fabriel. 'If I had destroyed you at Per Ramesse, when God intended, these sons would never have existed, nor your great granddaughter, who killed my son. Tell me where she went, and God may grant you peace in your graves.'

'And what will He grant you for killing all those children?'

'You think I wanted that?' Uziel cried. 'It was God—'

'It was *you!* I hear their cries every night, you murderous, demented old bastard! I see my son squirming and dying under your hand. Behold the slayer of babies.'

Uziel felt Fabriel's confusion deepening. *Why am I arguing with this demon?* He raised his arm again, felt Justine behind him, raising hers as well, and then, suddenly, he was blind.

The big one, striking at my eyes.

He let the bolt of energy fly, heard the clang of iron as one of the gates of the burial ground blew backward into the dark, stone cavern, and still he could not see. Fabriel screamed behind him, and his heart leapt with fear. Rubbing at his eyes, he reached out mentally, groping for the mind of Ramses, finding it, but then a powerful blow struck him from the side, hurling him across the chapel. Wood shattered across his flank as he fell – the altar. Vision came back, but he felt thick, now, stupid.

The arteries in my neck!

He fought back, opening the pinched blood vessels with his own powers of mind, but they narrowed again, cheating his brain of blood.

He saw Zane lunge at Fabriel, down among the chairs, fast as an eel. Terrified for his daughter, he struck out mentally at Zane.

'Look out!' Justine shouted, and then the air left him as Merrick smashed into him again, carrying him in a bull's rush back into the mural, plaster crunching under him. He lashed out with the white fire, but Merrick deflected his arm, and the vaulted ceiling of the chapel glowed white as bits of granite showered down.

Uziel lashed out again, but Merrick was fast, dashing to the side as a row of chairs burst into flames. A charred scent filled Uziel's nostrils and his hair crackled with ozone. Merrick rushed at him again. Uziel struck him down, but the phage rolled over, and then the chapel went dark again, as the blood flow to his retinas cut off.

We're too close to them. We can't win in here. Get out!

Pain seared his eyes and Uziel cried out, clawing at his pinched lids. In a teary haze, he saw that Fabriel had the one called Zane on his back, straddling him, but her eyes were glazed, the phage cutting off blood to her brain. Justine had Ramses pinned against a pillar as she rubbed at her eyes with the other hand. Turning back to Fabriel, he struck into Zane's mind, visualizing the neurons, gripping them in his mind, a sheaf of lights — red, black, ultraviolet and a golden white, buzzing together—

Then felt the she-phage, a trace in his mind, quite fresh!

Following her lingering luminescence, Uziel found himself observing an airfield from a narrow crack between two giant doors. His spine tingled — Zane's fear when he had looked out on this same runway. Zane in hiding, yes, inside a hangar of the airfield.

Father won't find me. I'll get away, as I always do . . .

His own *father?*

With astonishment, Uziel realized the one called Zane had hidden many times, over hundreds of years.

And now he'd given that experience to his daughter.

If I can unravel this memory, I'll know where she is!

Holding himself in the memory, Uziel saw that the planes on the runway were military. He back-pedaled from the hangar, getting images of a chain-link fence running along a busy highway, a McDonald's, a dark sky, a line of cars waiting to turn in at the gate . . . and *there*, a sign beside the guard station, precise tan letters on a brown background — *Andrews Air Force Base!*

A blow in the small of his back smashed Uziel from the memory. Merrick again, throwing him high. He crashed to the stone floor, an instant of withering pain. Groping mentally for Merrick's spine, he ripped at the neurons and the big phage went down, thrashing, but still striking back with Influence. Half in a fog, Uziel stumbled to Fabriel, who still sat astride Zane, her eyes dull. Zane's were pinched shut in agony, as light from Fabriel's hand pooled on the floor around him, too weak to kill, but immobilizing him with pain.

Lifting Fabriel from Zane, Uziel raced for the door. He could not win here, and he must get to the she-phage before she could do what she'd seen in her father's mind. He saw Justine, still against the great pillar, her hands locked around Ramses' throat, but not tightly enough.

Out! Justine. Leave them — we must go!

She released Ramses and ran after him. Outside, cold air shocked his face, clearing his mind. He wheeled south with Fabriel and Justine, driven by a rising exultation. The others didn't matter, he would kill them later. It was the she-phage who mattered, thinking she was safe, that she could kill an angel and get away.

Not while I still draw breath.

Chapter Twenty-One

Jenn could feel her heart pounding as she and Michael slipped into the cavernous darkness of Hangar 17. Almost free, but they hadn't made it yet. What if no planes took off tonight? Every second of waiting would be an agony, to be caught so close to escape, unbearable.

Sharp smells of aviation fuel and burnt insulation triggered an intense deja vu in her as she studied the hangar. It had changed little in the years since Zane had hidden here. The ceiling loomed high above them on the backs of steel girders. A huge, fat-bellied cargo jet dominated the center of the hangar, electric cords draping from its wings, wheeled stairways attending its flanks like bowing acolytes. She heard bat wings whispering through the vaulted darkness, and then the dainty footfalls of a mouse. The nape of her neck prickled – eerie, that a place she had never been to could be so familiar. She was inside Zane's skin.

And she did not like it.

'What next?' Michael asked.

'Wait for a plane to start up.' She could see it all clearly in her mind, each move to make. Would they get the chance?

Calm down, she told herself. Her hands were cold. She stuffed them into the pockets of her slacks, the white ones she'd worn to the hospital this morning, a thousand hours ago. Scared silly. Damn Uziel. If she had not looked him in the eye, come so close to death — but she had, and if she lived to two thousand, the memory would still scare her.

'Are you all right?'

'Come on.' She led him to the towering hangar doors. A gap of a few inches gave her a view of the runway. A medium-sized cargo-type jet sat at the head of the runway. The cockpit light was on, but she could see no one inside, and the engines were dead.

'How fast can you fly?' she asked Michael.

'Never clocked myself.'

'As fast as a jet?'

'No. Father couldn't catch up once we're airborne, if that's what you're worried about. But let's hope it isn't that close.'

'Amen.'

She closed her eyes. *Please let us make it!*

Michael squeezed her hand. 'Was that a prayer?'

Startled, she said, 'Are you reading me?'

'No. I've seen a lot of people pray.'

'Listen!' The rising growl of engines starting up; the door of the hangar vibrating suddenly against her shoulder. Pressing her face to the crack, she sighted the plane at the end of the runway. The air behind the engines shimmered. A ground crew was converging on the aircraft now, rolling stairs up to the door of the cargo bay.

'Let's go!'

'Too late.' Michael's voice was flat. 'I can feel Father. He's coming, fast. Fabriel and Mother are with him.'

The hackles rose on Jenn's neck as she felt it too, a faint touch that quickly grew stronger. Her mind blanked with panic.

'They're too close,' Michael cried. 'They'll cut us off!'

'We're going — it's our only chance.' She ran for the door, hearing Michael behind her, his footsteps drowned out by the rising pitch of the engines. Bursting from the hangar, she sprinted for the plane two hundred yards away. She could feel Uziel and the others closing from the north. Michael scooped her into his arms, lifting her from the tarmac, flying low.

Looking north, she saw Uziel, great wings flaring, only a few hundred yards away. Her heart stuttered in her chest.

Looking back at the plane, she saw the cargo door closing. 'Hurry, Michael – oh God, *hurry!*'

The distance to the plane shrank; she watched Uziel blaze toward them, and then something snapped inside her and she struck out at him, but the range was too great and he barely faltered.

Twenty yards to the plane, and Uziel under a hundred. The door nearly shut, and then Michael dove with her through the narrowing slice, the crewman jerking back at the gust of their passing. Turning, Jenn grabbed the door from the inside and slammed it the rest of the way shut. Terror struck through her knees and she nearly collapsed, hanging onto the door to stay upright.

Seconds crawled by and still the plane did not move. She could feel Uziel outside, waves of fury and anguish.

The plane began to roll.

Michael tensed beside her and his lips moved silently, and then she heard an echo of him in her mind—

No, Father!

I beg you, Michael, stand away from her.

He can get us through the metal, Jenn thought, terrified.

Leave us alone!

Come back to us, we love you. There's still time. You can stop this, please, son, please.

Michael's mother, Jenn realized.

The plane accelerated, lifting from the runway. She sank to the floor of the cargo bay. 'We made it!' she cried, then saw the anguish in Michael's eyes. 'Oh, Michael, I'm sorry—'

'Their choice.'

Kneeling beside her, he pulled her into his arms. She clung to him, listening to the wonderful, soothing roar of the airplane, feeling the vibration against her knees. After a moment, she rose and looked around. The cargo bay was filled with military vehicles, squat and square looking, larger than jeeps – *humvees*. Crates labeled 'Comm' and 'Amm' lined the walls.

'I wonder where we're going?' she said.

'Bogotá. This is for their military to use against the drug kingpins.' He waved an arm at the equipment.

'How do you—? Oh.' The minds of the crew. But why did Michael still look so grim?

Her heart sank as she realized what it was. Uziel will find out where we're headed, she thought. He'll call ahead. Other angels, his allies, will be waiting for us when we land.

'We *haven't* made it,' she said.

'Not yet.'

Chemosh imagined Uziel drifting in the sky above the overpass, searching in the dawning light, moving closer as he saw the mouth of the culvert. It made his flesh crawl. Was twenty feet of earth and half an inch of corrugated steel enough?

We held him off, but that's all. Next time he'll make sure we're in the open and pick us off.

Why wasn't he waiting when we left the cathedral?

Another image came, of Uziel hunting Jenn, instead; of Jenn dying alone, without her family around her. Was that it, why Uziel hadn't been waiting? Had he picked up on Jenn, somehow, as he'd left the cathedral? He would want her the most.

But if she'd been near the cathedral, he'd have sensed her to begin with.

I'm missing something, Chemosh thought.

Zane moved forward from the gloom, put his back to the other side of the culvert and slid down to his haunches. 'I'm afraid for Jenn.'

'She's intelligent and resourceful, and she has powers we do not.'

'So you're scared, too.'

'Terrified.'

Merrick moved up with them, settling beside his son. 'If we knew where she was . . .' He let the sentence hang.

'Actually, I might,' Zane said. 'I . . . let her into my mind to see an escape I made from Andrews Air Force Base more than twenty years ago. I stowed away on a military cargo plane.'

Chemosh felt the blood drain from his face.

'What's wrong?' Merrick asked.

'Uziel must have gone into our minds during the attack. I wasn't worried, because we didn't know where Jenn went. But if she was in your mind, he saw it, saw everything she saw. Damn! That's why he left so fast, without killing us.'

Zane rose, bumping his head. 'We have to get down there, now!'

'Hold on. We won't do Jenn any good if they pick us off coming out of here.'

'We can't just—'

'Wait, I'm thinking. If Uziel *got* Jenn at Andrews, the searchers will still be all over the city, looking to mop us up. But if he failed, he'll have moved the search to wherever the plane went.'

'If that's what happened,' Merrick said, 'we have to try and catch up, find out what plane she could have taken, and where.'

Zane said, 'She'd have hidden in the same hangar I used, off the same runway. It's unlikely more than one or two planes took off from there in the middle of the night. I'll go into the control tower and look at the logs. I'm sure as hell not going to sit in this hole any longer. If they get us coming out, they get us. Otherwise, we go after Jenn.'

Chemosh stood, too. 'Well, gentlemen, what are we waiting for?'

The cargo hold was getting colder every minute, the floor glittering with frost. The air seemed thinner too, though the hold was pressurized. Jenn sucked a breath, fighting a suffocating, trapped feeling. We can't be on this plane when it lands, she thought. What is Michael waiting for?

He sat across from her, his eyes closed, probably still

monitoring the mind of the pilot, waiting for some indication of where they were.

Panama, Jenn thought. That's what we want. It borders Colombia, and I know my way around there.

Zane's way around.

She felt a grim resignation. It hurt even to think about Zane, but she must hold him in her mind now – their survival might depend on it. The plane he'd hopped from Andrews Air Force Base twenty-five years ago had gone not to Bogotá but to Utah; she could remember hiding at night in a canyon among weirdly shaped pinnacles of red rock.

But a century before that, Zane had escaped Merrick in the jungles of Panama.

Impatient, Jenn entered the mind of the co-pilot. The three men in the cockpit were talking about Bogotá now, a whore-house the co-pilot had heard of. None of the men had any intention of actually going there, but Jenn found herself flushing at the images going through the co-pilot's mind, bawdy antics with slender, bronze-skinned women. As she started to back from his mind, he said, 'Oops – Panama's coming up, boys. Time to turn a little south.'

Jenn turned to Michael. He was already at the cargo door, his hand on the latch. When it opened, there would be a huge furore up in the cockpit, but there was no help for that.

'Grab my shoulders,' Michael said.

She gripped him loosely around the neck and wrapped her legs around his waist. The latch resisted for a second and then the cargo door slid open one foot, two. The thin air screamed past the opening, and litter on the floor gusted out past their feet, and then Michael leapt through. The slipstream smashed into them and she glimpsed the plane tearing away ahead, a dark shape that dwindled with shocking speed. The consternation of the flight crew faded in her mind as she lost sight of the plane.

Beyond Michael's shoulder, ocean glowed with an ultramarine intensity – and there, the darker edge was a shoreline. She made out scattered lights. At first there was no real sense of falling, but then the ocean began rapidly to etch with detail. A huge patch of moonlight glowed, swelling toward them. It was beautiful. Warm air, heavy with moisture, filled her lungs, and she felt the tension letting go inside her, a wonderful feeling of release. Let them wait in Bogotá. Let Uziel come down and find his lieutenants empty-handed.

Now we've made it, she thought. At least for awhile.

Michael began to brake their fall, veering toward the coastline. She looked with longing down at the glittering blue ocean.

'I haven't swum in ages,' she said into Michael's ear.

She felt some of the tension go out of his shoulders. 'Did you bring your suit?'

We're going to be alone together, really alone. She became aware of his strong back pressing into her breasts. Suddenly, she was kissing his ear, running her tongue into the delicate lobes, laughing as his head jerked then leaned back to her tongue. She could smell the sea, salt and kelp, see the moon glinting off waves — they were almost down! She sucked a deep breath, and then her feet broke the waves. She kept hold of Michael as they plunged down together into the cool, blue-black depths. She could not tell if she was rising or still sinking, and then a fish swam by, dropping below them, half visible through the swarming silvery bubbles churned up by their descent. Clutching Michael to her, she kissed him, taking a bubble of air from his mouth, and laughing it out again. She thought how wonderful it would be to make love to him down here.

Their heads broke the surface, and Michael grinned at her, water streaming down his face, his hair slicked back, gleaming in the moonlight.

'How long do we have before we need to get to shore?' she asked.

He sobered. 'Whoever meets the plane will read the minds of the crew and realize the cargo door opened in flight. They'll know just about where it happened. I'd say the sooner we get into the jungle and start losing ourselves, the better.'

'Did I say I wanted the truth?'

He touched her cheek, his eyes sad.

Jenn's teeth chattered, the water suddenly cold. Michael was right. She might, through Zane, know a jungle she'd never been in before, but the hunter this time was not Merrick but one who could drift along above the treetops, could sense her below even if he couldn't see her.

One who had only death in his heart.

Chapter Twenty-Two

When thou lookest into the mind of man, taste not the wine of his soul, lest ye drink deeply and become as the eater of blood. For the thoughts of man flow on sweet rivers but to drink thereof bringeth great harm to him and thee. Inasmuch as thou hast sworn to protect him, if thou takest the currents of his life into thyself, and the vigor thereof, thou hath broken thine oath before God. Therefore look only, that ye fall not as those others.

Codex Angelorum VI, 12

Jenn winced as Michael slapped aside a branch behind her. Couldn't he be quiet? She'd shown him how to hold branches away and slip under with no more than a rustle, but he seemed incapable of grasping the technique. His feet kept catching on vines, and every minute it seemed a rotting branch snapped with a loud report under his tromping feet. Two days in the jungle, and he was still as noisy as a bull elephant.

But why worry about noise?

Because Zane had, right here, a hundred years ago.

Spooky – she was not simply remembering Zane's passage here, she was, in a real sense, reliving it. If she had not absorbed Zane's trail skills, embedded in the memories, she'd be stumbling along as clumsily as Michael. This place should amaze her; instead, she felt a renewed sense of familiarity with the heavy, baking heat, the sudden rains, the density of the foliage — vegetation everywhere, plants growing right out of other plants, blanketing the ground in layer after rising layer and enshrouding the towering tree-trunks so thoroughly no bark was visible. Scant sunlight penetrated the canopy to this depth, and yet everything was a vibrant green. She had never seen so many shades of green before . . .

And yet, she *had*.

She listened to the clamorous calls of birds and monkeys in the canopy of the rain forest, high overhead. She didn't know their names, but she kept getting mental pictures of which animal went with which sound. That chittering in the tree-tops came from a black monkey with white at its throat and a saucy curve at the end of its tail. The strangled 'awwwwrk-ra-a-a-ack', cry went with a red, yellow, and blue bird that looked like a parrot, and another bird babbling 'pretty-pretty-pretty' with high-pitched enthusiasm was brown, with a long, curved beak. Its presence meant there was probably a grassy area or marsh not far away.

Sliding a hanging vine aside, she slipped ahead, continuing to practice Zane's silent stealth, even though she knew Uziel could sense them down here long before he could hear them. An avenging angel of death, drifting along two hundred feet above them, hidden by the canopy—

Cut it out!

She shivered, despite the heat.

'I'm beginning to understand why people slap mosquitoes,' Michael grumbled. 'They make a very irritating noise.'

She became aware of the constant whine around her ears, feathery touches on her neck and face as the insects landed and tried again and again to bite her. Her phage skin, which could resist the needle of a syringe, was impervious to them, as was Michael's, but the little pests had not given up in two days.

'Are we lost yet?' Michael asked.

'Very funny. We're heading in the general direction of Panama City. It's thirty or so miles that way.'

'Thank you, Amerigo Vespucci.'

'Stop griping. Walking is good for you.'

'How about stumbling, clawing, kicking and tearing?'

'It still beats flying. If you were carrying me above the canopy, your father could spot us from thirty miles away. As long as we stay down here, he'll have to get within a few miles to sense us, right?'

Michael grunted.

'We're coming to the cave, soon.'

'Good.'

It felt so natural to banter with him, or simply to be with him without talking. Hours had passed without a word, and yet she felt comfortable with their silences. We were together, she thought, long before I met him. When he walked into the break room, I had already begun, in a part of my mind too deep for words, to love him. She took a deep breath, letting it tingle sweetly in her lungs. They were running for their lives, but right at this moment, she felt an incredible happiness.

The air changed, turning heavy with the smells of warm dirt, chlorophyll, and fungi. She watched, entranced, as a butterfly with gorgeous, dark blue wings wobbled past her face. A grassy taste settled on her tongue and, seconds later, rain hissed down through the canopy, drenching her hair and sticking her clothes to her. Her socks, not yet dry from the last rain, began to squelch in her shoes and muck oozed up around her feet, clotting in the treads of her cross trainers – good, sensible shoes for the hard tiles of a medical ward, but less so in jungle muck. At least they weren't three-inch heels. Hearing Michael slip, she turned to see him floating in mid-air at waist level, his feet up, the fall an ordinary man would have taken stopped before he hit the ground. His exasperated expression made her want to laugh, but she resisted. Rain ran from the corners of his clenched lips, and his plastered hair dripped shining strings of water to the philodendrons. Slowly, he rotated back to vertical, planting his feet again, and she resumed course.

The rain ended, and the ground steamed all around her.

A huge brown animal burst from the undergrowth almost at her elbow — *a rat, two feet tall!*

She jumped back, then felt silly. Not a rat, of course not — way too big, and the muzzle was square and blunt. It stared at her with beady, piggish eyes, then dashed away into the dripping wall of green. Behind her, Michael laughed.

'And you call yourself an angel,' she said over her shoulder. How can you take pleasure in the fright of other people?'

'It's a sin,' he agreed. 'But I couldn't help myself. For a second, your shoulders were higher than your ears.'

Through the dripping fronds ahead, she saw a gray shape — rock, and she knew they were, at last, getting close to the cave. Hurrying ahead, she let Zane's memories guide her across a stream bed, now gushing with muddy water, past the slab and up a slope with no giant trees but lots of smaller ones, seeming to grow right out of the rock.

I'm on top of the cave!

She started down the other slope, and then her mucked-up heel slipped and she slid down the rock on her seat. At the bottom she sat, legs splayed, glad her once-white ducks were wet or they'd surely have torn. They were the only pants she had now, and she'd need them if they ever left this jungle.

Turning, she found herself peering into the dark mouth of a cave. It gave her an eerie feeling. Long ago, in those shadows, Zane had hidden from Merrick.

'You all right?'

'Of course.' Her rump stung fiercely, but no way was she going to admit it. The pain faded, and she stood, brushing the mud and grit from her pants. All at once, sunlight streamed down, dappling the ground around her;. looking up, she saw patches of blue sky. The rock here was unable to support large trees, and she realized with a jolt how exposed they were.

'Let's go in where it's dry.'

Michael followed her into the cave. The front part was high enough for them to stand; as soon as they entered the shade, the temperature dropped several degrees. With the rock over her head, she felt much safer.

'If it's all right with you,' she said, 'I'm going to take off these wet . . .' She saw that Michael was already stripping down, with no apparent self-consciousness. She watched, remaining still, her breath catching in her chest. He was magnificent: the tapered muscles of his thighs and calves, the narrow waist and tight rump, the way his back flared up into broad shoulders. Fine hair, more gold than red, dappled his chest and legs. He took no care to hide his manhood and she looked away, hoping he would not notice her face burning.

His angelhood.

She suppressed a giggle, feeling a pleasant heat in the pit of her stomach as she kicked off her shoes and skinned off her wet shirt and slacks. Underwear too? She could hardly do less than Michael. It seemed so strange to be naked in the presence of a male. Not since Hugh, a long time. Until a week ago, she hadn't thought about it, that part of her all but dead. But now . . .

She occupied herself wringing out her clothes, hearing him do the same.

And then she was out of things to do.

She sat on the floor of the cave. The smooth earth felt cool against her skin. She was hyper conscious of Michael behind her and wondered if he would touch her; instead, he sat beside her, arms on his knees, and gazed out at the sunlit mouth of the cave.

'This is a good place,' he said. 'Father could fly right over us and not know we were here.'

'After my clothes dry out,' she said, 'I'll take a look around, make sure Zane's escape routes away from the cave are still open.'

He was so close, she could feel a static tingle between their arms; the air of the cave swelled richly in her lungs. She felt a surge of desire for him, so strong it dizzied her. *Her* angel, who had forsaken everything else he loved for her. At this moment, nothing else in the world mattered but him. He was Caesar and she was Cleopatra, Prince Rainier and Princess Grace, Romeo and Juliet.

'Michael . . .'

He slid an arm behind her, warm along her back; with the other hand he turned her into him, angling his head down to find her lips. His firm mouth softened against hers. She slid a hand between his arm and body, feeling the contours of his ribs, running her thumb along the hard ridge under his chest muscles. She could taste him in his kiss, the blood-rich capillaries so close to her tongue. Lying back on the cool, firm earth, she let her head sink onto his firm biceps as he rolled to her and kissed her again. She wanted to lie like this, in his arms, just touching, and he seemed to sense it, because he did not move for a long time, until the cloak she'd kept over her carnal self dropped away and she felt ready for more, her body warming with its own heat. She pressed into him, as he gently lifted her leg along his side. He fitted her perfectly, and she said his name, to tell herself it was really him inside her, an angel. They moved together, and he pressed his face into her throat as the cave brightened and brightened around them; she felt herself slipping into his mind and could not stop it, as he could not hold himself from her, and the fullness of his love for her seemed to lift her from the hard ground, as though she too could defy gravity. She began to tremble with the ecstasy of his adoration; it filled her up and overflowed, making her adore him in return, and not just him, but herself and all of life.

'Michael!'

'How I've longed for you,' he murmured, and she lost all control, pulling herself against him, crying out in pleasure as a torrent of love swept away the last of her fear. She came in long, slow explosions that shot warmth all through her body and made her feel her own pounding blood.

The rapture lingered, as she lay with her head cradled on his stomach, aware only of his hand, stroking her hair. She longed suddenly for a part of him no amount of lovemaking could bring to her. 'I want to know you, Michael. Could I go into your mind?'

'Of course.'

Turning her head on his lap, she gazed into his eyes, a vivid dark blue in the shadows of the cave. She imagined herself drifting up into them, entering through the black holes at their centers, as the cave faded around her. She felt his love again, his passion for her, and wanted to linger in it, but instead moved herself through it, and began to see the world through his memories. She was on a street in Alexandria, but it was cobbled, not paved, no longer Old Town but a new one, and then the cobblestones, too, wavered and faded to dirt and she saw men in frock coats riding horses. She flew above the city of Washington, travelling backward through time as she watched it dwindle to a village and then a forest, tenanted by Indians. Back and back through his memories, gazing out over the harbor at Barcelona and the moors of the Scottish highlands, earlier territories of his family.

She saw Uziel through his eyes, a grand and awesome figure, loving to Michael, but she could feel the edge of fear he had also inspired throughout time in his son. Michael longs to love him without reservation, she realized, but Uziel has never let him close enough. He has kept Michael away from his heart of hearts, the wall is always there.

Saddened, she withdrew from Michael's mind. He loves his father so much, she thought, even though Uziel is hunting him now. And surely Uziel must love him, too.

She realized she was pitying the angel of death. She had never wanted so much to live, for a thousand years, and then five hundred more, all of it with Michael. That is what Uziel meant to take from her — she must harbor no illusions. At any moment, his shadow might cut across the sunlight out there and he *would* kill her.

How do I stop him?

'What are you thinking about?'

Quickly, she cast about for some less grim topic. She thought of Neil Hudson, wondered if he was still hanging on, if the brain activity she'd aroused in him had lasted. 'You tell me.'

He smiled down at her and, an instant later, looked hurt. 'A *patient?*'

'There, there. Earlier, I *was* thinking of you, when we, uhm, earlier.'

He gazed at her. 'You were wondering about Father, too. How to fight him if we have to.'

She looked away, uncomfortable. 'Michael, we don't have to talk about that now.'

'When, then?'

She shuddered as an image came of Michael and Uziel, locked together in mortal combat. If Michael fell, she would be destroyed whether she lived or died, and if he killed his father, how could he not be destroyed? 'I can't be the cause of you fighting your own father.'

'You are not the cause. He is.'

'Michael, if you survived, you would never be able to look at me without seeing your dead father's face. If we win only to lose ourselves and each other, maybe it would be better not to win.'

Michael put his hands on her shoulders. His eyes glistened with a tormented love that made her throat ache. 'If he finds us, he'll attack you. And then I'll have to fight him. But there might be one other way.' He held her shoulders, his eyes measuring her.

Her heart labored with foreboding. 'What?'

'When we enter minds, there is a way to take strength from the neural energy there. Tremendous strength.'

Jenn knew at once what he meant. After I attacked Rich, she thought, I felt strong as a god. It was like taking blood, only even more powerful.

Is that why, an hour later, I was able to kill Ariel?

Her stomach clenched. 'No,' she said.

'You could enter my mind and siphon off my core energy,' Michael urged. 'It would make you very powerful. If the two of us fight him, we'll each be weaker than him, but if you have all of my strength along with your own, you might be able to withstand him. You might even . . . win.' Michael swallowed, and she could see in his eyes what he really meant. *Kill my father.*

She stood. 'Michael, what if I took too much from you and you died? Even if that didn't happen, going into a mind and taking that . . . is evil.' She shuddered.

He got up too, and took her hands. 'Jenn,' he said softly. 'All right, yes, in most instances it would be evil.' But now one of us wants to take your life, and nothing is more evil than that. I am asking you, begging you to take strength from me. It is surely the lesser evil. You would not be violating me, you'd be expressly carrying out my will.'

Jenn heard him only dimly, struck by a sudden realization. To take energy had felt like taking blood. How strange that such a close parallel would exist between angels and phages. Except that angels apparently did not give in to their vampiristic urge. Was it their role as protectors that enabled them to resist? How many times had her own self-identity as a healer kept her from killing, her white medical coat armoring her against her nature? Without evil, there was no good, but was the relationship closer than anyone imagined, evil and good joined at the hip, brothers unable to exist without each other?

'Jenn?'

'You're asking me to vampirize you, without even knowing what I'm doing or how to control it. What would I be taking from you? The energy produced by your neurotransmitters? The brain couldn't function without that. If I go too far, you could die.'

'You won't go too far,' he said softly. 'And I would rather die than lose you.'

'Michael, I won't do it — don't ask me.'

'It's the only way. Don't say no. Just think about it, I beg you.'

He pulled her to him, and she held him, feeling his heart beat against hers, knowing if it ever stopped, her heart would die too.

Chapter Twenty-Three

Uziel tried to contain his frustration as he began searching another area of the jungle. A day gone already and he couldn't be sure he was even closing in on Michael and the she-phage. Checking the horizon on his left, he saw Achsah, one of the dozen he'd brought along from the Cherubini clan, drifting face down like a scuba diver intent on finding a fish in a thick bed of seaweed. Checking to his right, Uziel saw Fabriel hovering miles away, searching, searching.

But was there anyone to find?

The expanse of green below Uziel shimmered in the heat, a seamless, opaque canopy that hid the ground. Thousands of square miles of rain forest.

Or Michael and the she-phage could be in Bogotá.

Should I take half the Cherubini and join Justine there?

Uziel felt heavy with indecision, as if the hot, dense air had drained him of energy. The door to the cargo hold had opened during flight, when the plane was near Panama. They had almost certainly bailed out. Michael and the she-phage would not want to land with the plane, Uziel thought, knowing I'd have learned where it was going before it could come down.

But what if, realizing I'd think this way, they *stayed* with the plane?

Uziel groaned. It would be a desperate gamble, but if they'd done it, they might now be lost in the teeming throngs of Bogotá with only Justine to search for them. He might better have left her back in the States to try to find Merrick and the others.

God, please help me find them — if it's your will.

It *is* your will, isn't it?

No answer.

Of course not. God was not going to speak to him again until he had finished the work of Per Ramesse, eradicated Ramses and the blood eaters who had sprung from him.

If I fail, Uziel thought, I will never again sit at the left hand of God.

His head began to throb. So much jungle to search. Should he bring in more help? He could have a hundred here by this evening.

But could he keep control of that many?

The plan now was for whoever spotted the she-phage to back off at once and report to him. It made sense that Ariel's father would want to deal personally with the killer of his son. But the spotter would have picked up Michael, too, and that was going to be much harder to explain. I will say the she-phage has incredible powers, much like our own, Uziel thought, which is true. That she used those powers to cast a spell on Michael, also true. That only one who knows and loves Michael as I do has a chance of penetrating his confusion and saving him from her.

But will the spotter agree to keep that part quiet?

By now, all the clans know Michael is promised to Philippa Evangeline. Whoever finds him with the she-phage will be deeply shocked at first, and then face a decision: Accept my explanations and follow my urgings to keep silent so that Michael can recover himself and marry Philippa, or let it out who was found with the she-phage, knowing that Amator will then surely cancel the marriage and my family will suffer true scandal and isolation. Surely none of these young, innocent Cherubini believe we deserve that . . .

A spasm of dread passed through Uziel, a cold pressure, in his throat.

If I or one of mine can get to the she-phage first we can keep this quiet. The more help I use, the less likely that will be, but less help cuts down our chances of finding them at all.

Uziel drew a deep breath. It was not yet time to panic. He could make do with the dozen Cherubini, at least a little longer—

Father!

He looked around to see Fabriel hurrying toward him. Had she found the she-phage? Eagerness welled in him, then chilled into dread as he sensed her agitation.

What is it?

Amator Evangeline is coming, and Philippa is with him.

Jenn sat behind Michael in the cave, cradling him against her, mulling over her questions about him. She had known him almost a week now, and they'd talked for hours finding their way through the jungle, and then here in the cave. And he still had not mentioned God. He didn't seem religious in any usual sense of the word. Maybe religion was irrelevant if you were an actual angel of God. She was no angel, but she'd never been able to make it work for her. With so many contradictory versions of God, if you picked one, you were rejecting others. Every true believer was an unbeliever to someone else. Michael didn't talk about God, but he went through life being good, loving, principled, gentle, strong.

His father, on the other hand, seemed obsessed with God's will. And what had that obsession made of him? A ruthless killer, even of babies.

If there's truly a God, could he possibly prefer Uziel's way to Michael's?

Jenn thought of her own father and felt a pang of grief. She'd give anything not to know Zane was still a murderer. Her love for him was dying hard. She was in the habit of thinking of him every day, proud of how he'd mastered his urge to kill. Worrying, sometimes, yes, but never really doubting his word that he'd stopped. They'd become so close. On the run from Merrick, he'd missed her childhood, and so he'd had an insatiable appetite for the details of it — her first boyfriend, her favorite comic book characters, her little triumphs and spills, listening, leaning forward with that avid look.

He had lived a lie, betrayed her trust. It would hurt for a long time.

And now Michael, too, was losing his father—

He tensed against her, and then she heard it too, a soft footfall above, on top of the cave.

Uziel?

Terrified, she sprang up with Michael; in the same instant, a figure dropped down into the mouth of the cave.

Zane!

Uziel hated the nervousness he felt as he faced Amator Evangeline and his daughter in the simmering shade of hundred-foot trees. *I stood at the left hand of God,* Uziel thought. *Who is this fellow, that I should fear him?* But he did fear him. Why had Amator come all this way — Amator, personally?

'My family and I grieve with you for the death of your son.' Amator reached out his hands and Uziel took them. The head of the Evangeline Clan was slim and aristocratic, his broad forehead shadowing eyes blue as chips of ice. He had dressed in white cottons for the heat, his blond mane perfect, though he had just sped across the treetops. Behind his right shoulder, Philippa looked on with those striking eyes of hers, cool and grave. Almost as tall as her father, the long legs descending in flawless splendor from loose, khaki shorts. *She is beautiful,* Uziel thought. *And yet it's not a beauty that draws you.* Surprised at the thought, he nearly forgot to respond to her father.

'Thank you, Amator. Ariel was so young. We miss him terribly.'

'May God comfort you.' Amator's head tilted. 'I'm sure Michael must be devastated.'

Uziel's throat went dry. 'Inconsolable.'

'When you called and asked Philippa to delay her coming for a week, I must admit I had questions, but now I see. Michael, in his sensitivity, must have had a premonition of this evil.'

Uziel could think of nothing to say. Was Amator fishing?

'I, myself, have been aware of something,' Amator went on, 'these past few months. I can scarcely describe it — a creeping sense of uneasiness, as though the firmament itself were about to shift.'

'Yes,' Uziel said, realizing it was true. He had put his uneasiness off on his own issues, always with him. But there had been a tension in the air, an inner goading that had led him to intensify his prayers, without quite knowing why. God knows everything, he thought. He knew Ariel would be killed and that Michael was falling. It is his agitation we have been feeling. Though He will not speak, we are not beyond His eye.

Amator released his hands. 'Uziel, why did you not call us to help? We are about to become two branches of the same family. We must stand by each other.'

'I . . . thank you. I've . . . been off balance . . .'

'Of course. I understand. That's why I took it upon myself to come unasked. We are at your disposal. Tell us what to do.'

Uziel felt his heart pounding and hoped Amator could not hear it, this creature whose origins, like his own, disappeared beyond the veil of memory. I must be honest with him, or he'll see it. But I must also keep him and Philippa as far from the she-phage — and Michael — as possible. *Dear God, why do you torment me so?*

'Unfortunately, we have only a general idea where the she-phage who killed Ariel might be. The two most likely areas are here and Bogotá. Justine is there, and nearly alone. If you could go join her, it would be a great help.'

'Of course. You say nearly alone — is Michael by any chance with her?'

Uziel's dread deepened. 'No, he's somewhere up here.'

Amator smiled. 'It's just that Philippa was hoping to see him, offer her condolences and be at his side, as his future wife. You understand.'

Uziel glanced at her, found her lavender gaze sharp on him. He swallowed. 'Of course. As soon as I find him, I'll send him down to you.'

Philippa continued to stare at him, but Amator made a slight bow. 'Fine. And if we see him along the way, we'll take him with us, then.'

'Very good.' The words sounded distant in his own ears, spoken by someone else. Amator and Philippa lifted up through the trees. When they had disappeared, Uziel sank to his knees, clasping his hands together. *God, I beg you, if you never grant me another wish, don't let them find him . . .*

From the shadows of the cave, Jenn stared at her father, shocked and then angry. 'What are you doing here?'

He looked hurt. 'Jenn, please.'

'Answer my question.'

'I found what plane you'd caught and discovered you'd bailed out near Panama. I thought you might have the memory of my escape from Merrick here, so I came to help.'

'Your being here will not help us. It'll only make us easier to find.' She was aware of Michael, standing very still beside her. Her face burned, and she realized she was ashamed. Why did Zane have to come here, she thought, and remind Michael of where I come from, what all we phages want, deep down inside?

But surely his own capacity for vampirism tells him that already. I'm the one who doesn't want to be reminded.

She said, 'Uziel might be up there right now. What if he picked you up along the jungle trail?'

'If I'm that clumsy, how did you get here safely, yourself? Besides, I knew no angels were following me because I listened to the birds and animals.'

'What does that mean?'

'It's in the Bible. A man named Balaam was riding his donkey and it kept stopping in the middle of the path and refusing to go forward. It made him angry, and he cursed the donkey, then whipped it. Actually, the donkey had stopped because it had seen an angel blocking the path ahead. See, angels can hide themselves from us, but not from animals. So I just listened to the birds and monkeys in the treetops. They kept chattering, so I knew I was all right.'

'You read the Bible?' Michael said with surprise.

'On the plane down here,' Zane said. 'I'd have gotten a copy of the Koran and the Avesta, too, if the airport bookstore had had them. One thing I learned in five hundred years of running was to always do my homework.'

'He's trying to be funny,' Jenn said. 'And failing.'

Zane shrugged but looked stung.

'They *are* probably up there searching,' Michael said, 'so let's not make it any easier for them, shall we?' He motioned Zane into the cave.

Jenn saw that Zane meant to come to her, and she edged away from him. He stopped, looking forlorn. For a second, her heart melted, and then she remembered his hand drawing the knife over Sophie's wrist, felt it as if it were her own hand, and then, the worst part, her own desire, blending with her father's. A tremor of revulsion passed through her.

'Where are Merrick and Chemosh?' she asked.

'Panama City. Chemosh slipped into a branch of the Brinks company on the Via España and lifted the keys to one of the older armored trucks they've taken out of service. The truck is just sitting at the back of the lot, and he and Merrick are staying inside it as much as possible to avoid being detected from overhead. They're using the truck's phone to try and locate a helicopter to fly us all out of here.'

'I'm not going anywhere with you.'

'Jenn, please. I know I've hurt you—'

'Hurt me? You've destroyed everything good we had between us.' She felt tears welling up and fought them, determined he

273

should not see them and think he still had a hold on her heart. No. She wouldn't have it.

She stepped past him to the mouth of the cave.

Zane reached out a hand. 'Where are you going?'

'Out. Don't be here when I get back.'

And then, despite her effort to stop them, the tears came, bitter and scalding, and she ran from the cave.

Michael's heart ached for her. He saw that Zane meant to follow her. Leaping to the mouth of the cave, he blocked the phage's way.

The handsome face darkened. 'I have to go after her.'

'Don't you think you've hurt her enough?'

'But if Uziel is out there—'

'She'll feel him coming. She's a lot more capable than you think.'

Zane feinted with a leg and tried to jump past him on the other side. Michael caught his arm and threw him back inside the cave. Zane stumbled and nearly fell, then righted himself, glaring.

'You shouldn't have come here,' Michael said. 'Jenn is right. You must leave.'

'I'm not going to just sit around while your father tries to kill my daughter. And neither will my father and grandfather.'

'You can't stop it. You'll only die. Go back to Washington.'

Zane shook his head.

'How could you do it to her?'

'Do what?'

'The killing,' Michael said, disgusted.

Zane's gaze faltered, fell away, and then he stiffened. Michael could feel him trying to muster defiance, but the spark died in him and tears flooded his eyes. 'You have no idea what it's like. Do you think I want to be a killer? Never. But I'm always hungry for it – more hungry, even, than for the blood. Oh, you can satisfy it for a few days, a week, but it always comes back. In the beginning, five hundred years ago, I fought it for my father's sake. I drank from the dying on the battlefield, I tried to kill only when starving, and then only the most evil. I worshipped my father, I'd have done anything for him, but to deny what I was, that I could not do. So for five centuries, I had to run and hide from him, as you now hide from your own father.

'Then I found my daughter. She shines on me . . . and in her light I see a beast.' Zane began to weep again. 'You say you're an angel, an emissary of God. What sort of God would create me? What sadist gave me the hunger of a leopard but the heart of a man?'

Against his will, Michael felt compassion for Zane, so strong it startled him. What a tormented soul he was. 'I have no answer.'

Zane said, 'I have even asked God for help, but God never answers. Where is He . . . Michael? Can you at least tell me that?'

'No.'

'Don't you wonder?'

Michael remembered how he had felt just after Ariel's death. 'I wish God had been there to stop my brother from trying to kill Jenn.' He felt tears filling his own eyes. 'I miss Ariel — and yet I'm furious at him. I don't want to be. Is this a nightmare, Zane? Have you and I learned to dream without sleeping?'

'If only that could be true.' Zane gazed at him. 'Is it possible you really are an angel?'

Michael felt a weary impatience at the question. 'Does it matter what I am? Everyone is so concerned about what they are. No one is concerned enough about what they do. My father was always saying that he loved me. He never tired of saying it, how much love he feels for his family. How nice for him, these feelings he has. But what does he *do*? One time we went climbing together. We did not fly, we hugged the rocks and looked for places to put our feet, and picked our way up the ice and snow. At the top, we hugged each other and laughed like schoolboys. It was the finest day of my life, that one time. That was love. The rest of it has been the work, the duties we all have to him and to God. And now he is determined to destroy the noblest soul I have ever known. All those years, when I listened to what my father said, I told myself that he loved me. But now, when I finally wake up and look at what he does . . .' Michael felt a choking bitterness. He should not be saying such things to an enemy of his father, and yet he had the feeling that Zane might understand him better than anyone else could, this tormented being who had run from his own father for five hundred years.

'You have such pain,' Zane said wonderingly. 'Just like any man. But if you are an angel, too—'

'What?' Michael said. 'What would you have me *do*?'

'Take away my love of killing.'

Such desperate hope. Michael felt sorrow that he must dash it. 'I can't do that. No one can. I'm sorry.'

All light left Zane's eyes. Michael wanted to go to him, put a hand on his shoulder, but no, he was beyond consoling.

'Will you tell my daughter I *have* tried?' Zane said. 'That I've given it everything I had and that it is beyond my reach?'

Michael felt a sudden sharp unease. It sounded like the last line of a will and testament. Did Zane mean to end it all, to stop taking blood by any means and die?

But how could he? If he had that kind of strength, he would not have killed and would still have his daughter's love.

He realized Zane was waiting for an answer. 'You'd stop if you could, I can see that now.'

'Tell her.'

'Yes.'

Chapter Twenty-Four

Hundreds of yards from the cave, Jenn could still feel Zane's sorrow mingling with her own, a tightness in her chest, like a breath she could not release. A part of her wanted to hurry back, assure him that she loved him no matter what.

But in the end, it might not be a mercy.

Jenn expelled a breath, but the tight feeling in her chest remained.

She had a decision to make, and there was no escaping it.

She slipped between two giant trees, dizzied by their height, then headed downhill through thinning brush, toward the stream she could hear below. The brush parted and she saw it, a ribbon of muddy water only a few yards across. A hundred years ago it had been larger, and Zane had run along it for three miles to throw Merrick off his trail. Roots, twisted like arthritic fingers, choked the former banks of the creek; the gap was still wide enough to expose a winding channel of sky. Uneasy, she scanned it in both directions, but there was no sign of any searchers, just a few puffy clouds. The blue of the sky was deepening, sunset not far off. Backing into the protective fringe of vines and bushes, she sank to her haunches, weighed down by the two terrible choices. I know Zane is killing, she thought. If I don't stop him, more Sophies die. But the only way to stop him is to kill him, my own father. Merrick *had* to go after him. He raised him, gave him first blood. I'm just his daughter. I'm not responsible for what he does.

Tell that to his next victim.

She tried to imagine catching Zane, striking into him as she had Ariel, hearing his terrified cries as he fell. She felt sick to her stomach.

Maybe I won't have to. Maybe Uziel will kill me.

A crazy laugh bubbled up inside her. She pressed the sides of her head, fighting an urge to scream. I can't stand this, I just want to be back home. I want to go to the hospital and read charts and treat my patients—

She jerked her head back. The touch came again, like a cool finger tapping her forehead from inside. Through the gap between the trees, she saw a winged figure in the distance. Her blood froze. She held still, her heart pounding, hoping the foliage would hide her. Through the veil of leaves, she could see the angel drifting closer up the gap in the trees, great white wings trailing against the darkening sky.

Uziel?

Fighting an explosion of panic, she held herself still. A vacuum of sound descended on her, every bird and animal in the canopy above frightened to silence—

Zane wasn't joking!

Her forehead pulsed again, a cool mental touch.

The creature had detected her, and now it was homing in, hunting her as a hawk hunts a cowering rabbit. An overpowering urge to run seized her. If she could get back to the cave now—

But then she'd lead the creature to Michael. If it was Uziel, they'd fight, and she must not be the cause of that.

She must run away from the cave.

The touch came again, remaining now, a steady pressure on the inside of her forehead. Jenn bolted across the stream bed. Glancing back she saw the angel closing on her. She plunged into the undergrowth on the other side of the stream, panic and speed making her clumsy. Creepers tore at her ankles, bringing her down. Lunging up again, she heard a long ripping sound behind and realized the angel was now plunging down through the canopy toward her. She turned sharply, scrambling up a rocky slope, forcing her way through the clutching arms of the jungle. She could feel the angel clearly now . . . not Uziel!

Michael's sister!

Shoving back at the hammering presence in her mind, she threw it out. A resigned calm settled over her; stopping, she turned. Fabriel swung down through the trees at her, trailing an arc of pure, white light.

'Please,' Jenn said. 'I don't want to fight you.'

Fabriel's feet swung forward as she slowed, sinking to within inches of the tangled undergrowth. Jenn braced for her attack, but instead the angel gazed at her. Her blonde hair had been braided into a French twist behind her head, showing off her fine cheekbones. Her eyes were a clear aquamarine, lighter than Michael's but just as stunning.

'You touched my mind,' the angel said. 'You know who I am.'

'Michael's sister, Fabriel. He's told me about you. You're very beautiful.'

'Do you understand how it is that you can enter minds?'

Her voice was cool, neutral, but Jenn could imagine it as a melody. 'No. I don't know.'

'And yet it's how you killed Ariel.'

Jenn hardly dared move for fear of breaking the spell. Why wasn't Fabriel attacking?

Is she keeping me occupied while she calls her father?

Jenn forced herself to remain still. 'I'm so sorry for what happened with Ariel. I didn't mean even to hurt him, and I'd give anything if I could undo—'

Fabriel raised a hand, stopping her. 'I want you to think now, remember what happened between you and Ariel.'

'So you can look in my mind?'

Fabriel nodded.

A trick — a way to get in and then strike her down? Fear gave a cold lurch in her stomach. But she closed her eyes and thought of Ariel walking up the manicured slope of Arlington Cemetery with her, Ariel talking, Ariel attacking—

Fabriel gasped and tears spilled from her eyes. Her hands were clenched together now, as if in prayer. Bowing her head, she wept. Jenn found that she was crying too. Stepping forward, she raised a hand to Fabriel's shoulder, but the angel caught her wrist, staring at her, the blue eyes simmering beneath the sheen of tears.

'Can't you forgive me?' Jenn asked.

'It is not a matter of forgiving you. I see that it wasn't your fault. But I'm angry at you anyway.'

'I understand.'

'He was our baby. We miss him so much. I think it has made Father . . . a little crazy.'

'Are you calling him now?'

A shadow crossed Fabriel's face. 'No. I should, I must, but somehow, I don't want to. He *will* kill you.'

'All I want is to love his son.'

'I know. But you can never be together. Surely you see that.'

Jenn felt a quick, rebellious heat. 'What is our sin? Loving? Your father is wrong.'

Fabriel looked away into the jungle. 'It's pointless to talk about whether he's right or wrong, he believes he is right, and that God is willing him to do this. Do you have any idea who he is?'

'The angel of death.'

Fear flickered in Fabriel's eyes. 'That's right. If you stay with Michael, he'll fight Father to try and save you, fight him to the death, and the death will be Michael's.'

Jenn could not speak. Her throat closed as her mind showed it to her – Uziel raising his arm, Michael falling. Desperately she searched for some other outcome in her mind, could find none.

'You must leave him,' Fabriel said. 'If you love him, if you care for him at all, you must release him to us. Go now, as far and as fast as you can, and maybe I can persuade Father not to follow. I'll tell him you have given Michael up forever. I'll do my best, but you should know that I don't think it will be enough. I will pray he doesn't find you. No matter what happens, you will have saved Michael.'

Fabriel's voice sounded dull, distant, and Jenn realized she had covered her ears. She felt a smothering panic. Leave Michael, just as he had moved up from the deepest parts of her into the light of consciousness, where she could love him fully? Give up a thousand years with him?

But if it was the only way to save him . . .

I must, she thought.

'All right.' The words took everything, leaving her empty, parched.

Fabriel's eyes glistened. She held out her hands, and Jenn took them, numb against their warmth. 'Save him.'

'You have done that.'

Jenn felt a wrenching in her chest and realized some last part of her had tried to sob. No, she thought. No more pain. Turning toward Panama City, she began walking. She felt Fabriel's touch again in her mind, not cool this time, but warm as her hands, and with it, her forgiveness.

Michael put a hand on Zane's shoulder. The phage did not respond, just sat there, slumped against the wall of the cave as he had for the past half-hour, as if someone had switched him off.

'I'm worried about Jenn.'

Finally his head rose.

'I tried to reach her, and I couldn't. She's gone too far from the cave. You know the terrain around here—'

The dark eyes came back to life and Zane pushed up from the floor. 'Let's go.' Michael followed him from the cave. Zane forged ahead, disappearing between two trees, then reappearing to wave impatiently. Lifting from the ground, Michael flew between the trees, catching up, fear churning in his gut. Had Father found Jenn and snatched her up? I should never have let her go out, he thought.

Zane slipped through the underbrush down a long slope and Michael followed, trying not to think of Jenn lying dead in the jungle. Zane stopped to examine some creepers on the side of a tree, then loped on. Michael scrambled down through thinning brush to a stream, arriving just as Zane vanished ahead. Darkness was falling, and Michael felt his vision adjusting, brightening the tangle of growth and giving it a phosphorous tint.

'Here,' Zane hissed.

Michael pushed through another few yards and found him squatting, scowling at a tangled mat of vegetation. 'She was here,' he said. But the trail ends.'

'What do you mean?'

Zane looked sharply at him. 'I mean she came to this spot and no farther.'

'Could she have backtracked . . .' Michael realized panic was making him stupid. If she'd retraced her steps, they'd have run into her.

Zane stood, gripped his arm. 'Did they get my daughter? Did one of your family swoop down and pick her up?'

Michael could not speak. Zane must be right, what else could it be? He dropped to his knees. Someone screamed, and he knew it was him, but he could not stop.

Dazed, Jenn wandered down a back street of Panama City.

How had she gotten here?

Her stomach felt hollow with unease. Something had happened to her, but she could not remember what. Had it involved Michael? Was he all right?

She kept walking, not knowing what else to do, feeling her heart pound. If that was today's *La Prensa* back at the taxi stand, she had lost one night – an entire night and into the next morning, gone from her mind. The last thing she recalled before these streets was walking away from Fabriel into the jungle. Clearly, she had somehow made her way here, but why couldn't she remember?

Be calm, she told herself. Maybe it will come back to you.

The barred windows of a bodega etched a white-on-black after-image on her eyes, everything crisp and sharp in the morning light. A shower must have swept the air clean — yes, her clothes were damp, and the stuccoed wall beside her shone. She heard footsteps approaching; a man in a ruffled, light blue shirt untucked over black trousers tipped his straw hat to her and said, 'Buenos días, senorita.' Something in his eyes told her that few *gringas* ever walked down this street. Her fear deepened — not of men in straw hats, but of the hole in her memory. Was she in shock? Her hands did feel cold. Maybe she'd seen something horrible — *Uziel killing Michael?*

Dread gave her heart a quick, sharp squeeze. Angels could attack the nervous system and brain directly, and an attack by Uziel might well account for her memory loss. But how could she have survived?

At the corner, the street opened onto a market square where several dozen people browsed at a maze of sagging tables. She threaded her way through, inspecting the merchandise, afraid to look into herself. Men in cotton pants and T-shirts and women in loose blouses and flowing skirts lounged under awnings and umbrellas, selling jewelry, carvings of Jesus, the Madonna and various saints, and colorful mola needlework that featured bright, patchwork birds and flowers appliquéd onto darker backgrounds. Picking up a mug with 'Panama Canal' emblazoned in flaking gold on it, she examined it as if she were interested, a tourist, someone who belonged here. She tried to think what to do. Zane had said Chemosh and Merrick were here in town—

'Tree dollares, blondie.' The young man grinned at her with rotten teeth, holding up three fingers in case she did not understand even her own language.

Zane had said Merrick and Chemosh were staying in a Brinks armored car parked on the company's lot, using the armor to shield themselves—

And here I am, standing out in the open.

Where was the Brinks lot? A simple street name, Something-Spain . . .

'All right, two dollares,' the vendor said.

She pulled the bills, still damp with rain, from her pocket and held them back as the man reached for them.

'Can you direct me to Spain Avenue?'

He looked blank for a moment, then said, 'Ah, the Via España. Go up there one block to Avenida Central and turn right. It torn into Via España.'

'The Brinks office?'

His forehead creased in thought. 'Six or seven block, I think.'

She gave him the money and left the mug. Continuing through the market, she walked to the next block and turned right, moving briskly, trying to strip the fog from her mind. The sun seemed to have climbed much higher, warming her through her shirt. It gave her an uneasy feeling of time slippage – it seemed she'd only been in the market for a few minutes, but it must have been hours. Hadn't she already walked down this street? Yes, this same chain-link fence protecting the grounds of a hotel, a few palm trees and some painted rocks leading up to the wide veranda. On the street side of her, ancient compact cars and battered pickups growled past, fouling the air with exhaust and burning oil.

The street broadened up ahead and she could see fancier hotels and high-rise buildings. The Brinks office and lot must be up there, only a few more blocks. I promised Fabriel I would get out of here, she told herself, and never see Michael again. And that's what Merrick and Chemosh want, too.

She stopped on the sidewalk.

I have to know he's all right, she thought.

I have to say goodbye.

Across the street, she saw an alley. Darting through a break in the traffic, she halted inside the well of shade. She could take a minute, think.

A flash of recall startled her – of being above the jungle canopy, of seeing the moon gleam off the dark mat of vegetation.

Leaning against the alley wall, she stilled herself around the memory . . . yes, moonlight on treetops.

She touched her face, remembering the sweep of leaves across it, a tingling echo in her cheek. Had Uziel grabbed her and pulled her up through the canopy?

And then maybe she'd fought back and they'd dropped her.

Maybe, but it rang no bells.

Forget it, she thought. You're here and you want to know where Michael is. After you didn't come back to the cave, what would he do? Assume you were attacked; but when he couldn't find your body—

A woman screamed, raising the hackles on Jenn's neck.

There – again, but muffled, as if someone had clapped a hand over her mouth.

Jenn sprinted deeper into the alley toward the sound, finding a narrower side passage, following it between the grimy backs of three-story apartments. Clothes hung limp from lines above, strung across the gap to opposite windows, no room even for balconies. She heard the scream again, more clearly, and feet scuffling on pavement, just around the corner. As she rounded it, she saw them at the end of a cul de sac – four men holding a woman to the ground as they tore at her dress. One of them gripped her black hair, his other hand clamped over her mouth. The woman's face was turning dusky for lack of oxygen.

'You!' Jenn shouted.

The men froze for a second, then turned toward her, four feral faces, staring as if they could not believe their eyes. The woman twisted away from the stifling hand and sucked a breath. One of the men made a downward motion with his palm and rose from his crouch, walking toward Jenn.

'You want some too, *puta?*'

'Let her go.'

The man smiled. 'We trade 'er for you, that what you want, ey, babe?'

'That's right.'

He waved at the others. 'Let 'er go.'

A volley of Spanish came from the other three, but he stilled them with a look. The man holding her hair let go, and she staggered up, pulling at her dress, sobbing. She edged past the leader, pressing her back to one wall, knocking over a garbage can then breaking into a run. '*Gracias,*' she gasped as she passed, her eyes bright with relief. '*Llamaré policia.*'

Jenn's heart sank. Police — the last thing she needed or wanted.

And then a worse thought struck her. If angels were nearby, they'd be drawn to this. She must get out, quickly.

The leader had swaggered to a stop in front of her. Strike into his mind? She thought of Rich Sikorsky. No.

The man grabbed for her arm. Batting his hand aside, she took him by the inside of his biceps and flung him against the wall. His head snapped against the brick and he slid down, unconscious. The others rushed her. She grappled with them, feeling the slash of a knife into her lower back, the quick spurt of her blood. Infuriated, she kicked out, hearing bone snap, wincing at the scream. In a more careful flurry of elbows and fists, she laid them all out unconscious.

A shadow swept along the dim alley toward her.

Terror flashed through her. Looking up, she saw Uziel descending in a blaze of light, three other angels behind him. His left hand extended toward her. Frozen, she saw it flame; she threw herself mentally back at him, but he was too strong. She felt a fiery prickle along the nape of her neck and knew with an awful certainty that she was going to die. Uziel seemed to slow above her, hanging close, like a beautiful sculpture, lighting the alley with a bronze light; she gazed, paralyzed, into the smooth blackness of his eyes.

She cried out in her mind for Michael—

Then everything speeded up again as Uziel veered off at the last second, grazing the wall of the alley, tumbling down in a heap as a voice cried out in her mind: *Not here, Father. She was doing our work.*

Chapter Twenty-Five

Uziel lay in the dirt of the alley, dumbfounded, staring at Rafe. 'You struck me!'

Rafe settled beside him. 'Father—'

'You *struck* me . . . *You!*'

'But I had to stop you. That woman we saw running from the alley – these men were about to rape her. The phage saved her.'

'You think I don't know that?'

'The phage surely knew we were hunting her, and that the woman's terror might draw us, but she chose to help her anyway. She put the life of a normal above her own.'

Beyond Rafe, the two Cherubini drifted to the ground, checking the fallen men, but Uziel knew they must be listening to this, taking in every word. They were poised to agree with Rafe, he could feel it. Frustration burned in him. *I had her! And she wasn't with Michael. I could have killed her and sent the searchers home, then looked for Michael on my own while Amator and Philippa are still in Bogotá. It was the perfect chance!*

Galled, he listened to Jenn's panicked footsteps recede in the distance. He longed to go after her, but what if Rafe tried to stop him again, and the Cherubini joined in? With them hanging on him, the she-phage would escape anyway, and his authority would be destroyed, a far worse defeat than letting her run for the moment. *I know where she is, and that Michael isn't with her. She can't get far. Settle this, then you can bring the rest of the Cherubini in and sweep her up.*

'Did I do wrong, Father?'

Rafe's expression was penitent, and yet Uziel felt a chill at the sly thrust of the question. He rose and brushed himself off, giving himself time to answer. 'I know your heart is tender, son, and I love you for it, but you have just put your judgement above mine before God. It is God's will that I destroy this phage, but you prevented me and your reason is that she was doing good. Does that mean she *is* good? It's not uncommon for evil people to perform good deeds. Mobsters give to charity; Hitler loved dogs and built wonderful roads.'

'But *rape*, Father? If it has now become our job to punish evil, let's do it to this trash lying on the ground here.' Rafe's voice quivered with indignation.

'It has *not* become our job to punish evil, except where God tells us to. The she-phage is a mutant who has somehow developed powers meant only for angels. She has killed one of us, and seduced another, and there are far too few of us already. It is God's will I kill her before she becomes strong enough to destroy us all.'

Rafe's eyes widened. 'God has spoken to you, Father?'

Blood rushed to Uziel's face. He felt an overpowering urge to slap Rafe's face, but held back, knowing his anger came from his own doubt. How diabolical that Rafe should aggravate that uncertainty, chipping away at his faith like this. This is what I deserve, Uziel thought bleakly, for opening my heart after Ariel's funeral, admitting what I did at Per Ramesse, acknowledging I might be the reason why none of us has heard God's voice in so long. What would Rafe do if he knew that, in moments of weakness, I have actually feared I never heard it at all? My own son, maybe the only one I have left, and I have caused him to question . . .

And then Uziel realized what this was. God was using Rafe to test his faith. Faith was the only way back to hearing God's actual voice again. And what was faith but the moral strength to *know* God existed and had a plan for you, even if you couldn't prove it? Surely it was God's plan that a creature as dangerous and seductive as the she-phage should die. He must show Rafe — and God — his faith now.

'God *has* spoken to me, Rafe. He has commanded me to destroy the she-phage.'

Rafe looked down. 'I . . . I don't mean to question you, Father. Forgive me.'

Relief filled Uziel. 'Of course I forgive you.' Taking the hands of his remaining son, he felt an approving response in the two Cherubini. Yes; God had allowed the she-phage to slip away — for the moment — to test him. And I have passed the test, Uziel thought.

Now, quickly — bring in the others and get her.

Michael nursed a feeble spark of hope as he labored through the creepers and vines, struggling to keep up with Zane. Jenn is still alive, he thought. Please, God, she has to be.

Maybe the trail disappeared not because Jenn had been snatched up and killed by Father, but because she had left no trail. *I* didn't see any sign of her passage to begin with, Michael thought, not from the moment we left the cave. Only Zane did. And who says he's a perfect tracker? He didn't spend his life following trails but trying not to leave one, and Jenn has all his skills now . . .

But why would she leave me?

Seeing that Zane had stopped to study a philodendron plant, Michael slogged forward, his heart lifting. 'What is it?'

'This leaf was nicked not long ago, but almost certainly by an animal — a tapir's hoof or maybe the claw of a tiger.'

'There are tigers in here?' Michael said, surprised.

'Small ones.'

Zane continued to stare at the plant. He said, 'We've worked through a full circle around the point where Jenn's trail ended. I can't find any trace of her going beyond that point in any direction.'

'Then she went straight up,' Michael said. 'And the only way she could do that was if . . .' Sick at heart, he could not finish.

'But if your Father did get her, wouldn't he have read her mind as he killed her, to find out where you are?'

Hope stirred in Michael. 'You're right. Father would read her, and find out about the two of us being in the cave. He'd start from there and search outward. We're still close to the cave. He'd have found us by now. Which means he *didn't* get her.

'So where is she, and how in hell — you should pardon the expression — did she get there?'

'I don't know.' An unfocused energy filled Michael. He didn't know what to do, only that he had to do something, and he was tired of grubbing around on the jungle floor, where he was all but useless. 'I'm going up to search for her aura again. Stay here.'

'Where would I go?'

Michael rose up above the canopy, barely feeling the lash of leaves, the clawing branches. Breaking into the light, he hovered, concentrating, searching for any trace of Jenn. The canopy below him was silent. A few hundred yards away, bright blue and yellow birds rose and dived above the treetops. He could hear the distant chittering of monkeys. Closing his eyes, he groped for her in his mind.

And felt the barest contact.

Michael?

His heart leapt, and then he realized it was not Jenn but Fabriel. Turning, he saw her, near the horizon. Maybe she'd know something about Jenn. As she drew near, racing along across the treetops toward him, he could feel her joy, and also anxiety. Rushing up to him, Fabriel took his hands. He hugged her to him, then pulled back. 'Have you seen Jenn?'

'I . . . I found her yesterday, not far from here. Michael, you must forgive me, but I persuaded her to leave you — I couldn't

290

bear the thought of you battling Father over this. He would kill you, or you him. I couldn't bear either.'

Blood rushed to his face, a stinging heat. 'Damn it, Fabriel, I *love* her—'

'And she loves you, with total unselfishness. That's why she saw that you cannot be together. Michael, accept her sacrifice, I beg you. It's the only way.'

He wouldn't argue. It would serve no purpose and only delay what he had to know. 'Where did she go?'

Fabriel's eyes widened. 'Michael, haven't you heard a word I said?'

'Where did she *go*?'

'Last I saw, she was headed toward Panama City.'

'And Father?'

'I found him and told him Jenn had left you. I begged him to leave her be. I swore she'd have nothing more to do with you. I'd gotten where you were from Jenn's mind, and I told Father.'

'And?'

Fabriel looked miserable.

Michael felt his temper slipping. 'Fabriel, he didn't come to me, so what did he do?'

'He took the Cherubini and . . . headed for the city.'

'You told him?' Michael gripped her wrist, furious and terrified.

'No – please, Michael. I didn't tell him. But how else would she keep her promise to get away from you? She'd need to catch a plane or boat and Panama City's the closest place to do it. I went all the way to the city with him, trying to get him to turn back. When he wouldn't, I came to find you.'

'You did right. You should have done it sooner.' Releasing her, he turned away, sick with anger and hurt. 'Father had the chance to come to me, and instead he went after her.'

Fabriel was looking down now, peering into the canopy. 'Zane,' she whispered.

Surprised, Michael said, 'You know him?'

'We caught him and his father and Ramses at the National

Cathedral, but they escaped into the crypt and we had to go in after them. They're very capable in close, and they stood us off. I fought with Zane – do you have any idea what is in his heart?'

'He's a predator. The same God who made zebras, made lions.'

Fabriel looked shocked. 'I can't believe you would excuse him—'

'I don't excuse him, or condemn him. He loves his daughter with all his heart and wants to save her life. In that, we are the same, and it seems I'll need all the help I can get.'

Fabriel began to cry. She buried her face in her hands, and her shoulders shook. Michael's heart melted toward her. How awful this is for her. If I *were* to kill Father, or he me . . .

Fabriel dropped her hands. 'Oh! Michael, I almost forgot. Amator and Philippa are here – well, not right here. Father sent them to Bogotá to help Mother hunt Jenn down there.'

'I'll bet he did.' Michael groaned. Mother would not stay away from Father a moment longer than it took her to decide Bogotá would yield nothing. When she rejoined Father, with her would come two seasoned angels, one of them an immensely powerful ancient. If the Evangelines joined Uziel in attacking Jenn, she'd have no chance at all.

'Michael, Philippa came because she loves you—'

'She doesn't even know me. I pray I won't have to fight her, too.'

'Oh, Michael, you mustn't. It would mean war between our clans. Everyone would be drawn in.'

He looked at her, stabbed through by a terrible, dark foreboding. 'And how about you, dear sister? If it comes to a fight, will you help Father attack us?'

'Don't ask me,' she wailed. 'I can't face this. It's too terrible. Michael, go to Father – you go. Tell him you and Jenn are quits forever. Talk to him. Maybe you can—'

'Go back home, Fabriel, to Washington. This is Father's fight, not yours. If you won't help me, at least don't take his side.'

'Abandon Father and Mother?' She looked lost.

'Fabriel, I have to go.'

'No, I won't let you.' She grabbed his arm.

He put his hand on hers, aching with sadness. She let him go and turned away, weeping.

He longed to comfort her but there was no time. Plunging back down through the canopy, he found Zane.

'You were up there a long time.'

'My sister saw Jenn. She was headed for Panama City. So is Father. I have to go there before it's too late.'

'Take me with you.'

Michael hesitated. Jenn would not want to see Zane. And what would Uziel do if he caught the scent of Jenn's father, a true killer?

'Damn it, she's my daughter!'

Michael turned his back on Zane and said, 'Take hold of me and hang on.'

Chapter Twenty-Six

For this have I given thy kind dominion over the heavens,
thou and no other, that thou mayest defend mankind.

Codex Angelorum I, 5

In the baking heat of the Brinks truck, Uziel's cold gaze replayed
in Jenn's mind, the liquid black of his eyes. It gave her a flash of
her own body lying dead back in the alley. She shuddered. Beside
her Chemosh patted her knee and said, 'It's all right.'

No.

Clearly, Fabriel had not succeeded in calling her father off.

*Would she then have found Michael to tell him I was headed for Panama
City?*

Rising from the guard's bench, Jenn looked through the slit
into the driver's cab. Merrick, slouching behind the wheel, gazed
out at the street beyond the parking lot. He would look relaxed if
not for the constant panning of his eyes. Only ten blocks to the
alley, she thought. Uziel knows I'm around here somewhere.
He's got angels above right now, searching. It made the nerves in
her spine crawl.

'Two inches of hardened steel,' Chemosh said, pointing to
the roof of the van.

She nodded, unpersuaded.

There was no question of moving the truck. This was the

rendezvous point Zane had agreed to with Merrick and Che-mosh. If he showed up with Michael, he'd make sure they came here. Four hundred thousand people packed together in Panama City, four hundred thousand auras to get lost in, but they had to stay right here under Uziel's nose.

Moving to the other slit, at the back of the armored car, Jenn peered through the bulletproof glass at the back alley that exited the parking lot. Zane might slip in from there, habit making him use the shadows lengthening along the black asphalt for cover, though he'd be casting his own light to those above.

'How long will the helicopter pilot wait for us?'

'I'm the pilot.'

She turned, surprised. 'You don't even drive.'

'I don't *like* to drive. I do like to fly.'

So much I still don't know about him, she thought. If we make it out of here, I'm going to find out everything.

'Try not to worry. I had the chopper delivered to a pad at the bay. All we have to do is drive down there and get on.'

'And then?'

'Fly north, paralleling the canal zone, staying just above the jungle until we reach Colón, at the Atlantic entrance to the canal. Now that Uziel knows you're here, I doubt he'll dilute his forces to cover an airport more than fifty miles away. From Colón, I've got first class on a jet to Lyon, France.'

'For five?'

He nodded. 'I knew you wouldn't leave here without Michael. I've had fake passports made up for all of us.'

Gratitude brought a prickle of tears to her eyes. 'You've been busy.'

Chemosh shrugged. 'Easy enough in a place like this, the drug traffic what it is. You may find some cocaine dust on the floor of the chopper.'

'As long as we get out.' She watched the street behind the armored car. *Come on, Michael. Please.*

*   *   *

Uziel stood with Justine atop the vast, rust-flecked gate of the Miraflores Lock, trying to master his dread. He felt stiff with it, half frozen, as though his blood were slowly turning to ice. If Justine could just have stayed in Bogotá a little longer. There had been no choice but to let Amator and Philippa join the search over the city. What if one of them found Jenn and Michael was with her? Hours had passed, enough time for him to have found and rejoined her, as he must surely be trying to do.

Uziel bit back a groan, seeing Michael in the remorseless light of imagination, striking out at Amator or, worse, his cherished daughter. Amator had already had dark premonitions, and he would be proven right. It would mean war between us, Uziel thought. Would any take my side? I was thought to stand at the left hand of God. Some would join me, yes. But the horror . . .

His stomach plunged, and now he saw the nightmare — or memory — that always found him at his darkest moments, the great angels of heaven itself falling, spinning down in pulsing trails of light. Whatever had become of those who had not died?

Am I finally to know, by becoming one of them?

Uziel felt a pulse of weakness at his knees. He must stop this gnawing doubt before it ate him up inside. God is with me, he thought. I can only fail by doubting it.

Gazing north along the Canal, he watched the two Cherubini hovering and darting around the tanker in the lock. Bored crewmen lounged around on the deck while the Canal pilot eased the huge ship along. What would they think if they could suddenly see the heavenly searchers? Dear God, Uziel prayed, let the she-phage be in the hold of this ship.

It *would* be a clever thing to do, using the thick hull as a shield while she slipped away from the city. The she-phage was certainly clever.

But somehow the conviction clung that she was back in the city, probably not far from the alley, even though they'd not been able to find her in hours of searching. She'd found a basement, or a culvert.

Uziel felt Justine's hand on his shoulder. She said, 'What will we do if Michael's with her?'

'God's will.'

'What does that mean, God's will?'

'Justine!' His jaw clenched. How he hated being angry with her. But why must she, too, torment him? First Fabriel, then Rafe, and now her, reluctant, hanging on him, trying to drag down his resolve. Why couldn't they believe in him, as he believed in God?

'Michael *will* fight you.' Justine's voice quavered.

'He won't. I'm sure of it.'

'The she-phage has already killed one of us. How could she do that? What if she can fly, too, and rises up to attack us—?'

'She can't fly!' In a softer voice, he said, 'Justine, God gave angels dominion over the sky, only angels. It's inconceivable He would grant such powers to a blood eater. We will stay well above them this time, and they will not touch us. God will triumph. You must stop this questioning and have faith. I know what I'm doing. Don't you turn against me now.'

She circled in front of him, and he could see the pain in her face. 'I would never turn against you, my love. Don't you know that? I would follow you into hell.'

A chill went through him. 'All I ask is, if the she-phage is spotted, you bring Rafe and Fabriel. They're east of the city.'

'Must they take part?'

'We may not be able to prevail without them. And we can't let a second son fall to her.'

She touched his face with a sorrowful tenderness, as if she might never be able to touch it again. She's wrong, he thought. We're in hell now. But I'm going to get us out. I will hear God's voice again and know I have done right—

He felt a touch in his mind, excited and worried, both. His heart speeded up as he saw Melchiah, the young Cherubini who'd reminded him of Ariel, racing across the sky toward him.

What? What is it?

The she-phage. I picked up her trace and saw her getting into an armored truck in a parking lot on the Via España.

Uziel clasped his hands, ecstatic, *Thank you, God,* then realized there was more.

And?

The anxiety in the other mind peaked. *Your son was with her. I left my brother, Achsah, to watch. When I left, they were driving toward the bay.*

Uziel's heart plummeted. For a moment he was too stricken to speak.

I must contain it, he thought, like I planned.

As Melchiah drew close, Uziel saw that his face was clouded with confusion. He seized the young angel's hands. 'Listen to me, Melchiah. The she-phage has a very powerful mind – I told you that. What I had not wanted to tell you, for Michael's sake, is that she has used her powers to overcome his reason. You know that Amator and his daughter, whom Michael is to marry, are also searching the city. They must not learn you have seen the she-phage and Michael with her. If I can destroy the she-phage, his mind will clear, and he'll remember his goodness, his love for Philippa. But if she or her father become involved, Michael may, in his delusion, do things that may not be undone. It is God's work to prevent that.'

Melchiah hesitated, his young face troubled.

Desperate, Uziel said, 'I've lost one son, but you can help me save another – and a marriage that will bring all the angels closer together.'

Melchiah inclined his head. 'I and my brother will stay with you. I'll make sure he understands.'

Relief flooded Uziel. 'You will have a place of honor at their holy wedding.' Almost, he could believe it.

Jenn leapt from the Brinks truck as it was still rolling to a stop; at once she felt the distant touch, and her stomach clenched. Michael, piling out behind her, sensed it too – she could see it in his face.

She turned to Chemosh. 'I feel one of them.'

Chemosh paled. 'Has it located us?'

'I don't know.' She turned back to Michael. 'Do you know him?'

'No.'

She felt a small relief. At least it wasn't Uziel.

'Come on,' Chemosh urged.

The helicopter sat on a square of pavement, backlit by the dazzling bay. Chemosh ran for it, and Jenn followed with Merrick and Michael. Glancing around for Zane, she saw him holding back. To protect her? She stopped, twenty yards from the chopper, motioning sharply to him, 'Come on, damn it!' and he ran at last. Michael had waited, boosting her up into the small passenger cabin, and Zane behind her. Drop-down benches lined both walls of the cabin. She pulled Michael down beside her.

'Strap in,' Chemosh shouted over the rising roar of the blades. Buckling the safety harness around her, she felt the trace again, stronger now, despite the distorting energy of the rotors. Her throat tightened and she gasped a breath. *Uziel?*

No, but could he be far behind?

She slid into Michael's mind, feeling his alarm clamoring along her spine.

I think I can feel another one.

Father. He's behind the first one, catching up.

Jenn swallowed, feeling her heart hammer against her rib cage. *This isn't a jet — can he keep up?*

We'll find out. He clasped her hand. *Don't be afraid. It had to happen, sooner or later. If he catches us, we'll settle it.* His hand tightened on hers. *I love you, Jenn. More than anything.*

I love you. Her throat felt paralyzed. She could not have said it, but this was better anyway.

The chopper lurched and took off over the bay, speeding out to sea, not north as Chemosh had planned, but south. And then she realized he was making a wide arc away from Uziel. But the trace in her mind grew, cold as sleet.

We're not losing him.

No.

Chemosh glanced over his shoulder at her, the question in his eyes.

She shook her head.

The chopper veered back toward the coastline, heading inland to the north again, toward Colón. A straight run now; they would make it, or not. The banging thump of the rotors increased in pitch, then steadied, the chopper now going full out. They were over jungle now, the tops of the trees a blur just below the chopper.

Jenn picked up a third trace.

Mother. Michael's eyes closed.

She could feel Justine now, and Uziel, and one called Achsah, and a faint corona of others behind them – Fabriel and Rafe? – gaining, gaining.

Leaning forward, she shouted to Chemosh. 'How far?'

'Not sure. Twenty miles, maybe.'

We're not going to make it, Jenn thought. Bitterness flooded her parched mouth. She thought of the jet waiting in Colón; what would Lyon have been like? Trees touching over the streets, bread and wine in a café. *All I want is to love you.*

I won't let him hurt you.

She felt cold with alarm. *You mustn't fight him.*

Then you do it. Take my strength, Jenn, to magnify your own. It's the only way.

Looking out of a Plexiglas port, she saw a river winding away to the west. From the corner of her eye, she could see Zane gazing at her. *You can tell him now, it won't matter.* Leaning against the harness she touched his knee, mouthed, 'I love you.'

He clasped her hand, his eyes shiny.

The helicopter lurched; light filled the cab and Jenn felt heat burning through the metal, turning the cabin hot as a stove. Uziel was striking. The blades stuttered out of synch and the chopper banked sharply, the river filling the view, port side on.

Jenn's heart leapt into her throat as she saw the tops of trees flashing by a scant ten yards below.

Going to crash!

Michael shouted, 'Everyone, get out fast. Run to the jungle.'

With a shriek of metal, the skids of the chopper caught in the treetops. The chopper spun around, the blades dipping into the foliage. Jenn clutched the safety harness, holding on as the craft spun out of control. Her mind was strangely calm, lucid. Get clear, yes, as soon as the crash comes. There would be pain, but only for a few seconds. Save Michael, she thought, and your family.

A blade tore away and she saw a flash of water and then the sandy bank of the river, and then a crushing impact drove the air from her lungs and threw her against the harness. Flames burst around her, she couldn't see. Her ears rang, and then she heard Merrick shouting. Releasing the harness, she followed the sound of his voice, out of the flaming wreckage. Sand dragged at her running feet, and then she was out of the smoke.

Pain — her leg.

Looking down, she saw that one pantleg had torn away, exposing a deep gash. Someone brushed past her and she saw it was Merrick, in flames. Diving into the river, he surfaced, sputtering, half his hair and his eyebrows burned away.

'Get to shore — quickly!' she yelled.

Michael grabbed her hand and pulled her higher onto the narrow strip of sand formed by a bend in the river. Chemosh and Zane were already there. Blood coursed from a gash on Chemosh's forehead, but the wound healed before her eyes, sealing as he wiped the blood from his eyes. She felt Michael entering her mind — *They're coming. You know what to do!*

He gripped her hand. Distantly, she realized the sky was turning pink — sunset — and there they were, Uziel and five others, growing quickly from dark smudges to flaming, winged shapes. Fear drove into her gut, her knees buckled and she locked them straight again. The angels slowed, still a hundred yards above. *They won't fight. They'll stay out of range and execute us.*

'Father!'

She saw Michael, teeth bared, staring up at his hovering father. And then he stepped in front of her, shielding her.

'Move away!' Uziel cried. 'Save your soul, Michael.'

'This is not God's work!' *Fight him now, Jenn. Take from me and fight him with all you have.*

She reached into Michael's mind, touching the core of him, the sparking vigor of his life. A bright sense of wonder filled her, and for a second she could not think. She tore herself free. *No, Michael. It's your life. If I drink, I'll defile us both.*

She saw Uziel's left arm raising. She shoved Michael away.

Uziel gave a cry of triumph and the hand flamed, but she leapt away, feeling a shower of sand against her back, sharp as shrapnel. She struck back at Uziel, furious, finding his mind, propelling the force of her own into it, seeing him spin away, his hands clasped to his head. But he did not fall. Hammer blows from the other angels rained down, driving her to her knees.

And then one of the angels dived, screaming, at Merrick.

Fabriel, no! Uziel, crying out in dismay, and then Jenn felt the burning diminish in her mind and realized they were holding back for fear of hitting Fabriel who was locked together with Merrick now, feet churning in the sand, a slow, clumsy waltz.

They're not really fighting. She means to shield us!

But here came Uziel, diving down, pulling Fabriel off Merrick and flinging her aside. She sailed over the river and struck the water, sending up a sheet of spray. Uziel cried out in rage. Looking back, Jenn gasped as she saw Zane on his back, pinning the murderous left arm to his side as Uziel ascended again.

'No,' Jenn screamed, 'let go!'

She stared, paralyzed, as Uziel soared up. A stream of white fire flowed down from his pinioned hand into the river, raising a gout of steam, lavender in the setting sun. If he managed to get that arm free, lodge that lethal hand against Zane, he could rip the life from him, Jenn knew. He flew higher, Zane still clinging, and she saw with horror that the arm was bending up, breaking

Zane's grip. The left hand inched around until it gripped the back of Zane's neck. A burst of white light flared around Zane, and for an instant she saw the light hover above him, keeping his shape. She heard herself screaming—

And then the ground fell away, as she flew up toward Uziel.

But he had already let go. Zane's body fell without moving, the air taking his arms up gently until he hit the river and sank, and then she was on Uziel, inches from his face. His eyes went wide, and only then did she realize she was flying. Fury boiled in her; she gathered herself to strike into his brain.

He's Michael's father.

She pushed him instead, and he sailed back fifty yards, arms windmilling. She flew into his face again, driven by rage and anguish.

'No,' he gasped. 'It can't be!'

Silence muffled everything now. Looking down, she saw Zane floating toward the curve of riverbank. Was he moving, an arm reaching out? Had he, somehow, managed to survive the angel of death? Hope came, sweet as a breath. Turning back to Uziel, she saw the others drawing close, four angels ringing them at the points of the compass, eyes wide, not with horror but with wonder. Fabriel, streaming water, rose to them, her hands clasped. Jenn felt Michael beside her, radiant with joy. *She's one of us, Father, an angel of God. ONE OF US!*

Covering his eyes, Uziel wheeled away with a shriek, shrinking to a dot against the darkening sky.

No, don't leave us, come back! A lone, wailing voice – Justine.

But Uziel was gone.

Jenn dove to Zane, rolled now against the river bank. Merrick, bending over him, looked up and shook his head.

She was aware of scrambled images, sensations – Michael behind her, hands on her shoulders.

Zane's face, glowing in the last of the sunlight.

She had never before seen such peace on it. Kneeling in the shallows, she hugged her father and wept for all he had been and all he had longed to be.

Chapter Twenty-Seven

Near dawn, Jenn hovered above the dome of the US Capitol, wondering: If Uziel *was* in there, how would she know? Tons of concrete and marble to shield his aura, a maze of basement corridors, and the railway tunnel beneath.

She drifted down past the darkened office windows, scattering the floodlights that blazed up the wall at her with an ease that was nearly automatic now. Could she really be floating alongside this grand old building? It seemed a dream, beautiful, thrilling. *I'm flying!*

Anything?

Michael. Turning, she saw him far up the mall, above the Smithsonian Institution, a point of amber light against the black sky. *Not yet.*

You'd better get to the hospital. It's nearly seven.

I can stay a little longer.

That's all right. I don't think he's around here. Come give me a kiss.

He was keeping up a game front, but she knew how it hurt him; two weeks of searching, every night out here, up and down across the city, and no sign of his father. At least we know where mine is, Jenn thought. She could see in her mind the spot in the jungle where they'd buried Zane, at the foot of a towering tree, near the bend in the Chagres River where he'd given up his life. It would hurt for a long time. She missed him. But he had died in peace. Michael was sure, from something Zane had said to him, that he had wanted to die, had deliberately closed with Uziel, knowing it would happen. He had stopped himself from killing the only way he could.

I got to tell him I loved him, Jenn thought.

Michael can't tell his father anything.

It scared her to think of finding Uziel, of trying to bring him back. The angel of death. But what greatness he'd had, too, protecting people with all his might for over three thousand years. When I flew up in his face, she thought, he saw an angel — a fallen angel whom God had brought back to the light. At that moment, he realized he knew nothing about God. And then he screamed because he wasn't seeing me any more, he was seeing all those dead children.

Shaking the tragic memory off, she turned away from the Capitol and sped up the broad, grassy promenade of the mall. Without looking to the north, she knew that Justine was floating high above the Byzantine dome of the Shrine at Catholic University, the place she and Uziel had met each day for many years. She still believed he would come back to her there. Maybe.

Jenn saw Michael speeding to meet her. He took her in his arms and she soothed his back with her hands.

'Don't worry about me,' he said. 'I'm all right.'

'I do worry.'

'I have you,' he murmured. 'Truly, I have never been happier. Now you'd better go. Go on now.'

She thought of Neil Hudson, who just yesterday had said his first word since awakening from his coma. Rich Sikorsky, who was beginning to respond to the speech therapist. The new clinical chief, both smart and caring. Eagerness filled her, to be back where she belonged, doing what she loved. She did not know if she was really an angel or not. The clans, stunned by the news of her, had called a conclave. Amator Evangeline had proposed that phages were the defeated remnant of the war in heaven, fallen ones who retained vestiges of their former angelic power but whose origins had been lost — to them and to angels — beyond the veil of memory.

Or were both phages and angels simply two rare and closely related species of humanity around whom myths had grown up?

She did not have to know. What she did know was enough: She loved healing, and she had all the proper degrees and licenses, and she was just going to go ahead and do it.

'When are you coming?'

'My first patient isn't until ten,' he said. 'I'll be along. Maybe we can grab lunch.' She started to pull away, but he held onto her hand. 'This won't last forever, Jenn. Another week.'

'We'll hunt for him as long as you want.'

He shook his head. 'I miss him. I want to tell him I still love him and we all want him back. But more than anything, I want to be with you. I want to show you what great salads I can fix. I want to put wallpaper with silly cows on it in the little room you've been using for a study, and I want to make love to you so we can put a baby in that room.'

She kissed him, her heart full.

Uziel lay in the darkness of the crypt in the chapel of Joseph of Arimathea. The wrought-iron gate that sealed the burial area off from the chapel had been repainted and set back on its hinges, and a restorer from the National Gallery was at work on the mural of Mary and the dead Jesus. The fragrance of paint and linseed oil drifted back to Uziel in the darkness, a faint, discordant intrusion into the world to which he had fled. He was climbing Everest again, with Michael, inhaling the cold air, struggling for a foothold in the ice. Michael was telling him that if he slipped, he must fall — no fair flying. A blast of wind scoured his eyes, bringing a rush of tears.

He wondered if, when they reached the top of the mountain, they would see God.

And there was war in heaven . . . angels fought against the dragon; and the dragon fought, and his angels . . . and he was cast out into the earth, and his angels were cast out with him . . .

Revelation xii, 7, 9